"An exciting, intelligent, and mythic novel of duty, betrayal, greed, and love."
—*Booklist*

"Cornwell is certainly a step above most of the interpreters of myth."
—*USA Today*

"Thoroughly researched, infinitely detailed, and above all constantly embattled, this long adventure puts a new face on the Arthurian legend, and offers an intriguing picture puzzle presenting the famous story and its characters in a new guise."—*The Anniston Star*

"Splendid, white-hot storytelling."—*Kirkus Reviews*

"Cornwell's attention to historical detail, his penchant for lively storytelling, and his vivid characters make this a good choice."—*Library Journal*

Enemy of God

"Top-notch storyteller Cornwell continues where his acclaimed *The Winter King* left off, creating another compelling fictional history set in fifth-century Britain....Writing with brio, Cornwell puts a fresh perspective on these oft-told events."—*Publishers Weekly*

"Spellbinding. This complex and superbly wrought narrative easily eclipses the more sanitized and tepid versions of Arthur's exploits. Readers who have eagerly awaited the continuation of The Warlord Chronicles will not be disappointed."
—*Booklist*

The Winter King

"Great battle scenes and brilliant political intrigue swirl about a cast of legendary but very human characters. The redoubtable Cornwell strikes again."
—*Kirkus Reviews* (starred review)

"Cornwell takes us into the world of mystery, adventure, passion, and love with exquisite skill. This is a riveting, heart-topping tale that will enchant all those who read it."
—Deepak Chopra, author of *The Seven Spiritual Laws of Success* and *The Return of Merlin*

"A powerful and dramatic retelling of the Arthurian legend."—Sharon K. Penman, author of *When Christ and His Saints Slept*

"Without smoke and mirrors, the magic in *The Winter King* is conjured with the human heart."—*People*

"Everything works wonderfully well, from the battles to the courtly rituals. A winner."
—*New York Daily News*

The Warlord Chronicles: III

Excalibur

A NOVEL OF ARTHUR

BERNARD CORNWELL

St. Martin's Griffin
New York

Library of Congress Cataloging-in-Publication Data

Cornwell, Bernard.
  Excalibur: a novel of Arthur / Bernard Cornwell.
    p. cm.
  ISBN 0-312-18575-8 (hc)
  ISBN 0-312-20648-8 (pbk)
  1. Arthur, King—Fiction.   2. Britons—Kings and rulers—
Fiction.   3. Arthurian romances—Adaptations.   4. Great
Britain—History—To 1066—Fiction.   I. Title.
PR6053.075E93 1998
823'.914—dc21   98-10247
                                                                   CIP

First published in Great Britain by Michael Joseph Ltd.

10 9 8 7 6 5 4

Excalibur is for John and Sharon Martin

CHARACTERS

AELLE	A Saxon King
AGRICOLA	Warlord of Gwent
AMHAR	Bastard son of Arthur, twin to Loholt
ARGANTE	Princess of Demetia, daughter of Oengus mac Airem
ARTHUR	Bastard son of Uther, warlord of Dumnonia, later Governor of Siluria
ARTHUR-BACH	Arthur's grandchild, son of Gwydre and Morwenna
BALIG	Boatman, brother-in-law to Derfel
BALIN	One of Arthur's warriors
BALISE	Once a Druid of Dumnonia
BORS	Lancelot's champion and cousin
BROCHVAEL	King of Powys after Arthur's time
BUDIC	King of Broceliande, married to Arthur's sister Anna
BYRTHIG	King of Gwynedd
CADDWG	Boatman and sometime servant of Merlin
CEINWYN	Sister of Cuneglas, Derfel's partner
CERDIC	A Saxon King
CILDYDD	Magistrate of Aquae Sulis
CLOVIS	King of the Franks
CULHWCH	Arthur's cousin, a warrior
CUNEGLAS	King of Powys
CYWYLLOG	One-time lover of Mordred, servant to Merlin
DAFYDD	The clerk who translates Derfel's story
DERFEL	(*pronounced Dervel*) The narrator, one of Arthur's warriors, later a monk
DIWRNACH	King of Lleyn

EACHERN	One of Derfel's spearmen
EINION	Son of Culhwch
EMRYS	Bishop of Durnovaria, later Bishop of Silurian Isca
ERCE	A Saxon, Derfel's mother
FERGAL	Argante's Druid
GALAHAD	Half-brother to Lancelot, one of Arthur's warriors
GAWAIN	Prince of Broceliande, son of King Budic
GUINEVERE	Arthur's wife
GWYDRE	Arthur and Guinevere's son
HYGWYDD	Arthur's servant
IGRAINE	Queen of Powys after Arthur's time. Married to Brochvael
ISSA	Derfel's second-in-command
LANCELOT	Exiled King of Benoic, now allied to Cerdic
LANVAL	One of Arthur's warriors
LIOFA	Cerdic's champion
LLADARN	Bishop in Gwent
LOHOLT	Bastard son of Arthur, twin to Amhar
MARDOC	Son of Mordred and Cywyllog
MERLIN	Druid of Dumnonia
MEURIG	King of Gwent, son of Tewdric
MORDRED	King of Dumnonia
MORFANS	'The Ugly', one of Arthur's warriors
MORGAN	Arthur's sister, married to Sansum
MORWENNA	Derfel and Ceinwyn's daughter, married to Gwydre
NIALL	Commander of Argante's Blackshield guard
NIMUE	Merlin's priestess
OENGUS MAC AIREM	King of Demetia, leader of the Blackshields
OLWEN THE SILVER	Follower of Merlin and Nimue
PERDDEL	Cuneglas's son, later King of Powys
PEREDUR	Lancelot's son
PYRLIG	Derfel's bard
SAGRAMOR	Commander of one of Arthur's warbands

SANSUM	Bishop of Durnovaria, later Bishop at Dinnewrac monastery
SCARACH	Issa's wife
SEREN (1)	Derfel and Ceinwyn's daughter
SEREN (2)	Daughter of Gwydre and Morwenna, Arthur's granddaughter
TALIESIN	'Shining Brow', a famous bard
TEWDRIC	Once King of Gwent, now a Christian hermit
TUDWAL	Monk at Dinnewrac monastery
UTHER	Once King of Dumnonia, Mordred's grandfather, Arthur's father

PLACES

Names marked* are fictional

AQUAE SULIS	Bath, Avon
BEADEWAN	Baddow, Essex
BURRIUM	Usk, Gwent
CAER AMBRA *	Amesbury, Wiltshire
CAER CADARN *	South Cadbury, Somerset
CAMLANN	Real location not known; Dawlish Warren, Devon, suggested
CELMERESFORT	Chelmsford, Essex
CICUCIUM	Roman fort near Sennybridge, Powys
CORINIUM	Cirencester, Gloucestershire
DUN CARIC *	Castle Cary, Somerset
DUNUM	Hod Hill, Dorset
DURNOVARIA	Dorchester, Dorset
GLEVUM	Gloucester
GOBANNIUM	Abergavenny, Monmouthshire
ISCA (DUMNONIA)	Exeter, Devon
ISCA (SILURIA)	Caerleon, Gwent
LACTODURUM	Towcester, Northamptonshire
LEODASHAM	Leaden Roding, Essex
LINDINIS	Ilchester, Somerset
LYCCEWORD	Letchworth, Hertfordshire
MAI DUN	Maiden Castle, Dorset
MORIDUNUM	Carmarthen
MYNYDD BADDON	Real location not known; Little Solsbury Hill, near Bath, suggested
SORVIODUNUM	Old Sarum, Wiltshire
STEORTFORD	Bishop's Stortford, Hertfordshire

THUNRESLEA	Thundersley, Essex
VENTA	Winchester, Hampshire
WICFORD	Wickford, Essex
YNYS WAIR	Lundy Island, Bristol Channel
YNYS WYDRYN	Glastonbury, Somerset

PART ONE

The Fires of Mai Dun

WOMEN, HOW THEY do haunt this tale.

When I began writing Arthur's story I thought it would be a tale of men; a chronicle of swords and spears, of battles won and frontiers made, of ruined treaties and broken kings, for is that not how history itself is told? When we recite the genealogy of our kings we do not name their mothers and grandmothers, but say Mordred ap Mordred ap Uther ap Kustennin ap Kynnar and so on all the way back to the great Beli Mawr who is the father of us all. History is a story told by men and of men's making, but in this tale of Arthur, like the glimmer of salmon in peat-dark water, the women do shine.

Men do make history, and I cannot deny that it was men who brought Britain low. There were hundreds of us, and all of us were armed in leather and iron, and hung with shield and sword and spear, and we thought Britain lay at our command for we were warriors, but it took both a man and a woman to bring Britain low, and of the two it was the woman who did the greater damage. She made one curse and an army died, and this is her tale now for she was Arthur's enemy.

'Who?' Igraine will demand when she reads this.

Igraine is my Queen. She is pregnant, a thing that gives us all great joy. Her husband is King Brochvael of Powys, and I now live under his protection in the small monastery of Dinnewrac where I write Arthur's story. I write at the command of Queen Igraine, who is too young to have known the Emperor. That is what we called Arthur, the Emperor, *Amherawdr* in the British tongue, though Arthur himself rarely used the title. I write in the Saxon tongue, for I am a Saxon, and because Bishop Sansum, the saint who rules our small community at Dinnewrac, would never allow me to write Arthur's tale. Sansum hates Arthur, reviles his memory and calls him traitor, and so Igraine and I have told the saint that I am writing a gospel of our Lord Jesus Christ in the Saxon tongue and, because Sansum neither speaks Saxon nor can read any language, the deception has seen the tale safe this far.

The tale grows darker now and harder to tell. Sometimes, when I think of my beloved Arthur, I see his noontime as a sun-bright day, yet how quickly the clouds came! Later, as we shall see, the clouds parted and the sun mellowed his landscape once more, but then came the night and we have not seen the sun since.

It was Guinevere who darkened the noonday sun. It happened during the rebellion when Lancelot, whom Arthur had thought a friend, tried to usurp the throne of Dumnonia. He was helped in this by the Christians who had been deceived by their leaders, Bishop Sansum among them, into believing that it was their holy duty to scour the country of pagans and so prepare the island of Britain for the second coming of the Lord Jesus Christ in the year 500. Lancelot was also helped by the Saxon King Cerdic who launched a terrifying attack along the valley of the Thames in an attempt to divide Britain. If the Saxons had reached the Severn Sea then the British kingdoms of the north would have been cut off from those of the south, yet, by the grace of the Gods, we defeated not only Lancelot and his Christian rabble, but Cerdic also. But in the defeat Arthur discovered Guinevere's treachery. He found her naked in another man's arms, and it was as though the sun had vanished from his sky.

'I don't really understand,' Igraine said to me one day in late summer.

'What, dear Lady, do you not understand?' I asked.

'Arthur loved Guinevere, yes?'

'He did.'

'So why could he not forgive her? I forgave Brochvael over Nwylle.' Nwylle had been Brochvael's lover, but she had contracted a disease of the skin which had disfigured her beauty. I suspect, but have never asked, that Igraine used a charm to bring the disease to her rival. My Queen might call herself a Christian, but Christianity is not a religion that offers the solace of revenge to its adherents. For that you must go to the old women who know which herbs to pluck and what charms to say under a waning moon.

4

'You forgave Brochvael,' I agreed, 'but would Brochvael have forgiven you?'

She shuddered. 'Of course not! He'd have burned me alive, but that's the law.'

'Arthur could have burned Guinevere,' I said, 'and there were plenty of men who advised him to do just that, but he did love her, he loved her passionately, and that was why he could neither kill her nor forgive her. Not at first, anyway.'

'Then he was a fool!' Igraine said. She is very young and has the glorious certainty of the young.

'He was very proud,' I said, and maybe that did make Arthur a fool, but so it did the rest of us. I paused, thinking. 'He wanted many things,' I went on, 'he wanted a free Britain and the Saxons defeated, but in his soul he wanted Guinevere's constant reassurance that he was a good man. And when she slept with Lancelot it proved to Arthur that he was the lesser man. It wasn't true, of course, but it hurt him. How it hurt. I have never seen a man so hurt. She tore his heart.'

'So he imprisoned her?' Igraine asked me.

'He imprisoned her,' I said, and remembered how I had been forced to take Guinevere to the shrine of the Holy Thorn at Ynys Wydryn where Arthur's sister, Morgan, became her jailer. There was never any affection between Guinevere and Morgan. One was a pagan, the other a Christian, and the day I locked Guinevere into the shrine's compound was one of the few times I ever saw her weep. 'She will stay there,' Arthur told me, 'till the day she dies.'

'Men are fools,' Igraine declared, then gave me a sidelong glance. 'Were you ever unfaithful to Ceinwyn?'

'No,' I answered truthfully.

'Did you ever want to be?'

'Oh, yes. Lust does not vanish with happiness, Lady. Besides, what merit is there in fidelity if it is never tested?'

'You think there is merit in fidelity?' she asked, and I wondered which young, handsome warrior in her husband's caer had taken her eye. Her pregnancy would prevent any nonsense for the moment, but I feared what might happen after. Maybe nothing.

I smiled. 'We want fidelity in our lovers, Lady, so is it not obvious that they want it in us? Fidelity is a gift we offer to those we love. Arthur gave it to Guinevere, but she could not return it. She wanted something different.'

'Which was?'

'Glory, and he was ever averse to glory. He achieved it, but he would not revel in it. She wanted an escort of a thousand horsemen, bright banners to fly above her and the whole island of Britain prostrate beneath her. And all he ever wanted was justice and good harvests.'

'And a free Britain and the Saxons defeated,' Igraine reminded me drily.

'Those too,' I acknowledged, 'and he wanted one other thing. He wanted that thing more than all the others.' I smiled, remembering, and then thought that perhaps of all Arthur's ambitions, this last was the one he found most difficult to achieve and the one that the few of us who were his friends never truly believed he wanted.

'Go on,' Igraine said, suspecting that I was falling into a doze.

'He just wanted a piece of land,' I said, 'a hall, some cattle, a smithy of his own. He wanted to be ordinary. He wanted other men to look after Britain while he sought happiness.'

'And he never found it?' Igraine asked.

'He found it,' I assured her, but not in that summer after Lancelot's rebellion. It was a summer of blood, a season of retribution, a time when Arthur hammered Dumnonia into a surly submission.

Lancelot had fled southwards to his land of the Belgae. Arthur would dearly have loved to pursue him, but Cerdic's Saxon invaders were now the greater danger. They had advanced as far as Corinium by the rebellion's end, and might even have captured that city had the Gods not sent a plague to ravage their army. Men's bowels voided unstoppably, they vomited blood, they were weakened until they could not stand, and it was when the plague was at its worst that Arthur's forces struck them. Cerdic tried to rally his men, but the Saxons believed their Gods had deserted them and so they fled. 'But they'll be back,' Arthur told me when we stood among the bloody remnants of Cerdic's defeated rearguard. 'Next spring,' he said, 'they will be back.' He cleaned Excalibur's blade on his blood-stained cloak and slid her into the scabbard. He had grown a beard and it was grey. It made him look older, much older, while the pain of Guinevere's betrayal had made his long face gaunt, so that men who had never met Arthur until that summer found his appearance fearsome and he did nothing to soften that impression. He had ever been a patient man, but now his anger lay very close to the skin and it could erupt at the smallest provocation.

It was a summer of blood, a season of retribution, and Guinevere's fate was to be locked away in Morgan's shrine. Arthur had condemned his wife to a living grave and his guards were ordered to keep her there for ever. Guinevere, a Princess of the Henis-Wyren, was gone from the world.

'Don't be absurd, Derfel,' Merlin snapped at me a week later, 'she'll be out of there in two years! One, probably. If Arthur wanted her gone from his life he'd have put her to the flames, which is what he should have done. There's nothing like a good burning for improving a woman's behaviour, but it's no use telling Arthur that. The halfwit's in love with her! And he is a halfwit. Think about it! Lancelot alive, Mordred alive, Cerdic alive and Guinevere alive! If a soul wants to live for ever in this world it seems like a very good idea to become an enemy of Arthur. I am as well as can be expected, thank you for asking.'

'I did ask you earlier,' I said patiently, 'and you ignored me.'

'It's my hearing, Derfel. Quite gone.' He banged an ear. 'Deaf as a bucket. It's age, Derfel, sheer old age. I decay visibly.'

He did nothing of the sort. He looked better now than he had for a long time and his hearing, I am sure, was as acute as his sight – and that, despite his eighty or more years, was still as sharp as a hawk's. Merlin did not decay but seemed to have a new energy, one brought to him by the Treasures of Britain. Those thirteen Treasures were old, old as Britain, and for centuries they had been lost, but Merlin had at last succeeded in finding them. The power of the Treasures was to summon the ancient Gods back to Britain, a power that had never been tested, but now, in the year of Dumnonia's turmoil, Merlin would use them to work a great magic.

I had sought Merlin on the day I took Guinevere to Ynys Wydryn. It was a day of hard rain and I had climbed the Tor, half expecting to find Merlin on its summit, but discovered the hilltop

7

empty and sad. Merlin had once possessed a great hall on the Tor with a dream tower attached to it, but the hall had been burned. I had stood amidst the Tor's ruin and felt a great desolation. Arthur, my friend, was hurt. Ceinwyn, my woman, was far away in Powys. Morwenna and Seren my two daughters, were with Ceinwyn, while Dian, my youngest, was in the Otherworld, despatched there by one of Lancelot's swords. My friends were dead, or else far away. The Saxons were making ready to fight us in the new year, my house was ashes and my life seemed bleak. Maybe it was Guinevere's sadness that had infected me, but that morning, on Ynys Wydryn's rain-washed hill, I felt more alone than I had ever felt in all my life and so I knelt in the hall's muddy ashes and prayed to Bel. I begged the God to save us and, like a child, I begged Bel for a sign that the Gods did care about us.

That sign came a week later. Arthur had ridden eastwards to harry the Saxon frontier, but I had stayed at Caer Cadarn waiting for Ceinwyn and my daughters to come home. Some time in that week Merlin and his companion, Nimue, went to the great empty palace at nearby Lindinis. I had once lived there, guarding our King, Mordred, but when Mordred had come of age the palace had been given to Bishop Sansum as a monastery. Sansum's monks had been evicted now, chased by vengeful spearmen from the great Roman halls so that the big palace stood empty.

It was the local people who told us that the Druid was in the palace. They told stories of apparitions, of wonderful signs and of Gods walking in the night, and so I rode down to the palace, but found no sign of Merlin there. Two or three hundred people were camped outside the palace gates and they excitedly repeated the tales of night-time visions and, hearing them, my heart sank. Dumnonia had just endured the frenzy of a Christian rebellion fuelled by just such crazed superstition, and now it seemed the pagans were about to match the Christian madness. I pushed open the palace gates, crossed the big courtyard and strode through Lindinis's empty halls. I called Merlin's name, but there was no answer. I found a warm hearth in one of the kitchens, and evidence of another room recently swept, but nothing lived there except rats and mice.

Yet all that day more folk gathered in Lindinis. They came from every part of Dumnonia and there was a pathetic hope on all their faces. They brought their crippled and their sick, and they waited patiently until the dusk when the palace gates were flung open and they could walk, limp, crawl or be carried into the palace's outer courtyard. I could have sworn no one had been inside the vast building, but someone had opened the gates and lit great torches that illuminated the courtyard's arcades.

I joined the throng crowding into the courtyard. I was accompanied by Issa, my second-in-command, and the two of us stood draped in our long dark cloaks beside the gate. I judged the crowd to be country folk. They were poorly clothed and had the dark, pinched faces of those who must struggle to make a hard living from the soil, yet those faces were full of hope in the flaring torchlight. Arthur would have hated it, for he always resented giving supernatural hope to suffering people, but how this crowd needed hope! Women held up sick babies or pushed crippled children to the front, and all listened eagerly to the miraculous tales of Merlin's apparitions. This was the third night of the marvels and by now so many people wanted to witness the miracles that not all could get into the courtyard. Some perched on the wall behind me and others crammed the gateway, but none encroached on the arcade that ran around three sides of the courtyard, for that pillared and sheltered walkway was protected by four spearmen who used their long weapons to keep the crowd at bay. The four warriors were Blackshields, Irish spearmen from Demetia, the kingdom of Oengus mac Airem, and I wondered what they were doing so far from home.

The last daylight drained from the sky and bats flickered over the torches as the crowd settled on the flagstones to stare expectantly towards the palace's main door that lay opposite the courtyard gate. From time to time a woman moaned aloud. Children cried and were hushed. The four spearmen crouched at the corners of the arcade.

We waited. It seemed to me that we waited for hours and my mind was wandering, thinking of Ceinwyn and of my dead daughter Dian, when suddenly there was a great clash of iron inside the palace as though someone had struck a cauldron with a spear. The crowd gasped and some of the women stood and swayed in the torchlight. They waved their hands in the air and called on the Gods, but no apparitions appeared and the big palace doors stayed closed. I touched the iron in Hywelbane's hilt, and the sword felt reassuring. The edge of hysteria in the crowd was unsettling, but not so unsettling as the very circumstance of the occasion, for I had never known Merlin to need an audience for his magic. Indeed he despised those Druids who gathered crowds. 'Any trickster can impress halfwits,' he liked to say, but here, tonight, it seemed as if he was the one who wanted to impress the halfwits. He had the crowd on edge, he had it moaning and swaying, and when the great metallic crack sounded again they rose to their feet and began shouting Merlin's name.

Then the palace doors swung open and the crowd slowly fell silent.

For a few heartbeats the doorway was nothing but a black space, then a young warrior in the full panoply of battle walked out of the darkness to stand on the top step of the arcade.

There was nothing magical about him, except that he was beautiful. There was no other word for him. In a world of twisted limbs, crippled legs, goitred necks, scarred faces and weary souls, this warrior was beautiful. He was tall, thin and golden-haired, and he had a serene face that could only be described as kind, even gentle. His eyes were a startling blue. He wore no helmet so that his hair, which was as long as a girl's, hung straight down past his shoulders. He had a gleaming white breastplate, white greaves, and a white scabbard. The wargear looked expensive, and I wondered who he was. I thought I knew most of the warriors of Britain — at least those who could afford armour like this young man's — but he was a stranger to me. He smiled at the crowd, then raised both his hands and motioned that they were to kneel.

Issa and I stayed standing. Maybe it was our warrior's arrogance, or perhaps we just wanted to see across the intervening heads.

The long-haired warrior did not speak, but once the audience was down on its knees, he smiled his thanks at them and then walked around the arcade extinguishing the torches by taking them from their beckets and plunging them into water-filled barrels that stood ready. It was, I realized, a performance that had been carefully rehearsed. The courtyard became darker and darker until the only remaining light came from the two torches flanking the great palace door. There was little moon and the night was chilly dark.

The white warrior stood between the last two torches. 'Children of Britain,' he said, and he had a voice to match his beauty, a gentle voice, full of warmth, 'pray to your Gods! Within these walls are the Treasures of Britain and soon, very soon, their power will be unleashed, but now, so that you can see their power, we shall let the Gods speak to us.' With that he extinguished the last two torches and the courtyard was suddenly dark.

Nothing happened. The crowd mumbled, calling on Bel and Gofannon and Grannos and Don to show their power. My skin crawled and I clutched Hywelbane's hilt. Were the Gods circling us? I looked up to where a patch of stars glittered between the clouds and imagined the great Gods hovering in that upper air, and then Issa gasped and I looked down from the stars.

And I too gasped.

For a girl, hardly more than a child on the very edge of woman-hood, had appeared in the dark. She was a delicate girl, lovely in her youth and graceful in her loveliness, and she was as naked as a newborn. She was slender, with small high breasts and long thighs, and in one hand she carried a bunch of lilies and in the other a narrow-bladed sword.

And I just stared. For in the dark, the chill dark following the engulfment of the flames, the girl glowed. She actually glowed. She glistened with a shimmering white light. It was not a bright light, it did not dazzle, it was just there, like stardust brushed onto her white skin. It was a scattered, powdery radiance that touched her body and legs and arms and hair, though not her face. The lilies glowed, and the radiance glistened on the long thin blade of her sword.

The glowing girl walked the arcades. She seemed oblivious as the crowd in the courtyard held out their withered limbs and sick children. She ignored them, simply stepping delicately and lightly along the arcade with her shadowed face staring down at the stones. Her steps were feather light. She seemed self-absorbed, lost in her own dream, and the people moaned and called to her, but she did not look at them. She just walked on and the strange light glimmered on her body, and on her arms and legs, and on her long black hair that grew close about her face that was a black mask amidst the eerie glow, but somehow, instinctively perhaps, I sensed that her face was beautiful. She came close to where Issa and I were standing and there she suddenly lifted that jet black shadow of a face to stare in our direction. I smelt something that reminded me of the sea, and then, as suddenly as she had appeared, she vanished through a door and the crowd sighed.

'What was it?' Issa whispered to me.

'I don't know,' I answered. I was frightened. This was not madness, but something real, for I had seen it, but what was it? A Goddess? But why had I smelt the sea? 'Maybe it was one of Manawydan's spirits,' I told Issa. Manawydan was the God of the sea, and surely his nymphs would have that salt smell about them.

We waited a long time for the second apparition, and when it came it was far less impressive than the glowing sea nymph. A shape appeared on the palace roof, a black shape which slowly grew to be an armed, cloaked warrior in a monstrous helmet crested with the antlers of a great stag. The man was scarcely to be seen in the dark, but when a cloud slid from the moon we saw what he was and the crowd moaned as he stood above us with his arms outstretched and with his face hidden by the huge helmet's cheekpieces. He carried a spear and a sword. He stood for a second, then he too vanished, though I could have sworn I heard a tile slip from the roof's far side as he disappeared.

Then, just as he went, the naked girl appeared again, only this time it seemed as if she had simply materialized on the arcade's top step. One second there was darkness, then there was her long glowing body standing still and straight and shining. Again her face was in darkness so that it appeared as a shadow mask rimmed with her light-shot hair. She stood still for a few seconds, then did a slow dance, delicately pointing her toes as she stepped in an intricate pattern that circled and crossed the same spot of the arcade. She stared down as she danced. It seemed to me that the glistening unearthly light had been washed onto her skin, for I saw it was brighter in some places than others, but it was surely no human doing. Issa and I were on our knees now, for this had to be a sign from the Gods. It was light in darkness, beauty amidst the remnants. The nymph danced on, the light of her body slowly fading, and then, when she was only a hint of glistening loveliness in the arcade's shadow, she stopped, spread her arms and legs wide to face us boldly, and then she vanished.

A moment later two flaming torches were carried out from the palace. The crowd was shouting now, calling to their Gods and demanding to see Merlin, and at last he did appear from the palace entrance. The white warrior carried one of the flaming torches and one-eyed Nimue carried the second.

Merlin came to the top step and there stood tall in his long white robe. He let the crowd go on calling. His grey beard, which fell almost to his waist, was plaited into strands that were wrapped in black ribbons, just as his long white hair was plaited and bound. He carried his black staff and, after a while, he lifted it as a sign that the crowd should be silent. 'Did anything appear?' he asked anxiously.

'Yes, yes!' the crowd called back, and on Merlin's old, clever, mischievous face there came a look of pleased surprise, as though he had not known what might have happened in the courtyard.

He smiled, then stepped aside and beckoned with his free hand. Two small children, a boy and a girl, came from the palace carrying the Cauldron of Clyddno Eiddyn. Most of the Treasures of Britain were small things, commonplace even, but the Cauldron was a genuine Treasure and, of all the thirteen, the one with the most power. It was a great silver bowl decorated with a golden tracery of warriors and beasts. The two children struggled with the Cauldron's great weight, but managed to set it down beside the Druid. 'I have the Treasures of Britain!' Merlin announced, and the crowd sighed in response. 'Soon, very soon,' he went on, 'the power of the Treasures will be unleashed. Britain will be restored. Our enemies will be broken!' He paused to let the cheers echo in the courtyard. 'You have seen the power of the Gods tonight, but what you have seen is a small thing, an insignificant thing. Soon all Britain will see, but if we are to summon the Gods, then I need your help.'

The crowd shouted that he would have it and Merlin beamed approval at them. That benevolent smile made me suspicious. One part of me sensed that he was playing a game with these folk, but even Merlin, I told myself, could not make a girl glow in darkness. I had seen her, and I wanted to believe so badly, and the memory of that lissom, shining body convinced me that the Gods had not abandoned us.

'You must come to Mai Dun!' Merlin said sternly. 'You must

come for as long as you are able, and you must bring food. If you have weapons, you must bring them. At Mai Dun we shall work, and the work will be long and hard, but at Samain, when the dead walk, we shall summon the Gods together. You and I!' He paused, then held the tip of his staff towards the crowd. The black pole wavered, as if it was searching for someone in the throng, then it settled on me. 'Lord Derfel Cadarn!' Merlin called.

'Lord?' I answered, embarrassed to be singled out from the crowd.

'You will stay, Derfel. The rest of you go now. Go to your homes, for the Gods will not come again till Samain Eve. Go to your homes, see to your fields, then come to Mai Dun. Bring axes, bring food, and prepare to see your Gods in all their glory! Now, go! Go!'

The crowd obediently went. Many stopped to touch my cloak, for I was one of the warriors who had fetched the Cauldron of Clyddno Eiddyn from its hiding place on Ynys Mon and, to the pagans at least, that made me a hero. They touched Issa too, for he was another Warrior of the Cauldron, but when the crowd was gone he waited at the gate while I went to meet Merlin. I greeted him, but he brushed aside my enquiry as to his health, asking instead if I had enjoyed the evening's strange happenings.

'What was it?' I asked.

'What was what?' he asked innocently.

'The girl in the dark,' I said.

His eyes widened in mock astonishment. 'She was here again, was she? How very interesting! Was it the girl with wings, or the one who shines? The shining girl! I have no idea who she is, Derfel. I cannot unriddle every mystery of this world. You have spent too long with Arthur and like him you believe that everything must have a commonplace explanation, but alas, the Gods rarely choose to make themselves clear. Would you be useful and carry the Cauldron inside?'

I lifted the huge Cauldron and took it into the palace's pillared reception hall. When I had been there earlier in the day the room had been empty, but now there was a couch, a low table and four iron stands on which oil lamps stood. The young, handsome, white-armoured warrior, whose hair hung so long, smiled from the couch while Nimue, dressed in a shabby black robe, carried a lit taper to the lamps' wicks. 'This room was empty this afternoon,' I said accusingly.

'It must have seemed so to you,' Merlin said airily, 'but perhaps we simply chose not to show ourselves. Have you met the Prince Gawain?' He gestured to the young man who stood and bowed to me in greeting. 'Gawain is son of King Budic of Broceliande,' Merlin introduced the Prince, 'which makes him Arthur's nephew.'

'Lord Prince,' I greeted Gawain. I had heard of Gawain, but had never met him. Broceliande was the British kingdom across the sea in Armorica and of late, as the Franks pressed hard on their frontier, visitors from that kingdom had been rare.

'I am honoured to meet you, Lord Derfel,' Gawain said courteously, 'your fame has gone far from Britain.'

'Don't be absurd, Gawain,' Merlin snapped. 'Derfel's fame hasn't gone anywhere, except maybe to his fat head. Gawain is here to help me,' he explained to me.

'To do what?' I asked.

'Protect the Treasures, of course. He is a formidable spearman, or so I'm told. Is that true, Gawain? You're formidable?'

Gawain just smiled. He did not look very formidable, for he was still a very young man, maybe only fifteen or sixteen summers, and he did not yet need to shave. His long fair hair gave his face a girlish look, while his white armour, that I had earlier thought was so expensive, was now revealed to be nothing more than a coat of limewash painted on plain iron gear. If it had not been for his self-assurance and undeniable good looks, he would have been risible.

'So what have you been doing since last we met?' Merlin demanded of me, and it was then that I had told him of Guinevere and he had scoffed at my belief that she would be imprisoned for life. 'Arthur is a halfwit,' he insisted. 'Guinevere may be clever, but he doesn't need her. He needs something plain and stupid, something to keep his bed warm while he's worrying about the Saxons.' He sat on the couch and smiled as the two small children who had carried the Cauldron out to the courtyard now brought him a plate of bread and cheese with a flask of mead. 'Supper!' he said happily. 'Do join me, Derfel, for we wish to talk to you. Sit! You will find the floor quite comfortable. Sit beside Nimue.'

I sat. Nimue had ignored me thus far. The socket of her missing eye, that had been torn from her face by a king, was covered with an eye-patch, and her hair, that had been cut so short before we went south to Guinevere's sea palace, was growing back, though it was still short enough to give her a boyish look. She seemed angry, but Nimue always seemed angry. Her life was devoted to one thing only, the pursuit of the Gods, and she despised anything which deflected her from that search and maybe she thought Merlin's ironic pleasantries were somehow a waste of time. She and I had grown up together and in the years since our childhood I had more than once kept her alive, I had fed her and clothed her, yet still she treated me as though I was a fool.

'Who rules Britain?' she asked me abruptly.

'The wrong question!' Merlin snapped at her with unexpected vehemence, 'the wrong question!'

'Well?' she demanded of me, ignoring Merlin's anger.

'No one rules Britain,' I said.

'The right answer,' Merlin said vengefully. His bad temper had unsettled Gawain, who was standing behind Merlin's couch and looking anxiously at Nimue. He was frightened of her, but I cannot blame him for that. Nimue frightened most people.

'So who rules Dumnonia?' she asked me.

'Arthur does,' I answered.

Nimue gave Merlin a triumphant look, but the Druid just shook his head. 'The word is *rex*,' he said, '*rex*, and if either of you had the slightest notion of Latin you would know that *rex* means king, not emperor. The word for emperor is *imperator*. Are we to risk everything because you are uneducated?'

'Arthur rules Dumnonia,' Nimue insisted.

Merlin ignored her. 'Who is King here?' he demanded of me.

'Mordred, of course.'

'Of course,' he repeated. 'Mordred!' He spat at Nimue. 'Mordred!'

She turned away as though he was being tedious. I was lost, not understanding in the least what their argument meant, and I had no chance to ask for the two children appeared through the curtained doorway again to bring more bread and cheese. As they put the plates on the floor I caught a hint of sea smell, that waft of salt and seaweed that had accompanied the naked apparition, but then the children went back through the curtain and the smell vanished with them.

'So,' Merlin said to me with the satisfied air of a man who has won his argument, 'does Mordred have children?'

'Several, probably,' I answered. 'He was forever raping girls.'

'As kings do,' Merlin said carelessly, 'and princes too. Do you rape girls, Gawain?'

'No, Lord.' Gawain seemed shocked at the suggestion.

'Mordred was ever a rapist,' Merlin said. 'Takes after his father and grandfather in that, though I must say they were both a great deal gentler than young Mordred. Uther, now, he could never resist a pretty face. Or an ugly one if he was in the mood. Arthur, though, was never given to rape. He's like you in that, Gawain.'

'I am very glad to hear it,' Gawain said and Merlin rolled his eyes in mock exasperation.

'So what will Arthur do with Mordred?' the Druid demanded of me.

'He's to be imprisoned here, Lord,' I said, gesturing about the palace.

'Imprisoned!' Merlin seemed amused. 'Guinevere shut away, Bishop Sansum locked up, if life goes on like this then everyone in Arthur's life will soon be imprisoned! We shall all be on water and mouldy bread. What a fool Arthur is! He should knock Mordred's brains out.' Mordred had been a child when he inherited the kingship and Arthur had wielded the royal power as the boy grew, but when Mordred came of age, and true to the promise he had given to High King Uther, Arthur handed the kingdom to Mordred. Mordred misused that power, and even plotted Arthur's death, and it was that plot which had encouraged Sansum and Lancelot in their revolt. Mordred was to be imprisoned now, though Arthur was determined that Dumnonia's rightful King, in whom the blood of the Gods ran, should be treated with honour even if he was not to be allowed power. He would be kept under guard in this lavish palace, given all the luxuries he craved, but kept from mischief. 'So you think,' Merlin asked me, 'that Mordred does have whelps?'

'Dozens, I should think.'

'If you ever do think,' Merlin snapped. 'Give me a name, Derfel! Give me a name!'

I thought for a moment. I was in a better position than most men to know Mordred's sins for I had been his childhood guardian, a task I had done both reluctantly and badly. I had never succeeded in being a father to him, and though my Ceinwyn had tried to be a mother, she too had failed and the wretched boy had grown sullen and evil. 'There was a servant girl here,' I said, 'and he kept her company for a long time.'

'Her name?' Merlin demanded with a mouth full of cheese.

'Cywwylog.'

'Cywwylog!' He seemed amused by the name. 'And you say he fathered a child on this Cywwylog?'

'A boy,' I said, 'if it was his, which it probably was.'

'And this Cywwylog,' he said, waving a knife, 'where might she be?'

'Probably somewhere very close,' I answered. 'She never moved with us to Ermid's Hall and Ceinwyn always supposed that Mordred had given her money.'

'So he was fond of her?'

'I think he was, yes.'

'How gratifying to know that there is some good in the horrible boy. Cywwylog, eh? You can find her, Gawain?'

'I shall try, Lord,' Gawain said eagerly.

'Not just try, succeed!' Merlin snapped. 'What did she look like, Derfel, this curiously named Cywwylog?'

'Short,' I said, 'plumpish, black hair.'

'So far we have succeeded in whittling our search down to every girl in Britain beneath the age of twenty. Can you be more specific? How old would the child be now?'

'Six,' I said, 'and if I remember rightly, he had reddish hair.'

'And the girl?'

I shook my head. 'Pleasant enough, but not really memorable.'

'All girls are memorable,' Merlin said loftily, 'especially ones named Cywwylog. Find her, Gawain.'

'Why do you want to find her?' I asked.

'Do I poke my nose into your business?' Merlin demanded. 'Do I come and ask you foolish questions about spears and shields? Am I forever pestering you with idiotic enquiries about the manner in which you administer justice? Do I care about your harvests? Have

I, in short, made a nuisance of myself by interfering in your life, Derfel?'

'No, Lord.'

'So pray do not be curious about mine. It is not given for shrews to understand the ways of the eagle. Now eat some cheese, Derfel.'

Nimue refused to eat. She was brooding, angered by the way Merlin had dismissed her assertion that Arthur was the true ruler of Dumnonia. Merlin ignored her, preferring to tease Gawain. He did not mention Mordred again, nor would he talk about what he planned at Mai Dun, though he did finally speak of the Treasures as he escorted me towards the palace's outer gate where Issa still waited for me. The Druid's black staff clicked on the stones as we walked though the courtyard where the crowd had watched the apparitions come and go. 'I need people, you see,' Merlin said, 'because if the Gods are to be summoned then there is work to be done and Nimue and I cannot possibly do it all alone. We need a hundred folk, maybe more!'

'To do what?'

'You'll see, you'll see. Did you like Gawain?'

'He seems willing.'

'Oh, he's willing all right, but is that admirable? Dogs are willing. He reminds me of Arthur when he was young. All that eagerness to do good.' He laughed.

'Lord,' I said, anxious for reassurance, 'what will happen at Mai Dun?'

'We shall summon the Gods, of course. It's a complicated procedure and I can only pray I do it right. I do fear, of course, that it will not work. Nimue, as you might have gathered, believes I am doing it all wrong, but we shall see, we shall see.' He walked a couple of paces in silence. 'But if we do it right, Derfel, if we do it right, then what a sight we shall witness! The Gods coming in all their power. Manawydan striding from the sea, all wet and glorious. Taranis splintering the skies with lightning, Bel trailing fire from heaven, and Don cleaving the clouds with her spear of fire. That should scare the Christians, eh!' He danced a pair of clumsy steps for pure delight. 'The bishops will be pissing in their black robes then, eh?'

'But you cannot be sure,' I said, anxious for reassurance.

'Don't be absurd, Derfel. Why do you always want certainty of me? All I can do is perform the ritual and hope I get it right! But you witnessed something tonight, did you not? Does that not convince you?'

I hesitated, wondering if all I had witnessed was some trick. But what trick could make a girl's skin glow in the dark? 'And will the Gods fight the Saxons?' I asked.

'That is why we are summoning them, Derfel,' Merlin said patiently. 'The purpose is to restore Britain as she was in the old days before her perfection was soured by Saxons and Christians.' He stopped at the gate and stared out into the dark countryside. 'I do love Britain,' he said in a voice that was suddenly wan, 'I do so love this island. It is a special place.' He laid a hand on my shoulder. 'Lancelot burned your house. So where do you live now?'

'I have to build a place,' I said, though it would not be at Ermid's Hall where my little Dian had died.

'Dun Caric is empty,' Merlin said, 'and I will let you live there, though on one condition: that when my work is done and the Gods are with us, I may come to die in your house.'

'You may come and live there, Lord,' I said.

'To die, Derfel, to die. I am old. I have one task left, and that task will be attempted at Mai Dun.' He kept his hand on my shoulder. 'You think I do not know the risks I run?'

I sensed fear in him. 'What risks, Lord?' I asked awkwardly.

A screech owl sounded from the dark and Merlin listened with a cocked head for a repeat of the call, but none came. 'All my life,' he said after a while, 'I have sought to bring the Gods back to Britain, and now I have the means, but I don't know whether it will work. Or whether I am the man to do the rites. Or whether I'll even live to see it happen.' His hand tightened on my shoulder. 'Go, Derfel,' he said, 'go. I must sleep, for tomorrow I travel south. But come to Durnovaria at Samain. Come and witness the Gods.'

'I will be there, Lord.'

He smiled and turned away. And I walked back to the Caer in a daze, full of hope and beset by fears, wondering where the magic would take us now, or whether it would take us nowhere but to the feet of the Saxons who would come in the spring. For if Merlin could not summon the Gods then Britain was surely doomed.

Slowly, like a settling pool that had been stirred to turbidity, Britain calmed. Lancelot cowered in Venta, fearing Arthur's vengeance. Mordred, our rightful King, came to Lindinis where he was accorded every honour, but was surrounded by spearmen. Guinevere stayed at Ynys Wydryn under Morgan's hard gaze, while Sansum, Morgan's husband, was imprisoned in the guest quarters of Emrys, Bishop of Durnovaria. The Saxons retreated behind their frontiers, though once the harvest was gathered in each side raided the other savagely. Sagramor, Arthur's Numidian commander, guarded the Saxon frontier while Culhwch, Arthur's cousin and now once again one of his war leaders, watched Lancelot's Belgic border from our fortress at Dunum. Our ally, King Cuneglas of Powys, left a hundred spearmen under Arthur's command, then returned to his own kingdom, and on the way he met his sister, the Princess Ceinwyn, returning to Dumnonia. Ceinwyn was my woman as I was her man, though she had taken an oath never to marry. She came with our two daughters in the early autumn and I confess I was not truly happy until she returned. I met her on the road south of Glevum and I held her a long time in my arms, for there had been moments when I thought I would never see her again. She was a beauty, my Ceinwyn, a golden-haired Princess who once, long before, had been betrothed to Arthur and after he had abandoned that planned marriage to be with Guinevere, Ceinwyn's hand had been promised to other great princes, but she and I had run away together and I dare say we both did well by doing so.

We had our new house at Dun Caric, which lay just a short journey north of Caer Cadarn. Dun Caric means 'The Hill by the Pretty Stream', and the name was apt for it was a lovely place where I thought we would be happy. The hilltop hall was made of oak and roofed with rye-straw thatch and had a dozen outbuildings enclosed by a decayed timber palisade. The folk who lived in the small village at the foot of the hill believed the hall to be haunted, for Merlin had let an ancient Druid, Balise, live out his life in the place, but my spearmen had cleaned out the nests and vermin, then hauled out all Balise's ritual paraphernalia. I had no doubt that the villagers, despite their fear of the old hall, had already taken the cauldrons, tripods and anything else of real value, so we were left to dispose of the snakeskins, dry bones and desiccated corpses of birds, all of them thick with cobwebs. Many of the bones were human, great heaps of them, and we buried those remains in scattered pits so that the souls of the dead could not reknit and come back to stalk us.

Arthur had sent me dozens of young men to train into warriors and all that autumn I taught them the discipline of the spear and shield, and once a week, more out of duty than from pleasure, I visited Guinevere at nearby Ynys Wydryn. I carried her gifts of food and, as it got colder, a great cloak of bear fur. Sometimes I took her son, Gwydre, but she was never really comfortable with him. She was bored by his tales of fishing in Dun Caric's stream or hunting in our woods. She herself loved to hunt, but that pleasure was no longer permitted to her and so she took her exercise by walking around the shrine's compound. Her beauty did not fade, indeed her misery gave her large eyes a luminosity they had lacked before, though she would never admit to the sadness. She was too proud for that, though I could tell she was unhappy. Morgan galled her, besieging her with Christian preaching and constantly accusing her of being the scarlet whore of Babylon. Guinevere endured it patiently and the only complaint she ever made was in the early autumn when the nights lengthened and the first night frosts whitened the hollows and she told me that her chambers were being kept too cold. Arthur put a stop to that, ordering that Guinevere could burn as much fuel as she wished. He loved her still, though he hated to hear me mention her name. As for Guinevere, I did not know who she loved. She would always ask me for news of Arthur, but never once mentioned Lancelot.

Arthur too was a prisoner, but only of his own torments. His home, if he had one at all, was the royal palace at Durnovaria, but he preferred to tour Dumnonia, going from fortress to fortress and readying us all for the war against the Saxons that must come in the new year, though if there was any one place where he spent more time than another, it was with us at Dun Caric. We would see him coming from our hilltop hall, and a moment later a horn would sound in warning as his horsemen splashed across the stream.

Gwydre, his son, would run down to meet him and Arthur would lean down from Llamrei's saddle and scoop the boy up before spurring to our gate. He showed tenderness to Gwydre, indeed to all children, but with adults he showed a chill reserve. The old Arthur, the man of cheerful enthusiasm, was gone. He bared his soul only to Ceinwyn, and whenever he came to Dun Caric he would talk with her for hours. They spoke of Guinevere, who else? 'He still loves her,' Ceinwyn told me.

'He should marry again,' I said.

'How can he?' she asked. 'He doesn't think of anyone but her.'

'What do you tell him?'

'To forgive her, of course. I doubt she's going to be foolish again, and if she's the woman who makes him happy then he should swallow his pride and have her back.'

'He's too proud for that.'

'Evidently,' she said disapprovingly. She laid down her distaff and spindle. 'I think, maybe, he needs to kill Lancelot first. That would make him happy.'

Arthur tried that autumn. He led a sudden raid on Venta, Lancelot's capitol, but Lancelot had wind of the attack and fled to Cerdic, his protector. He took with him Amhar and Loholt, Arthur's sons by his Irish mistress, Ailleann. The twins had ever resented their bastardy and had allied themselves with Arthur's enemies. Arthur failed to find Lancelot, but he did bring back a rich haul of grain that was sorely needed because the turmoil of the summer had inevitably affected our harvest.

In mid autumn, just two weeks before Samain and in the days following his raid on Venta, Arthur came again to Dun Caric. He had become still thinner and his face even more gaunt. He had never been a man of frightening presence, but now he had become guarded so that men did not know what thoughts he had, and that reticence gave him a mystery, while the sadness in his soul added a hardness to him. He had ever been slow to anger, but now his temper flared at the smallest provocation. Most of all he was angry at himself for he believed he was a failure. His first two sons had abandoned him, his marriage had soured and Dumnonia had failed with it. He had thought he could make a perfect kingdom, a place of justice, security and peace, but the Christians had preferred slaughter. He

23

blamed himself for not seeing what was coming, and now, in the quiet after the storm, he doubted his own vision. 'We must just settle for doing the little things, Derfel,' he said to me that day.

It was a perfect autumn day. The sky was mottled with cloud so that patches of sunlight raced across the yellow-brown landscape that lay to our west. Arthur, for once, did not seek Ceinwyn's company, but led me to a patch of grass just outside Dun Caric's mended palisade from where he stared moodily at the Tor rearing on the skyline. He stared at Ynys Wydryn, where Guinevere lay. 'The little things?' I asked him.

'Defeat the Saxons, of course.' He grimaced, knowing that defeating the Saxons was no small thing. 'They are refusing to talk to us. If I send any emissaries they will kill them. They told me so last week.'

'They?' I asked.

'They,' he confirmed grimly, meaning both Cerdic and Aelle. The two Saxon Kings were usually at each other's throats, a condition we encouraged with massive bribery, but now, it seemed, they had learned the lesson that Arthur had taught the British kingdoms so well: that in unity alone lies victory. The two Saxon monarchs were joining forces to crush Dumnonia and their decision to receive no emissaries was a sign of their resolve, as well as a measure of self-protection. Arthur's messengers could carry bribes that might weaken their chieftains, and all emissaries, however earnestly they seek peace, serve to spy on the enemy. Cerdic and Aelle were taking no chances. They meant to bury their differences and join forces to crush us.

'I hoped the plague had weakened them,' I said.

'But new men have come, Derfel,' Arthur said. 'We hear their boats are landing every day, and every boat is filled with hungry souls. They know we are weak, so thousands of them will come next year, thousands upon thousands.' Arthur seemed to revel in the dire prospect. 'A horde! Maybe that is how we shall end, you and I? Two old friends, shield beside shield, cut down by barbarian axemen.'

'There are worse ways to die, Lord.'

'And better,' he said curtly. He was gazing towards the Tor, indeed whenever he came to Dun Caric he would always sit on this western slope; never on the eastern side, nor on the south slope facing Caer Cadarn, but always here, looking across the vale. I knew what he was thinking and he knew that I knew, but he would not mention her name for he did not want me to know that he woke each morning with thoughts of her and prayed every night for dreams of her. Then he was suddenly aware of my gaze and he looked down into the fields where Issa was training boys to be warriors. The autumn air was filled with the harsh clatter of spear staves clashing and of Issa's raw voice shouting to keep blades low and shields high. 'How are they?' Arthur asked, nodding at the recruits.

'Like us twenty years ago,' I said, 'and back then our elders said we would never make warriors, and twenty years from now those boys will be saying the same about their sons. They'll be good. One battle will season them, and after that they'll be as useful as any warrior in Britain.'

'One battle,' Arthur said grimly, 'we may only have one battle. When the Saxons come, Derfel, they will outnumber us. Even if Powys and Gwent send all their men, we shall be outnumbered.' He spoke a bitter truth. 'Merlin says I shouldn't worry,' Arthur added sarcastically, 'he says his business on Mai Dun will make a war unnecessary. Have you visited the place?'

'Not yet.'

'Hundreds of fools dragging firewood to the summit. Madness.' He spat down the slope. 'I don't put my trust in Treasures, Derfel, but in shield walls and sharp spears. And I have one other hope.' He paused.

'Which is?' I prompted him.

He turned to look at me. 'If we can divide our enemies one more time,' he said, 'then we still have a chance. If Cerdic comes on his own we can defeat him, so long as Powys and Gwent help us, but I can't defeat Cerdic and Aelle together. I might win if I had five years to rebuild our army, but I can't do it next spring. Our only hope, Derfel, is for our enemies to fall out.' It was our old way to make war. Bribe one Saxon King to fight the other, but from what Arthur had told me, the Saxons were taking good care to make sure it did not happen this winter. 'I will offer Aelle a permanent peace,' Arthur went on. 'He may keep all his present lands, and all the land he can take from Cerdic, and he and his descendants may rule those lands for ever. You understand me? I yield him that land in perpetuity, if he will only side with us in the coming war.'

I said nothing for a while. The old Arthur, the Arthur who had been my friend before that night in Isis's temple, would never have spoken those words for they were not true. No man would cede British land to the Sais. Arthur was lying in the hope that Aelle would believe the lie, and in a few years Arthur would break the promise and attack Aelle. I knew that, but I knew better than to challenge the lie, for then I could not pretend to believe in it myself. Instead I reminded Arthur of an ancient oath that had been buried on a stone beside a far-off tree. 'You've sworn to kill Aelle,' I reminded him. 'Is that oath forgotten?'

'I care for no oaths now,' he said coldly, then the temper broke through. 'And why should I? Does anyone keep their oaths to me?'

'I do, Lord.'

'Then obey me, Derfel,' he said curtly, 'and go to Aelle.'

I had known that demand was coming. I did not answer at first, but watched Issa shove his youngsters into a shaky-looking shield wall. Then I turned to Arthur. 'I thought Aelle had promised death to your emissaries?'

Arthur did not look at me. Instead he gazed at that far green mound. 'The old men say it will be a hard winter this year,' he said, 'and I want Aelle's answer before the snows come.'

'Yes, Lord,' I said.

He must have heard the unhappiness in my voice for he turned on me again. 'Aelle will not kill his own son.'

'We must hope not, Lord,' I said blandly.

'So go to him, Derfel,' Arthur said. For all he knew he had just condemned me to death, but he showed no regret. He stood and brushed the scraps of grass from his white cloak. 'If we can just beat Cerdic next spring, Derfel, then we can remake Britain.'

'Yes, Lord,' I said. He made it all sound so simple: just beat the Saxons, then remake Britain. I reflected that it had always been thus; one last great task, then joy would always follow. Somehow it never did, but now, in desperation and to give us one last chance, I must travel to see my father.

I AM A SAXON. My Saxon mother, Erce, while she was still pregnant, was taken captive by Uther and made a slave and I was born soon after. I was taken from my mother as a small child, but not before I had learned the Saxon tongue. Later, much later, on the very eve of Lancelot's rebellion, I found my mother and learned that my father was Aelle.

My blood then is pure Saxon, and half royal at that, though because I was raised among the Britons I feel no kinship with the Sais. To me, as to Arthur or to any other free-born Briton, the Sais are a plague carried to us across the Eastern Sea.

From whence they come, no one really knows. Sagramor, who has travelled more widely than any other of Arthur's commanders, tells me the Saxon land is a distant, fog-shrouded place of bogs and woodland, though he admits he has never been there. He just knows it is somewhere across the sea and they are leaving it, he claims, because the land of Britain is better, though I have also heard that the Saxons' homeland is under siege from other, even stranger, enemies who come from the world's farthest edge. But for whatever reason, for a hundred years now the Saxons have been crossing the sea to take our land and now they hold all eastern Britain. We call that stolen territory Lloegyr, the Lost Lands, and there is not a soul in free Britain who does not dream of taking back the Lost Lands. Merlin and Nimue believe that the lands will only be recovered by the Gods, while Arthur wishes to do it with the sword. And my task was to divide our enemies to make the task easier for either the Gods or for Arthur.

I travelled in the autumn when the oaks had turned to bronze, the beeches to red and the cold was misting the dawns white. I travelled alone, for if Aelle was to reward an emissary's coming with death then it was better that only one man should die. Ceinwyn had begged me to take a warband, but to what purpose? One band could not hope to take on the power of Aelle's whole army, and so, as the wind stripped the first yellow leaves from the elms, I rode eastwards. Ceinwyn had tried to persuade me to wait until after Samain, for if Merlin's invocations worked at Mai Dun then there would surely be no need for any emissaries to visit the Saxons, but Arthur would not countenance any delay. He had put his faith in Aelle's treachery and he wanted an answer from the Saxon King, and so I rode, hoping only that I would survive and that I would be back in Dumnonia by Samain Eve. I wore my sword and I had a shield hung on my back, but I carried no other weapons or armour.

I did not ride directly eastwards, for that route would have taken me dangerously close to Cerdic's land, so instead I went north into Gwent and then eastwards, aiming for the Saxon frontier where Aelle ruled. For a day and a half I journeyed through the rich farmlands of Gwent, passing villas and homesteads where smoke blew from roof holes. The fields were churned muddy by the hoofs of beasts being penned for the winter slaughter, and their lowing added a melancholy to my journey. The air had that first hint of winter and in the mornings the swollen sun hung low and pale in the mist. Starlings flocked on fallow fields.

The landscape changed as I rode eastwards. Gwent was a Christian country and at first I passed large, elaborate churches, but by the second day the churches were much smaller and the farms less prosperous until at last I reached the middle lands, the waste places where neither Saxon nor Briton ruled, but where both had their killing grounds. Here the meadows that had once fed whole families were thick with oak saplings, hawthorn, birch and ash, the villas were roofless ruins and the halls were stark burned skeletons. Yet some folk still lived here, and when I once heard footsteps running through a nearby wood I drew Hywelbane in fear of the masterless men who had their refuge in these wild valleys, but no one accosted me until that evening when a band of spearmen barred my path. They were men of Gwent and, like all King Meurig's soldiers, they wore the vestiges of old Rome's uniform; bronze breastplates, helmets crested with plumes of red-dyed horsehair, and rust-red cloaks. Their leader was a Christian named Carig and he invited me to their fortress that stood in a clearing on a high wooded ridge. Carig's job was to guard the frontier and he brusquely demanded to know my business, but enquired no further when I gave him my name and said I rode for Arthur.

Carig's fortress was a simple wooden palisade inside which was built a pair of huts that were thick with smoke from their open fires. I warmed myself as Carig's dozen men busied themselves with cooking a haunch of venison on a spit made from a captured Saxon spear. There were a dozen such fortresses within a day's march, all watching eastwards to guard against Aelle's raiders. Dumnonia had much the same precautions, though we kept an army permanently close to our border. The expense of such an army was exorbitant, and resented by those whose taxes of grain and leather and salt and fleeces paid for the troops. Arthur had always struggled to make the taxes fair and keep their burden light, though now, after the rebellion, he was ruthlessly levying a stiff penalty on all those wealthy men who had followed Lancelot. That levy fell disproportionately on Christians, and Meurig, the Christian King of Gwent, had sent a protest that Arthur had ignored. Carig, Meurig's loyal follower, treated me with a certain reserve, though he did do his best to warn me of what waited across the border. 'You do know, Lord,' he said, 'that the Sais are refusing to let men cross the frontier?'

'I had heard, yes.'

'Two merchants went by a week ago,' Carig said. 'They were carrying pottery and fleeces. I warned them, but,' he paused and shrugged, 'the Saxons kept the pots and the wool, but sent back two skulls.'

'If my skull comes back,' I told him, 'send it to Arthur.' I watched the venison fat drip and flare in the fire. 'Do any travellers come out of Lloegyr?'

'Not for weeks now,' Carig said, 'but next year, no doubt, you will see plenty of Saxon spearmen in Dumnonia.'

'Not in Gwent?' I challenged him.

'Aelle has no quarrel with us,' Carig said firmly. He was a nervous young man who did not much like his exposed position on Britain's frontier, though he did his duty conscientiously enough and his men, I noted, were well disciplined.

'You're Britons,' I told Carig, 'and Aelle's a Saxon, isn't that quarrel enough?'

Carig shrugged. 'Dumnonia is weak, Lord, the Saxons know that. Gwent is strong. They will attack you, not us.' He sounded horribly complacent.

'But once they have beaten Dumnonia,' I said, touching the iron in my sword hilt to avert the ill-luck implicit in my words, 'how long before they come north into Gwent?'

'Christ will protect us,' Carig said piously, and made the sign of the cross. A crucifix hung on the hut wall and one of his men licked his fingers then touched the feet of the tortured Christ. I surreptitiously spat into the fire.

I rode east next morning. Clouds had come in the night and the dawn greeted me with a thin cold rain that blew into my face. The Roman road, broken and weed-grown now, stretched into a dank wood and the further I rode the lower my spirits sank. Everything I had heard in Carig's frontier fort suggested that Gwent would not fight for Arthur. Meurig, the young King of Gwent, had ever been a reluctant warrior. His father, Tewdric, had known that the Britons must unite against their common enemy, but Tewdric had resigned his throne and gone to live as a monk beside the River Wye and his son was no warlord. Without Gwent's well-trained troops Dumnonia was surely doomed unless a glowing naked nymph presaged some miraculous intervention by the Gods. Or unless Aelle believed Arthur's lie. And would Aelle even receive me? Would he even believe that I was his son? The Saxon King had been kind enough to me on the few occasions we had met, but that meant nothing for I was still his enemy, and the longer I rode through that bitter drizzle between the towering wet trees, the greater my despair. I was sure Arthur had sent me to my death, and worse, that he had done it with the callousness of a losing gambler risking everything on one final cast on the throwboard.

At mid morning the trees ended and I rode into a wide clearing through which a stream flowed. The road forded the small water, but beside the crossing and stuck into a mound that stood as high as a man's waist, there stood a dead fir tree that was hung with offerings. The magic was strange to me so I had no idea whether the bedecked tree guarded the road, placated the stream or was

30

merely the work of children. I slid off my horse's back and saw that the objects hung from the brittle branches were the small bones of a man's spine. No child's play, I reckoned, but what? I spat beside the mound to avert its evil, touched the iron of Hywelbane's hilt, then led my horse through the ford.

The woods began again thirty paces beyond the stream and I had not covered half that distance when an axe hurtled out of the shadows beneath the branches. It turned as it came towards me, the day's grey light flickering from the spinning blade. The throw was bad, and the axe hissed past a good four paces away. No one challenged me, but nor did any other weapon come from the trees.

'I am a Saxon!' I shouted in that language. Still no one spoke, but I heard a mutter of low voices and the crackle of breaking twigs. 'I am a Saxon!' I called again, and wondered whether the hidden watchers were not Saxons but outlaw Britons, for I was still in the wasteland where the masterless men of every tribe and country hid from justice.

I was about to call in the British tongue that I meant no harm when a voice shouted from the shadows in Saxon. 'Throw your sword here!' a man commanded me.

'You may come and take the sword,' I answered.

There was a pause. 'Your name?' the voice demanded.

'Derfel,' I said, 'son of Aelle.'

I called my father's name as a challenge, and it must have unsettled them because once again I heard the low murmur of voices, and then, a moment later, six men pushed through the brambles to come into the clearing. All were in the thick furs that Saxons favoured as armour and all carried spears. One of them wore a horned helmet and he, evidently the leader, walked down the edge of the road towards me. 'Derfel,' he said, stopping a half dozen paces from me. 'Derfel,' he said again. 'I have heard that name, and it is no Saxon name.'

'It is my name,' I answered, 'and I am a Saxon.'

'A son of Aelle?' He was suspicious.

'Indeed.'

He considered me for a moment. He was a tall man with a mass of brown hair crammed into his horned helmet. His beard reached almost to his waist and his moustaches hung to the top edge of the leather breastplate he wore beneath his fur cloak. I supposed he was a local chieftain, or maybe a warrior deputed to guard this part of the frontier. He twisted one of his moustaches in his free hand, then let the strands unwind. 'Hrothgar, son of Aelle, I know,' he said musingly, 'and Cyrning, son of Aelle, I call a friend. Penda, Saebold and Yffe, sons of Aelle, I have seen in battle, but Derfel, son of Aelle?' He shook his head.

'You see him now,' I said.

He hefted his spear, noting that my shield was still hanging from my horse's saddle. 'Derfel, friend of Arthur, I have heard of,' he said accusingly.

'You see him also,' I said, 'and he has business with Aelle.'

'No Briton has business with Aelle,' he said, and his men growled their assent.

'I am a Saxon,' I retorted.

'Then what is your business?'

'That is for my father to hear and for me to speak. You are not part of it.'

He turned and gestured towards his men. 'We make it our business.'

'Your name?' I demanded.

He hesitated, then decided that imparting his name would do no harm. 'Ceolwulf,' he said, 'son of Eadbehrt.'

'So, Ceolwulf,' I said, 'do you think my father will reward you when he hears that you delayed my journey? What will you expect of him? Gold? Or a grave?'

It was a fine bluff, but it worked. I had no idea whether Aelle would embrace me or kill me, but Ceolwulf had sufficient fear of his King's wrath to give me grudging passage and an escort of four spearmen who led me deeper and deeper into the Lost Lands.

And so I travelled through places where few free Britons had stepped in a generation. These were the enemy heartlands, and for two days I rode through them. At first glance the country looked little different from British land, for the Saxons had taken over our fields and they farmed them in much the same manner as we did, though I noted their haystacks were piled higher and made squarer than ours, and their houses were built more stoutly. The Roman villas were mostly deserted, though here and there an estate still functioned. There were no Christian churches here, indeed no shrines at all that I could see, though we did once pass a British idol which had some small offerings left at its base. Britons still lived here and some even owned their own land, but most were slaves or else were wives to Saxons. The names of the places had all changed and my escort did not even know what they had been called when the British ruled. We passed through Lycceword and Steortford, then Leodasham and Celmeresfort, all strange Saxon names but all prosperous places. These were not the homes and farms of invaders, but the settlements of a fixed people. From Celmeresfort we turned south through Beadewan and Wicford, and as we rode my companions proudly told me that we now rode across farmland that Cerdic had yielded back to Aelle during the summer. The land was the price, they said, of Aelle's loyalty in the coming war that would take these people clean across Britain to the Western Sea. My escort was confident that they would win. They had all heard how Dumnonia had been weakened by Lancelot's rebellion, and that revolt had encouraged the Saxon Kings to unite in an effort to take all southern Britain.

Aelle's winter quarters were at a place the Saxons called Thunres-lea. It was a high hill in a flat landscape of clay fields and dark marshes, and from the hill's flat summit a man could stare south-wards across the wide Thames towards the misty land where Cerdic ruled. A great hall stood on the hill. It was a massive building of dark oak timbers, and fixed high on its steep pointed gable was Aelle's symbol: a bull's skull painted with blood. In the dusk the lonely hall loomed black and huge, a baleful place. Off to the east there was a village beyond some trees and I could see the flicker of a myriad fires there. It seemed I had arrived in Thunreslea at the time of a gathering, and the fires showed where folk camped. 'It's a feast,' one of my escort told me.

'In honour of the Gods?' I enquired.

'In honour of Cerdic. He's come to talk with our King.'

My hopes, that were already low, plummeted. With Aelle I stood some chance of survival, but with Cerdic, I thought, there was none. Cerdic was a cold, hard man, while Aelle had an emotional, even a generous, soul.

I touched Hywelbane's hilt and thought of Ceinwyn. I prayed

the Gods would let me see her again, and then it was time to slide off my weary horse's back, twitch my cloak straight, unhook the shield from my saddle's pommel and go to face my enemies.

Three hundred warriors must have been feasting on the rush-covered floor of that high, gaunt hall on its damp hilltop. Three hundred raucous, cheerful men, bearded and red-faced, who, unlike us Britons, saw nothing wrong in carrying weapons into a lord's feasting-hall. Three huge fires flared in the hall's centre and so thick was the smoke that at first I could not see the men sitting behind the long table at the hall's far end. No one noticed my entrance, for with my long fair hair and thick beard I looked like a Saxon spearman, but as I was led past the roaring fires a warrior saw the five-pointed white star on my shield and he remembered facing that symbol in battle. A growl erupted through the tumult of talk and laughter. The growl spread until every man in that hall was howling at me as I walked towards the dais on which the high table stood. The howling warriors put down their horns of ale and began to beat their hands against the floor or against their shields so that the high roof echoed with the death-beat.

The crash of a blade striking the table ended the noise. Aelle had stood, and it was his sword that had driven splinters from the long rough table where a dozen men sat behind heaped plates and full horns. Cerdic was beside him, and on Cerdic's other side was Lancelot. Nor was Lancelot the only Briton there. Bors, his cousin, slouched beside him while Amhar and Loholt, Arthur's sons, sat at the table's end. All of them were enemies of mine, and I touched Hywelbane's hilt and prayed for a good death.

Aelle stared at me. He knew me well enough, but did he know I was his son? Lancelot looked astonished to see me, he even blushed, then he beckoned to an interpreter, spoke to him briefly and the interpreter leant towards Cerdic and whispered in the monarch's ear. Cerdic also knew me, but neither Lancelot's words, nor his recognition of an enemy, changed the impenetrable expression on his face. It was a clerk's face, clean-shaven, narrow-chinned, and with a high broad forehead. His lips were thin and his sparse hair was combed severely back to a knot behind his skull, but the otherwise unremarkable face was made memorable by his eyes. They were pale eyes, merciless eyes, a killer's eyes.

34

Aelle seemed too astonished to speak. He was much older than Cerdic, indeed he was a year or two beyond fifty which made him an old man by any reckoning, but he still looked formidable. He was tall, broad-chested, and had a flat, hard face, a broken nose, scarred cheeks and a full black beard. He was dressed in a fine scarlet robe and had a thick gold torque at his neck and more gold about his wrists, but no finery could disguise the fact that Aelle was first and foremost a soldier, a great bear of a Saxon warrior. Two fingers were missing from his right hand, struck off in some long-ago battle where, I daresay, he had taken a bloody revenge. He finally spoke. 'You dare come here?'

'To see you, Lord King,' I answered and went down on one knee. I bowed to Aelle, then to Cerdic, but ignored Lancelot. To me he was a nothing, a client King of Cerdic's, an elegant British traitor whose dark face was filled with loathing for me.

Cerdic speared a piece of meat on a long knife, brought it towards his mouth, then hesitated. 'We are receiving no messengers from Arthur,' he said casually, 'and any who are foolish enough to come are killed.' He put the meat in his mouth, then turned away as though he had disposed of me as a piece of trivial business. His men bayed for my death.

Aelle again silenced the hall by banging his sword blade on the table. 'Do you come from Arthur?' he challenged me.

I decided the Gods would forgive an untruth. 'I bring you greetings, Lord King,' I said, 'from Erce, and the filial respect of Erce's son who is also, to his joy, your own.'

The words meant nothing to Cerdic. Lancelot, who had listened to a translation, again whispered urgently to his interpreter and that man spoke once more to Cerdic. I did not doubt that he had encouraged what Cerdic now uttered. 'He must die,' Cerdic insisted. He spoke very calmly, as though my death were a small thing. 'We have an agreement,' he reminded Aelle.

'Our agreement says we shall receive no embassies from our enemies,' Aelle said, still staring at me.

'And what else is he?' Cerdic demanded, at last showing some temper.

'He is my son,' Aelle said simply, and a gasp sounded all around the crowded hall. 'He is my son,' Aelle said again, 'are you not?'

'I am, Lord King.'

'You have more sons,' Cerdic told Aelle carelessly, and gestured towards some bearded men who sat at Aelle's left hand. Those men – I presumed they were my half-brothers – just stared at me in confusion. 'He brings a message from Arthur!' Cerdic insisted. 'That dog,' he pointed his knife towards me, 'always serves Arthur.'

'Do you bring a message from Arthur?' Aelle asked.

'I have a son's words for a father,' I lied again, 'nothing more.'

'He must die!' Cerdic said curtly, and all his supporters in the hall growled their agreement.

'I will not kill my own son,' Aelle said, 'in my own hall.'

'Then I may?' Cerdic asked acidly. 'If a Briton comes to us then he must be put to the sword.' He spoke those words to the whole hall. 'That is agreed between us!' Cerdic insisted and his men roared their approval and beat spear shafts against their shields. 'That thing,' Cerdic said, flinging a hand towards me, 'is a Saxon who fights for Arthur! He is vermin, and you know what you do with vermin!' The warriors bellowed for my death and their hounds added to the clamour with howls and barks. Lancelot watched me, his face unreadable, while Amhar and Loholt looked eager to help put me to the sword. Loholt had an especial hatred for me, for I had held his arm while his father had struck off his right hand.

Aelle waited until the tumult had subsided. 'In my hall,' he said, stressing the possessive word to show that he ruled here, not Cerdic, 'a warrior dies with his sword in his hand. Does any man here wish to kill Derfel while he carries his sword?' He looked about the hall, inviting someone to challenge me. No one did, and Aelle looked down at his fellow King. 'I will break no agreement with you, Cerdic. Our spears will march together and nothing my son says can prevent that victory.'

Cerdic picked a scrap of meat from between his teeth. 'His skull,' he said, pointing to me, 'will make a fine standard for battle. I want him dead.'

'Then you kill him,' Aelle said scornfully. They might have been allies, but there was little affection between them. Aelle resented the younger Cerdic as an upstart, while Cerdic believed the older man lacked ruthlessness.

Cerdic half smiled at Aelle's challenge. 'Not me,' he said mildly, 'but my champion will do the work.' He looked down the hall, found the man he wanted and pointed a finger. 'Liofa! There is vermin here. Kill it!'

The warriors cheered again. They relished the thought of a fight, and doubtless before the night was over the ale they were drinking would cause more than a few deadly battles, but a fight to the death between a King's champion and a King's son was a far finer entertainment than any drunken brawl and a much better amusement than the melody of the two harpists who watched from the hall's edges.

I turned to see my opponent, hoping he would prove to be already half drunk and thus easy meat for Hywelbane, but the man who stepped through the feasters was not at all what I had expected. I thought he would be a huge man, not unlike Aelle, but this champion was a lean, lithe warrior with a calm, shrewd face that carried not a single scar. He gave me an unworried glance as he let his cloak fall, then he pulled a long thin-bladed sword from its leather scabbard. He wore little jewellery, nothing but a plain silver torque, and his clothes had none of the finery that most champions affected. Everything about him spoke of experience and confidence, while his unscarred face suggested either monstrous good luck or uncommon skill. He also looked frighteningly sober as he came to the open space in front of the high table and bowed to the Kings.

Aelle looked troubled. 'The price for speaking with me,' he told me, 'is to defend yourself against Liofa. Or you may leave now and go home in safety.' The warriors jeered that suggestion.

'I would speak with you, Lord King,' I said.

Aelle nodded, then sat. He still looked unhappy and I guessed that Liofa had a fearsome reputation as a swordsman. He had to be good, or else he would not be Cerdic's champion, but something about Aelle's face told me that Liofa was more than just good.

Yet I too had a reputation, and that seemed to worry Bors who was whispering urgently in Lancelot's ear. Lancelot, once his cousin had finished, beckoned to the interpreter who in turn spoke with Cerdic. The King listened, then gave me a dark look. 'How do we know,' he asked, 'that this son of yours, Aelle, is not wearing some charm of Merlin's?'

The Saxons had always feared Merlin, and the suggestion made them growl angrily.

Aelle frowned. 'Do you have one, Derfel?'

'No, Lord King.'

Cerdic was not convinced. 'These men would recognize Merlin's magic,' he insisted, waving at Lancelot and Bors; then he spoke to the interpreter, who passed on his orders to Bors. Bors shrugged, stood up and walked round the table and off the dais. He hesitated as he approached me, but I spread my arms as though to show that I meant him no harm. Bors examined my wrists, maybe looking for strands of knotted grass or some other amulet, then tugged open the laces of my leather jerkin. 'Be careful of him, Derfel,' he muttered in British, and I realized, with surprise, that Bors was no enemy after all. He had persuaded Lancelot and Cerdic that I needed to be searched just so that he could whisper his warning to me. 'He's quick as a weasel,' Bors went on, 'and he fights with both hands. Watch the bastard when he seems to slip.' He saw the small golden brooch that had been a present from Ceinwyn. 'Is it charmed?' he asked me.

'No.'

'I'll keep it for you anyway,' he said, unpinning the brooch and showing it to the hall, and the warriors roared their anger that I might have been concealing the talisman. 'And give me your shield,' Bors said, for Liofa had none.

I slipped the loops from my left arm and gave the shield to Bors. He took it and placed it against the dais, then balanced Ceinwyn's brooch on the shield's top edge. He looked at me as if to make sure I had seen where he put it and I nodded.

Cerdic's champion gave his sword a cut in the smoky air. 'I have killed forty-eight men in single combat,' he told me in a mild, almost bored voice, 'and lost count of the ones who have fallen to me in battle.' He paused and touched his face. 'In all those fights,' he said, 'I have not once taken a scar. You may yield to me now if you want your death to be swift.'

'You may give me your sword,' I told him, 'and spare yourself a beating.'

The exchange of insults was a formality. Liofa shrugged away my offer and turned to the kings. He bowed again and I did the

38

same. We were standing ten paces apart in the middle of the open space between the dais and the nearest of the three big fires, and on either flank the hall was crammed with excited men. I could hear the chink of coins as wagers were placed.

Aelle nodded to us, giving his permission for the fight to begin. I drew Hywelbane and raised her hilt to my lips. I kissed one of the little slivers of pig bone that were set there. The two bone scraps were my real talismans and they were far more powerful than the brooch, for the pig bones had once been a part of Merlin's magic. The scraps of bone gave me no magical protection, but I kissed the hilt a second time, then faced Liofa.

Our swords are heavy and clumsy things that do not hold their edge in battle and so become little more than great iron clubs that take considerable strength to wield. There is nothing delicate about sword fighting, though there is skill. The skill lies in deception, in persuading an opponent that a blow will come from the left and, when he guards that side, striking from the right, though most sword fights are not won by such skill, but by brute strength. One man will weaken and so his guard will be beaten down and the winner's sword will hack and beat him to death.

But Liofa did not fight like that. Indeed, before or since, I have never fought another quite like Liofa. I sensed the difference as he approached me, for his sword blade, though as long as Hywelbane, was much slimmer and lighter. He had sacrificed weight for speed, and I realized that this man would be as fast as Bors had warned me, lightning fast, and just as I realized that, so he attacked, only instead of sweeping the blade in a great curve he lunged with it, trying to rake its point through the muscles of my right arm.

I walked away from the lunge. These things happen so fast that afterwards, trying to remember the passages of a fight, the mind cannot pin down each move and counter-stroke, but I had seen a flicker in his eye, saw that his sword could only stab forward and I had moved just as he whipped the stab towards me. I pretended that the speed of his lunge had given me no surprise and I made no parry, but just walked past him and then, when I reckoned he must be off balance I snarled and backswung Hywelbane in a blow that would have disembowelled an ox.

He leapt backwards, not off balance at all, and spread his arms

39

wide so that my blow scythed a harmless six inches from his belly. He waited for me to swing again, but instead I was waiting for him. Men were shouting at us, calling for blood, but I had no ears for them. I kept my gaze fixed on Liofa's calm grey eyes. He hefted the sword in his right hand, flicked it forward to touch my blade, then swung at me.

I parried easily, then countered his backswing which followed as naturally as the day follows the night. The clangour of the swords was loud, but I could feel that there was no real effort in Liofa's blows. He was offering me the fight I might have expected, but he was also judging me as he edged forward and as he swung blow after blow. I parried the cuts, sensing when they became harder, and just when I expected him to make a real effort he checked a blow, let go of the sword in mid-air, snatched it with his left hand and slashed it straight down towards my head. He did it with the speed of a viper striking.

Hywelbane caught that downward cut. I do not know how she did it. I had been parrying a sideways blow and suddenly there was no sword there, but only death above my skull, yet somehow my blade was in the right place and his lighter sword slid down to Hywelbane's hilt and I tried to convert the parry into a counter-cut, but there was no force in my response and he leapt easily backwards. I kept going forward, cutting as he had cut, only doing it with all my strength so that any one of the blows would have gutted him, and the speed and force of my attacks gave him no choice but to retreat. He parried the blows as easily as I had parried his, but there was no resistance in the parries. He was letting me swing, and instead of defending with his sword he was protecting himself by constantly retreating. He was also letting me exhaust my strength on thin air instead of on bone and muscle and blood. I gave a last massive cut, checked the blade in mid swing and twisted my wrist to lunge Hywelbane at his belly.

His sword edged towards the lunge, then whipped back at me as he sidestepped. I made the same quick sidestep, so that each of us missed. Instead we clashed, breast to breast, and I smelt his breath. There was a faint smell of ale, though he was certainly not drunk. He froze for a heartbeat, then courteously moved his sword arm aside and looked quizzically at me as if to suggest that we agree

40

to break apart. I nodded, and we both stepped backwards, swords held wide, while the crowd talked excitedly. They knew they were watching a rare fight. Liofa was famous among them, and I dare say my name was not obscure, but I knew I was probably out-matched. My skills, if I had any, were a soldier's skills. I knew how to break a shield wall, I knew how to fight with spear and shield, or with sword and shield, but Liofa, Cerdic's champion, had only one skill and that was to fight man on man with a sword. He was lethal.

We drew back six or seven paces, then Liofa skipped forward, as light on his feet as a dancer, and cut at me fast. Hywelbane met the cut hard and I saw him draw back from the solid parry with a flinch. I was faster than he expected, or maybe he was slower than usual for even a small amount of ale will slow a man. Some men only fight drunk, but those who live longest fight sober.

I wondered about that flinch. He had not been hurt, yet I had obviously worried him. I cut at him and he leapt back, and that leap gave me another pause to think. What had made him flinch? Then I remembered the weakness of his parries and I realized he dared not risk his blade against mine, for it was too light. If I could strike that blade with all my force then it would as like as not break and so I slashed again, only this time I kept slashing and I roared at him as I stamped towards him. I cursed him by air, by fire and by sea. I called him woman, I spat on his grave and on the dog's grave where his mother was buried, and all the while he said not a word, but just let his sword meet mine and slide away and always he backed away and those pale eyes watched me.

Then he slipped. His right foot seemed to slide on a patch of rushes and his leg went out from under him. He fell backwards and reached out with his left hand to check himself and I roared his death and raised Hywelbane high.

Then I stepped away from him, without even trying to finish the killing blow.

I had been warned of that slip by Bors and I had been waiting for it. To watch it was marvellous, and I had very nearly been fooled for I could have sworn the slip was an accident, but Liofa was an acrobat as well as a sword fighter and the apparently unbalanced slip turned into a sudden supple motion that swept his sword around to where my feet should have been. I can still hear that long slim blade hissing as it swept just inches above the floor rushes. The blow should have sliced into my ankles, crippling me, only I was not there.

I had stepped back and now watched him calmly. He looked up ruefully. 'Stand, Liofa,' I said, and my voice was steady, telling him that all my rage had been a pretence.

I think he knew then that I was truly dangerous. He blinked once or twice and I guessed he had used his best tricks on me, but none had worked, and his confidence was sapped. But not his skill, and he came forward hard and fast to drive me back with a dazzling succession of short cuts, quick lunges and sudden sweeps. I let the sweeps go unparried, while the other attacks I touched away as best I could, deflecting them and trying to break his rhythm, but at last one cut beat me squarely. I caught it on my left forearm and the leather sleeve broke the sword's force, though I bore a bruise for the best part of a month afterwards. The crowd sighed. They had watched the fight keenly and were eager to see the first blood drawn. Liofa ripped the blade back from my forearm, trying to saw its edge through the leather to the bone, but I flicked my arm out of the way, lunged with Hywelbane and so drove him back.

He waited for me to follow up the attack, but it was my turn to play the tricks now. I deliberately did not move towards him, but instead let my sword drop a few inches as I breathed heavily. I shook my head, trying to flick the sweat-soaked hanks of hair from my forehead. It was hot beside that great fire. Liofa watched me cautiously. He could see I was out of breath, he saw my sword falter, but he had not killed forty-eight men by taking risks. He gave me one of his quick cuts to test my reaction. It was a short swing that demanded a parry, but would not thump home like an axe biting into flesh. I parried it late, deliberately late, and let the tip of Liofa's sword strike my upper arm as Hywelbane clanged on the thicker part of his blade. I grunted, feigned a swing, then pulled my blade back as he stepped easily away.

Again I waited for him. He lunged, I struck his sword aside, but this time I did not try to counter his attack with one of my own. The crowd had fallen silent, sensing this fight was about to end. Liofa tried another lunge and again I parried. He preferred the lunge, for that would kill without endangering his precious blade, but I knew that if I parried those quick stabs often enough he would eventually kill me the old way instead. He tried two more lunges and I knocked the first clumsily aside, stepped back from the second, then cuffed at my eyes with my left sleeve as though the sweat was stinging them.

He swung then. He shouted aloud for the first time as he gave a mighty swing that came from high above his head and angled down towards my neck. I parried it easily, but staggered as I slid his scything blow safely over my skull with Hywelbane's blade, then I let her drop a little and he did what I expected him to do.

He backswung with all his force. He did it fast and well, but I knew his speed now and I was already bringing Hywelbane up in a counter-stroke that was just as fast. I had both hands on her hilt and I put all my strength into that slashing upward blow that was not aimed at Liofa, but at his sword.

The two swords met plumb.

Only this time there was no ringing sound, but a crack.

For Liofa's blade had broken. The outer two thirds of it sheared clean away to fall among the rushes, leaving only a stump in his hand. He looked horrified. Then, for a heartbeat, he seemed tempted to attack me with the remnants of his sword, but I gave Hywelbane two fast cuts that drove him back. He could see now that I was not tired at all. He could also see that he was a dead man, but still he tried to parry Hywelbane with his broken weapon, but she beat that feeble metal stump aside and then I stabbed.

And held the blade still at the silver torque about his throat. 'Lord King?' I called, but keeping my eyes on Liofa's eyes. There was a silence in the hall. The Saxons had seen their champion beaten and they had no voices left. 'Lord King!' I called again.

'Lord Derfel?' Aelle answered.

'You asked me to fight King Cerdic's champion, you did not ask me to kill him. I beg his life of you.'

Aelle paused. 'His life is yours, Derfel.'

'Do you yield?' I asked Liofa. He did not answer at once. His pride was still seeking a victory, but while he hesitated I moved Hywelbane's tip from his throat to his right cheek. 'Well?' I prompted him.

'I yield,' he said, and threw down the stump of his sword.

I thrust with Hywelbane just hard enough to gouge the skin and flesh away from his cheekbone. 'A scar, Liofa,' I said, 'to remind you that you fought the Lord Derfel Cadarn, son of Aelle, and that you lost.' I left him bleeding. The crowd was cheering. Men are strange things. One moment they had been baying for my blood, now they were shouting plaudits because I had spared their champion's life. I retrieved Ceinwyn's brooch, then picked up my shield and gazed up at my father. 'I bring you greetings from Erce, Lord King,' I said.

'And they are welcome, Lord Derfel,' Aelle said, 'they are welcome.'

He gestured to a chair on his left that one of his sons had vacated and thus I joined Arthur's enemies at their high table. And feasted.

At the feast's end Aelle took me to his own chamber that lay behind the dais. It was a great room, high-beamed, with a fire burning at its centre and a bed of furs beneath the gable wall. He closed the door where he had set guards, then beckoned that I should sit on a wooden chest beside the wall while he walked to the far end of the chamber, loosened his drawers, and urinated into a sink hole in the earthen floor. 'Liofa's fast,' he said to me as he pissed.

'Very.'

'I thought he'd beat you.'

'Not fast enough,' I said, 'or else the ale slowed him. Now spit in it.'

'Spit in what?' my father demanded.

'Your urine. To prevent bad luck.'

'My Gods take no note of piss or spit, Derfel,' he said in amusement. He had invited two of his sons into the room and those two, Hrothgar and Cyrning, watched me curiously. 'So what message,' Aelle demanded, 'does Arthur send?'

'Why should he send any?'

'Because you wouldn't be here otherwise. You think you were whelped by a fool, boy? So what does Arthur want? No, don't tell me, let me guess.' He tied the rope belt of his trews, then went to sit in the room's only chair, a Roman armchair made of black wood

44

and inset with ivory, though much of the ivory pattern had lifted from its setting. 'He will offer me security of land, is that it,' Aelle asked, 'if I attack Cerdic next year?'

'Yes, Lord.'

'The answer is no,' he growled. 'A man offers me what is already mine! What kind of an offer is that?'

'A perpetual peace, Lord King,' I said.

Aelle smiled. 'When a man promises something for ever, he is playing with the truth. Nothing is for ever, boy, nothing. Tell Arthur my spears march with Cerdic next year.' He laughed. 'You wasted your time, Derfel, but I'm glad you came. Tomorrow we shall talk of Erce. You want a woman for the night?'

'No, Lord King.'

'Your Princess will never know,' he teased me.

'No, Lord King.'

'And he calls himself a son of mine!' Aelle laughed and his sons laughed with him. They were both tall and, though their hair was darker than mine, I suspect they resembled me, just as I suspected that they had been brought to the chamber to witness the conversation and so pass on Aelle's flat refusal to the other Saxon leaders. 'You can sleep outside my door,' Aelle said, waving his sons out of the chamber, 'you'll be safe there.' He waited as Hrothgar and Cyrning went out of the room, then checked me with a hand. 'Tomorrow,' my father said in a lower voice, 'Cerdic goes home, and he takes Lancelot with him. Cerdic will be suspicious that I let you live, but I will survive his suspicions. We shall talk tomorrow, Derfel, and I'll have a longer answer for your Arthur. It won't be the answer he wants, but maybe it's one he can live with. Go now, I have company coming.'

I slept in the narrow space between the dais and my father's door. In the night a girl slipped past me to Aelle's bed while in the hall the warriors sang and fought and drank and eventually slept, though it was dawn before the last man began snoring. That was when I woke to hear the cockerels calling on Thunreslea's hill, and I strapped on Hywelbane, picked up my cloak and shield, and stepped past the embers of the fires to go out into the raw chill air. A mist clung to the high plateau, thickening to a fog as the land dropped down to where the Thames widened into the sea. I walked

45

away from the hall to the hill's edge from where I stared down into the whiteness above the river.

'My Lord King,' a voice said behind me, 'ordered me to kill you if I found you alone.'

I turned to see Bors, Lancelot's cousin and champion. 'I owe you thanks,' I said.

'For warning you about Liofa?' Bors shrugged as though his warning had been a small thing. 'He's quick, isn't he? Quick and lethal.' Bors came to stand beside me where he bit into an apple, decided it was pulpy and so threw it away. He was another big warrior, another scarred and black-bearded spearman who had stood in too many shield walls and seen too many friends cut down. He gave a belch. 'I never minded fighting to give my cousin Dumnonia's throne,' he said, 'but I never wanted to fight for a Saxon. And I didn't want to watch you being cut down to amuse Cerdic.'

'But next year, Lord,' I said, 'you will be fighting for Cerdic.'

'Will I?' he asked me. He sounded amused. 'I don't know what I shall do next year, Derfel. Maybe I'll sail away to Lyonesse? They tell me the women there are the most beautiful in all the world. They have hair of silver, bodies of gold and no tongues.' He laughed, then took another apple from a pouch and polished it against his sleeve. 'My Lord King now,' he said, meaning Lancelot, 'he'll fight for Cerdic, but what other choice does he have? Arthur won't welcome him.'

I realized then what Bors was hinting. 'My Lord Arthur,' I said carefully, 'has no quarrel with you.'

'Nor I with him,' Bors said through a mouthful of apple. 'So maybe we shall meet again, Lord Derfel. It's a great pity I couldn't find you this morning. My Lord King would have rewarded me richly if I had killed you.' He grinned and walked away.

Two hours later I watched Bors leave with Cerdic, going down the hill where the clearing mist shredded among red-leaved trees. A hundred men went with Cerdic, most of them suffering from the night's feast, just like Aelle's men who formed an escort for their departing guests. I rode behind Aelle whose own horse was being led while he walked beside King Cerdic and Lancelot. Just behind them walked two standard-bearers, one carrying Aelle's blood-spattered bull skull on a staff, the other hoisting aloft Cerdic's red-painted wolf skull that was hung with a dead man's flayed skin. Lancelot ignored me. Earlier in the morning, when we had unexpectedly encountered each other close to the hall, he had simply looked through me and I made nothing of the encounter. His men had murdered my youngest daughter, and though I had killed the murderers, I would still have liked to avenge Dian's soul on Lancelot himself, but Aelle's hall was not the place to do it. Now, from a grassy ridge above the muddy banks of the Thames, I watched as Lancelot and his few retainers walked towards Cerdic's waiting ships.

Only Amhar and Loholt dared challenge me. The twins were sullen youths who hated their father and despised their mother. In their own eyes they were princes, but Arthur, who disdained titles, refused to give them the honour and that had only increased their resentment. They believed they had been cheated of royal rank, of land, of wealth and of honour, and they would fight for anyone who tried to defeat Arthur whom they blamed for all their ill-fortune. The stump of Loholt's right arm was sheathed in silver, to which he had attached a pair of bear's claws. It was Loholt who turned back to me. 'We shall meet next year,' he told me.

I knew he was spoiling for a fight, but I kept my voice mild. 'I look forward to the meeting.'

He held up his silver-sheathed stump, reminding me how I had held his arm as his father had struck with Excalibur. 'You owe me a hand, Derfel.'

I said nothing. Amhar had come to stand beside his brother. They both had their father's big-boned, long-jawed face, but in them it had been soured so that they showed none of Arthur's strength. Instead they looked cunning, almost wolf-like.

'Did you not hear me?' Loholt demanded.

'Be glad,' I told him, 'that you still have one hand. And as for my debt to you, Loholt, I shall pay it with Hywelbane.'

They hesitated, but they could not be certain that Cerdic's guards would support them if they drew their swords, and so at last they contented themselves with spitting at me before turning and strutting down to the muddy beach where Cerdic's two boats waited.

47

This shore beneath Thunreslea was a miserable place, half land and half sea, where the meeting of the river and the ocean had spawned a dull landscape of mudbanks, shoals and tangling sea-creeks. Gulls cried as Cerdic's spearmen plunged across the glutinous foreshore, waded into the shallow creek and hauled themselves over the wooden gunwales of their longboats. I saw Lancelot lift the hem of his cloak as he picked his delicate way through the foul-smelling mud. Loholt and Amhar followed him and, once they reached their boat, they turned and pointed their fingers at me, a gesture designed to cast ill-luck. I ignored them. The ship's sails were already raised, but the wind was light and the two high-prowed boats had to be manoeuvred out of the narrow ebbing creek with long oars wielded by Cerdic's spearmen. Once the boats' wolf-crested prows were facing towards the open water the warrior-oarsmen began a chant that offered a rhythm to their strokes. '*Hwaet* for your mother,' they chanted, 'and *hwaet* for your girl, and *hwaet* for your lover who you *hwaet* on the floor,' and with every '*hwaet*' they shouted louder and pulled on their long oars and the two ships gained speed until at last the mist curled about their sails that were crudely painted with wolves' skulls. 'And *hwaet* for your mother,' the chant began again, only now the voices were thinner through the vapour, 'and *hwaet* for your girl,' and the low hulls became vague in the mist until, at last, the ships vanished in the whitened air, 'and *hwaet* for your lover who you *hwaet* on the floor.' The sound came as if from nowhere, and then faded with the splashing of their oars.

Two of Aelle's men heaved their lord onto his horse. 'Did you sleep?' he asked me as he settled himself in his saddle.

'Yes, Lord King.'

'I had better things to do,' he said curtly. 'Now follow me.' He kicked back his heels and turned his horse along the shore where the creeks rippled and sucked as the tide ebbed. This morning, in honour of his departing guests, Aelle had dressed as a warrior King. His iron helmet was trimmed with gold and crowned with a fan of black feathers, his leather breastplate and long boots were dyed black, while from his shoulders there fell a long black bearskin cloak that dwarfed his small horse. A dozen of his men followed us on horseback, one of them carrying the bull-skull standard.

Aelle, like me, rode clumsily. 'I knew Arthur would send you,' he said suddenly and, when I made no answer, he turned to me. 'So you found your mother?'

'Yes, Lord King.'

'How is she?'

'Old,' I said truthfully, 'old, fat and sick.'

He sighed at that news. 'They start as young girls so beautiful they can break the hearts of a whole army, and after they've had a couple of children they all look old, fat and sick.' He paused, thinking about that. 'But somehow I thought that would never happen to Erce. She was very beautiful,' he said wistfully, then grinned, 'but thank the Gods there's a constant supply of the young ones, eh?' He laughed, then gave me another glance. 'When you first told me your mother's name I knew you were my son.' He paused. 'My firstborn son.'

'Your firstborn bastard,' I said.

'So? Blood is blood, Derfel.'

'And I am proud to have yours, Lord King.'

'And so you should be, boy, though you share it with enough others. I have not been selfish with my blood.' He chuckled, then turned his horse onto a mudbank and whipped the animal up its slippery slope to where a fleet of boats lay stranded. 'Look at them, Derfel!' my father said, reining in his horse and gesturing at the boats, 'look at them! Useless now, but nearly every one came this summer and every one was filled to the gunwales with folk.' He kicked his heels back again and we rode slowly past that sorry line of stranded boats.

There might have been eighty or ninety craft on the mudbank. All of them were double-ended, elegant ships, but all were now decaying. Their planks were green with slime, their bilges were flooded and their timbers black with rot. Some of the boats, which must have been there longer than a year, were nothing but dark skeletons. 'Threescore folk in every boat, Derfel,' Aelle said, 'at least threescore, and every tide brought more of them. Now, when the storms are haunting the open sea, they don't come, but they are building more boats and those will arrive in the spring. And not just here, Derfel, but all up the coast!' he swept his arm to encompass all Britain's eastern shore, 'boats and boats! All filled with our people, all wanting a home, all wanting land.' He spoke the last word fiercely, then turned his horse away from me without waiting for any response. 'Come!' he shouted, and I followed his horse across the tide-rippled mud of a creek, up a shingle bank and then through patches of thorn as we climbed the hill on which his great hall stood.

Aelle curbed his beast on a shoulder of the hill where he waited for me, then, when I joined him, he mutely pointed down into a saddle of land. An army was there. I could not count them, so many men were gathered in that fold of land, and these men, I knew, were but a part of Aelle's army. The Saxon warriors stood in a great crowd and when they saw their King on the skyline they burst into a huge roar of acclamation and began to beat their spear shafts against their shields so that the whole grey sky was filled with their terrible clattering. Aelle raised his scarred right hand and the noise died away. 'You see, Derfel?' he asked me.

'I see what you choose to show me, Lord King,' I answered evasively, knowing exactly what message I was being given by the stranded boats and the mass of armoured men.

'I am strong now,' Aelle said, 'and Arthur is weak. Can he even raise five hundred men? I doubt it. The spearmen of Powys will come to his aid, but will they be enough? I doubt it. I have a thousand trained spearmen, Derfel, and twice as many hungry men who will wield an axe to gain a yard of ground they can call their own. And Cerdic has more men still, far more, and he needs land even more desperately than I do. We both need land, Derfel, we both need land, and Arthur has it, and Arthur is weak.'

'Gwent has a thousand spearmen,' I said, 'and if you invade Dumnonia Gwent will come to its aid.' I was not sure of that, but it would do no harm to Arthur's cause to sound confident. 'Gwent, Dumnonia and Powys,' I said, 'all will fight, and there are still others who will come to Arthur's banner. The Blackshields will fight for us, and spearmen will come from Gwynedd and Elmet, even from Rheged and Lothian.'

Aelle smiled at my boastfulness. 'Your lesson is not yet done, Derfel,' he said, 'so come.' And again he spurred on, still climbing the hill, but now he inclined east towards a grove of trees. He dismounted by the wood, gestured for his escort to stay where they were, then led me along a narrow damp path to a clearing where two small wooden buildings stood. They were little more than huts with pitched roofs of rye-thatch and low walls made from untrimmed tree trunks. 'See?' he said, pointing to the nearer hut's gable.

I spat to avert the evil, for there, high on the gable, was a wooden cross. Here, in pagan Lloegyr, was one of the last things I had ever expected to see: a Christian church. The second hut, slightly lower than the church, was evidently living quarters for the priest who greeted our arrival by crawling out through the low door of his hovel. He wore the tonsure, had a monk's black robe and a tangled brown beard. He recognized Aelle and bowed low. 'Christ's greetings, Lord King!' the man called in badly accented Saxon.

'Where are you from?' I asked in the British tongue.

He looked surprised to be spoken to in his native language. 'From Gobannium, Lord,' he told me. The monk's wife, a draggled creature with resentful eyes, crawled from the hovel to stand beside her man.

'What are you doing here?' I asked him.

'The Lord Christ Jesus has opened King Aelle's eyes, Lord,' he said, 'and invited us to bring the news of Christ to his people. I am here with my brother priest Gorfydd to preach the gospel to the Sais.'

I looked at Aelle, who was smiling slyly. 'Missionaries from Gwent?' I asked.

'Feeble creatures, are they not?' Aelle said, gesturing the monk and his wife back into their hut. 'But they think they will turn us from the worship of Thunor and Seaxnet and I am content to let them think as much. For now.'

'Because,' I said slowly, 'King Meurig has promised you a truce so long as you let his priests come to your people?'

Aelle laughed. 'He is a fool, that Meurig. He cares more for the souls of my people than for the safety of his land, and two priests are a small price for keeping Gwent's thousand spearmen idle while we take Dumnonia.' He put an arm about my shoulders and led me back towards the horses. 'You see, Derfel? Gwent will not fight, not while their King believes there is a chance of spreading his religion among my people.'

'And is the religion spreading?' I asked.

He snorted. 'Among a few slaves and women, but not many, and it won't spread far. I'll see to that. I saw what that religion did to Dumnonia, and I'll not allow it here. Our old Gods are good enough for us, Derfel, so why should we need new ones? That's half the trouble with the Britons. They've lost their Gods.'

'Merlin has not,' I said.

That checked Aelle. He turned in the shadow of the trees and I saw the worry on his face. He had always been fearful of Merlin. 'I hear tales,' he said uncertainly.

'The Treasures of Britain,' I said.

'What are they?' he demanded.

'Nothing much, Lord King,' I said, honestly enough, 'just a tattered collection of old things. Only two are of any real value; a sword and a cauldron.'

'You have seen them?' he asked fiercely.

'Yes.'

'What will they do?'

I shrugged. 'No one knows. Arthur believes they will do nothing, but Merlin says they command the Gods and that if he performs the right magic at the right time then the old Gods of Britain will do his bidding.'

'And he'll unleash those Gods on us?'

'Yes, Lord King,' I said, and it would be soon, very soon, but I did not say that to my father.

Aelle frowned. 'We have Gods too,' he said.

'Then call them, Lord King. Let the Gods fight the Gods.'

'Gods aren't fools, boy,' he growled, 'why should they fight when men can do their killing for them?' He began walking again. 'I am old now,' he told me, 'and in all my years I have never seen the Gods. We believe in them, but do they care about us?' He gave me a worried look. 'Do you believe in these Treasures?'

'I believe in Merlin's power, Lord King.'

'But Gods walking the earth?' He thought about it for a while, then shook his head. 'And if your Gods come, why should ours not come to protect us? Even you, Derfel,' he spoke sarcastically, 'would find it hard to fight Thunor's hammer.' He had led me out

52

of the trees and I saw that both his escort and our horses were gone. 'We can walk,' Aelle said, 'and I shall tell you all about Dumnonia.'

'I know about Dumnonia, Lord King.'

'Then you know, Derfel, that its King is a fool, and that its ruler does not want to be a King, not even a, whatever it is you call him, a kaiser?'

'An emperor,' I said.

'An emperor,' he repeated, mocking the word with his pronunciation. He was leading me along a path beside the woods. No one else was in sight. To our left the ground fell away to the misted levels of the estuary, while to our north were the deep, dank woods. 'Your Christians are rebellious,' Aelle summed up his argument, 'your King is a crippled fool and your leader refuses to steal the throne from the fool. In time, Derfel, and sooner rather than later, another man will want that throne. Lancelot nearly took it, and a better man than Lancelot will try soon enough.' He paused, frowning. 'Why did Guinevere open her legs to him?' he asked.

'Because Arthur wouldn't become King,' I said bleakly.

'Then he is a fool. And next year he'll be a dead fool unless he accepts a proposal.'

'What proposal, Lord King?' I asked, stopping beneath a fiery red beech.

He stopped and placed his hands on my shoulders. 'Tell Arthur to give the throne to you, Derfel.'

I stared into my father's eyes. For a heartbeat I thought he must be jesting, then saw he was as earnest as a man could be. 'Me?' I asked, astonished.

'You,' Aelle said, 'and you swear loyalty to me. I shall want land from you, but you can tell Athur to give the throne to you, and you can rule Dumnonia. My people will settle and farm the land, and you shall govern them, but as my client King. We shall make a federation, you and I. Father and son. You rule Dumnonia and I rule Aengeland.'

'Aengeland?' I asked, for the word was new to me.

He took his hands from my shoulders and gestured about the countryside. 'Here! You call us Saxons, but you and I are Aengles. Cerdic is a Saxon, but you and I are the Aenglish and our country

53

is Aengeland. This is Aengeland!' He said it proudly, looking about that damp hilltop.

'What of Cerdic?' I asked him.

'You and I will kill Cerdic,' he said frankly, then plucked my elbow and began walking again, only now he led me onto a track that led between the trees where pigs rooted for beechmast among the newly fallen leaves. 'Tell Arthur what I suggest,' Aelle said. 'Tell him he can have the throne rather than you if that's what he wants, but whichever of you takes it, you take it in my name.'

'I shall tell him, Lord King,' I said, though I knew Arthur would scorn the proposal. I think Aelle knew that too, but his hatred of Cerdic had driven him to the suggestion. He knew that even if he and Cerdic did capture all southern Britain there would still have to be another war to determine which of them should be the Bretwalda, which is their name for the High King. 'Supposing,' I said, 'that Arthur and you attack Cerdic together next year instead?'

Aelle shook his head. 'Cerdic's spread too much gold among my chiefs. They won't fight him, not while he offers them Dumnonia as a prize. But if Arthur gives Dumnonia to you, and you give it to me, then they won't need Cerdic's gold. You tell Arthur that.'

'I shall tell him, Lord King,' I said again, but I still knew Arthur would never agree to the proposal for it would mean breaking his oath to Uther, the oath that promised to make Mordred King, and that oath lay at the taproot of all Arthur's life. Indeed I was so certain that he would not break the oath that, despite my words to Aelle, I doubted I would even mention the proposal to Arthur.

Aelle now led me into a wide clearing where I saw that my horse was waiting, and with it an escort of mounted spearmen. In the centre of the clearing there was a great rough stone the height of a man, and though it was nothing like the trimmed sarsens of Dumnonia's ancient temples, nor like the flat boulders on which we acclaimed our Kings, it was plain that it must be a sacred stone, for it stood all alone in the circle of grass and none of the Saxon warriors ventured close to it, though one of their own sacred objects, a great bark-stripped tree trunk with a crudely carved face, had been planted in the soil nearby. Aelle led me towards the great rock, but stopped short of it and fished in a pouch that hung from his sword belt. He brought out a small leather bag that he unlaced, then tipped something onto his palm. He held the object out to me and I saw that it was a tiny golden ring in which a small chipped agate was set. 'I was going to give this to your mother,' he told me, 'but Uther captured her before I had the chance, and I've kept it ever since. Take it.'

I took the ring. It was a simple thing, country made. It was not Roman work, for their jewels are exquisitely fashioned, nor was it Saxon made, for they like their jewellery heavy, but the ring had probably been made by some poor Briton who had fallen to a Saxon blade. The square green stone was not even set straight, but still the tiny ring possessed an odd and fragile loveliness. 'I never gave it to your mother,' Aelle said, 'and if she's fat, then she can't wear it now. So give it to your Princess of Powys. I hear she is a good woman?'

'She is, Lord King.'

'Give it to her,' Aelle said, 'and tell her that if our countries do come to war then I shall spare the woman wearing that ring, her and all her family.'

'Thank you, Lord King,' I said, and put the little ring in my pouch.

'I have one last gift for you,' he said and put an arm on my shoulders and led me to the stone. I was feeling guilty that I had not brought him any gift, indeed in my fear of coming into Lloegyr the thought had not even occurred to me, but Aelle overlooked the omission. He stopped beside the boulder. 'This stone once belonged to the Britons,' he told me, 'and was sacred to them. There's a hole in it, see? Come to the side, boy, look.'

I walked to the side of the stone and saw there was indeed a great black hole running into the heart of the stone.

'I talked once with an old British slave,' Aelle said, 'and he told me that by whispering into that hole you can talk with the dead.'

'But you don't believe that?' I asked him, having heard the scepticism in his voice.

'We believe we can talk to Thunor, Woden and Seaxnet through that hole,' Aelle said, 'but for you? Maybe you can reach the dead, Derfel.' He smiled. 'We shall meet again, boy.'

'I hope so, Lord King,' I said, and then I remembered my

mother's strange prophecy, that Aelle would be killed by his son, and I tried to dismiss it as the ravings of a mad old woman, but the Gods often choose such women as their mouthpieces and I suddenly had nothing to say.

Aelle embraced me, crushing my face into the collar of his great fur cape. 'Has your mother long to live?' he asked me.

'No, Lord King.'

'Bury her,' he said, 'with her feet to the north. It is the way of our people.' He gave me a last embrace. 'You'll be taken safe home,' he said, then stepped back. 'To talk to the dead,' he added gruffly, 'you must walk three times round the stone, then kneel to the hole. Give my granddaughter a kiss from me.' He smiled, pleased to have surprised me by revealing such an intimate knowledge of my life, and then he turned and walked away.

The waiting escort watched as I walked thrice round the stone, then as I knelt and leaned to the hole. I suddenly wanted to weep and my voice choked as I whispered my daughter's name. 'Dian?' I whispered into the stone's heart, 'my dear Dian? Wait for us, my darling, and we will come to you. Dian.' My dead daughter, my lovely Dian, murdered by Lancelot's men. I told her we loved her, I sent her Aelle's kiss, then I leaned my forehead on the cold rock and thought of her little shadowbody all alone in the Otherworld. Merlin, it is true, had told us that children play happily beneath the apples of Annwn in that death world, but I still wept as I imagined her suddenly hearing my voice. Did she look up? Was she, like me, crying?

I rode away. It took me three days to reach Dun Caric and there I gave Ceinwyn the little golden ring. She had always liked simple things and the ring suited her far better than some elaborate Roman jewel. She wore it on the small finger of her right hand which was the only finger it fitted. 'I doubt it will save my life, though,' she said ruefully.

'Why not?' I asked.

She smiled, admiring the ring. 'What Saxon will pause to look for a ring? Rape first and plunder after, isn't that the spearman's rule?'

'You won't be here when the Saxons come,' I said. 'You must go back to Powys.'

She shook her head. 'I shall stay. I can't always run to my brother when trouble comes.'

I let that argument rest until the time came and instead sent messengers to Durnovaria and Caer Cadarn to let Arthur know I had returned. Four days later he came to Dun Caric, where I reported Aelle's refusal to him. Arthur shrugged as if he had expected nothing else. 'It was worth a try,' he said dismissively. I did not tell him of Aelle's offer to me, for in his sour mood he would probably think I was tempted to accept and he might never have trusted me again. Nor did I tell him that Lancelot had been at Thunreslea, for I knew how he hated even the mention of that name. I did tell him about the priests from Gwent and that news made him scowl. 'I suppose I shall have to visit Meurig,' he said bleakly, staring at the Tor. Then he turned to me. 'Did you know,' he asked me accusingly, 'that Excalibur is one of the Treasures of Britain?'

'Yes, Lord,' I admitted. Merlin had told me so long before, but he had sworn me to secrecy for fear that Arthur might destroy the sword to demonstrate his lack of superstition.

'Merlin has demanded its return,' Arthur said. He had always known that demand might come, right from the distant day when Merlin had given the young Arthur the magical sword.

'You will give it to him?' I asked anxiously.

He grimaced. 'If I don't, Derfel, will that stop Merlin's nonsense?'

'If it is nonsense, Lord,' I said, and I remembered that shimmering naked girl and told myself she was a harbinger of wondrous things.

Arthur unbuckled the belt with its cross-hatched scabbard. 'You take it to him, Derfel,' he said grudgingly, 'you take it to him.' He pushed the precious sword into my hands. 'But tell Merlin I want her back.'

'I will, Lord,' I promised. For if the Gods did not come on Samain Eve then Excalibur would have to be drawn and carried against the army of all the Saxons.

But Samain Eve was very near now, and on that night of the dead the Gods would be summoned.

And next day I carried Excalibur south to make it happen.

MAI DUN IS A GREAT hill that lies to the south of Durnovaria and at one time it must have been the greatest fortress in all Britain. It has a wide, gently domed summit stretching east and west around which the old people built three huge walls of steeply embanked turf. No one knows when it was built, or even how, and some believe that the Gods themselves must have dug the ramparts for that triple wall seems much too high, and its ditches far too deep, for mere human work, though neither the height of the walls nor the depth of the ditches prevented the Romans from capturing the fortress and putting its garrison to the sword. Mai Dun has lain empty since that day, but for a small stone temple of Mithras that the victorious Romans built at the eastern end of the summit plateau. In summer the old fortress is a lovely place where sheep graze the precipitous walls and butterflies flicker above the grass, wild thyme and orchids, but in late autumn, when the nights close in early and the rains sweep across Dumnonia from the west, the summit can be a chill bare height where the wind bites hard.

The main track to the summit leads to the maze-like western gate and the path was slippery with mud as I carried Excalibur to Merlin. A horde of common folk trudged with me. Some had great bundles of firewood on their backs, others were carrying skins of drinking water while a few were goading oxen that dragged great tree trunks or pulled sledges heaped with trimmed branches. The oxen's flanks ran with blood as they struggled to haul their loads up the steep, treacherous path to where, high above me on the outermost grass rampart, I could see spearmen standing guard. The presence of those spearmen confirmed what I had been told in Durnovaria, that Merlin had closed Mai Dun to all except those who came to work.

Two spearmen guarded the gate. Both were Irish Blackshield

warriors, hired from Oengus mac Airem, and I wondered how much of Merlin's fortune was being spent on readying this desolate grass fort for the coming of the Gods. The men recognized that I was not one of the folk working at Mai Dun and came down the slope to meet me. 'You have business here, Lord?' one of them asked respectfully. I was not in armour, but I wore Hywelbane and her scabbard alone marked me as a man of rank.

'I have business with Merlin,' I said.

The Blackshield did not stand aside. 'Many folk come here, Lord,' he said, 'and claim to have business with Merlin. But does Lord Merlin have business with them?'

'Tell him,' I said, 'that Lord Derfel has brought him the last Treasure.' I tried to imbue the words with a due sense of ceremony, but they did not seem to impress the Blackshields. The younger man climbed away with the message while the older chatted to me. Like most of Oengus's spearmen he seemed a cheerful rogue. The Blackshields came from Demetia, a kingdom Oengus had made on Britain's west coast, but though they were invaders, Oengus's Irish spearmen were not hated like the Saxons. The Irish fought us, they stole from us, they enslaved us and they took our land, but they spoke a language close to ours, their Gods were our Gods and, when they were not fighting us, they mingled easily enough with the native Britons. Some, like Oengus himself, now seemed more British than Irish, for his native Ireland, which had always taken pride in never having been invaded by the Romans, had now succumbed to the religion the Romans had brought. The Irish had adopted Christianity, though the Lords Across the Sea, who were those Irish kings like Oengus who had taken land in Britain, still clung to their older Gods, and next spring, I reflected, unless Merlin's rites brought those Gods to our rescue, these Blackshield spearmen would doubtless fight for Britain against the Saxons.

It was young Prince Gawain who came from the summit to meet me. He strode down the track in his limewashed wargear, though his splendour was spoilt when his feet shot out from under him on a muddy patch and he bumped a few yards on his bottom. 'Lord Derfel!' he called as he scrambled up again, 'Lord Derfel! Come, come! Welcome!' He beamed a wide smile as I approached. 'Is not this the most exciting thing?' he demanded.

'I don't know yet, Lord Prince.'

'A triumph!' he enthused, carefully stepping around the muddy patch that had caused his downfall. 'A great work! Let us pray it will not be in vain.'

'All Britain prays for that,' I said, 'except maybe the Christians.'

'In three days' time, Lord Derfel,' he assured me, 'there will be no more Christians in Britain, for all will have seen the true Gods by then. So long,' he added anxiously, 'as it does not rain.' He looked up at the dismal clouds and suddenly seemed close to tears.

'Rain?' I asked.

'Or maybe it is cloud that will deny us the Gods. Rain or cloud, I am not sure, and Merlin is impatient. He doesn't explain, but I think rain is the enemy, or maybe it is cloud.' He paused, still miserable. 'Both, perhaps. I asked Nimue, but she doesn't like me,' he sounded very woeful, 'so I am not sure, but I am beseeching the Gods for clear skies. And of late it has been cloudy, very cloudy, and I suspect the Christians are praying for rain. Have you really brought Excalibur?'

I unwrapped the cloth from the scabbarded sword and held the hilt towards him. For a moment he dared not touch it, then he gingerly reached out and drew Excalibur from its scabbard. He stared reverently at the blade, then touched with his finger the chased whorls and incised dragons that decorated the steel. 'Made in the Otherworld,' he said in a voice full of wonder, 'by Gofannon himself!'

'More likely forged in Ireland,' I said uncharitably, for there was something about Gawain's youth and credulity that was driving me to puncture his pious innocence.

'No, Lord,' he assured me earnestly, 'it was made in the Otherworld.' He pushed Excalibur back into my hands. 'Come, Lord,' he said, trying to hurry me, but he only slipped in the mud again and flailed for balance. His white armour, so impressive at a distance, was shabby. Its limewash was mud-streaked and fading, but he possessed an indomitable self-confidence that prevented him from appearing ridiculous. His long golden hair was bound in a loose plait that hung down to the small of his back. As we negotiated the entrance passage that twisted between the high grass banks I asked Gawain how he had met Merlin. 'Oh, I've known

Merlin all my life!' the Prince answered happily. 'He came to my father's court, you see, though not so much of late, but when I was just a little boy he was always there. He was my teacher.'

'Your teacher?' I sounded surprised and so I was, but Merlin was always secretive and he had never mentioned Gawain to me.

'Not my letters,' Gawain said, 'the women taught me those. No, Merlin taught me what my fate is to be.' He smiled shyly. 'He taught me to be pure.'

'To be pure!' I gave him a curious glance. 'No women?'

'None, Lord,' he admitted innocently. 'Merlin insists. Not now, anyway, though after, of course.' His voice tailed away and he actually blushed.

'No wonder,' I said, 'that you pray for clear skies.'

'No, Lord, no!' Gawain protested. 'I pray for clear skies so that the Gods will come! And when they do, they will bring Olwen the Silver with them.' He blushed again.

'Olwen the Silver?'

'You saw her, Lord, at Lindinis.' His handsome face became almost ethereal. 'She treads lighter than a breath of wind, her skin shines in the dark and flowers grow in her footsteps.'

'And she is your fate?' I asked, suppressing a nasty little stab of jealousy at the thought of that shining, lissom spirit being given to young Gawain.

'I am to marry her when the task is done,' he said earnestly, 'though for now my duty is to guard the Treasures, but in three days I shall welcome the Gods and lead them against the enemy. I am to be the liberator of Britain.' He made this outrageous boast very calmly, as though it was a commonplace task. I said nothing, but just followed him past the deep ditch that lies between Mai Dun's middle and inner walls and I saw that its trench was filled with small makeshift shelters made from branches and thatch. 'In two days,' Gawain saw where I was looking, 'we shall pull those shelters down and add them to the fires.'

'Fires?'

'You'll see, Lord, you'll see.'

Though at first, when I reached the summit, I could make no sense of what I saw. The crest of Mai Dun is an elongated grassy space in which a whole tribe with all its livestock could shelter in time of war, but now the hill's western end was crossed and latticed with a complicated arrangement of dry hedges. 'There!' Gawain said proudly, pointing to the hedges as if they were his own accomplishment.

The folk carrying the firewood were being directed towards one of the nearer hedges where they threw down their burdens and trudged off to collect still more timber. Then I saw that the hedges were really great ridges of wood being heaped ready for burning. The heaps were taller than a man, and there seemed to be miles of them, but it was not until Gawain led me up onto the innermost rampart that I saw the design of the hedges.

They filled all the western half of the plateau and at their centre were five piles of firewood that made a circle in the middle of an empty space some sixty or seventy paces across. That wide space was surrounded by a spiralling hedge which twisted three full turns, so that the whole spiral, including the centre, was over a hundred and fifty paces wide. Outside the spiral was an empty circle of grass that was girdled by a ring of six double spirals, each uncoiling from one circular space and coiling again to enclose another so that twelve fire-ringed spaces lay in the intricate outer ring. The double spirals touched each other so that they would make a rampart of fire all about the massive design. 'Twelve smaller circles,' I asked Gawain, 'for thirteen Treasures?'

'The Cauldron, Lord, will be at the centre,' he said, his voice filled with awe.

It was a huge accomplishment. The hedges were tall, well above the height of a man, and all were dense with fuel; indeed there must have been enough firewood on that hilltop to keep the fires of Durnovaria burning through nine or ten winters. The double spirals at the western end of the fortress were still being completed and I could see men energetically stamping down the wood so that the fire would not blaze briefly, but would burn long and fierce. There were whole tree trunks waiting for the flames inside the banked timbers. It would be a fire, I thought, to signal the ending of the world.

And in a way, I supposed, that was exactly what the fire was intended to mark. It would be the end of the world as we knew it, for if Merlin was right then the Gods of Britain would come to this high place. The lesser Gods would go to the smaller circles of the outer ring while Bel would descend to the fiery heart of Mai Dun where his Cauldron waited. Great Bel, God of Gods, the Lord of Britain, would come in a great rush of air with the stars roiling in his wake like autumn leaves tossed by a storm wind. And there, where the five individual fires marked the heart of Merlin's circles of flame, Bel would step again in Ynys Prydain, the Isle of Britain. My skin suddenly felt cold. Till this moment I had not really understood the magnitude of Merlin's dream, and now it almost overwhelmed me. In three days, just three days, the Gods would be here.

'We have over four hundred folk working on the fires,' Gawain told me earnestly.

'I can believe it.'

'And we marked the spirals,' he went on, 'with fairy rope.'

'With what?'

'A rope, Lord, knotted from the hair of a virgin and merely one strand in width. Nimue stood in the centre and I paced about the perimeter and my Lord Merlin marked my steps with elf stones. The spirals had to be perfect. It took a week to do, for the rope kept breaking and every time it did we needed to begin again.'

'Maybe it wasn't fairy rope after all, Lord Prince?' I teased him.

'Oh, it was, Lord,' Gawain assured me. 'It was knotted from my own hair.'

'And on Samain Eve,' I said, 'you light the fires and wait?'

'Three hours on three, Lord, the fires must burn, and at the sixth hour we begin the ceremony.' And sometime after that the night would turn to day, the sky would fill with fire and the smoky air would be lashed into turmoil by the Gods' beating wings.

Gawain had been leading me along the fort's northern wall, but now gestured down to where the small Temple of Mithras stood just to the east of the firewood rings. 'You can wait there, Lord,' he said, 'while I fetch Merlin.'

'Is he far off?' I asked, thinking that Merlin might be in one of the temporary shelters thrown up on the plateau's eastern end.

'I'm not certain where he is,' Gawain confessed, 'but I know he went to fetch Anbarr, and I think I know where that might be.'

'Anbarr?' I asked. I only knew Anbarr from stories where he was a magical horse, an unbroken stallion reputed to gallop as fast across water as he could across land.

'I will ride Anbarr alongside the Gods,' Gawain said proudly, 'and carry my banner against the enemy.' He pointed to the temple where a huge flag leaned unceremoniously against the low tiled roof. 'The banner of Britain,' Gawain added, and he led me down to the temple where he unfurled the standard. It was a vast square of white linen on which was embroidered the defiant red dragon of Dumnonia. The beast was all claws, tail and fire. 'It's really the banner of Dumnonia,' Gawain confessed, 'but I don't think the other British Kings will mind, do you?'

'Not if you drive the Sais into the sea,' I said.

'That is my task, Lord,' Gawain said very solemnly. 'With the help of the Gods, of course, and of that,' he touched Excalibur that was still under my arm.

'Excalibur!' I sounded surprised, for I could not imagine any man other than Arthur carrying the magical blade.

'What else?' Gawain asked me. 'I am to carry Excalibur, ride Anbarr, and drive the enemy from Britain.' He smiled delightedly, then gestured at a bench beside the temple door. 'If you will wait, Lord, I shall seek Merlin.'

The temple was guarded by six Blackshield spearmen, but as I had come to the place in Gawain's company they made no effort to stop me ducking under the doorway's low lintel. I was not exploring the little building from curiosity, but rather because Mithras was my chief God in those days. He was the soldier's God, the secret God. The Romans had brought his worship to Britain and even though they had long gone, Mithras was still a favourite amongst warriors. This temple was tiny, merely two small rooms that were windowless to imitate the cave of Mithras's birth. The outer room was filled with wooden boxes and wicker baskets which, I suspected, contained the Treasures of Britain, though I lifted none of the lids to look. Instead I crawled through the inner door into the black sanctuary and saw, glimmering there, the great silver-gold Cauldron of Clyddno Eiddyn. Beyond the Cauldron, and only just visible in the small grey light that seeped through the two low doors, was the altar of Mithras. Either Merlin or Nimue, who both ridiculed Mithras, had placed a badger's skull

64

on the altar to avert the God's attention. I swept the skull away, then knelt beside the Cauldron and said a prayer. I begged Mithras to help our other Gods and I prayed he would come to Mai Dun and lend his terror to the slaughter of our enemies. I touched the hilt of Excalibur to his stone and wondered when a bull had last been sacrificed in this place. I imagined the Roman soldiers forcing the bull to its knees, then shoving its rump and tugging its horns to cram it through the low doors until, once in the inner sanctuary, it would stand and bellow with fear, smelling nothing but the spearmen all about it in the dark. And there, in the terrifying dark, it would be hamstrung. It would bellow again, collapse, but still thrash its great horns at the worshippers, but they would overpower it and drain its blood and the bull would slowly die and the temple would fill with the stink of its dung and blood. Then the worshippers would drink the bull's blood in memory of Mithras, just as he had commanded us. The Christians, I was told, had a similar ceremony, but they claimed that nothing was killed in their rites, though few pagans believed it for death is the due we owe to the Gods in return for the life they give us.

I stayed on my knees in the dark, a warrior of Mithras come to one of his forgotten temples, and there, as I prayed, I smelt the same sea smell that I remembered from Lindinis, the seaweed and salt tang that had touched our nostrils as Olwen the Silver had stalked so slim and delicate and lovely down Lindinis's arcade. For a moment I thought a God was present, or maybe that Olwen the Silver had come to Mai Dun herself, but nothing stirred; there was no vision, no glowing naked skin, just the thin sea-salt smell and the soft whisper of the wind outside the temple.

I turned back through the inner door and there, in the outer room, the smell of the sea was stronger. I tugged open box lids and lifted sacking covers from the wicker baskets, and I thought I had found the source of the sea smell when I discovered that two of the baskets were filled with salt that had become heavy and clotted in the damp autumn air, but the sea smell did not come from the salt, but from a third basket that was crammed with wet bladderwrack. I touched the seaweed, then licked my finger and tasted salt water. A great clay pot was stoppered next to the basket and, when I lifted the lid, I found the pot was filled with sea water, presumably to keep the bladderwrack moist, and so I dug into the basket of seaweed and found, just beneath the surface, a layer of shellfish. The fish had long, narrow, elegant double-sided shells, and looked something like mussels, only these were a little larger than mussels and their shells were a greyish white instead of black. I lifted one, smelt it and supposed that it was merely some delicacy that Merlin liked to eat. The shellfish, perhaps resenting my touch, cracked open its shell and pissed a squirt of liquid onto my hand. I put it back into the basket and covered the layer of living shellfish with the seaweed.

I was just turning to the outer door, planning to wait outside, when I noticed my hand. I stared at it for several heartbeats, thinking that my eyes deceived me, but in the wan light by the outer door I could not be certain so I ducked back through the inner door to where the great Cauldron waited by the altar and there, in the darkest part of Mithras's temple, I held my right hand before my face.

And saw that it was glowing.

I stared. I did not really want to believe in what I saw, but my hand did glow. It was not luminous, not an inner light, but a wash of unmistakable brightness on my palm. I drew a finger through the wet patch left by the shellfish and so made a dark streak through the shimmering surface. So Olwen the Silver had been no nymph, no messenger from the Gods after all, but a human girl smeared with the juices of shellfish. The magic was not of the Gods, but of Merlin, and all my hopes seemed to die in that dark chamber.

I wiped my hand on my cloak and went back to the daylight. I sat down on the bench by the temple door and gazed at the inner rampart where a group of small children tumbled and slid in boisterous play. The despair that had haunted me on my journey into Lloegyr returned. I so wanted to believe in the Gods, yet was so filled with doubt. What did it matter, I asked myself, that the girl was human, and that her inhuman luminous shimmer was a trick of Merlin's? That did not negate the Treasures, but whenever I had thought about the Treasures, and whenever I had been tempted to doubt their efficacy, I had reassured myself with the memory of that shining naked girl. And now, it seemed, she was no harbinger of the Gods at all, but merely one of Merlin's illusions.

'Lord?' A girl's voice disturbed my thoughts. 'Lord?' she asked again, and I looked up to see a plump, dark-haired young woman smiling nervously at me. She was dressed in a simple robe and cloak, had a ribbon round her short dark curls and was holding the hand of a small red-haired boy. 'You don't remember me, Lord?' she asked, disappointed.

'Cywwylog,' I said, recalling her name. She had been one of our servants at Lindinis where she had been seduced by Mordred. I stood. 'How are you?' I asked.

'Good as can be, Lord,' she said, pleased that I had remembered her. 'And this is little Mardoc. Takes after his father, doesn't he?' I looked at the boy. He was, perhaps, six or seven years old and was sturdy, round-faced, and had stiff bristling hair just like his father, Mordred. 'But not in himself, he don't take after his father,' Cywwylog said, 'he's a good little boy, he is, good as gold, Lord. Never been a minute's trouble, not really, have you, my darling?' She stooped and gave Mardoc a kiss. The boy was embarrassed by the show of affection, but grinned anyway. 'How's the Lady Ceinwyn?' Cywwylog asked me.

'Very well. She'll be pleased we met.'

'Always kind to me, she was,' Cywwylog said. 'I would have gone to your new home, Lord, only I met a man. Married now, I am.'

'Who is he?'

'Idfael ap Meric, Lord. He serves Lord Lanval now.'

Lanval commanded the guard that kept Mordred in his gilded prison. 'We thought you left our household,' I confessed to Cywwylog, 'because Mordred gave you money.'

'Him? Give me money!' Cywwylog laughed. 'I'll live to see the stars fall before that happens, Lord. I was a fool back then,' Cywwylog confessed to me cheerfully. 'Of course I didn't know what kind of a man Mordred was, and he weren't really a man, not then, and I suppose I had my head turned, him being the King, but I wasn't the first girl, was I? and I dare say I won't be the last. But it all turned out for the best. My Idfael's a good man, and he don't mind young Mardoc being a cuckoo in his nest. That's what you are, my lovely,' she said, 'a cuckoo!' And she stooped and cuddled Mardoc who squirmed in her arms and then burst out laughing when she tickled him.

'What are you doing here?' I asked her.

'Lord Merlin asked us to come,' Cywwylog said proudly.' He's taken a liking to young Mardoc, he has. He spoils him! Always feeding him, he is, and you'll get fat, yes, you will, you'll be fat like a pig!' And she tickled the boy again who laughed, struggled and at last broke free. He did not run far, but stood a few feet away from where he watched me with his thumb in his mouth.

'Merlin asked you to come?' I asked.

'Needed a cook, Lord, that's what he said, and I dare say I'm as good a cook as the next woman, and with the money he offered, well, Idfael said I had to come. Not that Lord Merlin eats much. He likes his cheese, he does, but that doesn't need a cook, does it?'

'Does he eat shellfish?'

'He likes his cockles, but we don't get many of those. No, it's mostly cheese he eats. Cheese and eggs. He's not like you, Lord, you were a great one for meat, I remember?'

'I still am,' I said.

'They were good days,' Cywwylog said. 'Little Mardoc here is the same age as your Dian. I often thought they'd make good playmates. How is she?'

'She's dead, Cywwylog,' I said.

Her face dropped. 'Oh, no, Lord, say that isn't true?'

'She was killed by Lancelot's men.'

She spat onto the grass. 'Wicked men, all of them. I am sorry, Lord.'

'But she's happy in the Otherworld,' I assured her, 'and one day we'll all join her there.'

'You will, Lord, you will. But the others?'

'Morwenna and Seren are fine.'

'That's good, Lord.' She smiled. 'Will you be staying here for the Summons?'

'The Summons?' That was the first time I had heard it called that. 'No,' I said, 'I haven't been asked. I thought I'd probably watch from Durnovaria.'

'It'll be something to see,' she said; then she smiled and thanked me for talking to her and afterwards she pretended to chase Mardoc who ran away from her squealing with delight. I sat, pleased to have met her again, and then wondered what games Merlin was playing. Why had he wanted to find Cywwylog? And why hire a cook, when he had never before employed someone to prepare his meals?

A sudden commotion beyond the ramparts broke my thoughts and scattered the playing children. I stood up just as two men appeared dragging on a rope. Gawain hurried into sight an instant later, and then, at the rope's end, I saw a great fierce black stallion. The horse was trying to pull free and very nearly dragged the two men back off the wall, but they snatched at the halter and were hauling the terrified beast forward when the horse suddenly bolted down the steep inner wall and pulled the men behind him. Gawain shouted at them to take care, then half slid and half ran after the great beast. Merlin, apparently unconcerned by the small drama, followed with Nimue. He watched as the horse was led to one of the eastern shelters, then he and Nimue came down to the temple. 'Ah, Derfel!' he greeted me carelessly. 'You look very glum. Is it toothache?'

'I brought you Excalibur,' I said stiffly.

'I can see that with my own eyes. I'm not blind, you know. A little deaf at times, and the bladder is feeble, but what can one expect at my age?' He took Excalibur from me, drew its blade a few inches from the scabbard, then kissed the steel. 'The sword of Rhydderch,' he said in awe, and for a second his face bore an oddly ecstatic look, then he abruptly slammed the sword home and let Nimue take it from him. 'So you went to your father,' Merlin said to me. 'Did you like him?'

'Yes, Lord.'

'You always were an absurdly emotional fellow, Derfel,' Merlin said, then glanced at Nimue who had drawn Excalibur free of its sheath and was holding the naked blade tight against her thin body. For some reason Merlin seemed upset at this and he plucked the scabbard away from her and then tried to take the sword back. She would not let it go and Merlin, after struggling with her for a few heartbeats, abandoned the attempt. 'I hear you spared Liofa?' he said, turning back to me. 'That was a mistake. A very dangerous beast, Liofa is.'

'How do you know that I spared him?'

Merlin gave me a reproachful look. 'Maybe I was an owl in the

69

rafters of Aelle's hall, Derfel, or perhaps I was a mouse in his floor rushes?' He lunged at Nimue and this time he did succeed in wresting the sword from her grip. 'Mustn't deplete the magic,' he muttered, sliding the blade clumsily back into its scabbard. 'Arthur did not mind yielding the sword?' he asked me.

'Why should he, Lord?'

'Because Arthur is dangerously close to scepticism,' Merlin said, stooping to push Excalibur into the temple's low doorway. 'He believes we can manage without the Gods.'

'Then it's a pity,' I said sarcastically, 'that he never saw Olwen the Silver glowing in the dark.'

Nimue hissed at me. Merlin paused, then slowly turned and straightened from the doorway to give me a sour look. 'Why, Derfel, is that a pity?' he asked in a dangerous voice.

'Because if he had seen her, Lord, then surely he would believe in the Gods? So long, of course, as he didn't discover your shellfish.'

'So that's it,' he said. 'You've been questing about, haven't you? You've been shoving your fat Saxon nose where it oughtn't to be shoved and you found my piddocks.'

'Piddocks?'

'The shellfish, fool, they're called piddocks. At least, the vulgar call them that.'

'And they glow?' I asked.

'Their juices do have a luminous quality,' Merlin admitted airily. I could see he was annoyed at my discovery, but he was doing his best not to show any irritation. 'Pliny mentions the phenomenon, but then he mentions so much that it's very hard to know quite what to believe. Most of his notions are arrant nonsense, of course. All that rubbish about Druids cutting mistletoe on the sixth day of a new moon! I'd never do that, never! The fifth day, yes, and sometimes the seventh, but the sixth? Never! And he also recommends, as I recall, wrapping a woman's breast band about the skull to cure an aching head, but the remedy doesn't work. How could it? The magic is in the breasts, not in the band, so it is clearly far more efficacious to bury the aching head in the breasts themselves. The remedy has never failed me, that's for sure. Have you read Pliny, Derfel?'

'No, Lord.'

'That's right, I never taught you Latin. Remiss of me. Well, he does discuss the piddock and he noted that the hands and mouths of those who ate the creature glowed afterwards, and I confess I was intrigued. Who would not be? I was reluctant to explore the phenomenon further, for I have wasted a great deal of my time on Pliny's more credulous notions, but that one turned out to be accurate. Do you remember Caddwg? The boatman who rescued us from Ynys Trebes? He is now my piddock hunter. The creatures live in holes in the rocks, which is inconvenient of them, but I pay Caddwg well and he assiduously winkles them out as a proper piddock hunter should. You look disappointed, Derfel.'

'I thought, Lord,' I began, then faltered, knowing I was about to be mocked.

'Oh! You thought the girl came from the heavens!' Merlin finished the sentence for me, then hooted with derision. 'Did you hear that, Nimue? Our great warrior, Derfel Cadarn, believed our little Olwen was an apparition!' He drew out the last word, giving it a portentous tone.

'He was supposed to believe that,' Nimue said drily.

'I suppose he was, come to think of it,' Merlin admitted. 'It's a good trick, isn't it, Derfel?'

'But just a trick, Lord,' I said, unable to hide my disappointment.

Merlin sighed. 'You are absurd, Derfel, entirely absurd. The existence of tricks does not imply the absence of magic, but magic is not always granted to us by the Gods. Do you understand nothing?' This last question was asked angrily.

'I know I was deceived, Lord.'

'Deceived! Deceived! Don't be so pathetic. You're worse than Gawain! A Druid in his second day of training could deceive you! Our job is not to satisfy your infantile curiosity, but to do the work of the Gods, and those Gods, Derfel, have gone far from us. They have gone far! They're vanishing, melting into the dark, going into the abyss of Annwn. They have to be summoned, and to summon them I needed labourers, and to attract labourers I needed to offer a little hope. Do you think Nimue and I could build the fires all on our own? We needed people! Hundreds of people! And smearing a girl with piddock juice brought them to us, but all you can do is bleat about being deceived. Who cares what you think? Why don't

71

you go and chew a piddock? Maybe that will enlighten you.' He kicked at Excalibur's hilt, which still protruded from the temple. 'I suppose that fool Gawain showed you everything?'

'He showed me the rings of fire, Lord.'

'And now you want to know what they're for, I suppose?'

'Yes, Lord.'

'Anyone of average intelligence could work it out for himself,' Merlin said grandly. 'The Gods are far away, that's obvious, or otherwise they would not be ignoring us, but many years ago they gave us the means of summoning them: the Treasures. The Gods are now so far gone into Annwn's chasm that the Treasures by themselves do not work. So we have to attract the Gods' attention, and how do we do that? Simple! We send a signal into the abyss, and that signal is simply a great pattern of fire, and in the pattern we place the Treasures, and then we do one or two other things which don't really matter very much, and after that I can die in peace instead of having to explain the most elementary matters to absurdly credulous halfwits. And no,' he said before I had even spoken, let alone asked a question, 'you cannot be up here on Samain Eve. I want only those I can trust. And if you come here again I shall order the guards to use your belly for spear practice.'

'Why not just surround the hill with a ghost fence?' I asked. A ghost fence was a line of skulls, charmed by a Druid, across which no one would dare trespass.

Merlin stared at me as though my wits were gone. 'A ghost fence! On Samain Eve! It is the one night of the year, halfwit, on which ghost fences do not work! Do I have to explain everything to you? A ghost fence, fool, works because it harnesses the souls of the dead to frighten the living, but on Samain Eve the souls of the dead are freed to wander and so cannot be harnessed. On Samain Eve a ghost fence is about as much use to the world as your wits.'

I took his reproof calmly. 'I just hope you don't get clouds,' I said instead, trying to placate him.

'Clouds?' Merlin challenged me. 'Why should clouds worry me? Oh, I see! That dimwit Gawain talked to you and he gets everything wrong. If it is cloudy, Derfel, the Gods will still see our signal because their sight, unlike ours, is not constrained by clouds, but if it is too cloudy then it is likely to rain,' he made his voice into that of a man explaining something very simple to a small child, 'and heavy rain will put out all the big fires. There, that was really difficult for you to work out for yourself, wasn't it?' He glared angrily at me, then turned away to stare at the rings of firewood. He leaned on his black staff, brooding at the huge thing he had done on Mai Dun's summit. He was silent for a long time, then suddenly shrugged. 'Have you ever thought,' he asked, 'what might have happened if the Christians had succeeded in putting Lancelot on the throne?' His anger had gone, to be replaced by a melancholy.

'No, Lord,' I said.

'Their year 500 would have come and they would all have been waiting for that absurd nailed God of theirs to come in glory.' Merlin had been gazing at the rings as he spoke, but now he turned to look at me. 'What if he had never come?' he asked in puzzlement. 'Suppose the Christians were all ready, all in their best cloaks, all washed and scrubbed and praying, and then nothing happened?'

'Then in the year 501,' I said, 'there would be no Christians.'

Merlin shook his head. 'I doubt that. It's the business of priests to explain the inexplicable. Men like Sansum would have invented a reason, and people would believe them because they want to believe so very badly. Folk don't give up hope because of disappointment, Derfel, they just redouble their hope. What fools we all are.'

'So you're frightened,' I said, feeling a sudden stab of pity for him, 'that nothing will happen at Samain?'

'Of course I'm frightened, you halfwit. Nimue isn't.' He glanced at Nimue, who was watching us both with a sullen look. 'You're full of certainty, my little one, aren't you?' Merlin mocked her, 'but as for me, Derfel, I wish this had never been necessary. We don't even know what's supposed to happen when we light the fires. Maybe the Gods will come, but perhaps they'll bide their time?' He gave me a fierce look. 'If nothing happens, Derfel, that doesn't mean that nothing happened. Do you understand that?'

'I think so, Lord.'

'I doubt you do. I don't even know why I bother wasting explanations on you! Might as well lecture an ox on the finer points of rhetoric! Absurd man that you are. You can go now. You've delivered Excalibur.'

'Arthur wants it back,' I said, remembering to deliver Arthur's message.

'I'm sure he does, and maybe he will get it back when Gawain's finished with it. Or maybe not. What does it matter? Stop worrying me with trifles, Derfel. And goodbye.' He stalked off, angry again, but stopped after a few paces to turn and summon Nimue. 'Come, girl!'

'I shall make sure Derfel leaves,' Nimue said, and with those words she took my elbow and steered me towards the inner rampart.

'Nimue!' Merlin shouted.

She ignored him, dragging me up the grass slope to where the path led along the rampart. I stared at the complex rings of firewood. 'It's a lot of work you've done,' I said lamely.

'And all wasted if we don't perform the proper rituals,' Nimue said waspishly. Merlin had been angry with me, but his anger was mostly feigned and it had come and gone like lightning, but Nimue's rage was deep and forceful and had drawn her white, wedge-shaped face tight. She had never been beautiful, and the loss of her eye had given her face a dreadful cast, but there was a savagery and intelligence in her looks that made her memorable, and now, on that high rampart in the west wind, she seemed more formidable than ever.

'Is there some danger,' I asked, 'that the ritual will not be done properly?'

'Merlin's like you,' she said angrily, ignoring my question. 'He's emotional.'

'Nonsense,' I said.

'And what do you know, Derfel?' she snapped. 'Do you have to endure his bluster? Do you have to argue with him? Do you have to reassure him? Do you have to watch him making the greatest mistake of all history?' She spat these questions at me. 'Do you have to watch him waste all this effort?' She waved a thin hand at the fires. 'You are a fool,' she added bitterly. 'If Merlin farts, you think it's wisdom speaking. He's an old man, Derfel, and he has not long to live, and he is losing his power. And power, Derfel, comes from inside.' She beat her hand between her small breasts. She had stopped on the rampart's top and turned to face me. I was a strapping soldier, she a tiny slip of a woman, yet she overpowered

74

me. She always did. In Nimue there ran a passion so deep and dark and strong that almost nothing could withstand it.

'Why do Merlin's emotions threaten the ritual?' I asked.

'They just do!' Nimue said, and turned and walked on.

'Tell me,' I demanded.

'Never!' she snapped. 'You're a fool.'

I walked behind her. 'Who is Olwen the Silver?' I asked her.

'A slave girl we purchased in Demetia. She was captured from Powys and she cost us over six gold pieces because she's so pretty.'

'She is,' I said, remembering her delicate step through Lindinis's hushed night.

'Merlin thinks so, too,' Nimue said scornfully. 'He quivers at the sight of her, but he's much too old these days, and besides we have to pretend she's a virgin for Gawain's sake. And he believes us! But that fool will believe anything! He's an idiot!'

'And he'll marry Olwen when this is all over?'

Nimue laughed. 'That's what we've promised the fool, though once he discovers she's slave born and not a spirit he might change his mind. So maybe we'll sell her on. Would you like to buy her?' She gave me a sly look.

'No.'

'Still faithful to Ceinwyn?' she said mockingly. 'How is she?'

'She's well,' I said.

'And is she coming to Durnovaria to watch the summons?'

'No,' I said.

Nimue turned to give me a suspicious look. 'But you will?'

'I'll watch, yes.'

'And Gwydre,' she asked, 'will you bring him?'

'He wants to come, yes. But I shall ask his father's permission first.'

'Tell Arthur he should let him come. Every child in Britain should witness the coming of the Gods. It will be a sight never to be forgotten, Derfel.'

'So it will happen?' I asked, 'despite Merlin's faults?'

'It will happen,' Nimue said vengefully, 'despite Merlin. It will happen because I will make it happen. I'll give that old fool what he wants whether he likes it or not.' She stopped, turned and seized my left hand to stare with her one eye at the scar on its palm. That scar bound me by oath to do her bidding and I sensed she was about to make some demand of me, but then some impulse of caution stopped her. She took a breath, stared at me, then let my scarred hand drop. 'You can find your own way now,' she said in a bitter tone, then walked away.

I went down the hill. The folk still trudged to Mai Dun's summit with their loads of firewood. For nine hours, Gawain had said, the fires must burn. Nine hours to fill a sky with flame and bring the Gods to earth. Or maybe, if the rites were done wrong, the fires would bring nothing.

And in three nights we would discover which it would be.

Ceinwyn would have liked to come to Durnovaria to witness the summoning of the Gods, but Samain Eve is the night when the dead walk the earth and she wanted to be certain that we left gifts for Dian and she thought the place to leave those gifts was where Dian had died, and so she took our two living daughters to the ruins of Ermid's Hall and there among the hall's ashes she placed a jug of diluted mead, some buttered bread and a handful of the honey-covered nuts Dian had always loved so much. Dian's sisters put some walnuts and hard-boiled eggs in the ashes, then they all sheltered in a nearby forester's hut guarded by my spearmen. They did not see Dian, for on Samain Eve the dead never show themselves, but to ignore their presence is to invite misfortune. In the morning, Ceinwyn told me later, the food was all gone and the jug was empty.

I was in Durnovaria where Issa joined me with Gwydre. Arthur had given his son permission to watch the summoning and Gwydre was excited. He was eleven years old that year, full of joy and life and curiosity. He had his father's lean build, but he had taken his good looks from Guinevere for he had her long nose and bold eyes. There was mischief in him, but no evil, and both Ceinwyn and I would have been glad if his father's prophecy came true and he married our Morwenna. That decision would not be taken for another two or three years, and until then Gwydre would live with us. He wanted to be on the summit of Mai Dun, and was disappointed when I explained that no one was permitted to be there other than those who would perform the ceremonies. Even the folk who had built the great fires were sent away during the day. They, like the hundreds of other curious folk who had come from all over Britain, would watch the summons from the fields beneath the ancient fort.

Arthur arrived on the morning of Samain Eve and I saw the joy with which he greeted Gwydre. The boy was his one source of happiness in those dark days. Arthur's cousin, Culhwch, arrived from Dunum with a half-dozen spearmen. 'Arthur told me I shouldn't come,' he told me with a grin, 'but I wouldn't miss this.' Culhwch limped to greet Galahad who had spent the last months with Sagramor, guarding the frontier against Aelle's Saxons, and while Sagramor had obeyed Arthur's orders to stay at his post, he had asked Galahad to go to Durnovaria to carry news of the night's events back to his forces. The high expectations worried Arthur, who feared his followers would feel a terrible disappointment if nothing happened.

The expectations only increased, for that afternoon King Cuneglas of Powys rode into the town and brought with him a dozen men including his son Perddel who was now a self-conscious youth trying to grow his first moustaches. Cuneglas embraced me. He was Ceinwyn's brother and a more decent, honest man never lived. He had called on Meurig of Gwent on his journey south and now confirmed that monarch's reluctance to fight the Saxons. 'He believes his God will protect him,' Cuneglas said grimly.

'So do we,' I said, gesturing out of Durnovaria's palace window to the lower slopes of Mai Dun that were thick with people hoping to be close to whatever the momentous night might bring. Many of the folk had tried to climb to the top of the hill, but Merlin's Blackshield spearmen were keeping them all at a distance. In the field just to the north of the fortress a brave group of Christians prayed noisily that their God would send rain to defeat the heathen rites, but they were chased away by an angry crowd. One Christian woman was beaten insensible, and Arthur sent his own soldiers to keep the peace.

'So what happens tonight?' Cuneglas asked me.

'Maybe nothing, Lord King.'

'I've come this far to see nothing?' Culhwch grumbled. He was a squat, bellicose, foul-mouthed man whom I counted among my

77

closest friends. He had limped ever since a Saxon blade had scored deep into his leg in the battle against Aelle's Saxons outside London, but he made no fuss about the thickly scarred wound and claimed he was still as formidable a spearman as ever. 'And what are you doing here?' he challenged Galahad. 'I thought you were a Christian?'

'I am.'

'So you're praying for rain, are you?' Culhwch accused him. It was raining even as we spoke, though it was nothing more than a light drizzle that spat from the west. Some men believed fair weather would follow the drizzle, but inevitably there were pessimists who forecast a deluge.

'If it does pour with rain tonight,' Galahad needled Culhwch, 'will you admit my God is greater than yours?'

'I'll slit your throat,' Culhwch growled, who would do no such thing for he, like me, had been a friend of Galahad for many years.

Cuneglas went to talk with Arthur, Culhwch disappeared to discover whether a red-haired girl still plied for trade in a tavern by Durnovaria's north gate, while Galahad and I walked with young Gwydre into the town. The atmosphere was merry, indeed it was as if a great autumn fair had filled Durnovaria's streets and spilt onto the surrounding meadows. Merchants had set up stalls, the taverns were doing a brisk business, jugglers dazzled the crowds with their skills and a score of bards chanted songs. A performing bear lumbered up and down Durnovaria's hill beneath Bishop Emrys's house, becoming ever more dangerous as folk fed it bowls of mead. I glimpsed Bishop Sansum peering through a window at the great beast, but when he saw me he jerked back inside and pulled the wooden shutter closed. 'How long will he stay a prisoner?' Galahad asked me.

'Till Arthur forgives him,' I said, 'which he will, for Arthur always forgives his enemies.'

'How very Christian of him.'

'How very stupid of him,' I said, making sure that Gwydre was not in earshot. He had gone to look at the bear. 'But I can't see Arthur forgiving your half-brother,' I went on. 'I saw him a few days ago.'

'Lancelot?' Galahad asked, sounding surprised. 'Where?'

'With Cerdic.'

Galahad made the sign of the cross, oblivious to the scowls it attracted. In Durnovaria, as in most towns in Dumnonia, the majority of folk were Christian, but today the streets were thronged with pagans from the countryside and many were eager to pick fights with their Christian enemies. 'You think Lancelot will fight for Cerdic?' Galahad asked me.

'Does he ever fight?' I responded caustically.

'He can.'

'Then if he fights at all,' I said, 'it will be for Cerdic.'

'Then I pray I am given the chance to kill him,' Galahad said, and again crossed himself.

'If Merlin's scheme works,' I said, 'there won't be a war. Just a slaughter led by the Gods.'

Galahad smiled. 'Be honest with me, Derfel, will it work?'

'That's what we're here to see,' I said evasively, and it struck me suddenly that there must be a score of Saxon spies in the town who would have come to see the same thing. Those men would probably be followers of Lancelot, Britons who could mingle unnoticed in the expectant throng that swelled all day. If Merlin failed, I thought, then the Saxons would take heart and the spring battles would be all the harder.

The rain began to fall more steadily and I called Gwydre and the three of us ran back to the palace. Gwydre begged his father for permission to watch the summoning from the fields close under Mai Dun's ramparts, but Arthur shook his head. 'If it rains like this,' Arthur told him, 'then nothing will happen anyway. You'll just catch cold, and then –' he stopped abruptly. And then your mother will be angry with me, he had been about to say.

'Then you'll pass the cold to Morwenna and Seren,' I said, 'and I'll catch it from them, and I'll give it your father, and then the whole army will be sneezing when the Saxons come.'

Gwydre thought about that for a second, decided it was nonsense, and tugged his father's hand. 'Please!' he said.

'You can watch from the upper hall with the rest of us,' Arthur insisted.

'Then can I go back and watch the bear, father? It's getting

79

drunk and they're going to put dogs on it. I'll stand under a porch to keep dry. I promise. Please, father?'

Arthur let him go and I sent Issa to guard him, then Galahad and I climbed to the palace's upper hall. A year before, when Guinevere had still sometimes visited this palace, it had been elegant and clean, but now it was neglected, dusty and forlorn. It was a Roman building and Guinevere had tried to restore it to its ancient splendour, but it had been plundered by Lancelot's forces in the rebellion and nothing had been done to repair the damage. Cuneglas's men had made a fire on the hall's floor and the heat of the logs was buckling the small tiles. Cuneglas himself was standing at the wide window from where he was staring gloomily across Durnovaria's thatch and tile towards the slopes of Mai Dun that were almost hidden by veils of rain. 'It is going to let up, isn't it?' he appealed to us as we entered.

'It'll probably get worse,' Galahad said, and just at that moment a rumble of thunder sounded to the north and the rain perceptibly hardened until it was bouncing four or five inches from the rooftops. The firewood on Mai Dun's summit would be getting a soaking, but so far only the outer layers would be drenched while the timber deep in the heart of the fires would still be dry. Indeed that inner timber would stay dry through an hour or more of this heavy rain, and dry timber at the heart of a fire will soon burn the damp from the outer layers, but if the rain persisted into the night then the fires would never blaze properly. 'At least the rain will sober up the drunks,' Galahad observed.

Bishop Emrys appeared in the hall door, the black skirts of his priest's robe drenched and muddy. He gave Cuneglas's fearsome pagan spearmen a worried glance, then hurried over to join us at the window. 'Is Arthur here?' he asked me.

'He's somewhere in the palace,' I said, then introduced Emrys to King Cuneglas and added that the Bishop was one of our good Christians.

'I trust we are all good, Lord Derfel,' Emrys said, bowing to the King.

'To my mind,' I said, 'the good Christians are the ones who did not rebel against Arthur.'

'Was it a rebellion?' Emrys asked. 'I think it was a madness,

80

Lord Derfel, brought on by pious hope, and I daresay that what Merlin is doing this day is exactly the same thing. I suspect he will be disappointed, just as many of my poor folk were disappointed last year. But in tonight's disappointment, what might happen? That's why I'm here.'

'What will happen?' Cuneglas asked.

Emrys shrugged. 'If Merlin's Gods fail to appear, Lord King, then who will be blamed? The Christians. And who will be slaughtered by the mob? The Christians.' Emrys made the sign of the cross. 'I want Arthur's promise to protect us.'

'I'm sure he'll give it gladly,' Galahad said.

'For you, Bishop,' I added, 'he will.' Emrys had stayed loyal to Arthur, and he was a good man, even if he was as cautious in his advice as he was ponderous in his old body. Like me, the Bishop was a member of the Royal Council, the body that ostensibly advised Mordred, though now that our King was a prisoner in Lindinis, the council rarely met. Arthur saw the counsellors privately, then made his own decisions, but the only decisions that really needed to be made were those that prepared Dumnonia for the Saxon invasion and all of us were content to let Arthur carry that burden.

A fork of lightning slithered between the grey clouds, and a moment later a crack of thunder sounded so loud that we all involuntarily ducked. The rain, already hard, suddenly intensified, beating furiously on the roofs and churning streamlets of muddy water down Durnovaria's streets and alleys. Puddles spread on the hall floor.

'Maybe,' Cuneglas observed dourly, 'the Gods don't want to be summoned?'

'Merlin says they are far off,' I said, 'so this rain isn't their doing.'

'Which is proof, surely, that a greater God is behind the rain,' Emrys argued.

'At your request?' Cuneglas enquired acidly.

'I did not pray for rain, Lord King,' Emrys said. 'Indeed, if it will please you, I shall pray for the rain to cease.' And with that he closed his eyes, spread his arms wide and raised his head in prayer. The solemnity of the moment was somewhat spoilt by a drop of rainwater that came through the roof tiles to fall straight onto his tonsured forehead, but he finished his prayer and made the sign of the cross.

And miraculously, just as Emrys's pudgy hand formed the sign of the cross on his dirty gown, the rain began to relent. A few flurries still came hard on the west wind, but the drumming on the roof ceased abruptly and the air between our high window and Mai Dun's crest began to clear. The hill still looked dark under the grey clouds, and there was nothing to be seen on the old fortress except for a handful of spearmen guarding the ramparts and, below them, a few pilgrims who had lodged themselves as high as they dared on the hill's slopes. Emrys was not certain whether to be pleased or downcast at the efficacy of his prayer, but the rest of us were impressed, especially as a rift opened in the western clouds and a watery shaft of sunlight slanted down to turn the slopes of Mai Dun green.

Slaves brought us warmed mead and cold venison, but I had no appetite. Instead I watched as the afternoon sank into evening and as the clouds grew ragged. The sky was clearing, and the west was becoming a great furnace blaze of red above distant Lyonesse. The sun was sinking on Samain Eve, and all across Britain and even in Christian Ireland folk were leaving food and drink for the dead who would cross the gulf of Annwn on the bridge of swords. This was the night when the ghostly procession of shadowbodies came to visit the earth where they had breathed and loved and died. Many had died on Mai Dun and tonight that hill would be thick with their wraiths; then, inevitably, I thought of Dian's little shadowbody wandering among the ruins of Ermid's Hall.

Arthur came to the hall and I thought how different he looked without Excalibur hanging in its cross-hatched scabbard. He grunted when he saw the rain had stopped, then listened to Bishop Emrys's plea. 'I'll have my spearmen in the streets,' he assured the Bishop, 'and so long as your folks don't taunt the pagans, they'll be safe.' He took a horn of mead from a slave, then turned back to the Bishop. 'I wanted to see you anyway,' he said, and told the Bishop his worries about King Meurig of Gwent. 'If Gwent won't fight,' Arthur warned Emrys, 'then the Saxons will outnumber us.'

Emrys blanched. 'Gwent won't let Dumnonia fall, surely!'

'Gwent has been bribed, Bishop,' I told him, and described how Aelle had allowed Meurig's missionaries into his territory. 'So long as Meurig thinks there's a chance of converting the Sais,' I said, 'he won't lift a sword against them.'

'I must rejoice at the thought of evangelizing the Saxons,' Emrys said piously.

'Don't,' I warned him. 'Once those priests have served Aelle's purpose he'll cut their throats.'

'And afterwards cut ours,' Cuneglas added grimly. He and Arthur had decided to make a joint visit to the King of Gwent, and Arthur now urged Emrys to join them. 'He'll listen to you, Bishop,' Arthur said, 'and if you can convince him that Dumnonia's Christians are more threatened by the Saxons than they are by me, then he might change his mind.'

'I shall come gladly,' Emrys said, 'very gladly.'

'And at the very least,' Cuneglas said grimly, 'young Meurig will need to be persuaded to let my army cross his territory.'

Arthur looked alarmed. 'He might refuse?'

'So my informants say,' Cuneglas said, then shrugged. 'But if the Saxons do come, Arthur, I shall cross his territory whether he gives permission or not.'

'Then there'll be war between Gwent and Powys,' Arthur noted sourly, 'and that will help only the Sais.' He shuddered. 'Why did Tewdric ever give up the throne?' Tewdric was Meurig's father, and though Tewdric had been a Christian he had always led his men against the Saxons at Arthur's side.

The last red light in the west faded. For a few moments the world was suspended between light and dark, and then the gulf swallowed us. We stood in the window, chilled by the damp wind, and watched the first stars prick through the chasms in the clouds. The waxing moon was low over the southern sea where its light was diffused around the edges of a cloud that hid the stars forming the head of the snake constellation. It was nightfall on Samain Eve and the dead were coming.

A few fires lit Durnovaria's houses, but the country beyond was utterly black except where a shaft of moonlight silvered a patch of trees on the shoulder of a distant hill. Mai Dun was nothing but a looming shadow in the darkness, a blackness at the dead night's black heart. The dark deepened, more stars appeared and the moon flew wild between ragged clouds. The dead were streaming over the bridge of swords now and were here among us, though we could not see them, or hear them, but they were here, in the palace, in the streets, in every valley and town and household of Britain, while on the battlefields, where so many souls had been torn from their earthly bodies, the dead were wandering as thick as starlings. Dian was under the trees at Ermid's Hall, and still the shadowbodies streamed across the bridge of swords to fill the isle of Britain. One day, I thought, I too would come on this night to see my children and their children and their children's children. For all time, I thought, my soul would wander the earth each Samain Eve.

The wind calmed. The moon was again hidden by a great bank of cloud that hung above Armorica, but above us the skies were clearer. The stars, where the Gods lived, blazed in the emptiness. Culhwch had come back to the palace and he joined us at the window where we crowded to watch the night. Gwydre had returned from the town, though after a while he got bored with staring into a damp darkness and went to see his friends among the palace's spearmen.

'When do the rites begin?' Arthur asked.

'Not for a long time yet,' I warned him. 'The fires must burn for six hours before the ceremony starts.'

'How does Merlin count the hours?' Cuneglas asked.

'In his head, Lord King,' I answered.

The dead glided among us. The wind had dropped to nothing and the stillness made the dogs howl in the town. The stars, framed by the silver-edged clouds, seemed unnaturally bright.

And then, quite suddenly, from the dark within the night's harsh dark, from Mai Dun's wide walled summit, the first fire blazed and the summoning of the Gods had begun.

For a moment that one flame leapt pure and bright above Mai Dun's ramparts, then the fires spread until the wide bowl formed by the grassy banks of the fortress walls was filled with a dim and smoky light. I imagined men thrusting torches deep into the high, wide hedges, then running with the flame to carry the fire out into the central spiral or along the outer rings. The fires caught slowly at first, the flames fighting against the hissing wet timbers above them, but the heat gradually boiled away the damp and the glow of the blaze became brighter and brighter until the fire had at last gripped all that great pattern and the light flared huge and triumphant in the night. The crest of the hill was now a ridge of fire, a boiling tumult of flame above which the smoke was touched red as it churned skywards. The fires were bright enough to cast flickering shadows in Durnovaria where the streets were filled with people; some had even climbed onto rooftops to watch the distant conflagration.

'Six hours?' Culhwch asked me with disbelief.

'So Merlin told me.'

Culhwch spat. 'Six hours! I could go back to the redhead.' But he did not move, indeed none of us moved; instead we watched that dance of flame above the hill. It was the balefire of Britain, the end of history, the summons to the Gods, and we watched it in a tense silence as though we expected to see the livid smoke torn apart by the descent of the Gods.

It was Arthur who broke the tension. 'Food,' he said gruffly. 'If we have to wait six hours, then we might as well eat.'

There was small conversation during that meal, and most of what there was concerned King Meurig of Gwent and the terrible possibility that he would keep his spearmen out of the coming war. If, I kept thinking, there would be war at all, and I constantly glanced out of the window to where the flames leapt and the smoke boiled. I tried to gauge the passing of the hours, but in truth I had no idea whether one hour passed or two before the meal ended and we were once again standing beside the big open window to gaze at Mai Dun where, for the first time ever, the Treasures of Britain had been assembled. There was the Basket of Garanhir which was a willow-woven dish that might carry a loaf and some fishes, though the weave was now so ragged that any respectable woman would long ago have consigned the basket to the fire. The Horn of Bran Galed was an ox horn that was black with age and chipped at its tin-rimmed edges. The Chariot of Modron had been broken over the years and was so small that none but a child could ever ride in it, if indeed it could ever be reassembled. The Halter of Eiddyn was an ox halter of frayed rope and rusted iron rings that even the poorest peasant would hesitate to use. The Knife of Laufrodedd was blunt and broad-bladed and had a broken wooden handle, while the Whetstone of Tudwal was an abraded thing any craftsman would be ashamed to possess. The Coat of Padarn was threadbare and patched, a beggar's garment, but still in better repair than the Cloak of Rhegadd which was supposed to grant its wearer invisibility, but which was now scarcely more than a cobweb. The Dish of Rhygenydd was a flat wooden platter cracked beyond all use, while the Throwboard of Gwenddolau was an old, warped piece of wood on which the gaming marks had worn almost clean away. The Ring of Eluned looked like a common warrior-ring, the simple metal circles that spearmen liked to make from their dead enemy's weapons, but all of us had thrown away better-looking warrior-rings than the Ring of Eluned. Only two of the Treasures had any intrinsic value. One was the Sword of Rhydderch, Excalibur, that had been forged in the Otherworld by Gofannon himself, and the other was the Cauldron of Clyddno Eiddyn. Now all of them, the tawdry and the splendid alike, were ringed by fire to signal to their distant Gods.

The sky was still clearing, though some clouds were still heaped above the southern horizon where, as we went deeper into that night of the dead, lightning began to flicker. That lightning was the first sign of the Gods and, in fear of them, I touched the iron of Hywelbane's hilt, but the great flashes of light were far, far away, perhaps above the distant sea or even further off above Armorica. For an hour or more the lightning raked the southern sky, but always in silence. Once a whole cloud seemed lit from within, and we all gasped and Bishop Emrys made the sign of the cross.

The distant lightning faded, leaving only the great fire raging within Mai Dun's ramparts. It was a signal fire to cross the Gulf of Annwn, a blaze to reach into the darkness between the worlds. What were the dead thinking, I wondered? Was a horde of shadow-souls clustering around Mai Dun to witness the summoning of the Gods? I imagined the reflections of those flames flickering along the steel blades of the bridge of swords and maybe reaching into the Otherworld itself and I confess I was frightened. The lightning had vanished, and nothing now seemed to be happening other then the great fire's violence, but all of us, I think, were aware that the world trembled on the brink of change.

Then, sometime in the passing of those hours, the next sign came. It was Galahad who first saw it. He crossed himself, stared out of the window as though he could not believe what he was seeing, then pointed up above the great plume of smoke that was casting a veil across the stars. 'Do you see it?' he asked, and we all pressed into the window to gaze upwards.

And I saw that the lights of the night sky had come.

We had all seen such lights before, though not often, but their arrival on this night was surely significant. At first there was just a shimmering blue haze in the dark, but slowly the haze strengthened and grew brighter, and a red curtain of fire joined the blue to hang like a rippled cloth among the stars. Merlin had told me that such lights were common in the far north, but these were hanging in the south, and then, gloriously, abruptly, the whole space above our heads was shot through with blue and silver and crimson cascades. We all went down into the courtyard to see better, and there we stood awestruck as the heavens glowed. From the courtyard we could no longer see the fires of Mai Dun, but their light filled the southern sky, just as the weirder lights arched gloriously above our heads.

'Do you believe now, Bishop?' Culhwch asked.

Emrys seemed unable to speak, but then he shuddered and touched the wooden cross hanging about his neck. 'We have never,' he said quietly, 'denied the existence of other powers. It is just that we believe our God to be the only true God.'

'And the other Gods are what?' Cuneglas asked.

Emrys frowned, unwilling at first to answer, but honestly made him speak. 'They are the powers of darkness, Lord King.'

'The powers of light, surely,' Arthur said in awe, for even Arthur was impressed. Arthur, who would prefer that the Gods never touched us at all, was seeing their power in the sky and he was filled with wonderment. 'So what happens now?' he asked.

He had put the question to me, but it was Bishop Emrys who answered. 'There will be death, Lord,' he said.

'Death?' Arthur asked, unsure that he had heard correctly.

Emrys had gone to stand under the arcade, as though he feared the strength of the magic that flickered and flowed so bright across the stars. 'All religions use death, Lord,' he said pedantically, 'even ours believes in sacrifice. It is just that in Christianity it was the Son of God who was killed so that no one again would ever need to be knifed on an altar, but I can think of no religion that does not use death as part of its mystery. Osiris was killed,' he suddenly realized he was speaking of Isis's worship, the bane of Arthur's life, and hurried on, 'Mithras died, too, and his worship requires the death of bulls. All our Gods die, Lord,' the Bishop said, 'and all religions except Christianity recreate those deaths as part of their worship.'

'We Christians have gone beyond death,' Galahad said, 'into life.'

'Praise God we have,' Emrys agreed, making the sign of the cross, 'but Merlin has not.' The lights in the sky were brighter now; great curtains of colours through which, like threads in a tapestry, flickers of white light streaked and dropped. 'Death is the most powerful magic,' the Bishop said disapprovingly. 'A merciful God would not allow it, and our God ended it by his own Son's death.'

'Merlin doesn't use death,' Culhwch said angrily.

'He does,' I spoke softly. 'Before we went to fetch the Cauldron he made a human sacrifice. He told me.'

'Who?' Arthur asked sharply.

'I don't know, Lord.'

'He was probably telling stories,' Culhwch said, gazing upwards, 'he likes to do that.'

'Or more likely he was telling the truth,' Emrys said. 'The old religion demanded much blood, and usually it was human. We know so little, of course, but I remember old Balise telling me that the Druids were fond of killing humans. They were usually prisoners. Some were burned alive, others put into death pits.'

'And some escaped,' I added softly, for I myself had been thrown into a Druid's death pit as a small child and my escape from that horror of dying, broken bodies had led to my adoption by Merlin.

Emrys ignored my comment. 'On other occasions, of course,' he went on, 'a more valuable sacrifice was required. In Elmet and Cornovia they still speak of the sacrifice made in the Black Year.'

'What sacrifice was that?' Arthur asked.

'It could just be a legend,' Emrys said, 'for it happened too long ago for memory to be accurate.' The Bishop was speaking about the Black Year in which the Romans had captured Ynys Mon and so torn the heart from the Druids' religion, a dark event that had happened more than four hundred years in our past. 'But folk in those parts still talk of King Cefydd's sacrifice,' Emrys continued. 'It's a long time since I heard the tale, but Balise always believed it. Cefydd, of course, was facing the Roman army and it seemed likely he would be overwhelmed, so he sacrificed his most valuable possession.'

'Which was?' Arthur demanded. He had forgotten the lights in the sky and was staring fixedly at the Bishop.

'His son, of course. It was ever thus, Lord. Our own God sacrificed His Son, Jesus Christ, and even demanded that Abraham kill Isaac, though, of course, He relented in that desire. But Cefydd's Druids persuaded him to kill his son. It didn't work, of course. History records that the Romans killed Cefydd and all his army and then destroyed the Druid's groves on Ynys Mon.' I sensed the Bishop was tempted to add some thanks to his God for that destruction, but Emrys was no Sansum and thus was tactful enough to keep his thanks unspoken.

Arthur walked to the arcade. 'What is happening on that hilltop, Bishop?' he asked in a low voice.

'I cannot possibly tell, Lord,' Emrys said indignantly.

'But you think there is killing?'

'I think it is possible, Lord,' Emrys said nervously. 'I think it likely, even.'

'Killing who?' Arthur demanded, and the harshness of his voice made every man in the courtyard turn from the glory in the sky to stare at him.

'If it is the old sacrifice, Lord, and the supreme sacrifice,' Emrys said, 'then it will be the son of the ruler.'

'Gawain, son of Budic,' I said softly, 'and Mardoc.'

'Mardoc?' Arthur swung on me.

'A child of Mordred's,' I answered, suddenly understanding why Merlin had asked me about Cywyllog, and why he had taken the child to Mai Dun, and why he had treated the boy so well. Why had I not understood before? It seemed obvious now.

'Where's Gwydre?' Arthur asked suddenly.

For a few heartbeats no one answered, then Galahad gestured towards the gatehouse. 'He was with the spearmen,' Galahad said, 'while we had supper.'

But Gwydre was there no longer, nor was he in the room where Arthur slept when he was in Durnovaria. He was nowhere to be found, and no one recalled having seen him since dusk. Arthur utterly forgot the magical lights as he searched the palace, hunting from the cellars to the orchard, but finding no sign of his son. I was thinking about Nimue's words to me on Mai Dun when she had encouraged me to bring Gwydre to Durnovaria, and remembering her argument with Merlin in Lindinis about who truly ruled Dumnonia, and I did not want to believe my suspicions, but could not ignore them. 'Lord,' I caught Arthur's sleeve. 'I think he's been taken to the hill. Not by Merlin, but by Nimue.'

'He's not a king's son,' Emrys said very nervously.

'Gwydre is the son of a ruler!' Arthur shouted, 'does anyone here deny that?' No one did and suddenly no one dared say a thing. Arthur turned towards the palace. 'Hygwydd! A sword, spear, shield, Llamrei! Quick!'

'Lord!' Culhwch intervened.

'Quiet!' Arthur shouted. He was in a fury now and it was me he vented his rage on for I had encouraged him to allow Gwydre to come to Durnovaria. 'Did you know what was to happen?' he asked me.

'Of course not, Lord. I still don't know. You think I would hurt Gwydre?'

Arthur stared grimly at me, then turned away. 'None of you need come,' he said over his shoulder, 'but I am riding to Mai Dun to fetch my son.' He strode across the courtyard to where Hygwydd, his servant, was holding Llamrei while a groom saddled her. Galahad followed him quietly.

I confess that for a few seconds I did not move. I did not want to move. I wanted the Gods to come. I wanted all our troubles to be ended by the beat of great wings and the miracle of Beli Mawr striding the earth. I wanted Merlin's Britain.

And then I remembered Dian. Was my youngest daughter in the palace courtyard that night? Her soul must have been on the earth, for it was Samain Eve, and suddenly there were tears at my eyes as I recalled the agony of a child lost. I could not stand in Durnovaria's palace courtyard while Gwydre died, nor while Mardoc suffered. I did not want to go to Mai Dun, but I knew I could not face Ceinwyn if I did nothing to prevent the death of a child and so I followed Arthur and Galahad.

Culhwch stopped me. 'Gwydre is a whore's son,' he growled too softly for Arthur to hear.

I chose not to quarrel about the lineage of Arthur's son. 'If Arthur goes alone,' I said instead, 'he'll be killed. There are two score of Blackshields on that hill.'

'And if we go, we make ourselves into the enemies of Merlin,' Culhwch warned me.

'And if we don't go,' I said, 'we make an enemy of Arthur.'

Cuneglas came to my side and put a hand on my shoulder. 'Well?'

'I'm riding with Arthur,' I answered. I did not want to, but I could not do otherwise. 'Issa!' I shouted. 'A horse!'

'If you're going,' Culhwch grumbled, 'I suppose I'll have to come. Just to make sure you're not hurt.' Then suddenly all of us were shouting for horses, weapons and shields.

Why did we go? I have thought so often about that night. I can still see the flickering lights shaking the heavens, and smell the smoke streaming from Mai Dun's summit, and feel the great weight of magic that pressed on Britain, yet still we rode. I know I was in confusion on that flame-riven night. I was driven by a sentimentality about a child's death, and by Dian's memory, and by my guilt because I had encouraged Gwydre to be at Durnovaria, but above all there was my affection for Arthur. And what, then, of my affection for Merlin and Nimue? I suppose I had never thought they needed me, but Arthur did, and on that night when Britain was trapped between the fire and the light, I rode to find his son.

Twelve of us rode. Arthur, Galahad, Culhwch, Derfel and Issa were the Dumnonians, the others were Cuneglas and his followers. Today, where the story is still told, children are taught that Arthur, Galahad and I were the three ravagers of Britain, but there were twelve riders in that night of the dead. We had no body armour, just our shields, but every man carried a spear and a sword.

Folk shrank to the sides of the firelit street as we rode towards Durnovaria's southern gate. The gate was open, as it was left open every Samain Eve to give the dead access to the town. We ducked under the gate beams then galloped south and west between fields filled with people who stared enthralled at the boiling mix of flame and smoke that streamed from the hill's summit.

Arthur set a terrifying pace and I clung to my saddle pommel, fearful of being thrown. Our cloaks streamed behind, our sword scabbards banged up and down, while above us the heavens were filled with smoke and light. I could smell the burning wood and hear the crackle of the flames long before we reached the hill's slope.

No one tried to stop us as we urged the horses uphill. It was not till we reached the intricate tangle of the gateway maze that any spearmen opposed us. Arthur knew the fortress, because when he and Guinevere had lived in Durnovaria they had often come to its summit in the summertime and he led us unerringly through the twisting passage and it was there that three Blackshields levelled their spears to halt us. Arthur did not hesitate. He rammed his heels back, aimed his own long spear and let Llamrei run. The Blackshields twisted aside, shouting helplessly as the big horses thundered past.

The night was all noise and light now. The noise was of a mighty fire and the splitting of whole trees in the heart of the hungry flames. Smoke shrouded the lights in the sky. There were spearmen shouting at us from the ramparts, but none opposed us as we burst through the inner wall onto Mai Dun's summit.

And there we were stopped, not by Blackshields, but by a blast of searing heat. I saw Llamrei rear and twist away from the flames, saw Arthur clinging to her mane and saw her eyes flash red with reflected fire. The heat was like a thousand smithy furnaces; a bellowing blast of scorching air that made us all flinch and reel away. I could see nothing inside the flames, for the centre of Merlin's design was hidden by the seething walls of fire. Arthur kicked Llamrei back towards me. 'Which way?' he shouted.

I must have shrugged.

'How did Merlin get inside?' Arthur asked.

I made a guess. 'The far side, Lord.' The temple was on the eastern side of the fire-maze and I suspected a passage must surely have been left through the outer spirals.

Arthur hauled on his rein and urged Llamrei up the slope of the inner rampart to the path that ran along its crest. The Blackshields scattered rather than face him. We rode up the rampart after Arthur, and though our horses were terrified of the great fire to their right, they followed Llamrei through the whirling sparks and smoke. Once a great section of fire collapsed as we galloped past and my horse swerved away from the inferno onto the outer face of the inner rampart. For a second I thought she was going to tumble down into the ditch and I was hanging desperately out of the saddle with my left hand tangled in her mane, but somehow she found her footing, regained the path and galloped on.

Once past the northern tip of the great fire rings Arthur turned down onto the summit plateau again. A glowing ember had landed on his white cloak and started the wool smouldering, and I rode alongside him and beat the small fire out. 'Where?' he called to me.

'There, Lord,' I pointed to the spirals of fire nearest to the temple. I could see no gap there, but as we drew closer it was apparent that there had been a gap which had been closed with firewood, though that new wood was not nearly so thickly stacked as the rest and there was a narrow space where the fire, rather than being eight or ten feet tall, was no higher than a man's waist. Beyond that low gap lay the open space between the outer and inner spirals, and in that space we could see more Blackshields waiting.

Arthur walked Llamrei towards the gap. He was leaning forward, speaking to the horse, almost as if he was explaining to her what he wanted. She was frightened. Her ears kept pricking back, and she took short nervous steps, but she did not shy from the raging fires that burned on either side of the only passage into the heart of the hilltop fire. Arthur stopped her a few paces short of the gap and calmed her, though her head kept tossing and her eyes were wide and white. He let her look at the gap, then he patted her neck, spoke to her again, and wheeled away.

He trotted in a wide circle, spurred her into a canter, then spurred her again as he aimed at the gap. She tossed her head and I thought she would baulk, but then she seemed to make up her mind and flew at the flames. Cuneglas and Galahad followed. Culhwch cursed at the risk we were taking, then all of us kicked our horses in Llamrei's wake.

Arthur crouched over the mare's neck as she pounded towards the fire. He was letting Llamrei choose her pace and she slowed again. I thought she would shy away, then I saw she was gathering herself for the leap between the flames. I was shouting, trying to cover my fear, then Llamrei jumped and I lost sight of her as the wind snatched a cloak of flaming smoke over the gap. Galahad was next into the space, but Cuneglas's horse swerved away. I was galloping hard behind Culhwch, and the heat and clamour of the fires was filling the noisy air. I think I half wanted my horse to refuse, but she kept on and I closed my eyes as the flame and smoke surrounded me. I felt the horse rise, heard her whinny, then we thumped down inside the outer ring of flame and I felt a vast relief and wanted to shout in triumph.

Then a spear ripped into my cloak just behind my shoulder. I had been so intent on surviving the fire that I had not thought about what waited for us inside the flame ring. A Blackshield had lunged at me and had missed, but now he abandoned the spear and ran to pull me from the saddle. He was too close for my own spear blade to be of use so I simply rammed the staff down at his head and kicked my horse on. The man seized my spear. I let it go, drew Hywelbane and hacked back once. I glimpsed Arthur circling on Llamrei and flailing left and right with his sword, and now I did the same. Galahad kicked a man in the face, speared another, then spurred away. Culhwch had seized a Blackshield's helmet crest and was dragging the man towards the fire. The man tried desperately to untie the chin strap, then screamed as Culhwch hurled him at the flames before wheeling away.

Issa was through the gap now, and so were Cuneglas and his six followers. The surviving Blackshields had fled towards the centre of the maze of fire and we followed them, trotting between two leaping walls of flame. The borrowed sword in Arthur's hand was red with light. He kicked Llamrei and she began to canter and the Blackshields, knowing they must be caught, ran aside and dropped their spears to show they would fight no more.

We had to ride halfway around the circle to find the entrance to the inner spiral. The gap between the inner and outer fires was a good thirty paces across, wide enough to let us ride without being roasted alive, but the space inside the spiral's passage was less than ten paces in width, and these were the biggest fires, the fiercest, and we all hesitated at the entrance. We could still see nothing of what happened within the circle. Did Merlin know we were here? Did the Gods? I looked up, half expecting a vengeful spear to hurtle down from heaven, but there was only the twisting canopy of smoke shrouding the fire-tortured, light-cascading sky.

And so we rode into the last spiral. We rode hard and fast, galloping in a tightening curve between the roaring blast of leaping flames. Our nostrils filled with smoke as embers scorched our faces, but turn by turn we drew ever nearer to the mystery's centre.

The noise of the fires obscured our coming. I think that Merlin and Nimue had no idea that their ritual was about to be ended for they did not see us. Instead the guards at the circle's centre saw us first and they shouted in warning and ran to oppose us, but Arthur came out of the fires like a demon cloaked in smoke. Indeed, his clothes streamed smoke as he shouted a challenge and rammed Llamrei hard into the Blackshields' hasty, half-formed shield wall. He broke that wall by sheer speed and weight, and the rest of us followed, swords swinging, while the handful of loyal Blackshields scattered.

Gwydre was there. And Gwydre lived.

He was in the grip of two Blackshields who, seeing Arthur, let the boy go free. Nimue screamed at us, winging curses across the central ring of five fires as Gwydre ran sobbing to his father's side. Arthur leaned down and with a strong arm lifted his son onto the saddle. Then he turned to look at Merlin.

Merlin, his face streaming with sweat, gazed calmly at us. He was halfway up a ladder that was leaning against a gallows made of two tree trunks struck upright in the ground and crossed by a third, and that gallows now stood in the very centre of the five fires that formed the middle ring. The Druid was in a white robe and the sleeves of that robe were red with blood from their cuffs to the elbow. In his hand was a long knife, but on his face, I swear, there was a momentary look of utter relief.

The boy Mardoc lived, though he would not have lived for long. The child was already naked, all but for a strip of cloth that had been tied about his mouth to silence his screams, and he was hanging from the gallows by his ankles. Next to him, also hanging by the ankles, was a pale, thin body that looked very white in the flamelight, except that the corpse's throat had been cut almost to the spine and all the man's blood had run down into the Cauldron, and still it ran to drip from the lank, reddened ends of Gawain's long hair. The hair was so long that its gory tresses fell inside the golden rim of the silver Cauldron of Clyddno Eiddyn, and it was only by that long hair that I knew it was Gawain who hung there, for his handsome face was sheeted with blood, hidden by blood, cloaked in blood.

Merlin, still with the long knife that had killed Gawain in his hand, seemed dumbstruck by our coming. His look of relief had vanished and now I could not read his face at all, but Nimue was shrieking at us. She held up her left palm, the one with the scar that was the twin of the scar on my left palm. 'Kill Arthur!' she shouted at me. 'Derfel! You are my sworn man! Kill him! We can't stop now!'

A sword blade suddenly glittered by my beard. Galahad held it, and Galahad smiled gently at me. 'Don't move, my friend,' he said.

He knew the power of oaths. He knew, too, that I would not kill Arthur, but he was trying to spare me Nimue's vengeance. 'If Derfel moves,' he called to Nimue, 'I shall cut his throat.'

'Cut it!' she screamed. 'This is a night for the death of kings' sons!'

'Not my son,' Arthur said.

'You are no King, Arthur ap Uther,' Merlin spoke at last. 'Did you think I would kill Gwydre?'

'Then why is he here?' Arthur asked. He had one arm around Gwydre, while the other held his reddened sword. 'Why is he here?' Arthur demanded again, more angrily.

For once Merlin had nothing to say and it was Nimue who answered. 'He is here, Arthur ap Uther,' she said with a sneer, 'because the death of that miserable creature may not suffice.' She pointed at Mardoc who was wriggling helplessly on the gallows. 'He is the son of a King, but not the rightful heir.'

'So Gwydre would have died?' Arthur asked.

'And come to life!' Nimue said belligerently. She had to shout to be heard above the angry splintering noise of the fires. 'Do you not know the power of the Cauldron? Place the dead in the bowl of Clyddno Eiddyn and the dead walk again, they breathe again, they live.' She stalked towards Arthur, a madness in her one eye. 'Give me the boy, Arthur.'

'No.' Arthur pulled Llamrei's rein and the mare leapt away from Nimue. She turned on Merlin. 'Kill him!' she screamed, pointing at Mardoc. 'We can try him at least. Kill him!'

'No!' I shouted.

'Kill him!' Nimue screeched, and then, when Merlin made no move, she ran towards the gallows. Merlin seemed unable to move, but then Arthur turned Llamrei again and headed Nimue off. He let his horse ram her so that she tumbled to the turf.

'Let the child live,' Arthur said to Merlin. Nimue was clawing at him, but he pushed her away and, when she came back, all teeth and hooked hands, he swung the sword close to her head and that threat calmed her.

Merlin moved the bright blade so that it was close to Mardoc's throat. The Druid looked almost gentle, despite his blood-soaked sleeves and the long blade in his hand. 'Do you think, Arthur ap

Uther, that you can defeat the Saxons without the help of the Gods?' he asked.

Arthur ignored the question. 'Cut the boy down,' he commanded.

Nimue turned on him. 'Do you wish to be cursed, Arthur?'

'I am cursed,' he answered bitterly.

'Let the boy die!' Merlin shouted from the ladder. 'He's nothing to you, Arthur. A by-blow of a King, a bastard born to a whore.'

'And what else am I?' Arthur shouted, 'but a by-blow of a King, a bastard born to a whore?'

'He must die,' Merlin said patiently, 'and his death will bring the Gods to us, and when the Gods are here, Arthur, we shall put his body in the Cauldron and let the breath of life return.'

Arthur gestured at the horrid, life-drained body of Gawain, his nephew. 'And one death is not enough?'

'One death is never enough,' Nimue said. She had run around Arthur's horse to reach the gallows where she now held Mardoc's head still so that Merlin could slit his throat.

Arthur walked Llamrei closer to the gallows. 'And if the Gods do not come after two deaths, Merlin,' he asked, 'how many more?'

'As many as it needs,' Nimue answered.

'And every time,' Arthur spoke loudly, so we could all hear him, 'that Britain is in trouble, every time there is an enemy, every time there is a plague, every time that men and women are frightened, we shall take children to the scaffold?'

'If the Gods come,' Merlin said, 'there will be no more plague or fear or war.'

'And will they come?' Arthur asked.

'They are coming!' Nimue screamed. 'Look!' And she pointed upwards with her free hand, and we all looked and I saw that the lights in the sky were fading. The bright blues were dimming to purple black, the reds were smoky and vague, and the stars were brightening again beyond the dying curtains. 'No!' Nimue wailed, 'no!' And she drew out the last cry into a lament that seemed to last for ever.

Arthur had taken Llamrei right up to the gallows. 'You call me the *Amherawdr* of Britain,' he said to Merlin, 'and an emperor must rule or cease to be emperor, and I will not rule in a Britain where children must be killed to save the lives of adults.'

'Don't be absurd!' Merlin protested. 'Sheer sentimentality!'

'I would be remembered,' Arthur said, 'as a just man, and there is already too much blood on my hands.'

'You will be remembered,' Nimue spat at him, 'as a traitor, as a ravager, as a coward.'

'But not,' Arthur said mildly, 'by the descendants of this child,' and with that he reached up and slashed with his sword at the rope that held Mardoc's ankles. Nimue screamed as the boy fell, then she leapt at Arthur again with her hands hooked like claws, but Arthur simply backhanded her hard and fast across the head with the flat of his sword blade so that she spun away dazed. The force of the blow could easily be heard above the crackling of flames. Nimue staggered, slack-jawed and with her one eye unfocused, and then she dropped.

'Should have done that to Guinevere,' Culhwch growled to me.

Galahad had left my side, dismounted, and now freed Mardoc's bonds. The child immediately began screaming for his mother.

'I never could abide noisy children,' Merlin said mildly, then he shifted the ladder so that it rested beside the rope holding Gawain to the beam. He climbed the rungs slowly. 'I don't know,' he said as he clambered upwards, 'whether the Gods have come or not. You all of you expected too much, and maybe they are here already. Who knows? But we shall finish without the blood of Mordred's child,' and with that he sawed clumsily at the rope holding Gawain's ankles. The body swayed as he cut so that the blood-soaked hair slapped at the Cauldron's edge, but then the rope parted and the corpse dropped heavily into the blood that splashed up to stain the Cauldron's rim. Merlin climbed slowly down the ladder, then ordered the Blackshields who had been watching the confrontation to fetch the great wicker baskets of salt that were standing a few yards away. The men scooped the salt into the Cauldron, packing it tight around Gawain's hunched and naked body.

'What now?' Arthur asked, sheathing his sword.

'Nothing,' Merlin said. 'It is over.'

'Excalibur?' Arthur demanded.

'She is in the southernmost spiral,' Merlin said, pointing that way, 'though I suspect you will have to wait for the fires to burn out before you can retrieve her.'

'No!' Nimue had recovered enough to protest. She spat blood from the inside of her cheek that had been split open by Arthur's blow. 'The Treasures are ours!'

'The Treasures,' Merlin said wearily, 'have been gathered and used. They are nothing now. Arthur may have his sword. He'll need it.' He turned and threw his long knife into the nearest fire, then turned to watch as the two Blackshields finished packing the Cauldron. The salt turned pink as it covered Gawain's hideously wounded body. 'In the spring,' Merlin said, 'the Saxons will come, and then we shall see if there was any magic here this night.'

Nimue screamed at us. She wept and raved, she spat and cursed, she promised us death by air, by fire, by land and by sea. Merlin ignored her, but Nimue was never ready to accept half measures and that night she became Arthur's enemy. That night she began to work on the curses that would give her revenge on the men who stopped the Gods coming to Mai Dun. She called us the ravagers of Britain and she promised us horror.

We stayed on the hill all night. The Gods did not come, and the fires burned so fiercely that it was not till the following afternoon that Arthur could retrieve Excalibur. Mardoc was given back to his mother, though I later heard he died that winter of a fever.

Merlin and Nimue took the other Treasures away. An ox-cart carried the Cauldron with its ghastly contents. Nimue led the way and Merlin, like an old obedient man, followed her. They took Anbarr, Gawain's uncut, unbroken black horse, and they took the great banner of Britain, and where they went none of us knew, but we guessed it would be a wild place to the west where Nimue's curses could be honed through the storms of winter.

Before the Saxons came.

It is odd, looking back, to remember how Arthur was hated then. In the summer he had broken the hopes of the Christians and now, in the late autumn, he had destroyed the pagan dreams. As ever, he seemed surprised by his unpopularity. 'What else was I supposed to do?' he demanded of me. 'Let my son die?'

'Cefydd did,' I said unhelpfully.

'And Cefydd still lost the battle!' Arthur said sharply. We were riding north. I was going home to Dun Caric, while Arthur, with

Cuneglas and Bishop Emrys, was travelling on to meet King Meurig of Gwent. That meeting was the only business that mattered to Arthur. He had never trusted the Gods to save Britain from the Sais, but he reckoned that eight or nine hundred of Gwent's well-trained spearmen could tip the balance. His head seethed with numbers that winter. Dumnonia, he reckoned, could field six hundred spearmen of whom four hundred had been tested in battle. Cuneglas would bring another four hundred, the Blackshield Irish another hundred and fifty and to those we could add maybe a hundred masterless men who might come from Armorica or the northern kingdoms to seek plunder. 'Say twelve hundred men,' Arthur would guess, then he would worry the figure up or down according to his mood, but if his mood was optimistic he sometimes dared add eight hundred men from Gwent to give us a total of two thousand men, yet even that, he claimed, might not be enough because the Saxons would probably field an even larger army. Aelle could assemble at least seven hundred spears, and his was the weaker of the two Saxon kingdoms. We estimated Cerdic's spears at a thousand, and rumours were reaching us that Cerdic was buying spearmen from Clovis, the King of the Franks. Those hired men were being paid in gold, and had been promised more gold when victory yielded them the treasury of Dumnonia. Our spies also reported that the Saxons would wait until after the Feast of Eostre, their spring festival, to give the new boats time to come from across the sea. 'They'll have two and a half thousand men,' Arthur reckoned, and we had only twelve hundred if Meurig would not fight. We could raise the levy, of course, but no levy would stand against properly trained warriors, and our levy of old men and boys would be opposed by the Saxon *fyrd*.

'So without Gwent's spearmen,' I said gloomily, 'we're doomed.'

Arthur had rarely smiled since Guinevere's treachery, but he smiled now. 'Doomed? Who says that?'

'You do, Lord. The numbers do.'

'You've never fought and won when you've been outnumbered?'

'Yes, Lord, I have.'

'So why can't we win again?'

'Only a fool seeks a battle against a stronger enemy, Lord,' I said.

'Only a fool seeks a battle,' he said vigorously. 'I don't want to fight in the spring. It's the Saxons who want to fight, and we have no choice in the matter. Believe me, Derfel, I don't wish to be outnumbered, and whatever I can do to persuade Meurig to fight, I will do, but if Gwent won't march then we shall have to beat the Saxons by ourselves. And we can beat them! Believe that, Derfel!'

'I believed in the Treasures, Lord.'

He gave a derisory bark of laughter. 'This is the Treasure I believe in,' he said, patting Excalibur's hilt. 'Believe in victory, Derfel! If we march against the Saxons like beaten men then they'll give our bones to the wolves. But if we march like winners we'll hear them howl.'

It was a fine bravado, but it was hard to believe in victory. Dumnonia was shrouded with gloom. We had lost our Gods, and folk said it was Arthur who had driven them away. He was not just the enemy of the Christian God, now he was the enemy of all the Gods and men said that the Saxons were his punishment. Even the weather presaged disaster for, on the morning after I parted from Arthur, it began to rain and it seemed as though that rain would never stop. Day after day brought low grey clouds, a chill wind, and insistent driving rain. Everything was wet. Our clothes, our bedding, our firewood, the floor-rushes, the very walls of our houses seemed greasy with damp. Spears rusted in their racks, stored grain sprouted or grew mouldy, and still the rain drove relentlessly from the west. Ceinwyn and I did our best to seal Dun Caric's hall. Her brother had brought her a gift of wolf pelts from Powys and we used them to line the timber walls, but the very air beneath the roof beams seemed sodden. Fires burned sullen to grudge us a spitting and smoky warmth that reddened our eyes. Both our daughters were cross-grained that early winter. Morwenna, the eldest, who was usually the most placid and contented of children, became shrewish and so insistently selfish that Ceinwyn took a belt to her. 'She misses Gwydre,' Ceinwyn told me afterwards. Arthur had decreed that Gwydre would not leave his side, and so the boy had gone with his father to meet King Meurig. 'They should marry next year,' Ceinwyn added. 'That will cure her.'

'If Arthur will let Gwydre marry her,' I responded gloomily. 'He has no great love for us these days.' I had wanted to accompany

Arthur into Gwent, but he had peremptorily refused me. There had been a time when I had thought myself his closest friend, but now he growled at me rather than welcomed me. 'He thinks I risked Gwydre's life,' I said.

'No,' Ceinwyn disagreed. 'He's been distant with you ever since the night when he discovered Guinevere.'

'Why would that change things?'

'Because you were with him, my dear,' Ceinwyn said patiently, 'and with you he cannot pretend that nothing has changed. You were a witness to his shame. He sees you and he remembers her. He's also jealous.'

'Jealous?'

She smiled. 'He thinks you are happy. He thinks now that if he had married me then he too would be happy.'

'He probably would,' I said.

'He even suggested it,' Ceinwyn said carelessly.

'He did what?' I erupted.

She soothed me. 'It wasn't serious, Derfel. The poor man needs reassurance. He thinks that because one woman rejected him all women might, and so he asked me.'

I touched Hywelbane's hilt. 'You never told me.'

'Why should I? There was nothing to tell. He asked a very clumsy question and I told him I was sworn to the Gods to be with you. I told him very gently, and afterwards he was very ashamed. I also promised him that I would not tell you, and I've now broken that promise which means I shall be punished by the Gods.' She shrugged as if to suggest that the punishment would be deserved and thus accepted. 'He needs a wife,' she added wryly.

'Or a woman.'

'No,' Ceinwyn said. 'He isn't a casual man. He can't lie with a woman and walk away afterwards. He confuses desire with love. When Arthur gives his soul he gives everything, and he cannot give just a little bit of himself.'

I was still angry. 'What did he think I would do while he married you?'

'He thought you would rule Dumnonia as Mordred's guardian,' Ceinwyn said. 'He had this odd idea that I would go with him to Broceliande and there we would live like children under the sun, and you would stay here and defeat the Saxons.' She laughed.

'When did he ask?'

'The day he ordered you to go and see Aelle. I think he thought I'd run away with him while you were gone.'

'Or he hoped Aelle would kill me,' I said resentfully, remembering the Saxon promise to slaughter any emissary.

'He was very ashamed afterwards,' Ceinwyn assured me earnestly. 'And you're not to tell him I told you.' She made me promise that, and I kept the promise. 'It really wasn't important,' she added, ending the conversation. 'He'd have been truly shocked if I'd have said yes. He asked, Derfel, because he is in pain and men in pain behave desperately. What he really wants is to run away with Guinevere, but he can't, because his pride won't let him and he knows we all need him to defeat the Saxons.'

We needed Meurig's spearmen to do that, but we heard no news of Arthur's negotiations with Gwent. Weeks passed and still no certain news came from the north. A travelling priest from Gwent told us that Arthur, Meurig, Cuneglas and Emrys had talked for a week in Burrium, Gwent's capital, but the priest knew nothing of what had been decided. The priest was a small, dark man with a squint and a wispy beard that he moulded with beeswax into the shape of a cross. He had come to Dun Caric because there was no church in the small village and he wanted to establish one. Like many such itinerant priests he had a band of women; three drab creatures who clustered protectively about him. I first heard of his arrival when he began to preach outside the smithy beside the stream and I sent Issa and a pair of spearmen to stop his nonsense and bring him up to the hall. We fed him a gruel of sprouted barley grains that he ate greedily, spooning the hot mixture into his mouth and then hissing and spluttering because the food burned his tongue. Scraps of gruel lodged on his odd-shaped beard. His women refused to eat until he had finished.

'All I know, Lord,' he answered our impatient questions, 'is that Arthur has now travelled west.'

'Where?'

'To Demetia, Lord. To meet Oengus mac Airem.'

'Why?'

He shrugged. 'I don't know, Lord.'

'Does King Meurig make preparations for war?' I asked.

'He is prepared to defend his territory, Lord.'

'And to defend Dumnonia?'

'Only if Dumnonia recognizes the one God, the true God,' the priest said, crossing himself with the wooden spoon and splattering his dirty gown with scraps of the barley gruel. 'Our King is fervent for the cross and his spears won't be offered to pagans.' He looked up at the ox-skull that was nailed onto one of our high beams and made the sign of the cross again.

'If the Saxons take Dumnonia,' I said, 'then Gwent won't be far behind.'

'Christ will protect Gwent,' the priest insisted. He gave the bowl to one of his women who scooped up his scant leavings with a dirty finger. 'Christ will protect you, Lord,' the priest continued, 'if you humble yourself before Him. If you renounce your Gods and are baptized then you will have victory in the new year.'

'Then why was Lancelot not victorious last summer?' Ceinwyn asked.

The priest looked at her with his good eye while the other wandered off into the shadows. 'King Lancelot, Lady, was not the Chosen One. King Meurig is. It says in our scriptures that one man will be chosen and it seems King Lancelot was not that man.'

'Chosen to do what?' Ceinwyn asked.

The priest stared at her; she was still such a beautiful woman, so golden and calm, the star of Powys. 'Chosen, Lady,' he said, 'to unite all the peoples of Britain under the living God. Saxon and Briton, Gwentian and Dumnonian, Irish and Pict, all worshipping the one true God and all living in peace and love.'

'And what if we decide not to follow King Meurig?' Ceinwyn asked.

'Then our God will destroy you.'

'And that,' I asked, 'is the message you have come here to preach?'

'I can do no other, Lord. I am commanded.'

'By Meurig?'

'By God.'

'But I am the lord of the land both sides of the stream,' I said, 'and of all the land southwards to Caer Cadarn and northwards to

Aquae Sulis and you do not preach here without my permission.'

'No man can countermand God's word, Lord,' the priest said.

'This can,' I said, drawing Hywelbane.

His women hissed. The priest stared at the sword, then spat into the fire. 'You risk God's wrath.'

'You risk my wrath,' I said, 'and if, at sundown tomorrow, you are still on the land I govern I shall give you as a slave to my slaves. You may sleep with the beasts tonight, but tomorrow you will go.'

He grudgingly left next day, and as if to punish me the first snow of the winter came with his leaving. That snow was early, promising a bitter season. At first it fell as sleet, but by nightfall it had become a thick snow that had whitened the land by dawn. It grew colder over the next week. Icicles hung inside our roof and now began the long winter struggle for warmth. In the village the folk slept with their beasts, while we fought the bitter air with great fires that made the icicles drip from the thatch. We put our winter cattle into the beast sheds, and killed the others, packing their meat in salt as Merlin had stored Gawain's blood-drained body. For two days the village echoed with the distraught bellowing of oxen being dragged to the axe. The snow was spattered red and the air stank of blood, salt and dung. Inside the hall the fires roared, but they gave us small warmth. We woke cold, we shivered inside our furs and we waited in vain for a thaw. The stream froze so that we had to chip our way through the ice to draw each day's water.

We still trained our young spearmen. We marched them through the snow, hardening their muscles to fight the Saxon. On the days when the snow fell hard and the wind whirled the flakes thick about the snow-crusted gables of the village's small houses, I had the men make their shields out of willow boards that were covered with leather. I was making a warband, but as I watched them work I feared for them, wondering how many would live to see the summer sun.

A message came from Arthur just before the solstice. At Dun Caric we were busy preparing the great feast that would last all through the week of the sun's death when Bishop Emrys arrived. He rode a horse with hoofs swathed in leather and was escorted by six of Arthur's spearmen. The Bishop told us he had stayed in Gwent, arguing with Meurig, while Arthur had gone on to Demetia.

'King Meurig has not utterly refused to help us,' the Bishop told us, shivering beside the fire where he had made a space for himself by pushing two of our dogs aside. He held his plump, red-chapped hands towards the flames. 'But his conditions for that help are, I fear, unacceptable.' He sneezed. 'Dear Lady, you are most kind,' he said to Ceinwyn who had brought him a horn of warmed mead.

'What conditions?' I asked.

Emrys shook his head sadly. 'He wants Dumnonia's throne, Lord.'

'He wants what?' I exploded.

Emrys held up a plump, chapped hand to still my anger. 'He says that Mordred is unfit to rule, that Arthur is unwilling to rule, and that Dumnonia needs a Christian king. He offers himself.'

'Bastard,' I said. 'The treacherous, lily-livered little bastard.'

'Arthur can't accept, of course,' Emrys said, 'his oath to Uther ensures that.' He sipped the mead and sighed appreciatively. 'So good to be warm again.'

'So unless we give Meurig the kingdom,' I said angrily, 'he won't help us?'

'So he says. He insists God will protect Gwent and that, unless we acclaim him king, we must defend Dumnonia by ourselves.'

I walked to the hall door, pulled aside the leather curtain and stared at the snow that was heaped high on the points of our wooden palisade. 'Did you talk to his father?' I asked Emrys.

'I did see Tewdric,' the Bishop said. 'I went with Agricola, who sends you his best wishes.'

Agricola had been King Tewdric's warlord, a great warrior who fought in Roman armour and with a chill ferocity. But Agricola was an old man now, and Tewdric, his master, had given up the throne and shaved his head into a priest's tonsure, thus yielding the power to his son. 'Is Agricola well?' I asked Emrys.

'Old, but vigorous. He agrees with us, of course, but . . .' Emrys shrugged. 'When Tewdric abdicated his throne, he gave up his power. He says he cannot change his son's mind.'

'Will not,' I grumbled, going back to the fire.

'Probably will not,' Emrys agreed. He sighed. 'I like Tewdric, but for now he is busy with other problems.'

'What problems?' I demanded too vehemently.

'He would like to know,' Emrys answered diffidently, 'whether in heaven we will eat like mortals, or whether we shall be spared the need for earthly nourishment. There is a belief, you must understand, that angels do not eat at all, that indeed they are spared all gross and worldly appetites, and the old King is trying to replicate that manner of life. He eats very little, indeed he boasted to me that he once managed three whole weeks without defecating and felt a great deal more holy afterwards.' Ceinwyn smiled, but said nothing, while I just stared at the Bishop with disbelief. Emrys finished the mead. 'Tewdric claims,' he added dubiously, 'that he will starve himself into a state of grace. I confess I am not convinced, but he does seem a most pious man. We should all be as blessed.'

'What does Agricola say?' I asked.

'He boasts of how frequently he defecates. Forgive me, Lady.'

'It must have been a joyous reunion for the two of them,' Ceinwyn said drily.

'It was not immediately useful,' Emrys admitted. 'I had hoped to persuade Tewdric to change his son's mind, but alas,' he shrugged, 'all we can do now is pray.'

'And keep our spears sharp,' I said wanly.

'That, too,' the Bishop agreed. He sneezed again and made the sign of the cross to nullify the ill-luck of the sneeze.

'Will Meurig let Powys's spearmen cross his land?' I asked.

'Cuneglas told him that if he refused permission then he would cross anyway.'

I groaned. The last thing we needed was for one British kingdom to fight another. For years such warfare had weakened Britain and had allowed the Saxons to take valley after valley and town after town, though of late it had been the Saxons who fought each other, and we who had taken advantage of their enmity to inflict defeats on them; but Cerdic and Aelle had learned the lesson that Arthur had beaten into the Britons, that victory came with unity. Now it was the Saxons who were united and the British who were divided.

'I think Meurig will let Cuneglas cross,' Emrys said, 'for he does not want war with anyone. He just wants peace.'

'We all want peace,' I said, 'but if Dumnonia falls then Gwent will be the next country to feel the Saxon blades.'

'Meurig insists not,' the Bishop said, 'and he is offering sanctuary to any Dumnonian Christian who wishes to avoid the war.'

That was bad news, for it meant that anyone who had no stomach to face Aelle and Cerdic need only claim the Christian faith to be given refuge in Meurig's kingdom. 'Does he really believe his God will protect him?' I asked Emrys.

'He must, Lord, for what other use is God? But God, of course, may have other ideas. It is so very hard to read His mind.' The Bishop was now warm enough to risk shedding the big cloak of bear fur from his shoulders. Beneath it he wore a sheepskin jerkin. He put his hand inside the jerkin and I assumed he was scratching for a louse, but instead he brought out a folded parchment that was tied with a ribbon and sealed with a melted drop of wax. 'Arthur sent this to me from Demetia,' he said, offering me the parchment, 'and asked that you should deliver it to the Princess Guinevere.'

'Of course,' I said, taking the parchment. I confess I was tempted to break the seal and read the document, but resisted the temptation. 'Do you know what it says?' I asked the Bishop.

'Alas, Lord, no,' Emrys said, though without looking at me, and I suspected the old man had broken the seal and did know the letter's contents, but was unwilling to admit that small sin. 'I'm sure it is nothing important,' the Bishop said, 'but he particularly asked that she should receive it before the solstice. Before he returns, that is.'

'Why did he go to Demetia?' Ceinwyn asked.

'To assure himself that the Blackshields will fight this spring, I assume,' the Bishop said, but I detected an evasion in his voice. I suspected the letter would contain the real reason for Arthur's visit to Oengus mac Airem, but Emrys could not reveal that without also admitting that he had broken the seal.

I rode to Ynys Wydryn next day. It was not far, but the journey took most of the morning for in places I had to lead my horse and mule through drifts of snow. The mule was carrying a dozen of the wolf pelts that Cuneglas had brought us and they proved a welcome gift because Guinevere's timber-walled prison room was full of cracks through which the wind hissed cold. I discovered her crouched beside a fire that burned in the centre of the room. She straightened when I was announced, then dismissed her two attendants to the kitchens. 'I am tempted,' she said, 'to become a kitchenmaid myself. The kitchen is at least warm, but sadly full of canting Christians. They can't break an egg without praising their wretched God.' She shivered and drew her cloak tight about her slender shoulders. 'The Romans,' she said, 'knew how to keep warm, but we seem to have lost that skill.'

'Ceinwyn sent you these, Lady,' I said, dropping the skins on the floor.

'You will thank her for me,' Guinevere said and then, despite the cold, she went and pushed open the shutters of a window so that daylight could come into the room. The fire swayed under the rush of cold air and sparks whirled up to the blackened beams. Guinevere was robed in thick brown wool. She was pale, but that haughty, green-eyed face had lost none of its power or pride. 'I had hoped to see you sooner,' she chided me.

'It has been a difficult season, Lady,' I said, excusing my long absence.

'I want to know, Derfel, what happened at Mai Dun,' she said.

'I shall tell you, Lady, but first I am ordered to give you this.' I took Arthur's parchment from the pouch at my belt and gave it to her. She tore the ribbon away, levered up the wax seal with a fingernail and unfolded the document. She read it in the glare of the light reflected from the snow through the window. I saw her face tighten, but she showed no other reaction. She seemed to read the letter twice, then folded it and tossed it onto a wooden chest. 'So tell me of Mai Dun,' she said.

'What do you know already?' I asked.

'I know what Morgan chooses to tell me, and what that bitch chooses is a version of her wretched God's truth.' She spoke loudly enough to be overheard by anyone eavesdropping on our conversation.

'I doubt that Morgan's God was disappointed by what happened,' I said, then told her the full story of that Samain Eve. She stayed silent when I had finished, just staring out of the window at the snow-covered compound where a dozen hardy pilgrims knelt before the holy thorn. I fed the fire from the pile of logs beside the wall.

'So Nimue took Gwydre to the summit?' Guinevere asked.

'She sent Blackshields to fetch him. To kidnap him, in truth. It wasn't difficult. The town was full of strangers and all kinds of spearmen were wandering in and out of the palace.' I paused. 'I doubt he was ever in real danger, though.'

'Of course he was!' she snapped.

Her vehemence took me aback. 'It was the other child who was to be killed,' I protested, 'Mordred's son. He was stripped, ready for the knife, but not Gwydre.'

'And when that other child's death had accomplished nothing, what would have happened then?' Guinevere asked. 'You think Merlin wouldn't have hung Gwydre by his heels?'

'Merlin would not do that to Arthur's son,' I said, though I confess there was no conviction in my voice.

'But Nimue would,' Guinevere said, 'Nimue would slaughter every child in Britain to bring the Gods back, and Merlin would have been tempted. To get so close,' she held a finger and thumb a coin's breadth apart, 'and with only Gwydre's life between Merlin and the return of the Gods? Oh, I think he would have been tempted.' She walked to the fire and opened her robe to let the warmth inside its folds. She wore a black gown beneath the robe and had not a single jewel in sight. Not even a ring on her fingers. 'Merlin,' she said softly, 'might have felt a pang of guilt for killing Gwydre, but not Nimue. She sees no difference between this world and the Otherworld, so what does it matter to her if a child lives or dies? But the child that matters, Derfel, is the ruler's son. To gain what is most precious you must give up what is most valuable, and what is valuable in Dumnonia is not some bastard whelp of Mordred's. Arthur rules here, not Mordred. Nimue wanted Gwydre dead. Merlin knew that, only he hoped that the lesser deaths would suffice. But Nimue doesn't care. One day, Derfel, she'll assemble the Treasures again and on that day Gwydre will have his blood drained into the Cauldron.'

'Not while Arthur lives.'

'Not while I live either!' she proclaimed fiercely, and then, recognizing her helplessness, she shrugged. She turned back to the window and let the brown robe drop. 'I haven't been a good mother,' she said unexpectedly. I did not know what to say, so said nothing. I had never been close to Guinevere, indeed she treated me with the same rough mix of affection and derision that she might have extended to a stupid but willing dog, but now, perhaps because she had no one else with whom to share her thoughts, she offered them to me. 'I don't even like being a mother,' she admitted. 'These women, now,' she indicated Morgan's white-robed women who hurried through the snow between the shrine's buildings, 'they all worship motherhood, but they're all as dry as husks. They weep for their Mary and tell me that only a mother can know true sadness, but who wants to know that?' She asked the question fiercely. 'It's all such a waste of life!' She was bitterly angry now. 'Cows make good mothers and sheep suckle perfectly adequately, so what merit lies in motherhood? Any stupid girl can become a mother! It's all that most of them are fit for! Motherhood isn't an achievement, it's an inevitability!' I saw she was weeping despite her anger. 'But it was all Arthur ever wanted me to be! A suckling cow!'

'No, Lady,' I said.

She turned on me angrily, her eyes bright with tears. 'You know more than I about this, Derfel?'

'He was proud of you, Lady,' I said awkwardly. 'He revelled in your beauty.'

'He could have had a statue made of me if that's all he wanted! A statue with milk ducts that he could clamp his infants onto!'

'He loved you,' I protested.

She stared at me and I thought she was about to erupt into a blistering anger, but instead she smiled wanly. 'He worshipped me, Derfel,' she said tiredly, 'and that is not the same thing as being loved.' She sat suddenly, collapsing onto a bench beside the wooden chest. 'And being worshipped, Derfel, is very tiresome. But he seems to have found a new goddess now.'

'He's done what, Lady?'

'You didn't know?' She seemed surprised, then plucked up the letter. 'Here, read it.'

I took the parchment from her. It carried no date, just the superscription Moridunum, showing that it had been written from Oengus mac Airem's capital. The letter was in Arthur's solid handwriting and was as cold as the snow that lay so thick on the windowsill. 'You should know, Lady,' he had written, 'that I am renouncing you as my wife and taking Argante, daughter of Oengus mac Airem, instead. I do not renounce Gwydre, only you.' That was all. It was not even signed.

'You really didn't know?' Guinevere asked me.

'No, Lady,' I said. I was far more astonished than Guinevere. I had heard men say that Arthur should take another wife, but he had said nothing to me and I felt offended that he had not trusted me. I felt offended and disappointed. 'I didn't know,' I insisted.

'Someone opened the letter,' Guinevere said in wry amusement. 'You can see they left a smudge of dirt on the bottom. Arthur wouldn't do that.' She leaned back so that her springing red hair was crushed against the wall. 'Why is he marrying?' she asked.

I shrugged. 'A man should be married, Lady.'

'Nonsense. You don't think any the less of Galahad because he's never married.'

'A man needs . . .' I began, then my voice tailed away.

'I know what a man needs,' Guinevere said with amusement. 'But why is Arthur marrying now? You think he loves this girl?'

'I hope so, Lady.'

She smiled. 'He's marrying, Derfel, to prove that he doesn't love me.'

I believed her, but I dared not agree with her. 'I'm sure it's love, Lady,' I said instead.

She laughed at that. 'How old is this Argante?'

'Fifteen?' I guessed. 'Maybe only fourteen?'

She frowned, thinking back. 'I thought she was meant to marry Mordred?'

'I thought so too,' I answered, for I remembered Oengus offering her as a bride to our King.

'But why should Oengus marry the child to a limping idiot like Mordred when he can put her into Arthur's bed?' Guinevere said. 'Only fifteen, you think?'

'If that.'

'Is she pretty?'

'I've never seen her, Lady, but Oengus says she is.'

'The Uí Liatháin do breed pretty girls,' Guinevere said. 'Was her sister beautiful?'

'Iseult? Yes, in a way.'

'This child will need to be beautiful,' Guinevere said in an amused voice. 'Arthur won't look at her otherwise. All men have to envy him. That much he does demand of his wives. They must be beautiful and, of course, much better behaved than I was.' She laughed and looked sideways at me. 'But even if she's beautiful and well behaved it won't work, Derfel.'

'It won't?'

'Oh, I'm sure the child can spit out babies for him if that's what he wants, but unless she's clever he'll get very bored with her.' She turned to gaze into the fire. 'Why do you think he wrote to tell me?'

'Because he thinks you should know,' I said.

She laughed at that. 'I should know? Why do I care if he beds some Irish child? I don't need to know, but he does need to tell me.' She looked at me again. 'And he'll want to know how I reacted, won't he?'

'Will he?' I asked in some confusion.

'Of course he will. So tell him, Derfel, that I laughed.' She stared defiantly at me, then suddenly shrugged. 'No, don't. Tell him I wish him all happiness. Tell him whatever you like, but ask one favour of him.' She paused, and I realized how she hated asking for favours. 'I do not want to die, Derfel, by being raped by a horde of lice-ridden Saxon warriors. When Cerdic comes next spring, ask Arthur to move my prison to a safer place.'

'I think you'll be safe here, Lady,' I said.

'Tell me why you think that?' she demanded sharply.

I took a moment to collect my thoughts. 'When the Saxons come,' I said, 'they'll advance along the Thames valley. Their aim is to reach the Severn Sea and that is their quickest route.'

Guinevere shook her head. 'Aelle's army will come along the Thames, Derfel, but Cerdic will attack in the south and hook up north to join Aelle. He'll come through here.'

'Arthur says not,' I insisted. 'He believes they don't trust each other, so they'll want to stay close together to guard against treachery.'

Guinevere dismissed that with another abrupt shake of her head. 'Aelle and Cerdic aren't fools, Derfel. They know they have to trust each other long enough to win. After that they can fall out, but not before. How many men will they bring?'

114

'We think two thousand, maybe two and a half.'

She nodded. 'The first attack will be on the Thames, and that will be large enough to make you think it is their main attack. And once Arthur has gathered his forces to oppose that army, Cerdic will march in the south. He'll run wild, Derfel, and Arthur will have to send men to oppose him, and when he does, Aelle will attack the rest.'

'Unless Arthur lets Cerdic run wild,' I said, not believing her forecast for a moment.

'He could do that,' she agreed, 'but if he does then Ynys Wydryn will be in Saxon hands and I do not want to be here when that happens. If he won't release me, then beg him to imprison me in Glevum.'

I hesitated. I saw no reason not to pass on her request to Arthur, but I wanted to make certain that she was sincere. 'If Cerdic does come this way, Lady,' I ventured, 'he's liable to bring friends of yours in his army.'

She gave me a murderous look. She held it for a long time before speaking. 'I have no friends in Lloegyr,' she said at last, icily.

I hesitated, then decided to forge on. 'I saw Cerdic not two months ago,' I said, 'and Lancelot was in his company.'

I had never mentioned Lancelot's name to her before and her head jerked as though I had struck her. 'What are you saying, Derfel?' she asked softly.

'I am saying, Lady, that Lancelot will come here in the spring. I am suggesting, Lady, that Cerdic will make him lord of this land.'

She closed her eyes and for a few seconds I was not certain whether she was laughing or crying. Then I saw it was laughter that had made her shudder. 'You are a fool,' she said, looking at me again. 'You're trying to help me! Do you think I love Lancelot?'

'You wanted him to be King,' I said.

'What does that have to do with love?' she asked derisively. 'I wanted him to be King because he's a weak man and a woman can only rule in this world through such a feeble man. Arthur isn't weak.' She took a deep breath. 'But Lancelot is, and perhaps he will rule here when the Saxons come, but whoever controls Lancelot it will not be me, nor any woman now, but Cerdic, and Cerdic, I hear, is anything but weak.' She stood, crossed to me and plucked the letter from my hands. She unfolded it, read it a last time, then tossed the parchment into the fire. It blackened, shrivelled, then burst into flame. 'Go,' she said, watching the flames, 'and tell Arthur that I wept at his news. That's what he wants to hear, so tell him. Tell him I wept.'

I left her. In the next few days the snow thawed, but the rains came again and the bare black trees dripped onto a land that seemed to be rotting in the misty damp. The solstice neared, though the sun never showed. The world was dying in dark, damp despair. I waited for Arthur's return, but he did not summon me. He took his new bride to Durnovaria and there he celebrated the solstice. If he cared what Guinevere thought of his new marriage, he did not ask me.

We gave the feast of the winter solstice in Dun Caric's hall and there was not a person present who did not suspect it would be our last. We made our offerings to the midwinter sun, but knew that when the sun rose again it would not bring life to the land, but death. It would bring Saxon spears and Saxon axes and Saxon swords. We prayed, we feasted and we feared that we were doomed. And still the rain would not stop.

PART TWO

Mynydd Baddon

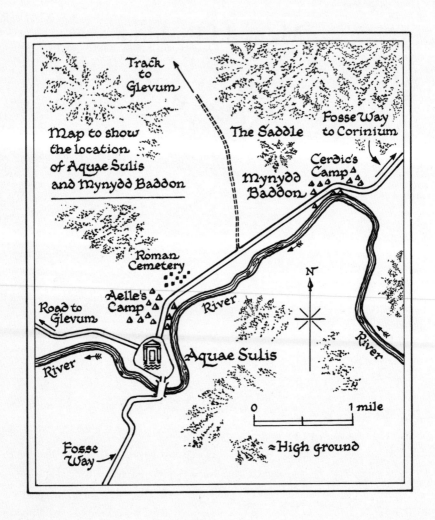

Track
to
Glevum

Map to show
the location
of Aquae Sulis
and Mynydd Baddon

The Saddle

Fosse Way
to Corinium

Cerdic's
Camp

Mynydd
Baddon

Roman
Cemetery

Aelle's
Camp

Road to
Glevum

River

N

River

River

Aquae Sulis

0   1 mile

Fosse
Way

≈ High ground

'W HO?' IGRAINE DEMANDED as soon as she had read the first sheet of the latest pile of parchments. She has learned some of the Saxon tongue in the last few months and is very proud of herself for that achievement, though in truth it is a barbarous language and much less subtle than the British.

'Who?' I echoed her question.

'Who was the woman who guided Britain to destruction? It was Nimue, wasn't it?'

'If you give me time to write the tale, dear Lady, you will find out.'

'I knew you were going to say that. I don't even know why I asked.' She sat on the wide ledge of my windowsill with one hand on her swollen belly and with her head cocked to one side as though she were listening. After a while a look of mischievous delight came to her face. 'The baby's kicking,' she said, 'do you want to feel it?'

I shuddered. 'No.'

'Why not?'

'I was never interested in babies.'

She made a face at me. 'You'll love mine, Derfel.'

'I will?'

'He's going to be lovely!'

'How do you know,' I enquired, 'that it is a boy?'

'Because no girl can kick this hard, that's why. Look!' And my Queen smoothed the blue dress tight over her belly and laughed when the smooth dome flickered. 'Tell me about Argante,' she said, letting go of the dress.

'Small, dark, thin, pretty.'

Igraine made a face at the inadequacy of my description. 'Was she clever?'

I thought about it. 'She was sly, so yes, she had a sort of cleverness, but it was never fed by education.'

My Queen gave that statement a scornful shrug. 'Is education so important?'

'I think it is, yes. I always regret I never learned Latin.'

'Why?' Igraine asked.

'Because so much of mankind's experience is written in that tongue, Lady, and one of the things an education gives us is access to all the things other folks have known, feared, dreamed and achieved. When you are in trouble it helps to discover someone who has been in the same predicament before. It explains things.'

'Like what?' Igraine demanded.

I shrugged. 'I remember something Guinevere once said to me. I didn't know what it meant, because it was in Latin, but she translated it, and it explained Arthur exactly. I've never forgotten it either.'

'Well? Go on.'

'*Odi at amo*,' I quoted the unfamiliar words slowly, '*excrucior*.'

'Which means?'

'I hate and I love, it hurts. A poet wrote the line, I forget which poet, but Guinevere had read the poem and one day, when we were talking about Arthur, she quoted the line. She understood him exactly, you see.'

'Did Argante understand him?'

'Oh, no.'

'Could she read?'

'I'm not sure. I don't remember. Probably not.'

'What did she look like?'

'She had very pale skin,' I said, 'because she refused to go into the sun. She liked the night, Argante did. And she had very black hair, as shiny as a raven's feathers.'

'You say she was small and thin?' Igraine asked.

'Very thin, and quite short,' I said, 'but the thing I remember most about Argante is that she very rarely smiled. She watched everything and missed nothing, and there was always a calculating look on her face. People mistook that look for cleverness, but it wasn't cleverness at all. She was merely the youngest of seven or eight daughters and so she was always worried that she would be left out. She was looking for her share all the time, and all the time she believed she was not receiving it.'

Igraine grimaced. 'You make her sound horrid!'

'She was greedy, bitter and very young,' I said, 'but she was also beautiful. She had a delicacy that was very touching.' I paused and sighed. 'Poor Arthur. He did pick his women very badly. Except for Ailleann, of course, but then he didn't pick her. She was given to him as a slave.'

'What happened to Ailleann?'

'She died in the Saxon War.'

'Killed?' Igraine shuddered.

'Of the plague,' I said. 'It was a very normal death.'

Christ.

That name does look odd on the page, but I shall leave it there. Just as Igraine and I were talking about Ailleann, Bishop Sansum came into the room. The saint cannot read, and because he would utterly disapprove of my writing this story of Arthur, Igraine and I pretend that I am making a gospel in the Saxon tongue. I say he cannot read, but Sansum does have the ability to recognize some few words and Christ is one of them. Which is why I wrote it. He saw it, too, and grunted suspiciously. He looks very old these days. Almost all his hair has gone, though he still has two white tufts like the ears of Lughtigern, the mouse lord. He has pain when he passes urine, but he will not submit his body to the wise-women for healing, for he claims they are all pagans. God, the saint claims, will cure him, though at times, God forgive me, I pray that the saint might be dying for then this small monastery would have a new bishop. 'My Lady is well?' he asked Igraine after squinting down at this parchment.

'Thank you, Bishop, I am.'

Sansum poked about the room, looking for something wrong, though what he expected to find I cannot tell. The room is very simple; a cot, a writing table, a stool and a fire. He would have liked to criticize me for burning a fire, but today is a very mild winter's day and I am saving what small fuel the saint permits me to have. He flicked at a scrap of dust, decided not to comment on it and so peered at Igraine instead. 'Your time must be very near, Lady?'

'Less than two moons, they say, Bishop,' Igraine said, and made the sign of the cross against her blue dress.

'You will know, of course, that our prayers will echo throughout heaven on your Ladyship's behalf,' Sansum said, without meaning a word of it.

'Pray, too,' Igraine said, 'that the Saxons are not close.'

'Are they?' Sansum asked in alarm.

'My husband hears they are readying to attack Ratae.'

'Ratae is far away,' the Bishop said dismissively.

'A day and a half?' Igraine said, 'and if Ratae falls, what fortress lies between us and the Saxons?'

'God will protect us,' the Bishop said, unconsciously echoing the long-dead belief of the pious King Meurig of Gwent, 'as God will protect your Ladyship at the hour of your trial.' He stayed a few more minutes, but had no real business with either of us. The saint is bored these days. He lacks mischief to foment. Brother Maelgwyn, who was the strongest of us and who carried much of the monastery's physical labour, died a few weeks ago and, with his passing, the Bishop lost one of his favourite targets for contempt. He finds little pleasure in tormenting me for I endure his spite patiently, and besides, I am protected by Igraine and her husband.

At last Sansum went and Igraine made a face at his retreating back. 'Tell me, Derfel,' she said when the saint was out of earshot, 'what should I do for the birth?'

'Why on earth do you ask me?' I said in amazement. 'I know nothing about childbirth, thank God! I've never even seen a child born, and I don't want to.'

'But you know about the old things,' she said urgently, 'that's what I mean.'

'The women in your caer will know much more than I do,' I said, 'but whenever Ceinwyn gave birth we always made sure there was iron in the bed, women's urine on the doorstep, mugwort on the fire, and, of course, we had a virgin girl ready to lift the newborn child from the birth-straw. Most important of all,' I went on sternly, 'there must be no men in the room. Nothing brings so much ill-luck as having a man present at a birth.' I touched the protruding nail in my writing desk to avert the evil fortune of even mentioning such an unlucky circumstance. We Christians, of course, do not believe that touching iron will affect any fortune, whether evil or good, but the nailhead on my desk is still much polished by my touching. 'Is it true about the Saxons?' I asked.

Igraine nodded. 'They're getting closer, Derfel.'

I rubbed the nailhead again. 'Then warn your husband to have sharp spears.'

'He needs no warning,' she said grimly.

I wonder if the war will ever end. For as long as I have lived the Britons have fought the Saxons, and though we did win one great victory over them, in the years since that victory we have seen more land lost and, with the land, the stories that were attached to the valleys and hilltops have been lost as well. History is not just a tale of men's making, but is a thing tied to the land. We call a hill by the name of a hero who died there, or name a river after a princess who fled beside its banks, and when the old names vanish, the stories go with them and the new names carry no reminder of the past. The Sais take our land and our history. They spread like a contagion, and we no longer have Arthur to protect us. Arthur, scourge of the Sais, Lord of Britain and the man whose love hurt him more than any wound from sword or spear. How I do miss Arthur.

The winter solstice is when we prayed that the Gods would not abandon the earth to the great darkness. In the bleakest of winters those prayers often seemed like pleas of despair, and that was never more so than in the year before the Saxons attacked when our world was deadened beneath a shell of ice and crusted snow. For those of us who were adepts of Mithras the solstice had a double meaning, for it is also the time of our God's birth, and after the big solstice feast at Dun Caric I took Issa west to the caves where we held our most solemn ceremonies and there I inducted him into the worship of Mithras. He endured the ordeals successfully and so was welcomed into that band of elite warriors who keep the God's mysteries. We feasted afterwards. I killed the bull that year, first hamstringing the beast so that it could not move, then swinging the axe in the low cave to sever its spine. The bull, I recall, had a shrivelled liver, which was reckoned a bad omen, but there were no good omens that cold winter.

Forty men attended the rites, despite the bitter weather. Arthur, though long an initiate, did not arrive, but Sagramor and Culhwch had come from their frontier posts for the ceremonies. At the end of the feasting, when most of the warriors were sleeping off the effects of the mead, we three withdrew to a low tunnel where the smoke was not thick and we could talk privately.

Both Sagramor and Culhwch were certain that the Saxons would attack directly along the valley of the Thames. 'What I hear,' Sagramor told us, 'is that they're filling London and Pontes with food and supplies.' He paused to tear some meat from a bone with his teeth. It had been months since I had seen Sagramor, and I found his company reassuring; the Numidian was the toughest and most fearsome of all Arthur's warlords, and his prowess was reflected in his narrow, axe-sharp face. He was the most loyal of men, a staunch friend, and a wondrous teller of stories, but above everything he was a natural warrior who could outfox and outfight any enemy. The Saxons were terrified of Sagramor, believing he was a dark demon from their Otherworld. We were happy that they should live in such numbing fear and it was a comfort that, even though outnumbered, we would have his sword and his experienced spearmen on our side.

'Won't Cerdic attack in the south?' I asked.

Culhwch shook his head. 'He's not making any show of it. Nothing stirring in Venta.'

'They don't trust each other,' Sagramor spoke of Cerdic and Aelle. 'They daren't let one another out of their sight. Cerdic fears we'll buy off Aelle, and Aelle fears that Cerdic will cheat him of the spoils, so they're going to stick closer than brothers.'

'So what will Arthur do?' I asked.

'We hoped you'd tell us that,' Culhwch answered.

'Arthur doesn't speak to me these days,' I said, not bothering to hide my bitterness.

'That makes two of us,' Culhwch growled.

'Three,' Sagramor said. 'He comes to see me, he asks questions, he rides on raids and then he goes away. He says nothing.'

'Let's hope he's thinking,' I said.

'Too busy with that new bride, probably,' Culhwch offered sourly.

'Have you met her?' I asked.

'An Irish kitten,' he said dismissively, 'with claws.' Culhwch told us he had visited Arthur and his new bride on his way north to this meeting with Mithras. 'She's pretty enough,' he said grudgingly. 'If you took her slave you'd probably want to make sure she stayed in your own kitchen for a while. Well, I would. You wouldn't, Derfel.' Culhwch often teased me about my loyalty to Ceinwyn, though I was not so very unusual in my fidelity. Sagramor had taken a captured Saxon for a wife and, like me, was famously loyal to his woman. 'What use is a bull that only serves one cow?' Culhwch now asked, but neither of us responded to his jibe.

'Arthur is frightened,' Sagramor said instead. He paused, gathering his thoughts. The Numidian spoke the British tongue well, though with a wretched accent, but it was not his natural language, and he often spoke slowly to make certain he was expressing his exact ideas. 'He has defied the Gods, and not just at Mai Dun, but by taking Mordred's power. The Christians hate him and now the pagans say he is their enemy. Do you see how lonely that makes him?'

'The trouble with Arthur is that he doesn't believe in the Gods,' Culhwch said dismissively.

'He believes in himself,' Sagramor said, 'and when Guinevere betrayed him, he took a blow to the heart. He is ashamed. He lost much pride, and he's a proud man. He thinks we all laugh at him, and so he is distant from us.'

'I don't laugh at him,' I protested.

'I do,' Culhwch said, flinching as he straightened his wounded leg. 'Stupid bastard. Should have taken his sword belt to Guinevere's back a few times. That would have taught the bitch a lesson.'

'Now,' Sagramor went on, blithely ignoring Culhwch's predictable opinion, 'he fears defeat. For what is he if he is not a soldier? He likes to think he is a good man, that he rules because he is a natural ruler, but it is the sword that has carried him to power. In his soul he knows that, and if he loses this war then he loses the thing he cares about most; his reputation. He will be remembered as the usurper who was not good enough to hold what he usurped. He is terrified of a second defeat for his reputation.'

'Maybe Argante can heal the first defeat,' I said.

'I doubt it,' Sagramor said. 'Galahad tells me that Arthur didn't really want to marry her.'

'Then why did he?' I asked gloomily.

Sagramor shrugged. 'To spite Guinevere? To please Oengus? To show us that he doesn't need Guinevere?'

'To slap bellies with a pretty girl?' Culhwch suggested.

'If he even does that,' Sagramor said.

Culhwch stared at the Numidian in apparent shock. 'Of course he does,' Culhwch said.

Sagramor shook his head. 'I hear he doesn't. Only rumour, of course, and rumour is least trustworthy when it comes to the ways of a man and his woman. But I think this Princess is too young for Arthur's tastes.'

'They're never too young,' Culhwch growled. Sagramor just shrugged. He was a far more subtle man than Culhwch and that gave him a much greater insight into Arthur, who liked to appear so straightforward, but whose soul was in truth as complicated as the twisted curves and spooling dragons that decorated Excalibur's blade.

We parted in the morning, our spear and sword blades still reddened with the blood of the sacrificed bull. Issa was excited. A few years before he had been a farm boy, but now he was an adept of Mithras and soon, he had told me, he would be a father for Scarach, his wife, was pregnant. Issa, given confidence by his initiation into Mithras, was suddenly sure we could beat the Saxons without Gwent's help, but I had no such belief. I might not have liked Guinevere, but I had never thought her a fool, and I was worried about her forecast that Cerdic would attack in the south. The alternative made sense, of course; Cerdic and Aelle were reluctant allies and would want to keep a careful eye on each other. An overwhelming attack along the Thames would be the quickest way to reach the Severn Sea and so split the British kingdoms into two parts, and why should the Saxons sacrifice their advantage of numbers by dividing their forces into two smaller armies that Arthur might defeat one after the other? Yet if Arthur expected just one attack, and only guarded against that one attack, the advantages of a southern assault were overwhelming. While Arthur was tangled with one Saxon army in the Thames valley, the other could hook around his right flank and reach the Severn almost unopposed. Issa, though, was not worried by such things. He only imagined himself in the shield wall where, ennobled by Mithras's acceptance, he would cut down Saxons like a farmer reaping hay.

The weather stayed cold after the season of the solstice. Day after day dawned frozen and pale with the sun little more than a reddened disc hanging low in the southern clouds. Wolves scavenged deep into the farmlands, hunting for our sheep that we had penned into hurdle folds, and one glorious day we hunted down six of the grey beasts and so secured six new wolf tails for my warband's helmets. My men had begun to wear such tails on their helmet crests in the deep woods of Armorica where we had fought the Franks and, because we had raided them like scavenging beasts, they had called us wolves and we had taken the insult as a compliment. We were the Wolftails, though our shields, instead of bearing a wolf mask, were painted with a five-pointed star as a tribute to Ceinwyn.

Ceinwyn was still insistent that she would not flee to Powys in the spring. Morwenna and Seren could go, she said, but she would stay. I was angry at that decision. 'So the girls can lose both mother and father?' I demanded.

'If that's what the Gods decree, yes,' she said placidly, then shrugged. 'I may be being selfish, but that is what I want.'

'You want to die? That's selfish?'

'I don't want to be so far away, Derfel,' she said. 'Do you know what it's like to be in a distant country when your man is fighting? You wait in terror. You fear every messenger. You listen to every rumour. This time I shall stay.'

'To give me something else to worry about?'

'What an arrogant man you are,' she said calmly. 'You think I can't look after myself?'

'That little ring won't keep you safe from Saxons,' I said, pointing to the scrap of agate on her finger.

'So I shall keep myself safe. Don't worry, Derfel, I won't be under your feet, and I won't let myself be taken captive.'

Next day the first lambs were born in a sheepfold hard under Dun Caric's hill. It was very early for such births, but I took it as a good sign from the Gods. Before Ceinwyn could forbid it, the firstborn of those lambs was sacrificed to ensure that the rest of the lambing season would go well. The little beast's bloody pelt was nailed to a willow beside the stream and beneath it, next day, a wolfsbane bloomed, its small yellow petals the first flash of colour in the turning year. That day, too, I saw three kingfishers flickering bright by the icy edges of the stream. Life was stirring. In the dawn, after the cockerels had woken us, we could again hear the songs of thrushes, robins, larks, wrens and sparrows.

Arthur sent for us two weeks after those first lambs were born. The snow had thawed, and his messenger had struggled through the muddy roads to bring us the summons that demanded our presence at the palace of Lindinis. We were to be there for the feast of Imbolc, the first feast after the solstice and one that is devoted to the Goddess of fertility. At Imbolc we drive newborn lambs through burning hoops and afterwards, when they think no one is watching, the young girls will leap through the smouldering hoops and touch their fingers to the ashes of Imbolc's fires and smear the grey dust high between their thighs. A child born in November is called a child of Imbolc and has ash as its mother and fire as its father. Ceinwyn and I arrived in the afternoon of Imbolc Eve as the wintry sun was throwing long shadows across the pale grass. Arthur's spearmen surrounded the palace, guarding him against the sullen hostility of people who remembered Merlin's magical invocation of the glowing girl in the palace courtyard.

To my surprise, I discovered the courtyard was prepared for Imbolc. Arthur had never cared for such things, leaving most religious observances to Guinevere, and she had never celebrated the crude country festivals like Imbolc; but now a great hoop of plaited straw stood ready for the flames in the centre of the yard while a handful of newborn lambs were penned with their mothers in a small hurdle enclosure. Culhwch greeted us, giving a sly nod to the hoop. 'A chance for you to have another baby,' he said to Ceinwyn.

'Why else would I be here?' she responded, giving him a kiss. 'And how many do you have now?'

'Twenty-one,' he said proudly.

'From how many mothers?'

'Ten,' he grinned, then slapped my back. 'We're to get our orders tomorrow.'

'We?'

'You, me, Sagramor, Galahad, Lanval, Balin, Morfans,' Culhwch shrugged, 'everyone.'

'Is Argante here?' I asked.

'Who do you think put up the hoop?' he asked. 'This is all her idea. She's brought a Druid out of Demetia, and before we all eat tonight we have to worship Nantosuelta.'

'Who?' Ceinwyn asked.

'A Goddess,' Culhwch said carelessly. There were so many Gods and Goddesses that it was impossible for anyone but a Druid to know all their names and neither Ceinwyn nor I had ever heard of Nantosuelta before.

We did not see either Arthur or Argante until after dark when Hygwydd, Arthur's servant, summoned us all into the courtyard that was lit with pitch-soaked torches flaming in their iron beckets. I remembered Merlin's night here, and the crowd of awed folk who had lifted their maimed and sick babies to Olwen the Silver. Now an assembly of lords and their ladies waited awkwardly on either side of the plaited hoop, while set on a dais at the courtyard's western end were three chairs draped with white linen. A Druid stood beside the hoop and I presumed he was the sorcerer whom Argante had fetched from her father's kingdom. He was a short, squat man with a wild black beard in which tufts of fox hair and bunches of small bones were plaited. 'He's called Fergal,' Galahad told me, 'and he hates Christians. He spent all afternoon casting spells against me, then Sagramor arrived and Fergal almost fainted with horror. He thought it was Crom Dubh come in person.' Galahad laughed.

Sagramor could have indeed been that dark God, for he was dressed in black leather and had a black-scabbarded sword at his hip. He had come to Lindinis with his big, placid Saxon wife, Malla, and the two stood apart from the rest of us at the far side of the courtyard. Sagramor worshipped Mithras but had little time for the British Gods, while Malla still prayed to Woden, Eostre, Thunor, Fir and Seaxnet: all Saxon deities.

All Arthur's leaders were there, though, as I waited for Arthur,

129

I thought of the men who were missing. Cei, who had grown up with Arthur in distant Gwynedd, had died in Dumnonian Isca during Lancelot's rebellion. He had been murdered by Christians. Agravain, who for years had been the commander of Arthur's horsemen, had died during the winter, struck down by a fever. Balin had taken over Agravain's duties, and he had brought three wives to Lindinis, together with a tribe of small stocky children who stared in horror at Morfans, the ugliest man of Britain, whose face was now so familiar to the rest of us that we no longer noticed his hare lip, goitred neck or twisted jaw. Except for Gwydre, who was still a boy, I was probably the youngest man there and that realization shocked me. We needed new warlords, and I decided then and there that I would give Issa his own band of men as soon as the Saxon war was over. If Issa lived. If I lived.

Galahad was looking after Gwydre and the two of them came to stand with Ceinwyn and me. Galahad had always been a handsome man, but now, as he grew into his middle years, those good looks possessed a new dignity. His hair had turned from its bright gold into grey, and he now wore a small pointed beard. He and I had always been close, but in that difficult winter he was probably closer to Arthur than to anyone else. Galahad had not been present at the sea palace to see Arthur's shame, and that, together with his calm sympathy, made him acceptable to Arthur. Ceinwyn, keeping her voice low so that Gwydre could not hear, asked him how Arthur was. 'I wish I knew,' Galahad said.

'He's surely happy,' Ceinwyn observed.

'Why?'

'A new wife?' Ceinwyn suggested.

Galahad smiled. 'When a man makes a journey, dear Lady, and has his horse stolen in the course of it, he frequently buys a replacement too hastily.'

'And doesn't ride it thereafter, I hear?' I put in brutally.

'Do you hear that, Derfel?' Galahad answered, neither confirming nor denying the rumour. He smiled. 'Marriage is such a mystery to me,' he added vaguely. Galahad himself had never married. Indeed he had never really settled since Ynys Trebes, his home, had fallen to the Franks. He had been in Dumnonia ever since and he had seen a generation of children grow to adulthood in that time, but he still seemed like a visitor. He had rooms in the palace at Durnovaria, but kept little furniture there and scant comfort. He rode errands for Arthur, travelling the length of Britain to resolve problems with other kingdoms, or else riding with Sagramor in raids across the Saxon frontier, and he seemed happiest when he was thus kept busy. I had sometimes suspected that he was in love with Guinevere, but Ceinwyn had always mocked that thought. Galahad, she said, was in love with perfection and was too fastidious to love an actual woman. He loved the idea of women, Ceinwyn said, but could not bear the reality of disease and blood and pain. He showed no revulsion at such things in battle, but that, Ceinwyn declared, was because in battle it was men who were bloody and men who were fallible, and Galahad had never idealized men, only women. And maybe she was right. I only knew that at times my friend had to be lonely, though he never complained. 'Arthur's very proud of Argante,' he now said mildly, though in a tone which suggested he was leaving something unsaid.

'But she's no Guinevere?' I suggested.

'She's certainly no Guinevere,' Galahad agreed, grateful that I had voiced the thought, 'though she's not unlike her in some ways.'

'Such as?' Ceinwyn asked.

'She has ambitions,' Galahad said dubiously. 'She thinks Arthur should cede Siluria to her father.'

'Siluria isn't his to yield!' I said.

'No,' Galahad agreed, 'but Argante thinks he could conquer it.'

I spat. To conquer Siluria, Arthur would need to fight Gwent and even Powys, the two countries that jointly ruled the territory. 'Mad,' I said.

'Ambitious, if unrealistic,' Galahad corrected me.

'Do you like Argante?' Ceinwyn asked him directly.

He was spared the need to answer because the palace door was suddenly thrown open and Arthur at last appeared. He was robed in his customary white, and his face that had grown so gaunt over the last months looked suddenly old. That was a cruel fate, for on his arm, robed in gold, was his new bride and that new bride was little more than a child.

That was the first time I saw Argante, Princess of the Uí Liatháin and Iseult's sister, and in many ways she resembled the doomed

Iseult. Argante was a fragile creature poised between girlhood and womanhood, and on that night of Imbolc's Eve she looked closer to childhood than adulthood for she was swathed in a great cloak of stiff linen that had surely once belonged to Guinevere. The robe was certainly too big for Argante, who walked awkwardly in its golden folds. I remembered seeing her sister hung with jewels and thinking that Iseult had looked like a child arrayed in its mother's gold and Argante gave the same impression of being dressed up for play and, just like a child pretending to adulthood, she carried herself with a self-absorbed solemnity to defy her innate lack of dignity. She wore her glossy black hair in a long tress that was twisted about her skull and held in place with a brooch of jet, the same colour as the shields of her father's feared warriors, and the adult style sat uneasily on her young face, just as the heavy golden torque about her neck seemed too massive for her slender throat. Arthur led her to the dais and there bowed her into the left-hand chair and I doubt there was a single soul in the courtyard, whether guest, Druid or guard, who did not think how like father and daughter they appeared. There was a pause once Argante was seated. It was an awkward moment, as though a piece of ritual had been forgotten and a solemn ceremony was in danger of becoming ridiculous, but then there was a scuffle in the doorway, a snigger of laughter, and Mordred came into view.

Our King limped on his clubbed foot and with a sly smile on his face. Like Argante he was playing a role, but unlike her he was an unwilling player. He knew that every man in that courtyard was Arthur's man and that all hated him, and that while they pretended he was their King he lived only by their sufferance. He climbed the dais. Arthur bowed and we all followed suit. Mordred, his stiff hair as unruly as ever and his beard an ugly fringe to his round face, nodded curtly, then sat in the centre chair. Argante gave him a surprisingly friendly glance, Arthur took the last chair, and there they sat, Emperor, King and child bride.

I could not help thinking that Guinevere would have done all this so much better. There would have been heated mead to drink, more fires for warmth, and music to drown the awkward silences, but on this night no one seemed to know what was supposed to happen, until Argante hissed at her father's Druid. Fergal glanced about nervously, then scuttled across the courtyard to snatch up one of the becketed torches. He used the torch to ignite the hoop, then muttered incomprehensible incantations as the flames seized the straw.

The five newborn lambs were carried from the pen by slaves. The ewes called miserably for their missing offspring that wriggled in the slaves' arms. Fergal waited until the hoop was a complete circle of fire, then ordered the lambs be herded through the flames. Confusion followed. The lambs, having no idea that the fertility of Dumnonia depended on their obedience, scattered in every direction except towards the fire and Balin's children happily joined the whooping hunt and only succeeded in compounding the confusion, but at last, one by one, the lambs were collected and shooed towards the hoop, and in time all five were persuaded to jump through the circlet of fire, but by then the courtyard's intended solemnity had been shattered. Argante, who was doubtless accustomed to seeing such ceremonies performed much better in her native Demetia, frowned, but the rest of us laughed and chatted. Fergal restored the night's dignity by suddenly uttering a feral scream that froze us all. The Druid was standing with his head thrown back so that he stared up at the clouds, and in his right hand there was lifted a broad flint knife, and in his left, where it struggled helplessly, was a lamb.

'Oh, no,' Ceinwyn protested and turned away. Gwydre grimaced and I put an arm about his shoulders.

Fergal bellowed his challenge at the night, then held both lamb and knife high over his head. He screamed again, then savaged the lamb, striking and tearing at its little body with the clumsy, blunt knife, the lamb struggled ever more weakly and bleated to its mother that called hopelessly back, and all the while blood poured from its fleece onto Fergal's raised face and onto his wild, bone-hung, fox-plaited beard. 'I am very glad,' Galahad murmured in my ear, 'that I do not live in Demetia.'

I glanced at Arthur while this extraordinary sacrifice was being performed and I saw a look of utter revulsion on his face. Then he saw that I was watching him and his face stiffened. Argante, her mouth open eagerly, was leaning forward to watch the Druid. Mordred was grinning.

133

The lamb died and Fergal, to the horror of us all, began to prance about the courtyard, shaking the corpse and screaming prayers. Blood droplets spattered us. I threw my cloak protectively over Ceinwyn as the Druid, his own face streaming with rivulets of blood, danced past. Arthur plainly had no idea that this barbarous killing had been arranged. He had doubtless thought his new bride had planned some decorous ceremony to precede the feast, but the rite had become an orgy of blood. All five lambs were slaughtered, and when the last small throat had been cut by the black flint blade, Fergal stepped back and gestured at the hoop. 'Nantosuelta awaits you,' he called to us, 'here she is! Come to her!' Clearly he expected some response, but none of us moved. Sagramor stared up at the moon and Culhwch hunted a louse in his beard. Small flames flickered along the hoop and scraps of burning straw fluttered down to where the torn bloody corpses lay on the courtyard's stones, and still none of us moved. 'Come to Nantosuelta!' Fergal called hoarsely.

Then Argante stood. She shrugged off the stiff golden robe to reveal a simple blue woollen dress that made her look more childlike than ever. She had narrow boyish hips, small hands and a delicate face as white as the lambs' fleeces had been before the black knife took their little lives. Fergal called to her. 'Come,' he chanted, 'come to Nantosuelta, Nantosuelta calls you, come to Nantosuelta,' and on he crooned, summoning Argante to her Goddess. Argante, almost in a trance now, stepped slowly forward, each step a separate effort so that she moved and stopped, moved and stopped, as the Druid beguiled her onwards. 'Come to Nantosuelta,' Fergal intoned, 'Nantosuelta calls you, come to Nantosuelta.' Argante's eyes were closed. For her, at least, this was an awesome moment, though the rest of us were all, I think, embarrassed. Arthur looked appalled, and no wonder, for it seemed that he had only exchanged Isis for Nantosuelta, though Mordred, who had once been promised Argante as his own bride, watched with an eager face as the girl shuffled forward. 'Come to Nantosuelta, Nantosuelta calls you,' Fergal beckoned her on, only now his voice had risen to a mock female screech.

Argante reached the hoop and as the heat of the last flames touched her face she opened her eyes and almost seemed surprised to find herself standing beside the Goddess's fire. She looked at Fergal, then ducked swiftly through the smoky ring. She smiled triumphantly and Fergal clapped her, inviting the rest of us to join the applause. Politely we did so, though our unenthusiastic clapping ceased as Argante crouched down beside the dead lambs. We were all silent as she dipped a delicate finger into one of the knife wounds. She withdrew her finger and held it up so that we could all see the blood thick on its tip. Then she turned so that Arthur could see. She stared at him as she opened her mouth, baring small white teeth, then slowly placed the finger between her teeth and closed her lips around it. She sucked it clean. Gwydre, I saw, was staring in disbelief at his stepmother. She was not much older than Gwydre. Ceinwyn shuddered, her hand firmly clasping mine.

Argante was still not finished. She turned, wet her finger with blood again, and stabbed the bloody finger into the hot embers of the hoop. Then, crouching still, she groped under the hem of her blue dress, transferring the blood and ashes to her thighs. She was ensuring that she would have babies. She was using Nantosuelta's power to start her own dynasty and we were all witnesses to that ambition. Her eyes were closed again, almost in ecstasy, then suddenly the rite was over. She stood, her hand visible again, and beckoned Arthur. She smiled for the first time that evening, and I saw she was beautiful, but it was a stark beauty, as hard in its way as Guinevere's, but without Guinevere's tangle of bright hair to soften it.

She beckoned to Arthur again, for it seemed the ritual demanded that he too must pass through the hoop. For a second he hesitated, then he looked at Gwydre and, unable to take any more of the superstition, he stood up and shook his head. 'We shall eat,' he said harshly, then softened the curt invitation by smiling at his guests; but at that moment I glanced at Argante and saw a look of utter fury on her pale face. For a heartbeat I thought she would scream at Arthur. Her small body was tensed rigid and her fists were clenched, but Fergal, who alone except for me seemed to have noticed her rage, whispered in her ear and she shuddered as the anger passed. Arthur had noticed nothing. 'Bring the torches,' he ordered the guards, and the flames were carried inside the palace to illuminate the feasting-hall. 'Come,' Arthur called to the rest of

135

us and we gratefully moved towards the palace doors. Argante hesitated, but again Fergal whispered to her and she obeyed Arthur's summons. The Druid stayed beside the smoking hoop.

Ceinwyn and I were the last of the guests to leave the courtyard. Some impulse had held me back, and I touched Ceinwyn's arm and drew her aside into the arcade's shadow from where we saw that one other person had also stayed in the courtyard. Now, when it seemed empty of all but the bleating ewes and the blood-soaked Druid, that person stepped from the shadows. It was Mordred. He limped past the dais, across the flagstones, and stopped beside the hoop. For a heartbeat he and the Druid stared at each other, then Mordred made an awkward gesture with his hand, as though seeking permission to step through the glowing remnants of the fire circle. Fergal hesitated, then nodded abruptly. Mordred ducked his head and stepped through the hoop. He stooped at the far side and wet his finger in blood, but I did not wait to see what he did. I drew Ceinwyn into the palace where the smoking flames lit the great wall-paintings of Roman Gods and Roman hunts. 'If they serve lamb,' Ceinwyn said, 'I shall refuse to eat.'

Arthur served salmon, boar and venison. A harpist played. Mordred, his late arrival unnoticed, took his place at the head table where he sat with a sly smile on his blunt face. He spoke to no one and no one spoke to him, but at times he glanced across at the pale, thin Argante who alone in the room seemed to take no pleasure from the feast. I saw her catch Mordred's eye once and they exchanged exasperated shrugs as if to suggest that they despised the rest of us, but other than that one glance, she merely sulked and Arthur was embarrassed for her, while the rest of us pretended not to notice her mood. Mordred, of course, enjoyed her sullenness.

Next morning we hunted. A dozen of us rode, all men. Ceinwyn liked to hunt, but Arthur had asked her to spend the morning with Argante and Ceinwyn had reluctantly agreed.

We drew the western woods, though without much hope for Mordred frequently hunted among these trees and the huntsman doubted we would find game. Guinevere's deerhounds, now in Arthur's care, loped off among the black trunks and managed to start a doe which gave us a fine gallop through the woods, but the huntsman called off the hounds when he saw that the animal was pregnant. Arthur and I had ridden at a tangent to the chase, thinking to head off the prey at the edge of the woods, but we reined in when we heard the horns. Arthur looked about him, as if expecting to find more company, then grunted when he saw I was alone with him. 'A strange business, last night,' he said awkwardly. 'But women like these things,' he added dismissively.

'Ceinwyn doesn't,' I said.

He gave me a sharp look. He must have been wondering if she had told me about his proposal of marriage, but my face betrayed nothing and he must have decided she had not spoken. 'No,' he said. He hesitated again, then laughed awkwardly. 'Argante believes I should have stepped through the flames as a way of marking the marriage, but I told her I don't need dead lambs to tell me I'm married.'

'I never had a chance to congratulate you on your marriage,' I said very formally, 'so let me do so now. She's a beautiful girl.'

That pleased him. 'She is,' he said, then blushed. 'But only a child.'

'Culhwch says they should all be taken young, Lord,' I said lightly.

He ignored my levity. 'I hadn't meant to marry,' he said quietly. I said nothing. He was not looking at me, but staring across the fallow fields. 'But a man should be married,' he said firmly, as if trying to convince himself.

'Indeed,' I agreed.

'And Oengus was enthusiastic. Come spring, Derfel, he'll bring all his army. And they're good fighters, the Blackshields.'

'None better, Lord,' I said, but I reflected that Oengus would have brought his warriors whether Arthur had married Argante or not. What Oengus had really wanted, of course, was Arthur's alliance against Cuneglas of Powys, whose lands Oengus's spearmen were forever raiding, but doubtless the wily Irish King had suggested to Arthur that the marriage would guarantee the arrival of his Blackshields for the spring campaign. The marriage had plainly been arranged in haste and now, just as plainly, Arthur was regretting it.

'She wants children, of course,' Arthur said, still thinking of the horrid rites that had bloodied Lindinis's courtyard.

'Don't you, Lord?'

'Not yet,' he said curtly. 'Better to wait, I think, till the Saxon business is over.'

'Speaking of which,' I said, 'I have a request from the Lady Guinevere.' Arthur gave me another sharp look, but said nothing. 'Guinevere fears,' I went on, 'that she will be vulnerable if the Saxons attack in the south. She begs you to move her prison to a safer place.'

Arthur leaned forward to fondle his horse's ears. I had expected him to be angry at the mention of Guinevere, but he showed no irritation. 'The Saxons might attack in the south,' he said mildly, 'in fact I hope they do, for then they'll split their forces into two and we can pluck them one at a time. But the greater danger, Derfel, is if they make one single attack along the Thames, and I must plan for the greater, not the lesser, danger.'

'But it would surely be prudent,' I urged him, 'to move whatever is valuable from southern Dumnonia?'

He turned to look at me. His gaze was mocking, as though he despised me for showing sympathy to Guinevere. 'Is she valuable, Derfel?' he asked. I said nothing and Arthur turned away from me to stare across the pale fields where thrushes and blackbirds hunted the furrows for worms. 'Should I kill her?' he suddenly asked me.

'Kill Guinevere?' I responded, shocked at the suggestion, then decided that Argante was probably behind his words. She must have resented that Guinevere still lived after committing an offence for which her sister had died. 'The decision, Lord,' I said, 'is not mine, but surely, if it was death she deserved, it should have been given months ago? Not now.'

He grimaced at that advice. 'What will the Saxons do with her?' he asked.

'She thinks they'll rape her. I suspect they'll put her on a throne.'

He glowered across the pale landscape. He knew I meant Lancelot's throne, and he was imagining the embarrassment of his mortal enemy on Dumnonia's throne with Guinevere beside him and Cerdic holding their power. It was an unbearable thought. 'If she's in any danger of capture,' he said harshly, 'then you will kill her.'

I could hardly believe what I had heard. I stared at him, but he refused to look me in the eyes. 'It's simpler, surely,' I said, 'to move her to safety? Can't she go to Glevum?'

'I have enough to worry about,' he snapped, 'without wasting thought on the safety of traitors.' For a few heartbeats his face looked as angry as I had ever seen it, but then he shook his head and sighed. 'Do you know who I envy?' he asked.

'Tell me, Lord.'

'Tewdric.'

I laughed. 'Tewdric! You want to be a constipated monk?'

'He's happy,' Arthur said firmly, 'he has found the life he always wanted. I don't want the tonsure and I don't care for his God, but I envy him all the same.' He grimaced. 'I wear myself out getting ready for a war no one except me believes we can win, and I want none of it. None of it! Mordred should be King, we took an oath to make him King, and if we beat the Saxons, Derfel, I'll let him rule.' He spoked defiantly, and I did not believe him. 'All I ever wanted,' he went on, 'was a hall, some land, some cattle, crops in season, timber to burn, a smithy to work iron, a stream for water. Is it too much?' He rarely indulged in such self-pity, and I just let his anger talk itself out. He had often expressed such a dream of a household tight in its own palisade, shielded from the world by deep woods and wide fields and filled with his own folk, but now, with Cerdic and Aelle gathering their spears, he must have known it was a hopeless dream. 'I can't hold Dumnonia for ever,' he said, 'and when we've beaten the Saxons it might be time to let other men bridle Mordred. As for me, I'll follow Tewdric into happiness.' He gathered his reins. 'I can't think about Guinevere now,' he said, 'but if she's in any danger, you deal with her.' And with that curt command he clapped his heels back and drove his horse away.

I stayed where I was. I was appalled, but if I had thought beyond my disgust at his order, I should surely have known what was in his mind. He knew I would not kill Guinevere, and he knew therefore that she was safe, but by giving me the harsh order he was not required to betray any affection for her. *Odi at amo, excrucior.*

We killed nothing that morning.

*

In the afternoon the warriors gathered in the feasting-hall. Mordred was there, hunched in the chair that served as his throne. He had nothing to contribute for he was a king without a kingdom, yet Arthur accorded him a proper courtesy. Arthur began, indeed, by saying that when the Saxons came Mordred would ride with him and that the whole army would fight beneath Mordred's banner of the red dragon. Mordred nodded his agreement, but what else could he do? In truth, and we all knew it, Arthur was not offering Mordred a chance of redeeming his reputation in battle, but ensuring that he could make no mischief. Mordred's best chance of regaining his power was to ally himself with our enemies by offering himself as a puppet king to Cerdic, but instead he would be a prisoner of Arthur's hard warriors.

Arthur then confirmed that King Meurig of Gwent would not fight. That news, though no surprise, was met by a growl of hatred. Arthur hushed the protest. Meurig, he said, was convinced that the coming war was not Gwent's battle, but the King had still given his grudging permission for Cuneglas to bring the army of Powys south across Gwent's land and for Oengus to march his Blackshields through his kingdom. Arthur said nothing of Meurig's ambition to rule Dumnonia, perhaps because he knew that such an announcement would only make us even angrier with the King of Gwent, and Arthur still hoped that somehow he could change Meurig's mind and so did not want to provoke more hatred between us and Gwent. The forces of Powys and Demetia, Arthur said, would converge on Corinium, for that walled Roman city was to be Arthur's base and the place where all our supplies were to be concentrated. 'We start supplying Corinium tomorrow,' Arthur said. 'I want it crammed with food, for it's there we shall fight our battle.' He paused. 'One vast battle,' he said, 'with all their forces against every man we can raise.'

'A siege?' Culhwch asked, surprised.

'No,' Arthur said. Instead, he explained, he intended to use Corinium as a lure. The Saxons would soon hear that the town was filled with salted meat, dried fish and grain, and, like any great horde on the march, they would be short of food themselves and so would be drawn to Corinium like a fox to a duckpond, and there he planned to destroy them. 'They will besiege it,' he said, 'and

Morfans will defend it.' Morfans, forewarned of that duty, nodded his agreement. 'But the rest of us,' Arthur went on, 'will be in the hills north of the city. Cerdic will know he has to destroy us and he'll break off his siege to do that. Then we'll fight him on ground of our choosing.'

The whole plan depended on both Saxon armies advancing up the valley of the Thames, and all the signs indicated that this was indeed the Saxon intention. They were piling supplies into London and Pontes, and making no preparations on the southern frontier. Culhwch, who guarded that southern border, had raided deep into Lloegyr and told us that he had found no concentration of spearmen, nor any indication that Cerdic was hoarding grain or meat in Venta or any other of the frontier towns. Everything pointed, Arthur said, to a simple, brutal and overwhelming assault up the Thames aimed at the shore of the Severn Sea with the decisive battle being fought somewhere near Corinium. Sagramor's men had already built great warning beacons on the hilltops on either side of the Thames valley, and still more beacons had been made on the hills spreading south and west into Dumnonia, and when we saw the smoke of those fires we were all to march to our places.

'That won't be until after Beltain,' Arthur said. He had spies in both Aelle's and Cerdic's halls, and all had reported that the Saxons would wait until after the feast of their Goddess Eostre which would be celebrated a whole week after Beltain. The Saxons wished the Goddess's blessing, Arthur explained, and they wanted to give the new season's boats time to come across the sea with their hulls packed with yet more hungry fighting men.

But after Eostre's feast, he said, the Saxons would advance and he would let them come deep into Dumnonia without a battle, though he planned to harass them all the way. Sagramor, with his battle-hardened spearmen, would retreat in front of the Saxon horde and offer whatever resistance he could short of a shield wall, while Arthur gathered the allied army at Corinium.

Culhwch and I had different orders. Our task was to defend the hills south of the Thames valley. We could not expect to defeat any determined Saxon thrust that came south through those hills, but Arthur did not expect any such attack. The Saxons, he said again and again, would keep marching westwards, ever westwards along the Thames, but they were bound to send raiding parties into the southern hills in search of grain and cattle. Our task was to stop those raiding parties, thus forcing the scavengers to go north instead. That would take the Saxons across the Gwentian border and might spur Meurig into a declaration of war. The unspoken thought in that hope, though each of us in that smoky room nevertheless understood it, was that without Gwent's well-trained spearmen the great battle near Corinium would be a truly desperate affair. 'So fight them hard,' Arthur told Culhwch and me. 'Kill their foragers, scare them, but don't be caught in battle. Harass them, frighten them, but once they're within a day's march of Corinium, leave them alone. Just march to join me.' He would need every spear he could gather to fight that great battle outside Corinium, and Arthur seemed sure that we could win it so long as our forces had the high ground.

It was, in its way, a good plan. The Saxons would be lured deep into Dumnonia and there be forced to attack up some steep hill, but the plan depended on the enemy doing exactly as Arthur wanted, and Cerdic, I thought, was not an obliging man. Yet Arthur seemed confident enough, and that, at least, was comforting.

We all went home. I made myself unpopular by searching all the houses in my district and confiscating grain, salted meat and dried fish. We left enough supplies to keep the folk alive, but sent the rest to Corinium where it would feed Arthur's army. It was a distasteful business, for peasants fear hunger almost as much as they fear enemy spearmen, and we were forced to search for hiding places and ignore the screams of women who accused us of tyranny. But better our searches, I told them, than Saxon ravages.

We also readied ourselves for battle. I laid out my wargear and my slaves oiled the leather jerkin, polished the mail coat, combed out the wolf-hair plume on the helmet and repainted the white star on my heavy shield. The new year came with the blackbird's first song. Missel thrushes called from the high twigs of the larches behind Dun Caric's hill, and we paid the children of the village to run with pots and sticks through the apple orchards to scare away the bullfinches that would steal the tiny fruit buds. Sparrows nested and the stream glinted with the returning salmon. The dusks were made noisy by flocks of pied wagtails. Within a few weeks there were blossoms on the hazel, dog violets in the woods and gold-touched cones on the sallow trees. Buck hares danced in the fields where the lambs played. In March there was a swarm of toads and I feared what it meant, but there was no Merlin to ask, for he, with Nimue, had vanished and it seemed we must fight without his help. Larks sang, and the predatory magpies hunted for new-laid eggs along hedgerows that still lacked their cover of foliage.

The leaves came at last, and with them news of the first warriors arriving south from Powys. They were few in number, for Cuneglas did not want to exhaust the food supplies being piled in Corinium, but their arrival gave promise of the greater army that Cuneglas would lead south after Beltain. Our calves were born, butter was churned and Ceinwyn busied herself cleaning out the hall after the long smoky winter.

They were odd and bittersweet days, for there was the promise of war in a new spring that was suddenly glorious with sun-drenched skies and flower-bright meadows. The Christians preach of 'the last days', by which they mean those times before the world's ending, and maybe folk will feel then as we did in that soft and lovely spring. There was an unreal quality to everyday life which made every small task special. Maybe this would be the last time we would ever burn winter straw from our bedding and maybe the last time we would ever heave a calf all bloody from its mother's womb into the world. Everything was special, because everything was threatened.

We also knew that the coming Beltain might be the last we would ever know as a family and so we tried to make it memorable. Beltain greets the new year's life, and on the eve of the feast we let all the fires die in Dun Caric. The kitchen fires, that had burned all winter long, went unfed all day and by night they were nothing but embers. We raked them out, swept the hearths clean, then laid new fires, while on a hill to the east of the village we heaped two great piles of firewood, one of them stacked about the sacred tree that Pyrlig, our bard, had selected. It was a young hazel that we had cut down and carried ceremonially through the village, across the stream and up the hill. The tree was hung with scraps of cloth, and all the houses, like the hall itself, were decked with new young hazel boughs.

That night, all across Britain, the fires were dead. On Beltain Eve darkness rules. The feast was laid in our hall, but there was no fire to cook it and no flame to light the high rafters. There was no light anywhere, except in the Christian towns where folks heaped their fires to defy the Gods, but in the countryside all was dark. At dusk we had climbed the hill, a mass of villagers and spearmen driving cattle and sheep that were folded into wattle enclosures. Children played, but once the great dark fell the smallest children fell asleep and their little bodies lay in the grass as the rest of us gathered about the unlit fires and there sang the Lament of Annwn.

Then, in the darkest part of the night, we made the new year's fire. Pyrlig made the flame by rubbing two sticks while Issa dribbled shavings of larch-wood kindling onto the spark that gave off a tiny wisp of smoke. The two men stooped to the tiny flame, blew on it, added more kindling, and at last a strong flame leapt up and all of us began to sing the Chant of Belenos as Pyrlig carried the new fire to the two heaps of firewood. The sleeping children awoke and ran to find their parents as the Beltain fires sprang high and bright.

A goat was sacrificed once the fires were burning. Ceinwyn, as ever, turned away as the beast's throat was cut and as Pyrlig scattered its blood on the grass. He tossed the goat's corpse onto the fire where the sacred hazel was burning, then the villagers fetched their cattle and sheep and drove them between the two great blazes. We hung plaited straw collars about the cows' necks, and then watched as young women danced between the fires to seek the blessing of the Gods on their wombs. They had danced through fire at Imbolc, but always did it again at Beltain. That was the first year Morwenna was old enough to dance between the fires and I felt a pang of sadness as I watched my daughter twirl and leap. She looked so happy. She was thinking of marriage and dreaming of babies, yet within a few weeks, I thought, she could be dead or enslaved. That thought filled me with a huge anger and I turned away from our fires and was startled to see the bright flames of other Beltain fires burning in the distance. All across Dumnonia the fires were burning to greet the newly arrived year.

My spearmen had brought two huge iron cauldrons to the hilltop and we filled their bellies with burning wood, then hurried down the hill with the two flaming pots. Once in the village the new fire was distributed, each cottage taking a flame from the fire and setting it to the waiting wood in the hearth. We went to the hall last and there carried the new fire into the kitchens. It was almost dawn by then, and the villagers crowded into the palisade to wait for the rising sun. The instant that its first brilliant shard of light showed above the eastern horizon, we sang the song of Lugh's birth; a joyous, dancing hymn of merriment. We faced the east as we sang our welcome to the sun, and right across the horizon we could see the dark dribble of Beltain smoke rising into the ever paler sky.

The cooking began as the hearth fires became hot. I had planned a huge feast for the village, thinking that this might be our last day of happiness for a long time. The common folk rarely ate meat, but on that Beltain we had five deer, two boars, three pigs and six sheep to roast; we had barrels of newly brewed mead and ten baskets of bread that had been baked on the old season's fires. There was cheese, honied nuts and oatcakes with the cross of Beltain scorched onto their crusts. In a week or so the Saxons would come, so this was a time to give a feast that might help our people through the horrors to come.

The villagers played games as the meat cooked. There were foot-races down the street, wrestling matches and a competition to see who could lift the heaviest weight. The girls wove flowers in their hair and, long before the feast began, I saw the couples slipping away. We ate in the afternoon, and while we feasted the poets recited and the village bards sang to us and the success of their compositions was judged by the amount of applause each generated. I gave gold to all the bards and poets, even the worst ones, and there were many of those. Most of the poets were young men who blushingly declaimed clumsy lines addressed to their girls, and the girls would look sheepish and the villagers would jeer, laugh and then demand that each girl reward the poet with a kiss, and if the kiss was too fleeting, the couple would be held face to face and made to kiss properly. The poetry became markedly better as we drank more.

I drank too much. Indeed we all feasted well and drank even better. At one point I was challenged to a wrestling match by the village's wealthiest farmer and the crowd demanded I accept and so, half drunk already, I clapped my hands on the farmer's body, and he did the same to me, and I could smell the reeking mead on his breath as he could doubtless smell it on mine. He heaved, I heaved back, and neither of us could move the other, so we stood there, locked head to head like battling stags, while the crowd mocked our sad display. In the end I tipped him over, but only because he was more drunk than I was. I drank still more, trying, perhaps, to obliterate the future.

By nightfall I was feeling sick. I went to the fighting platform we had built on the eastern rampart and there I leaned on the wall's top and stared at the darkening horizon. Twin wisps of smoke drifted from the hilltop where we had lit our night's new fires, though to my mead-fuddled mind it seemed as if there were at least a dozen smoke pyres. Ceinwyn climbed up to the platform and laughed at my dismal face. 'You're drunk,' she said.

'I am that,' I agreed.

'You'll sleep like a hog,' she said accusingly, 'and snore like one too.'

'It's Beltain,' I said in excuse, and waved my hand at the distant wisps of smoke.

She leaned on the parapet beside me. She had sloe blossom woven into her golden hair and looked as beautiful as ever. 'We must talk to Arthur about Gwydre,' she said.

'Marrying Morwenna?' I asked, then paused to collect my thoughts. 'Arthur seems so unfriendly these days,' I finally managed to say, 'and maybe he has a mind to marry Gwydre to someone else?'

'Maybe he has,' Ceinwyn said calmly, 'in which case we should find someone else for Morwenna.'

'Who?'

'That's exactly what I want you to think about,' Ceinwyn said, 'when you're sober. Maybe one of Culhwch's boys?' She peered down into the evening shadows at the foot of Dun Caric's hill. There was a tangle of bushes at the foot of the slope and she could see a couple busy among the leaves. 'That's Morfudd,' she said.

'Who?'

'Morfudd,' Ceinwyn said, 'the dairy girl. Another baby coming, I suppose. It really is time she married.' She sighed and stared at the horizon. She was silent for a long time, then she frowned.

'Don't you think there are more fires this year than last?' she asked.

I dutifully stared at the horizon, but in all honesty I could not distinguish between one spiring smoke trail and another. 'Possibly,' I said evasively.

She still frowned. 'Or maybe they aren't Beltain fires at all.'

'Of course they are!' I said with all the certitude of a drunken man.

'But beacons,' she went on.

It took a few heartbeats for the meaning of her words to sink in, then suddenly I did not feel drunk at all. I felt sick, but not drunk. I gazed eastwards. A score of plumes smudged their smoke against the sky, but two of the plumes were far thicker than the others and far too thick to be the remnants of fires lit the night before and allowed to die in the dawn.

And suddenly, sickeningly, I knew they were the warning beacons. The Saxons had not waited until after their feast of Eostre, but had come at Beltain. They knew we had prepared warning beacons, but they also knew that the fires of Beltain would be lit on hilltops all across Dumnonia, and they must have guessed that we would not notice the warning beacons among the ritual fires. They had tricked us. We had feasted, we had drunk ourselves insensible, and all the while the Saxons were attacking.

And Dumnonia was at war.

I WAS THE LEADER OF seventy experienced warriors, but I also
commanded a hundred and ten youngsters I had trained through
the winter. Those one hundred and eighty men constituted nearly
one third of all Dumnonia's spearmen, but only sixteen of them
were ready to march by dawn. The rest were either still drunk or
else so suffering that they ignored my curses and blows. Issa and
I dragged the worst afflicted to the stream and tossed them into
the chill water, but it did small good. I could only wait as, hour by
hour, more men recovered their wits. A score of sober Saxons could
have laid Dun Caric waste that morning.

The beacon fires still burned to tell us that the Saxons were
coming, and I felt a terrible guilt that I had failed Arthur so badly.
Later I learned that nearly every warrior in Dumnonia was similarly
insensible that morning, though Sagramor's hundred and twenty
men had stayed sober and they dutifully fell back in front of the
advancing Saxon armies, but the rest of us staggered, retched,
gasped for breath and gulped water like dogs.

By midday most of my men were standing, though not all, and
only a few were ready for a long march. My armour, shield and
war spears were loaded on a pack-horse, while ten mules carried
the baskets of food that Ceinwyn had been busy filling all morning.
She would wait at Dun Caric, either for victory or, more likely,
for a message telling her to flee.

Then, a few moments after midday, everything changed.

A rider came from the south on a sweating horse. He was
Culhwch's eldest son, Einion, and he had ridden himself and his
horse close to exhaustion in his frantic attempt to reach us. He half
fell from the saddle. 'Lord,' he gasped, then stumbled, found his
feet and gave me a perfunctory bow. For a few heartbeats he was
too breathless to speak, then the words tumbled out in frantic

excitement, but he had been so eager to deliver his message and had so anticipated the drama of the moment that he was quite unable to make any sense, though I did understand he had come from the south and that the Saxons were marching there.

I led him to a bench beside the hall and sat him down. 'Welcome to Dun Caric, Einion ap Culhwch,' I said very formally, 'and say all that again.'

'The Saxons, Lord,' he said, 'have attacked Dunum.'

So Guinevere had been right and the Saxons had marched in the south. They had come from Cerdic's land beyond Venta and were already deep inside Dumnonia. Dunum, our fortress close to the coast, had fallen in yesterday's dawn. Culhwch had abandoned the fort rather than have his hundred men overwhelmed, and now he was falling back in front of the enemy. Einion, a young man with the same squat build as his father, looked up at me woefully. 'There are just too many of them, Lord.'

The Saxons had made fools of us. First they had convinced us that they meant no mischief in the south, then they had attacked on our feast night when they knew we would mistake the distant beacon fires for the flames of Beltain, and now they were loose on our southern flank. Aelle, I guessed, was pushing down the Thames while Cerdic's troops were rampaging free by the coast. Einion was not certain that Cerdic himself led the southern attack, for he had not seen the Saxon King's banner of the red-painted wolf skull hung with a dead man's flayed skin, but he had seen Lancelot's flag of the sea eagle with the fish clutched in its talons. Culhwch believed that Lancelot was leading his own followers and two or three hundred Saxons besides.

'Where were they when you left?' I asked Einion.

'Still south of Sorviodunum, Lord.'

'And your father?'

'He was in the town, Lord, but he dare not be trapped there.'

So Culhwch would yield the fortress of Sorviodunum rather than be trapped. 'Does he want me to join him?' I asked.

Einion shook his head. 'He sent word to Durnovaria, Lord, telling the folk there to come north. He thinks you should protect them and take them to Corinium.'

'Who's at Durnovaria?' I asked.

'The Princess Argante, Lord.'

I swore softly. Arthur's new wife could not just be abandoned and I understood now what Culhwch was suggesting. He knew Lancelot could not be stopped, so he wanted me to rescue whatever was valuable in Dumnonia's heartland and retreat north towards Corinium while Culhwch did his best to slow the enemy. It was a desperately makeshift strategy, and at its end we would have yielded the greater part of Dumnonia to the enemy's forces, but there was still the chance that we could all come together at Corinium to fight Arthur's battle, though by rescuing Argante I abandoned Arthur's plans to harass the Saxons in the hills south of the Thames. That was a pity, but war rarely goes according to plan.

'Does Arthur know?' I asked Einion.

'My brother is riding to him,' Einion assured me, which meant Arthur would still not have heard the news. It would be late afternoon before Einion's brother reached Corinium, where Arthur had spent Beltain. Culhwch, meanwhile, was lost somewhere south of the great plain while Lancelot's army was – where? Aelle, presumably, was still marching west, and maybe Cerdic was with him, which meant Lancelot could either continue along the coast and capture Durnovaria, or else turn north and follow Culhwch towards Caer Cadarn and Dun Caric. But either way, I reflected, this landscape would be swarming with Saxon spearmen in only three or four days.

I gave Einion a fresh horse and sent him north to Arthur with a message that I would bring Argante to Corinium, but suggesting he might send horsemen to Aquae Sulis to meet us and then hurry her northwards. I then sent Issa and fifty of my fittest men south to Durnovaria. I ordered them to march fast and light, carrying only their weapons, and I warned Issa that he might expect to meet Argante and the other fugitives from Durnovaria coming north on the road. Issa was to bring them all to Dun Caric. 'With good fortune,' I told him, 'you'll be back here by tomorrow nightfall.'

Ceinwyn made her own preparations to leave. This was not the first time she had been a fugitive from war and she knew well enough that she and our daughters could take only what they could carry. Everything else must be abandoned, and so two spearmen dug a cave in the side of Dun Caric's hill and there she hid our gold and silver, and afterwards the two men filled the hole and disguised it with turf. The villagers were doing the same with cooking pots, spades, sharpening stones, spindles, sieves, anything, indeed, that was too heavy to carry and too valuable to lose. All over Dumnonia such valuables were being buried.

There was little I could do at Dun Caric except wait for Issa's return and so I rode south to Caer Cadarn and Lindinis. We kept a small garrison at Caer Cadarn, not for any military reason, but because the hill was our royal place and so deserved guarding. That garrison was composed of a score of old men, most of them crippled, and of the twenty only five or six would be truly useful in the shield wall, but I ordered them all north to Dun Caric, then turned the mare west towards Lindinis.

Mordred had sensed the dire news. Rumour passes at unimaginable speed in the countryside, and though no messenger had come to the palace, he still guessed my mission. I bowed to him, then politely requested that he be ready to leave the palace within the hour.

'Oh, that's impossible!' he said, his round face betraying his delight at the chaos that threatened Dumnonia. Mordred ever delighted in misfortune.

'Impossible, Lord King?' I asked.

He waved a hand about his throne room that was filled with Roman furniture, much of it chipped or with its inlay missing, but still lavish and beautiful. 'I have things to pack,' he said, 'people to see. Tomorrow, maybe?'

'You ride north to Corinium in one hour, Lord King,' I said harshly. It was important to move Mordred out of the Saxon path, which was why I had come here rather than ridden south to meet Argante. If Mordred had stayed he would undoubtedly have been used by Aelle and Cerdic, and Mordred knew it. For a moment he looked as though he would argue, then he ordered me out of the room and shouted for a slave to lay out his armour. I sought out Lanval, the old spearman whom Arthur had placed in charge of the King's guard. 'You take every horse in the stables,' I told Lanval, 'and escort the little bastard to Corinium. You give him to Arthur personally.'

Mordred left within the hour. The King rode in his armour and with his standard flying. I almost ordered him to furl the standard, for the sight of the dragon would only provoke more rumours in the country, but maybe it was no bad thing to spread alarm because folk needed time to prepare and to hide their valuables. I watched the King's horses clatter through the gate and turn north, then I went back into the palace where the steward, a lamed spearman named Dyrrig, was shouting at slaves to gather the palace's treasures. Candle-stands, pots and cauldrons were being carried to the back garden to be concealed in a dry well, while bedspreads, linens and clothes were being piled on carts to be hidden in the nearby woods. 'The furniture can stay,' Dyrrig told me sourly, 'the Saxons are welcome to it.'

I wandered through the palace's rooms and tried to imagine the Saxons whooping between the pillars, smashing the fragile chairs and shattering the delicate mosaics. Who would live here, I wondered? Cerdic? Lancelot? If anyone, I decided, it would be Lancelot, for the Saxons seemed to have no taste for Roman luxury. They left places like Lindinis to rot and built their own timber and thatch halls nearby.

I lingered in the throne room, trying to imagine it lined with the mirrors that Lancelot so loved. He existed in a world of polished metal so that he could ever admire his own beauty. Or perhaps Cerdic would destroy the palace to show that the old world of Britain was ended and that the new brutal reign of the Saxons had begun. It was a melancholy, self-indulgent moment, broken when Dyrrig shuffled into the room trailing his maimed leg. 'I'll save the furniture if you want,' he said grudgingly.

'No,' I said.

Dyrrig plucked a blanket off a couch. 'The little bastard left three girls here, and one of them's pregnant. I suppose I'll have to give them gold. He won't. Now, what's this?' He had stopped behind the carved chair that served as Mordred's throne and I joined him to see that there was a hole in the floor. 'Wasn't there yesterday,' Dyrrig insisted.

I knelt down and found that a complete section of the mosaic floor had been lifted. The section was at the edge of the room, where bunches of grapes formed a border to the central picture of a reclining God attended by nymphs, and one whole bunch of grapes had been carefully lifted out from the border. I saw that the small tiles had been glued to a piece of leather cut to the shape of the grapes, and beneath them there had been a layer of narrow Roman bricks that were now scattered under the chair. It was a deliberate hiding place, giving access to the flues of the old heating chamber that ran beneath the floor.

Something glinted at the bottom of the heating chamber and I leaned down and groped among the dust and debris to bring up two small gold buttons, a scrap of leather and what, with a grimace, I realized were mice droppings. I brushed my hands clean, then handed one of the buttons to Dyrrig. The other, which I examined, showed a bearded, belligerent, helmeted face. It was crude work, but powerful in the intensity of the stare. 'Saxon made,' I said.

'This one too, Lord,' Dyrrig said, and I saw that his button was almost identical to mine. I peered again into the heating chamber, but could see no more buttons or coins. Mordred had plainly hidden a hoard of gold there, but the mice had nibbled the leather bag so that when he lifted the treasure free a couple of the buttons had fallen out.

'So why does Mordred have Saxon gold?' I asked.

'You tell me, Lord,' Dyrrig said, spitting into the hole.

I carefully propped the Roman bricks on the low stone arches that supported the floor, then pulled the leather-backed tiles into place. I could guess why Mordred had gold, and I did not like the answer. Mordred had been present when Arthur revealed the plans of his campaign against the Saxons, and that, I thought, was why the Saxons had been able to catch us off balance. They had known we would concentrate our forces on the Thames, so all the while they had let us believe that was where the assault would come and Cerdic had slowly and secretly built up his forces in the south. Mordred had betrayed us. I could not be certain of that for two golden buttons did not constitute proof, but it made a grim sense. Mordred wanted his power back, and though he would not gain all that power from Cerdic he would certainly get the revenge on Arthur that he craved. 'How would the Saxons have managed to talk with Mordred?' I asked Dyrrig.

'Simple, Lord. There are always visitors here,' Dyrrig said. 'Merchants, bards, jugglers, girls.'

'We should have slit his throat,' I said bitterly, pocketing the button.

'Why didn't you?' Dyrrig asked.

'Because he's Uther's grandson,' I said, 'and Arthur would never permit it.' Arthur had taken an oath to protect Mordred, and that oath bound Arthur for life. Besides, Mordred was our real King, and in him ran the blood of all our Kings back to Beli Mawr himself, and though Mordred was rotten, his blood was sacred and so Arthur kept him alive. 'Mordred's task,' I said to Dyrrig, 'is to whelp an heir of a proper wife, but once he's given us a new King he would be well advised to wear an iron collar.'

'No wonder he doesn't marry,' Dyrrig said. 'And what happens if he never does? Suppose there's no heir?'

'That's a good question,' I said, 'but let's beat the Saxons before we worry about answering it.'

I left Dyrrig disguising the old dry well with brush. I could have ridden straight back to Dun Caric for I had looked after the urgent needs of the moment; Issa was on his way to escort Argante to safety, Mordred was safely gone north, but I still had one piece of unfinished business and so I rode north on the Fosse Way that ran beside the great swamps and lakes that edged Ynys Wydryn. Warblers were noisy among the reeds while sickle-winged martins were busy pecking beakfuls of mud to make their new nests beneath our eaves. Cuckoos called from the willows and birches that edged the marshland. The sun shone on Dumnonia, the oaks were in new green leaf and the meadows to my east were bright with cowslips and daisies. I did not ride hard, but let my mare amble until, a few miles north of Lindinis, I turned west onto the land bridge that reached towards Ynys Wydryn. So far I had been serving Arthur's best interests by ensuring Argante's safety and by securing Mordred, but now I risked his displeasure. Or maybe I did exactly what he had always wanted me to do.

I went to the shrine of the Holy Thorn, where I found Morgan preparing to leave. She had heard no definite news, but rumour had done its work and she knew Ynys Wydryn was threatened. I told her what little I knew and after she had heard that scanty news she peered up at me from behind her golden mask. 'So where is my husband?' she demanded shrilly.

'I don't know, Lady,' I said. So far as I knew Sansum was still a prisoner in Bishop Emrys's house in Durnovaria.

'You don't know,' Morgan snapped at me, 'and you don't care!'

'In truth, Lady, I don't,' I told her. 'But I assume he'll flee north like everyone else.'

'Then tell him we've gone to Siluria. To Isca.' Morgan, naturally, was quite prepared for the emergency. She had been packing the shrine's treasures in anticipation of the Saxon invasion, and boatmen were ready to carry those treasures and the Christian women across Ynys Wydryn's lakes to the coast where other boats were waiting to carry them north across the Severn Sea to Siluria. 'And tell Arthur I'm praying for him,' Morgan added, 'though he doesn't deserve my prayers. And tell him I have his whore safe.'

'No, Lady,' I said, for that was why I had ridden to Ynys Wydryn. To this day I am not exactly sure why I did not let Guinevere go with Morgan, but I think the Gods guided me. Or else, in the welter of confusion as the Saxons tore our careful preparations to tatters, I wanted to give Guinevere one last gift. We had never been friends, but in my mind I associated her with the good times, and though it was her foolishness that brought on the bad, I had seen how stale Arthur had been ever since Guinevere's eclipse. Or perhaps I knew that in this terrible time we needed every strong soul we could muster, and there were few souls as tough as that of the Princess Guinevere of Henis-Wyren.

'She comes with me!' Morgan insisted.

'I have orders from Arthur,' I insisted to Morgan, and that settled the matter, though in truth her brother's orders were terrible and vague. If Guinevere is in danger, Arthur had told me, I was to fetch her or maybe kill her, but I had decided to fetch her, and instead of sending her to safety across the Severn I would carry her still closer to the danger.

'It's rather like watching a herd of cows threatened by wolves,' Guinevere said when I reached her room. She was standing at the window from where she could see Morgan's women running to and fro between their buildings and the boats that waited beyond the shrine's western palisade. 'What's happening, Derfel?'

155

'You were right, Lady. The Saxons are attacking in the south.' I decided not to tell her that it was Lancelot who led that southern assault.

'Do you think they'll come here?' she asked.

'I don't know. I just know that we can't defend any place except where Arthur is, and he's at Corinium.'

'In other words,' she said with a smile, 'everything is confusion?' She laughed, sensing an opportunity in that confusion. She was dressed in her usual drab clothes, but the sun shone through the open window to give her splendid red hair a golden aura. 'So what does Arthur want to do with me?' she asked.

Death? No, I decided, he had never really wanted that. What he wanted was what his proud soul would not let him take for itself. 'I am just ordered to fetch you, Lady,' I answered instead.

'To go where, Derfel?'

'You can sail across the Severn with Morgan,' I said, 'or come with me. I'm taking folk north to Corinium and I dare say from there you can travel on to Glevum. You'll be safe there.'

She walked from the window and sat in a chair beside the empty hearth. 'Folk,' she said, plucking the word from my sentence. 'What folk, Derfel?'

I blushed. 'Argante. Ceinwyn, of course.'

Guinevere laughed. 'I would like to meet Argante. Do you think she'd like to meet me?'

'I doubt it, Lady.'

'I doubt it too. I imagine she'd prefer me to be dead. So, I can travel with you to Corinium, or go to Siluria with the Christian cows? I think I've heard enough Christian hymns to last me a lifetime. Besides, the greater adventure lies at Corinium, don't you think?'

'I fear so, Lady.'

'Fear? Oh, don't fear, Derfel.' She laughed with an exhilarating happiness. 'You all forget how good Arthur is when nothing goes right. It will be a joy to watch him. So when do we leave?'

'Now,' I said, 'or as soon as you're ready.'

'I'm ready,' she said happily, 'I've been ready to leave this place for a year.'

'Your servants?'

'There are always other servants,' she said carelessly. 'Shall we go?'

I only had the one horse and so, out of politeness, I offered it to her and walked beside her as we left the shrine. I have rarely seen a face as radiant as Guinevere's face was that day. For months she had been locked inside Ynys Wydryn's walls, and suddenly she was riding a horse in the open air, between new-leaved birch trees and under a sky unlimited by Morgan's palisade. We climbed to the land bridge beyond the Tor and once we were on that high bare ground she laughed and gave me a mischievous glance. 'What's to stop me riding away, Derfel?'

'Nothing at all, Lady.'

She whooped like a girl and kicked back her heels, then kicked again to force the tired mare into a gallop. The wind streamed in her red curls as she galloped free on the grassland. She shouted for the joy of it, curving the horse around me in a great circle. Her skirts blew back, but she did not care, she just kicked the horse again and so rode around and around until the horse was blowing and she was breathless. Only then did she curb the mare and slide out of the saddle. 'I'm so sore!' she said happily.

'You ride well, Lady,' I said.

'I dreamed of riding a horse again. Of hunting again. Of so much.' She patted her skirts straight, then gave me an amused glance. 'What exactly did Arthur order you to do with me?'

I hesitated. 'He was not specific, Lady.'

'To kill me?' she asked.

'No, Lady!' I said, sounding shocked. I was leading the mare by her reins and Guinevere was walking beside me.

'He certainly doesn't want me in Cerdic's hands,' she said tartly, 'I'd just be an embarrassment! I suspect he flirted with the idea of slitting my throat. Argante must have wanted that. I certainly would if I were her. I was thinking about that as I rode around you just now. Suppose, I thought, that Derfel has orders to kill me? Should I keep riding? Then I decided you probably wouldn't kill me, even if you did have orders. He'd have sent Culhwch if he wanted me dead.' She suddenly grunted and bent her knees to imitate Culhwch's limping walk. 'Culhwch would cut my throat,' she said, 'and wouldn't think twice about it.' She laughed, her new high spirits irrepressible. 'So Arthur wasn't specific?'

'No, Lady.'

'So truly, Derfel, this is your idea?' She waved at the countryside.

'Yes, Lady,' I confessed.

'I hope Arthur thinks you did the right thing,' she said, 'otherwise you'll be in trouble.'

'I'm in trouble enough already, Lady,' I confessed. 'The old friendship seems dead.'

She must have heard the bleakness in my voice, for she suddenly put an arm through mine. 'Poor Derfel. I suppose he's ashamed?'

I was embarrassed. 'Yes, Lady.'

'I was very bad,' she said in a rueful voice. 'Poor Arthur. But do you know what will restore him? And your friendship?'

'I'd like to know, Lady.'

She took her arm from mine. 'Grinding the Saxons into offal, Derfel, that's what will bring Arthur back. Victory! Give Arthur victory and he'll give us his old soul back.'

'The Saxons, Lady,' I warned her, 'are halfway to victory already.' I told her what I knew: that the Saxons were rampaging free to the east and south, our forces were scattered and that our only hope was to assemble our army before the Saxons reached Corinium, where Arthur's small warband of two hundred spearmen waited alone. I assumed Sagramor was retreating towards Arthur, Culhwch was coming from the south, and I would go north as soon as Issa returned with Argante. Cuneglas would doubtless march from the north and Oengus mac Airem would hurry from the west the moment they heard the news, but if the Saxons reached Corinium first, then all hope was gone. There was little enough hope even if we did win the race, for without Gwent's spearmen we would be so outnumbered that only a miracle could save us.

'Nonsense!' Guinevere said when I had explained the situation. 'Arthur hasn't even begun to fight! We're going to win, Derfel, we're going to win!' And with that defiant statement she laughed and, forgetting her precious dignity, danced some steps on the verge of the track. All seemed doom, but Guinevere was suddenly free and full of light and I had never liked her as much as I did at that moment. Suddenly, for the first time since I had seen the beacon fires smoking in the Beltain dusk, I felt a surge of hope.

The hope faded quickly enough, for at Dun Caric there was nothing but chaos and mystery. Issa had not returned and the small village beneath the hall was filled with refugees who were fleeing from rumour, though none had actually seen a Saxon. The refugees had brought their cattle, their sheep, their goats and their pigs, and all had converged on Dun Caric because my spearmen offered an illusion of safety. I used my servants and slaves to start new rumours that said Arthur would be withdrawing westwards to the country bordering Kernow, and that I had decided to cull the refugees' herds and flocks to provide rations for my men and those false rumours were enough to start most of the families walking towards the distant Kernow frontier. They should be safe enough on the great moors and by fleeing westwards their cattle and sheep would not block the roads to Corinium. If I had simply ordered them towards Kernow they would have been suspicious and lingered to make certain that I was not tricking them.

Issa was not with us by nightfall. I was still not unduly worried, for the road to Durnovaria was long and it was doubtless thronged with refugees. We made a meal in the hall and Pyrlig sang us the song of Uther's great victory over the Saxons at Caer Idern. When the song ended, and I had tossed Pyrlig a golden coin, I remarked that I had once heard Cynyr of Gwent sing that song, and Pyrlig was impressed. 'Cynyr was the greatest of all the bards,' he said wistfully, 'though some say Amairgin of Gwynedd was better. I wish I'd heard either of them.'

'My brother,' Ceinwyn remarked, 'says there is an even greater bard in Powys now. And just a young man, too.'

'Who?' Pyrlig demanded, scenting an unwelcome rival.

'Taliesin is his name,' Ceinwyn said.

'Taliesin!' Guinevere repeated the name, liking it. It meant 'shining brow'.

'I've never heard of him,' Pyrlig said stiffly.

'When we've beaten the Saxons,' I said, 'we shall demand a song of victory from this Taliesin. And from you too, Pyrlig,' I added hastily.

'I once heard Amairgin sing,' Guinevere said.

'You did, Lady?' Pyrlig asked, again impressed.

'I was only a child,' she said, 'but I remember he could make a hollow roaring sound. It was very frightening. His eyes would go very wide, he swallowed air, then he bellowed like a bull.'

'Ah, the old style,' Pyrlig said dismissively. 'These days, Lady, we seek harmony of words rather than mere volume of sound.'

'You should seek both,' Guinevere said sharply. 'I've no doubt this Taliesin is a master of the old style as well as being skilled at metre, but how can you hold an audience enthralled if all you offer them is clever rhythm? You must make their blood run cold, you must make them cry, you must make them laugh!'

'Any man can make a noise, Lady,' Pyrlig defended his craft, 'but it takes a skilled craftsman to imbue words with harmony.'

'And soon the only people who can understand the intricacies of the harmony,' Guinevere argued, 'are other skilled craftsmen, and so you become ever more clever in an effort to impress your fellow poets, but you forget that no one outside the craft has the first notion of what you're doing. Bard chants to bard while the rest of us wonder what all the noise is about. Your task, Pyrlig, is to keep the people's stories alive, and to do that you cannot be rarefied.'

'You would not have us be vulgar, Lady!' Pyrlig said and, in protest, struck the horsehair strings of his harp.

'I would have you be vulgar with the vulgar, and clever with the clever,' Guinevere said, 'and both, mark you, at the same time, but if you can only be clever then you deny the people their stories, and if you can only be vulgar then no lord or lady will toss you gold.'

'Except the vulgar lords,' Ceinwyn put in slyly.

Guinevere glanced at me and I saw she was about to launch an insult at me, and then she recognized the impulse herself and burst into laughter. 'If I had gold, Pyrlig,' she said instead, 'I would reward you, for you sing beautifully, but alas, I have none.'

'Your praise is reward enough, Lady,' Pyrlig said.

Guinevere's presence had startled my spearmen and all evening I saw small groups of men come to stare at her in wonderment. She ignored their gaze. Ceinwyn had welcomed her without any show of astonishment, and Guinevere had been clever enough to be kind to my daughters so that Morwenna and Seren both now slept on the ground beside her. They, like my spearmen, had been fascinated by the tall, red-haired woman whose reputation was as startling as her looks. And Guinevere was simply happy to be there. We had no tables or chairs in our hall, just the rush floor and woollen carpets, but she sat beside the fire and effortlessly dominated the hall. There was a fierceness in her eyes that made her daunting, her cascade of tangled red hair made her striking and her joy at being free was infectious.

'How long will she stay free?' Ceinwyn asked me later that night. We had given up our private chamber to Guinevere, and were in the hall with the rest of our people.

'I don't know.'

'So what do you know?' Ceinwyn asked.

'We wait for Issa, then we go north.'

'To Corinium?'

'I shall go to Corinium, but I'll send you and the families to Glevum. You'll be close enough to the fighting there and if the worst happens, you can go north into Gwent.'

I began to fret next day as Issa still did not appear. In my mind we were racing the Saxons towards Corinium, and the longer I was delayed, the more likely that race would be lost. If the Saxons could pick us off warband by warband then Dumnonia would fall like a rotted tree, and my warband, which was one of the strongest in the country, was stalled at Dun Caric because Issa and Argante had not appeared.

At midday the urgency was even greater for it was then that we saw the first distant smears of smoke against the eastern and southern sky. No one commented on the tall, thin plumes, but we all knew that we saw burning thatch. The Saxons were destroying as they came, and they were close enough now for us to see their smoke.

I sent a horseman south to find Issa while the rest of us walked the two miles across the fields to the Fosse Way, the great Roman road that Issa should have been using. I planned to wait for him, then continue up the Fosse Way to Aquae Sulis which lay some twenty-five miles northwards, and then to Corinium which was another thirty miles further on. Fifty-five miles of road. Three days of long, hard effort.

We waited in a field of molehills beside the road. I had over a hundred spearmen and at least that number of women, children, slaves and servants. We had horses, mules and dogs, all waiting. Seren, Morwenna and the other children picked bluebells in a nearby wood while I paced up and down the broken stone of the road. Refugees were passing constantly, but none of them, even those who had come from Durnovaria, had any news of the Princess Argante. A priest thought he had seen Issa and his men arrive in that city because he had seen the five-pointed star on some spearmen's shields, but he did not know if they were still there or had left. The one thing all the refugees were certain of was that the Saxons were near Durnovaria, though no one had actually seen a Saxon spearman. They had merely heard the rumours that had grown ever more wild as the hours passed. Arthur was said to be dead, or else he had fled to Rheged, while Cerdic was credited with possessing horses that breathed fire and magic axes that could cleave iron as though it were linen.

Guinevere had borrowed a bow from one of my huntsmen and was shooting arrows at a dead elm tree that grew beside the road. She shot well, putting shaft after shaft into the rotting wood, but when I complimented her on her skill, she grimaced. 'I'm out of practice,' she said, 'I used to be able to take a running deer at a hundred paces, now I doubt I'd hit a standing one at fifty.' She plucked the arrows from the tree. 'But I think I might hit a Saxon, given the chance.' She handed the bow back to my huntsman, who bowed and backed away. 'If the Saxons are near Durnovaria,' Guinevere asked me, 'what do they do next?'

'They come straight up this road,' I said.

'Not go further west?'

'They know our plans,' I said grimly, and told her about the golden buttons with the bearded faces that I had found in Mordred's quarters. 'Aelle's marching towards Corinium while the others run ragged in the south. And we're stuck here because of Argante.'

'Let her rot,' Guinevere said savagely, then shrugged. 'I know you can't. Does he love her?'

'I wouldn't know, Lady,' I said.

'Of course you'd know,' Guinevere said sharply. 'Arthur loves to pretend that he's ruled by reason, but he yearns to be governed by passion. He would turn the world upside down for love.'

'He hasn't turned it upside down lately,' I said.

'He did for me, though,' she said quietly, and not without a note of pride. 'So where are you going?'

I had walked to my horse that was cropping grass among the molehills. 'I'm going south,' I said.

'Do that,' Guinevere said, 'and we risk losing you too.'

She was right and I knew it, but frustration was beginning to boil inside me. Why had Issa not sent a message? He had fifty of my finest warriors and they were lost. I cursed the wasting day, cuffed a harmless boy who was strutting up and down pretending to be a spearman, and kicked at thistles. 'We could start north,' Ceinwyn suggested calmly, indicating the women and children.

'No,' I said, 'we must stay together.' I peered southwards, but there was nothing on the road except for more sad refugees trudging north. Most were families with one precious cow and maybe a calf, though many of this new season's calves were still too small to walk. Some calves, abandoned by the road, called piteously for their mothers. Others of the refugees were merchants trying to save their goods. One man had an ox-wagon filled with baskets of fuller's earth, another had hides, some had pottery. They glared at us as they passed, blaming us for not having stopped the Saxons sooner.

Seren and Morwenna, bored with their attempt to denude the wood of bluebells, had found a nest of leverets under some ferns and honeysuckle at the trees' edge. They excitedly called Guinevere to come and look, then gingerly stroked the little fur bodies that shivered under their touch. Ceinwyn watched them. 'She's made a conquest of the girls,' she said to me.

'A conquest of my spearmen too,' I said, and it was true. Just a few months ago my men had been cursing Guinevere as a whore, and now they gazed at her adoringly. She had set out to charm them, and when Guinevere decided to be charming, she could dazzle. 'Arthur will have a great deal of trouble putting her back behind walls after this,' I said.

'Which is probably why he wanted her released,' Ceinwyn observed. 'He certainly didn't want her dead.'

'Argante does.'

'I'm sure she does,' Ceinwyn agreed, then stared southwards with me, but there was still no sign of any spearmen on the long straight road.

Issa finally arrived at dusk. He came with his fifty spearmen, with the thirty men who had been the guards on the palace at Durnovaria, with the dozen Blackshields who were Argante's personal soldiers and with at least two hundred other refugees. Worse, he had brought six ox-drawn wagons and it was those heavy vehicles that had caused the delay. A heavily laden ox-wagon's highest speed is slower than an old man's walk, and Issa had fetched the wagons all the way north at their snail's pace. 'What possessed you?' I shouted at him. 'There isn't time to haul wagons!'

'I know, Lord,' he said miserably.

'Are you mad?' I was angry. I had ridden to meet him and now wheeled my mare on the verge. 'You've wasted hours!' I shouted.

'I had no choice!' he protested.

'You've got a spear!' I snarled. 'That gives you the right to choose what you want.'

He just shrugged and gestured towards the Princess Argante who rode atop the leading wagon. The wagon's four oxen, their flanks bleeding from the goads that had driven them all day, stopped in the road with their heads low.

'The wagons go no farther!' I shouted at her. 'You walk or ride from here!'

'No!' Argante insisted.

I slid off the mare and walked down the line of wagons. One held nothing but the Roman statues that had graced the palace courtyard in Durnovaria, another was piled with robes and gowns, while a third was heaped with cooking pots, beckets and bronze candle-stands. 'Get them off the road,' I shouted angrily.

'No!' Argante had leapt down from her high perch and now ran towards me. 'Arthur ordered me to bring them.'

'Arthur, Lady,' I turned on her, stifling my anger, 'does not need statues!'

'They come with us,' Argante shouted, 'otherwise I stay here!'

'Then stay here, Lady,' I said savagely. 'Off the road!' I shouted at the ox drivers. 'Move it! Off the road, now!' I had drawn Hywelbane and stabbed her blade at the nearest ox to drive the beast towards the verge.

'Don't go!' Argante screamed at the ox drivers. She tugged at one of the oxen's horns, pulling the confused beast back onto the road. 'I'm not leaving this for the enemy,' she shouted at me.

Guinevere watched from the roadside. There was a look of cool amusement on her face, and no wonder, for Argante was behaving like a spoiled child. Argante's Druid, Fergal, had hurried to his Princess's aid, protesting that all his magical cauldrons and ingredients were loaded on one of the wagons. 'And the treasury,' he added as an afterthought.

'What treasury?' I asked.

'Arthur's treasury,' Argante said sarcastically, as though by revealing the existence of the gold she won her argument. 'He wants it in Corinium.' She went to the second wagon, lifted some of the heavy robes and rapped a wooden box that was hidden beneath. 'The gold of Dumnonia! You'd give it to the Saxons?'

'Rather that than give them you and me, Lady,' I said and then I slashed with Hywelbane, cutting loose the oxen's harness. Argante screamed at me, swearing she would have me punished and that I was stealing her treasures, but I just sawed at the next harness as I snarled at the ox drivers to release their animals. 'Listen, Lady,' I said, 'we have to go faster than oxen can walk.' I pointed to the distant smoke. 'That's the Saxons! They'll be here in a few hours.'

'We can't leave the wagons!' she screamed. There were tears in her eyes. She might have been the daughter of a King, but she had grown up with few possessions and now, married to Dumnonia's ruler, she was rich and she could not let go of those new riches. 'Don't undo that harness!' she shouted at the drivers and they, confused, hesitated. I sawed at another leather trace and Argante began beating me with her fists, swearing that I was a thief and her enemy.

I pushed her gently away, but she would not go and I dared not be too forceful. She was in a tantrum now, swearing at me and hitting me with her small hands. I tried to push her away again, but she just spat at me, hit me again, then shouted at her Blackshield bodyguard to come to her aid.

Those twelve men were hesitant, but they were her father's warriors and sworn to Argante's service, and so they came towards me with levelled spears. My own men immediately ran to my defence. The Blackshields were terribly outnumbered, but they did not back down and their Druid was hopping in front of them, his fox-hair woven beard wagging and the small bones tied to its hairs clicking as he told the Blackshields that they were blessed and that their souls would go to a golden reward. 'Kill him!' Argante screamed at her bodyguard and pointing at me. 'Kill him now!'

'Enough!' Guinevere called sharply. She walked into the centre of the road and stared imperiously at the Blackshields. 'Don't be fools, put your spears down. If you want to die, take some Saxons with you, not Dumnonians.' She turned on Argante. 'Come here, child,' she said, and pulled the girl towards her and used a corner of her drab cloak to wipe away Argante's tears. 'You did quite right to try and save the treasury,' she told Argante, 'but Derfel is also right. If we don't hurry the Saxons will catch us.' She turned to me. 'Is there no chance,' she asked, 'that we can take the gold?'

'None,' I said shortly, nor was there. Even if I had harnessed spearmen to the wagons they would still have slowed us down.

'The gold is mine!' Argante screamed.

'It belongs to the Saxons now,' I said, and I shouted at Issa to get the wagons off the road and cut the oxen free.

Argante screamed a last protest, but Guinevere seized and hugged her. 'It doesn't become princesses,' Guinevere murmured softly, 'to show anger in public. Be mysterious, my dear, and never let men know what you're thinking. Your power lies in the shadows, but in the sunlight men will always overcome you.'

Argante had no idea who the tall, good-looking woman was, but she allowed Guinevere to comfort her as Issa and his men dragged the wagons onto the grass verge. I let the women take what cloaks and gowns they wanted, but we abandoned the cauldrons and tripods and candle-holders, though Issa did discover one of Arthur's war-banners, a huge sheet of white linen decorated with a great black bear embroidered in wool, and that we kept to stop it falling into the hands of the Saxons, but we could not take the gold.

Instead we carried the treasury boxes to a flooded drainage ditch in a nearby field and poured the coins into the stinking water in the hope that the Saxons would never discover it.

Argante sobbed as she watched the gold being poured into the black water. 'The gold is mine!' she protested a last time.

'And once it was mine, child,' Guinevere said very calmly, 'and I survived the loss, just as you now will.'

Argante pulled abruptly away to stare up at the taller woman. 'Yours?' she asked.

'Did I not name myself, child?' Guinevere asked with a delicate scorn. 'I'm the Princess Guinevere.'

Argante just screamed, then fled up the road to where her Blackshields had retreated. I groaned, sheathed Hywelbane, then waited as the last of the gold was concealed. Guinevere had found one of her old cloaks, a golden cascade of wool trimmed in bear fur, and had discarded the old dull garment she had worn in her prison. 'Her gold indeed,' she said to me angrily.

'It seems I have another enemy,' I said, watching Argante who was deep in conversation with her Druid and doubtless urging him to put a curse on me.

'If we share an enemy, Derfel,' Guinevere said with a smile, 'then that makes us allies at last. I like that.'

'Thank you, Lady,' I said, and reflected that it was not just my daughters and spearmen who were being charmed.

The last of the gold was sunk in the ditch and my men came back to the road and picked up their spears and shields. The sun flamed over the Severn Sea, filling the west with a crimson glow as we, at last, started northwards to the war.

We only made a few miles before the dark drove us off the road to find shelter, but at least we had reached the hills north of Ynys Wydryn. We stopped that night at an abandoned hall where we made a poor meal of hard bread and dried fish. Argante sat apart from the rest of us, protected by her Druid and her guards, and though Ceinwyn tried to draw her into our conversation she refused to be tempted and so we let her sulk.

After we had eaten I walked with Ceinwyn and Guinevere to the top of a small hill behind the hall where two of the old people's grave mounds stood. I begged the dead's forgiveness and climbed to the top of one of the mounds where Ceinwyn and Guinevere joined me. The three of us gazed southwards. The valley beneath us was prettily white with moon-glossed apple blossom, but we saw nothing on the horizon except the sullen glow of fires. 'The Saxons move fast,' I said bitterly.

Guinevere pulled her cloak tight around her shoulders. 'Where's Merlin?' she asked.

'Vanished,' I said. There had been reports that Merlin was in Ireland, or else in the northern wilderness, or perhaps in the wastes of Gwynedd, while still another tale claimed he was dead and that Nimue had cut down a whole mountainside of trees to make his balefire. It was just rumour, I told myself, just rumour.

'No one knows where Merlin is,' Ceinwyn said softly, 'but he'll surely know where we are.'

'I pray that he does,' Guinevere said fervently, and I wondered to what God or Goddess she prayed now. Still to Isis? Or had she reverted to the British Gods? And maybe, I shuddered at the thought, those Gods had finally abandoned us. Their balefire would have been the flames on Mai Dun and their revenge was the warbands that now ravaged Dumnonia.

We marched again at dawn. It had clouded over in the night and a thin rain started with the first light. The Fosse Way was crowded with refugees and even though I placed a score of armed warriors at our head who had orders to thrust all ox-wagons and herds off the road, our progress was still pitifully slow. Many of the children could not keep up and had to be carried on the pack animals that bore our spears, armour and food, or else hoisted onto the shoulders of the younger spearmen. Argante rode my mare while Guinevere and Ceinwyn walked and took it in turns to tell stories to the children. The rain became harder, sweeping across the hilltops in vast grey swathes and gurgling down the shallow ditches on either side of the Roman road.

I had hoped to reach Aquae Sulis at midday, but it was the middle of the afternoon before our bedraggled and tired band dropped into the valley where the city lay. The river was in spate and a choking mass of floating debris had become trapped against the stone piers of the Roman bridge to form a dam that had flooded the upstream fields on either bank. One of the duties of the city's magistrate was to keep the bridge spillways clear of just such debris, but the task had been ignored, just as he had ignored the upkeep of the city wall. That wall lay only a hundred paces north of the bridge and, because Aquae Sulis was not a fortress town, it had never been a formidable wall, but now it was scarcely an obstacle at all. Whole stretches of the wooden palisade on top of the earth and stone rampart had been torn down for firewood or building, while the rampart itself had become so eroded that the Saxons could have crossed the city wall without breaking stride. Here and there I could see frantic men trying to repair stretches of the palisade, but it would have taken five hundred men a full month to rebuild those defences.

We filed through the city's fine southern gate and I saw that though the town possessed neither the energy to preserve its ramparts nor the labour to keep the bridge from choking with flotsam, someone had found time to deface the beautiful mask of the Roman Goddess Minerva that had once graced the gate's arch. Where her face had been there was now just a calloused mass of hammered stone on which a crude Christian cross had been cut. 'It's a Christian town?' Ceinwyn asked me.

'Nearly all towns are,' Guinevere answered for me.

It was also a beautiful town. Or it had been beautiful once, though over the years the tiled roofs had fallen and been replaced by thick thatch and some houses had collapsed and were now nothing but piles of brick or stone, but still the streets were paved and the high pillars and lavishly carved pediment of Minerva's magnificent temple still soared above the petty roofs. My vanguard forced a brutal way through the crowded streets to reach the temple, which stood on a stepped pediment in the sacred heart of the city. The Romans had built an inner wall about that central shrine, a wall that encompassed Minerva's temple and the bath-house that had brought the city its fame and prosperity. The Romans had roofed in the bath, which was fed by a magical hot spring, but some of the roof tiles had fallen and wisps of steam now curled up from the holes like smoke. The temple itself, stripped of its lead gutters, was stained with rainwater and lichen, while the painted plaster inside the high portico had flaked and darkened; but despite the decay it was still possible to stand in the wide paved enclosure of the city's inner shrine and imagine a world where men could build such places and live without fear of spears coming from the barbarian east.

The city magistrate, a flurried, nervous, middle-aged man named Cildydd who wore a Roman toga to mark his authority, hurried out of the temple to greet me. I knew him from the time of the rebellion when, despite being a Christian himself, he had fled from the crazed fanatics who had taken over the shrines of Aquae Sulis. He had been restored to the magistracy after the rebellion, but I guessed his authority was slight. He carried a scrap of slate on which he had made scores of marks, evidently the numbers of the levy that was assembled inside the shrine's compound. 'Repairs are in hand!' Cildydd greeted me without any other courtesy. 'I have men cutting timbers for the walls. Or I did. The flooding is a problem, indeed it is, but if the rain stops?' He let the sentence trail away.

'The flooding?' I asked.

'When the river rises, Lord,' he explained, 'the water backs up through the Roman sewers. It's already in the lower part of the city. And not just water either, I fear. The smell, you see?' He sniffed delicately.

'The problem,' I said, 'is that the bridge arches are dammed with debris. It was your task to keep them clear. It was also your task to preserve the walls.' His mouth opened and closed without a word. He hefted the slate as if to demonstrate his efficiency, then just blinked helplessly. 'Not that it matters now,' I went on, 'the city can't be defended.'

'Can't be defended!' Cildydd protested. 'Can't be defended! It must be defended! We can't just abandon the city!'

'If the Saxons come,' I said brutally, 'you'll have no choice.'

'But we must defend it, Lord,' Cildydd insisted.

'With what?' I asked.

'Your men, Lord,' he said, gesturing at my spearmen who had taken refuge from the rain under the temple's high portico.

'At best,' I said, 'we can garrison a quarter mile of the wall, or what's left of it. So who defends the rest?'

'The levy, of course.' Cildydd waved his slate towards the drab

170

collection of men who waited beside the bath-house. Few had weapons and even fewer possessed any body armour.

'Have you ever seen the Saxons attack?' I asked Cildydd. 'They send big war-dogs first and they come behind with axes three feet long and spears on eight-foot shafts. They're drunk, they're maddened and they'll want nothing but the women and the gold inside your city. How long do you think your levy will hold?'

Cildydd blinked at me. 'We can't just give up,' he said weakly.

'Does your levy have any real weapons?' I asked, indicating the sullen-looking men waiting in the rain. Two or three of the sixty men had spears, I could see one old Roman sword, and most of the rest had axes or mattocks, but some men did not even possess those crude weapons, but merely held fire-hardened stakes that had been sharpened to black points.

'We're searching the city, Lord,' Cildydd said. 'There must be spears.'

'Spears or not,' I said brutally, 'if you fight here you'll all be dead men.'

Cildydd gaped at me. 'Then what do we do?' he finally asked.

'Go to Glevum,' I said.

'But the city!' He blanched. 'There are merchants, goldsmiths, churches, treasures.' His voice tailed away as he imagined the enormity of the city's fall, but that fall, if the Saxons came, was inevitable. Aquae Sulis was no garrison city, just a beautiful place that stood in a bowl of hills. Cildydd blinked in the rain. 'Glevum,' he said glumly. 'And you'll escort us there, Lord?'

I shook my head. 'I'm going to Corinium,' I said, 'but you go to Glevum.' I was half tempted to send Argante, Guinevere, Ceinwyn and the families with him, but I did not trust Cildydd to protect them. Better, I decided, to take the women and families north myself, then send them under a small escort from Corinium to Glevum.

But at least Argante was taken from my hands, for as I was brutally destroying Cildydd's slim hopes of garrisoning Aquae Sulis a troop of armoured horsemen clattered into the temple precinct. They were Arthur's men, flying his banner of the bear, and they were led by Balin who was roundly cursing the press of refugees. He looked relieved when he saw me, then astonished as he recognized

Guinevere. 'Did you bring the wrong Princess, Derfel?' he asked as he slid off his tired horse.

'Argante's inside the temple,' I said, jerking my head towards the great building where Argante had taken refuge from the rain. She had not spoken to me all day.

'I'm to take her to Arthur,' Balin said. He was a bluff, bearded man with the tattoo of a bear on his forehead and a jagged white scar on his left cheek. I asked him for news and he told me what little he knew and none of it was good. 'The bastards are coming down the Thames,' he said, 'we reckon they're only three days' march from Corinium, and there's no sign of Cuneglas or Oengus yet. It's chaos, Derfel, that's what it is, chaos.' He shuddered suddenly. 'What's the stink here?'

'The sewers are backing up,' I said.

'All over Dumnonia,' he said grimly. 'I have to hurry,' he went on, 'Arthur wants his bride in Corinium the day before yesterday.'

'Do you have orders for me?' I called after him as he strode towards the temple steps.

'Get yourself to Corinium! And hurry! And you're to send what food you can!' He shouted the last order as he disappeared through the temple's great bronze doors. He had brought six spare horses, enough to saddle Argante, her maids and Fergal the Druid, which meant that the twelve men of Argante's Blackshield escort were left with me. I sensed they were as glad as I was to be rid of their Princess.

Balin rode north in the late afternoon. I had wanted to be on the road myself, but the children were tired, the rain was incessant, and Ceinwyn persuaded me that we would make better time if we all rested this night under Aquae Sulis's roofs and marched fresh in the morning. I put guards on the bath-house and let the women and children go into the great steaming pool of hot water, then sent Issa and a score of men to hunt through the city for weapons to equip the levy. After that I sent for Cildydd and asked him how much food remained in the city. 'Scarcely any, Lord!' he insisted, claiming he had already sent sixteen wagons of grain, dried meat and salted fish north.

'You searched folk's houses?' I asked. 'The churches?'

'Only the city granaries, Lord.'

'Then let's make a proper search,' I suggested, and by dusk we had collected seven more wagon-loads of precious supplies. I sent the wagons north that same evening, despite the lateness of the hour. Ox-carts are slow and it was better that they should start the journey at dusk than wait for the morning.

Issa waited for me in the temple precinct. His search of the city had yielded seven old swords and a dozen boar spears, while Cildydd's men had turned up fifteen more spears, eight of them broken, but Issa also had news. 'There's said to be weapons hidden in the temple, Lord,' he told me.

'Who says?'

Issa gestured at a young bearded man who was dressed in a butcher's bloody apron. 'He reckons a hoard of spears was hidden in the temple after the rebellion, but the priest denies it.'

'Where's the priest?'

'Inside, Lord. He told me to get out when I questioned him.'

I ran up the temple steps and through the big doors. This had once been a shrine to Minerva and Sulis, the first a Roman and the second a British Goddess, but the pagan deities had been ejected and the Christian God installed. When I had last been in the temple there had been a great bronze statue of Minerva attended by flickering oil lamps, but the statue had been destroyed during the Christian rebellion and now only the Goddess's hollow head remained, and that had been impaled on a pole to stand as a trophy behind the Christian altar.

The priest challenged me. 'This is a house of God!' he roared. He was celebrating a mystery at his altar, surrounded by weeping women, but he broke off his ceremonies to face me. He was a young man, full of passion, one of those priests who had stirred up the trouble in Dumnonia and whom Arthur had allowed to live so that the bitterness of the failed rebellion would not fester. This priest, however, had clearly lost none of his insurgent fervour. 'A house of God!' he shouted again, 'and you defile it with sword and spear! Would you carry your weapons into your lord's hall? So why carry them into my Lord's house?'

'In a week,' I said, 'it will be a temple of Thunor and they'll be sacrificing your children where you stand. Are there spears here?'

'None!' he said defiantly. The women screamed and shrank away as I climbed the altar steps. The priest held a cross towards me. 'In the name of God,' he said, 'and in the name of His holy Son, and in the name of the Holy Ghost. No!' This last cry was because I had drawn Hywelbane and used her to strike the cross out of his hand. The scrap of wood skittered across the temple's marble floor as I rammed the blade into his tangled beard. 'I'll pull this place down stone by stone to find the spears,' I said, 'and bury your miserable carcass under its rubble. Now where are they?'

His defiance crumpled. The spears, which he had been hoarding in hope of another campaign to put a Christian on Dumnonia's throne, were concealed in a crypt beneath the altar. The entrance to the crypt was hidden, for it was a place where the treasures donated by folk seeking Sulis's healing power had once been concealed, but the frightened priest showed us how to lift the marble slab to reveal a pit crammed with gold and weapons. We left the gold, but carried the spears out to Cildydd's levy. I doubted the sixty men would be of any real use in battle, but at least a man armed with a spear looked like a warrior and, from a distance, they might give the Saxons pause. I told the levy to be ready to march in the morning and to pack as much food as they could find.

We slept that night in the temple. I swept the altar clear of its Christian trimmings and placed Minerva's head between two oil lamps so that she would guard us through the night. Rain dripped from the roof and puddled on the marble, but sometime in the small hours the rain stopped and the dawn brought a clearing sky and a fresh chill wind from the east.

We left the city before the sun rose. Only forty of the city's levy marched with us for the rest had melted away in the night, but it was better to have forty willing men than sixty uncertain allies. Our road was clear of refugees now, for I had spread the word that safety did not lie in Corinium but at Glevum, and so it was the western road that was crammed with cattle and folk. Our route took us east into the rising sun along the Fosse Way which here ran straight as a spear between Roman tombs. Guinevere translated the inscriptions, marvelling that men were buried here who had been born in Greece or Egypt or Rome itself. They were veterans of the Legions who had taken British wives and settled near the healing springs of Aquae Sulis, and their lichen-covered gravestones sometimes gave thanks to Minerva or to Sulis for the gift of years. After an hour we left the tombs behind and the valley narrowed as the steep hills north of the road came closer to the river meadows; soon, I knew, the road would turn abruptly north to climb into the hills that lay between Aquae Sulis and Corinium.

It was when we reached the narrow part of the valley that the ox drivers came running back. They had left Aquae Sulis the previous day, but their slow wagons had reached no further than the northwards bend in the road, and now, in the dawn, they had abandoned their seven loads of precious food. 'Sais!' one man shouted as he ran towards us. 'There are Sais!'

'Fool,' I muttered, then shouted at Issa to stop the fleeing men. I had allowed Guinevere to ride my horse, but now she slid off and I clumsily hauled my way onto the beast's back and spurred her forward.

The road turned northwards half a mile ahead. The oxen and their wagons had been abandoned just at the bend and I edged past them to peer up the slope. For a moment I could see nothing, then a group of horsemen appeared beside some trees at the crest. They were half a mile away, outlined against the brightening sky, and I could make out no details of their shields, but I guessed they were Britons rather than Saxons because our enemy did not deploy many horsemen.

I urged the mare up the slope. None of the horsemen moved. They just watched me, but then, away to my right, more men appeared at the hill's crest. These were spearmen and above them hung a banner that told me the worst.

The banner was a skull hung with what looked like rags, and I remembered Cerdic's wolf-skull standard with its ragged tail of flayed human skin. The men were Saxons and they barred our road. There were not many spearmen in sight, perhaps a dozen horsemen and fifty or sixty men on foot, but they had the high ground and I could not tell how many more might be hidden beyond the crest. I stopped the mare and stared at the spearmen, this time seeing the glint of sunlight on the broad axeblades some of the men carried. They had to be Saxons. But where had they come from? Balin had told me that both Cerdic and Aelle were advancing along the Thames, so it seemed likely that these men had come south from the wide river valley, but maybe they were some of Cerdic's spearmen who served Lancelot. Not that it really mattered who they were; all that mattered was that our road was blocked. Still more of the enemy appeared, their spears pricking the skyline all along the ridge.

I turned the mare to see Issa bringing my most experienced spearmen past the blockage at the road's turn. 'Saxons!' I called to him. 'Form a shield wall here!'

Issa gazed up at the distant spearmen. 'We fight them here, Lord?' he asked.

'No.' I dared not fight in such a bad place. We would be forced to struggle uphill, and we would ever be worried about our families behind us.

'We'll take the road to Glevum instead?' Issa suggested.

I shook my head. The Glevum road was thronged with refugees and if I had been the Saxon commander I would have wanted nothing more than to pursue an outnumbered enemy along that road. We could not outmarch him, for we would be obstructed by refugees, and he would find it a simple matter to cut through those panicked people to bring us death. It was possible, even likely, that the Saxons would not make any pursuit at all, but would be tempted to plunder the city instead, but it was a risk I dared not take. I gazed up the long hill and saw yet more of the enemy coming to the sun-bright crest. It was impossible to count them, but it was no small warband. My own men were making a shield wall, but I knew I could not fight here. The Saxons had more men and they had the high ground. To fight here was to die.

I twisted in the saddle. A half-mile away, just to the north of the Fosse Way, was one of the old people's fortresses, and its ancient earth wall – much eroded now – stood at the crest of a steep hill. I pointed to the grass ramparts. 'We'll go there,' I said.

'There, Lord?' Issa was puzzled.

'If we try to escape them,' I explained, 'they'll follow us. Our children can't move fast and eventually the bastards will catch us. We'll be forced to make a shield wall, put our families in the centre, and the last of us to die will hear the first of our women screaming. Better to go to a place where they'll hesitate to attack. Eventually they'll have to make a choice. Either they leave us alone and go north, in which case we follow, or else they fight, and if we're on a hilltop we stand a chance of winning. A better chance,' I added, 'because Culhwch will come this way. In a day or two we might even outnumber them.'

'So we abandon Arthur?' Issa asked, shocked at the thought.

'We keep a Saxon warband away from Corinium,' I said. But I was not happy with my choice, for Issa was right. I was abandoning Arthur, but I dared not risk the lives of Ceinwyn and my daughters. The whole careful campaign that Arthur had plotted was destroyed. Culhwch was cut off somewhere to the south, I was trapped at Aquae Sulis, while Cuneglas and Oengus mac Airem were still many miles away.

I rode back to find my armour and weapons. I had no time to don the body armour, but I pulled on the wolf-plumed helmet, found my heaviest spear and took up my shield. I gave the mare back to Guinevere and told her to take the families up the hill, then ordered the men of the levy and my younger spearmen to turn the seven food wagons round and get them up to the fortress. 'I don't care how you do it,' I said to them, 'but I want that food kept from the enemy. Haul the wagons up yourself if you have to!' I might have abandoned Argante's wagons, but in war a wagon-load of food is far more precious than gold and I was determined to keep those supplies from the enemy. If necessary, I would burn the wagons and their contents, but for the moment I would try to save the food.

I went back to Issa and took my place at the centre of the shield wall. The enemy ranks were thickening and I expected them to make a mad charge down the hill at any minute. They outnumbered us, but still they did not come and every moment that they hesitated was an extra moment in which our families and the precious wagon-loads of food could reach the hill's summit. I glanced behind constantly, watching the wagons' progress, and when they were just over halfway up the steep slope I ordered my spearmen back.

That retreat spurred the Saxons into an advance. They screamed a challenge and came fast down the hill, but they had left their attack too late. My men went back along the road, crossed a shallow ford where a stream tumbled from the hills towards the river, and now we had the higher ground for we were retreating uphill towards the fortress on its steep slope. My men kept their line straight, kept their shields overlapping and held their long spears steady, and that evidence of their training stopped the Saxon pursuit fifty yards short of us. They contented themselves with shouting challenges and insults, while one of their naked wizards, his hair spiked with cow dung, danced forward to curse us. He called us pigs, cowards and goats. He cursed us, and I counted them. They had one hundred and seventy men in their wall, and there were still more who had not yet come down the hill. I counted them and the Saxon war-leaders stood their horses behind their shield wall and counted us. I could see their banner clearly now and it was Cerdic's standard of a wolf skull hung with a dead man's flayed skin, but Cerdic himself was not there. This had to be one of his warbands come south from the Thames. The warband far outnumbered us, but its leaders were too canny to attack. They knew that they could beat us, but they also knew the dreadful toll that seventy experienced warriors would cull from their ranks. It was enough for them to have driven us away from the road.

We backed slowly up the hill. The Saxons watched us, but only their wizard followed us and after a while he lost interest. He spat at us and turned away. We jeered mightily at the enemy's timidity, but in truth I was feeling a huge relief that they had not attacked.

It took us an hour to heave the seven wagons of precious food over the ancient turf rampart and so onto the hill's gently domed top. I walked that domed plateau and discovered it to be a marvellous defensive position. The summit was a triangle, and on each of its three sides the ground fell steeply away so that any attacker would be forced to labour up into the teeth of our spears. I hoped the steepness of that slope would keep the Saxon warband from making any attack, and that in a day or two the enemy would leave and we would be free to find our way north to Corinium. We would arrive late, and Arthur would doubtless be angry with me, but for the moment I had kept this part of Dumnonia's army safe. We numbered over two hundred spearmen and we protected a crowd of women and children, seven wagons and two Princesses, and our refuge was a grassy hilltop high above a deep river valley. I found one of the levy and asked him the name of the hill.

'It's named like the city, Lord,' he said, apparently bemused that I should even want to know the name.

'Aquae Sulis?' I asked him.

'No, Lord! The old name! The name before the Romans came.'

'Baddon,' I said.

'And this is Mynydd Baddon, Lord,' he confirmed.

Mount Baddon. In time the poets would make that name ring through all of Britain. It would be sung in a thousand halls and fire the blood of children yet unborn, but for now it meant nothing to me. It was just a convenient hill, a grass-walled fort, and the place where, all unwillingly, I had planted my two banners in the turf. One showed Ceinwyn's star, while the other, which we had found and rescued from Argante's wagons, flaunted Arthur's banner of the bear.

So, in the morning light, where they flapped in the drying wind, the bear and the star defied the Saxons.

On Mynydd Baddon.

THE SAXONS WERE CAUTIOUS. They had not attacked us when they first saw us, and now that we were secure on Mynydd Baddon's summit they were content to sit at the southern base of the hill and simply watch us. In the afternoon a large contingent of their spearmen walked to Aquae Sulis, where they must have discovered an almost deserted city. I expected to see the flare and smoke of burning thatch, but no such fires appeared and at dusk the spearmen came back from the city laden with plunder. The shadows of nightfall darkened the river valley and, while we on Mynydd Baddon's summit were still in the last wash of daylight, our enemy's campfires studded the dark beneath us.

Still more fires showed in the hilly land to the north of us. Mynydd Baddon lay like an offshore island to those hills, and was separated from them by a high grassy saddle. I had half thought we might cross that high valley in the night, climb to the ridge beyond and make our way across the hills towards Corinium; so, before dusk, I sent Issa and a score of men to reconnoitre the route, but they returned to say there were mounted Saxon scouts all across the ridge beyond the saddle. I was still tempted to try and escape northwards, but I knew the Saxon horsemen would see us and that by dawn we would have their whole warband on our heels. I worried about the choice till deep into the night, then picked the lesser of the two evils: we would stay on Mynydd Baddon.

To the Saxons we must have appeared a formidable army. I now commanded two hundred and sixty-eight men and the enemy were not to know that fewer than a hundred of those were prime spearmen. Forty of the remainder were the city levy, thirty-six were battle-hardened warriors who had guarded Caer Cadarn or Durnovaria's palace, though most of those three dozen men were old and slow now, while a hundred and ten were unblooded youngsters. My seventy experienced spearmen and Argante's twelve Blackshields were among the best warriors in Britain, and though I did not doubt that the thirty-six veterans would be useful and that the youngsters might well prove formidable, it was still a pitifully small force with which to protect our hundred and fourteen women and seventy-nine children. But at least we had plenty of food and water, for we possessed the seven precious wagons and there were three springs on Mynydd Baddon's flanks.

By nightfall on that first day we had counted the enemy. There were about three hundred and sixty Saxons in the valley and at least another eighty on the land to the north. That was enough spearmen to keep us penned on Mynydd Baddon, but probably not enough to assault us. Each of the flat and treeless summit's three sides was three hundred paces in length, making a total that was far too great for my small numbers to defend, but if the enemy did attack we would see them coming from a long way off and I would have time to move spearmen to face their assault. I reckoned that even if they made two or three simultaneous assaults I could still hold, for the Saxons would have a terrible steep slope to climb and my men would be fresh, but if the enemy numbers increased then I knew I must be overwhelmed. My prayer was that these Saxons were nothing more than a strong foraging band, and once they had stripped Aquae Sulis and its river valley of whatever food they could find they would go back north to rejoin Aelle and Cerdic.

The next dawn showed that the Saxons were still in the valley, where the smoke of their campfires mingled with the river mist. As the mist thinned we saw they were cutting down trees to make huts; depressing evidence that they intended to stay. My own men were busy on the mount's slopes, chopping down the small hawthorns and the birch saplings that might give cover to an attacking enemy. They dragged the brush and small trees back to the summit and piled them as rudimentary breastworks on the remains of the old people's wall. I had another fifty men on the hill crest to the north of the saddle, where they were cutting firewood that we hauled back to the mount in one of the ox-wagons we had emptied of food. Those men brought back enough timber to make a long wooden hut of our own, though our hut, unlike the

Saxon shelters that were roofed with thatch or turf, was nothing but a ramshackle structure of untrimmed timbers stretched between four of the wagons and crudely thatched with branches, but it was large enough to shelter the women and children.

During the first night I had sent two of my spearmen north. Both of them were cunning rogues from among the unblooded youngsters and I ordered each to try and reach Corinium and tell Arthur of our plight. I doubted whether he could help us, but at least he would know what had happened. All next day I dreaded seeing those two young men again, fearing to see them being dragged as prisoners behind a Saxon horseman, but they vanished. Both, as I learned later, survived to reach Corinium.

The Saxons built their shelters and we piled more thorn and brush on our shallow wall. None of the enemy came near us, and we did not go down to challenge them. I divided the summit into sections, and assigned each to a troop of spearmen. My seventy experienced warriors, the best of my small army, guarded the angle of ramparts that faced due south towards the enemy. I split my youngsters into two troops, one on each flank of the experienced men, then gave the defence of the hill's northern side to the twelve Blackshields, supported by the levy and the guards from Caer Cadarn and Durnovaria. The Blackshields' leader was a scarred brute named Niall, a veteran of a hundred harvest raids whose fingers were thick with warrior rings, and Niall raised his own makeshift banner on the northern rampart. It was nothing but a branch-stripped birch sapling struck into the turf with a scrap of black cloak flying from its tip, but there was something wild and satisfyingly defiant about that ragged Irish flag.

I still had hopes of escaping. The Saxons might be making shelters in the river valley, but the high northern ground went on tempting me and on that second afternoon I rode my horse across the saddle of land beneath Niall's banner and so up to the opposing crest. A great empty stretch of moorland lay under the racing clouds. Eachern, an experienced warrior whom I had put in command of one of the bands of youngsters cutting timber on the crest, came to stand beside my mare. He saw that I was staring at the empty moor and guessed what was in my mind. He spat. 'Bastards are out there, so they are,' he said.

'You're sure?'

'They come and they go, Lord. Always horsemen.' He had an axe in his right hand and he pointed it westwards to where a valley ran north-west beside the moor. Trees grew thick in the small valley, though all we could see of them was their leafy tops. 'There's a road in those trees,' Eachern said, 'and that's where they're lurking.'

'The road must go towards Glevum,' I said.

'Goes to the Saxons first, Lord,' Eachern said. 'Bastards are there, so they are. I heard their axes.'

Which meant, I guessed, that the track in the valley was blocked with felled trees. I was still tempted. If we destroyed the food and left behind anything that could slow our march, then we might still break out of this Saxon ring and reach Arthur's army. All day my conscience had been nagging like a spur, for my clear duty was to be with Arthur and the longer I was stranded on Mynydd Baddon the harder his task was. I wondered if we could cross the moorland at night. There would be a half moon, enough to light the way, and if we moved fast we would surely outrun the main Saxon warband. We might be harried by a handful of Saxon horsemen, but my spearmen could deal with those. But what lay beyond the moor? Hilly country, for sure, and doubtless cut by rivers swollen by the recent rains. I needed a road, I needed fords and bridges, I needed speed or else the children would lag behind, the spearmen would slow to protect them and suddenly the Saxons would be on us like wolves outrunning a flock of sheep. I could imagine escaping from Mynydd Baddon, but I could not see how we were to cross the miles of country between us and Corinium without falling prey to enemy blades.

The decision was taken from me at dusk. I was still contemplating a dash north and hoping that by leaving our fires burning brightly we might deceive the enemy into thinking we remained on Mynydd Baddon's summit, but during the dusk of that second day still more Saxons arrived. They came from the north-east, from the direction of Corinium, and a hundred of them moved onto the moorland I had hoped to cross, then came south to drive my woodcutters out of the trees, across the saddle and so back onto Mynydd Baddon. Now we were truly trapped.

I sat that night with Ceinwyn beside a fire. 'It reminds me,' I said, 'of that night on Ynys Mon.'

'I was thinking of that,' she said.

It was the night we had discovered the Cauldron of Clyddno Eiddyn, and we had huddled in a jumble of rocks with the forces of Diwrnach all about us. None of us had expected to live, but then Merlin had woken from the dead and mocked me. 'Surrounded, are we?' he had asked me. 'Outnumbered, are we?' I had agreed to both propositions and Merlin had smiled. 'And you call yourself a lord of warriors!'

'You've landed us in a predicament,' Ceinwyn said, quoting Merlin, and she smiled at the memory, then sighed. 'If we weren't with you,' she went on, indicating the women and children about the fires, 'what would you do?'

'Go north. Fight a battle over there,' I nodded towards the Saxon fires that burned on the high ground beyond the saddle, 'then keep marching north.' I was not truly certain I would have done that, for such an escape would have meant abandoning any man wounded in the battle for the ridge, but the rest of us, unencumbered by women or children, could surely have outmarched the Saxon pursuit.

'Suppose,' Ceinwyn said softly, 'that you ask the Saxons to give the women and children safe passage?'

'They'll say yes,' I said, 'and as soon as you're out range of our spears they'll seize you, rape you, kill you and enslave the children.'

'Not really a good idea, then?' she asked gently.

'Not really.'

She leaned her head on my shoulder, trying not to disturb Seren who was sleeping with her head pillowed on her mother's lap. 'So how long can we hold?' Ceinwyn asked.

'I could die of old age on Mynydd Baddon,' I said, 'so long as they don't send more than four hundred men to attack us.'

'And will they?'

'Probably not,' I lied, and Ceinwyn knew I lied. Of course they would send more than four hundred men. In war, I have learned, the enemy will usually do whatever you fear the most, and this enemy would certainly send every spearman they had.

Ceinwyn lay silent for a while. Dogs barked among the distant

Saxon encampments, their sound coming clear through the still night. Our own dogs began to respond and little Seren shifted in her sleep. Ceinwyn stroked her daughter's hair. 'If Arthur's at Corinium,' she asked softly, 'then why are the Saxons coming here?'

'I don't know.'

'You think they'll eventually go north to join their main army?'

I had thought that, but the arrival of more Saxons had given me doubts. Now I suspected that we faced a big enemy warband that had been trying to march southwards around Corinium, looping deep into the hills to re-emerge at Glevum and so threaten Arthur's rear. I could think of no other reason why so many Saxons were in Aquae Sulis's valley, but that did not explain why they had not kept marching. Instead they were making shelters, which suggested they wanted to besiege us. In which case, I thought, perhaps we were doing Arthur a service by staying here. We were keeping a large number of his enemies away from Corinium, though if our estimation of the enemy forces was right then the Saxons had more than enough men to overwhelm both Arthur and us.

Ceinwyn and I fell silent. The twelve Blackshields had begun to sing, and when their song was done my men answered with the war chant of Illtydd. Pyrlig, my bard, accompanied the singing on his harp. He had found a leather breastplate and armed himself with a shield and spear, but the wargear looked strange on his thin frame. I hoped he would never have to abandon his harp and use the spear, for by then all hope would be lost. I imagined Saxons swarming across the hilltop, whooping their delight at finding so many women and children, then blotted the horrid thought out. We had to stay alive, we had to hold our walls, we had to win.

Next morning, under a sky of grey clouds through which a freshening wind brought snatches of rain from the west, I donned my wargear. It was heavy, and I had deliberately not worn it till now, but the arrival of the Saxon reinforcements had convinced me that we would have to fight and so, to put heart into my men, I chose to wear my finest armour. First, over my linen shirt and woollen trews, I pulled a leather tunic that fell to my knees. The leather was thick enough to stop a sword slash, though not a spear thrust. Over the tunic I pulled the precious coat of heavy Roman mail that my slaves had polished so that the small links seemed to shine. The mail coat was trimmed with golden loops at its hem, its sleeves and its neck. It was an expensive coat, one of the richest in Britain, and forged well enough to stop all but the most savage spear thrusts. My knee-length boots were sewn with bronze strips to cheat the lunging blade that comes low under the shield wall, and I had elbow-length gloves with iron plates to protect my forearms. My helmet was decorated with silver dragons that climbed up to its golden peak where the wolf-tail helm was fixed. The helmet came down over my ears, had a flap of mail to shield the back of my neck, and silvered cheekpieces that could be swung over my face so that an enemy did not see a man, but a metal-clad killer with two black shadows for eyes. It was the rich armour of a great warlord and it was designed to put fear into an enemy. I strapped Hywelbane's belt around the mail, tied a cloak about my neck and hefted my largest war spear. Then, thus dressed for battle and with my shield slung on my back, I walked the ring of Mynydd Baddon's walls so that all my men and all the watching enemy would see me and know that a lord of warriors waited for the fight. I finished my circuit at the southern peak of our defences and there, standing high above the enemy, I lifted the skirts of mail and leather to piss down the hill towards the Saxons.

I had not known Guinevere was close, and the first I knew was when she laughed and that laughter rather spoiled my gesture for I was embarrassed. She brushed away my apology. 'You do look fine, Derfel,' she said.

I swung the helmet's cheekpieces open. 'I had hoped, Lady,' I said, 'never to wear this gear again.'

'You sound just like Arthur,' she said wryly, then walked behind me to admire the strips of hammered silver that formed Ceinwyn's star on my shield. 'I never understand,' she said, coming back to face me, 'why you dress like a pigherder most of the time, but look so splendid for war.'

'I don't look like a pigherder,' I protested.

'Not like mine,' she said, 'because I can't abide having grubby people about me, even if they are swineherds, and so I always made certain they had decent clothes.'

'I had a bath last year,' I insisted.

'As recently as that!' she said, pretending to be impressed. She was carrying her hunter's bow and had a quiver of arrows at her back. 'If they come,' she said, 'I intend to send some of their souls to the Otherworld.'

'If they come,' I said, knowing that they would, 'all you'll see is helmets and shields and you'll waste your arrows. Wait till they raise their heads to fight our shield wall, then aim for their eyes.'

'I won't waste arrows, Derfel,' she promised grimly.

The first threat came from the north where the newly arrived Saxons formed a shield wall among the trees above the saddle that separated Mynydd Baddon from the high ground. Our most copious spring was in that saddle and perhaps the Saxons intended to deny us its use, for just after midday their shield wall came down into the small valley. Niall watched them from our ramparts. 'Eighty men,' he told me.

I brought Issa and fifty of my men across to the northern rampart, more than enough spearmen to see off eighty Saxons labouring uphill, but it soon became obvious that the Saxons did not intend to attack, but wanted to lure us down into the saddle where they could fight us on more equal terms. And no doubt once we were down there more Saxons would burst from the high trees to ambush us. 'You stay here,' I told my men, 'you don't go down! You stay!'

The Saxons jeered us. Some knew a few words of the British tongue, sufficient to call us cowards or women or worms. Sometimes a small group would climb halfway up our slope to tempt us to break ranks and rush down the hill, but Niall, Issa and I kept our men calm. A Saxon wizard shuffled up the wet slope towards us in short nervous rushes, jabbering incantations. He was naked beneath a wolfskin cape and had his hair dunged into a single tall spike. He shrilled his curses, wailed his charm words and then hurled a handful of small bones towards our shields, but still none of us moved. The wizard spat three times, then ran shivering down to the saddle, where a Saxon chieftain now tried to tempt one of us to single combat. He was a burly man with a tangled mane of greasy, dirt-matted golden hair that hung down past a lavish golden collar. His beard was plaited with black ribbons, his breastplate was of iron, his greaves of decorated Roman bronze, and his shield was painted with the mask of a snarling wolf. His helmet had bull's horns mounted on its sides and was surmounted by a wolf's skull to which he had tied a mass of black ribbons. He had strips of black fur tied around his upper arms and thighs, carried a huge double-bladed war axe, while from his belt hung a long sword and one of the short, broad-bladed knives called a *seax*, the weapon that gave the Saxons their name. For a time he demanded that Arthur himself come down and fight him, and when he tired of that he challenged me, calling me a coward, a chicken-hearted slave and the son of a leprous whore. He spoke in his own tongue which meant that none of my men knew what he said and I just let his words whip past me in the wind.

Then, in the middle of the afternoon, when the rain had ended and the Saxons were bored with trying to lure us down to battle, they brought three captured children to the saddle. The children were very young, no more than five or six years old, and they were held with *seaxs* at their throats. 'Come down,' the big Saxon chieftain shouted, 'or they die!'

Issa looked at me. 'Let me go, Lord,' he pleaded.

'It's my rampart,' Niall, the Blackshield leader, insisted. 'I'll fillet the bastard.'

'It's my hilltop,' I said. It was more than just my hilltop, it was also my duty to fight the first single combat of a battle. A king could let his champion fight but a warlord had no business sending men where he would not go himself, and so I closed the cheekpieces of my helmet, touched a gloved hand to the pork bones in Hywelbane's hilt, then pressed on my mail coat to feel the small lump made by Ceinwyn's brooch. Thus reassured I pushed through our crude timber palisade and edged down the steep slope. 'You and me!' I shouted at the tall Saxon in his own language, 'for their lives,' and I pointed my spear at the three children.

The Saxons roared approval that they had at last brought one Briton down from the hill. They backed away, taking the children with them, leaving the saddle to their champion and to me. The burly Saxon hefted the big axe in his left hand, then spat onto the buttercups. 'You speak our language well, pig,' he greeted me.

'It is a pig's language,' I said.

He tossed the axe high into the air where it turned, its blade flashing in the weak sunlight that was trying to break the clouds. The axe was long and its double-bladed head heavy, but he caught it easily by its haft. Most men would have found it hard to wield such a massive weapon for even a short time, let alone toss and catch it, but this Saxon made it look easy. 'Arthur dared not come and fight me,' he said, 'so I shall kill you in his stead.'

His reference to Arthur puzzled me, but it was not my job to disabuse the enemy if they thought Arthur was on Mynydd Baddon. 'Arthur has better things to do than to kill vermin,' I said, 'so he asked me to slaughter you, then bury your fat corpse with your feet pointing south so that through all time you will wander lonely and hurting, never able to find your Otherworld.'

He spat. 'You squeal like a spavined pig.' The insults were a ritual, as was the single combat. Arthur disapproved of both, believing insults to be a waste of breath and single combat a waste of energy, but I had no objection to fighting an enemy champion. Such combat did serve a purpose, for if I killed this man my troops would be hugely cheered and the Saxons would see a terrible omen in his death. The risk was losing the fight, but I was a confident man in those days. The Saxon was a full hand's breadth taller than I and much broader across his shoulders, but I doubted he would be fast. He looked like a man who relied on strength to win, while I took pride in being clever as well as strong. He looked up at our rampart that was now crowded with men and women. I could not see Ceinwyn there, but Guinevere stood tall and striking among the armed men. 'Is that your whore?' the Saxon asked me, holding his axe towards her. 'Tonight she'll be mine, you worm.' He took two steps nearer me so that he was just a dozen paces away, then tossed the big axe up in the air again. His men were cheering him from the northern slope, while my men were shouting raucous encouragements from the ramparts.

'If you're frightened,' I said, 'I can give you time to empty your bowels.'

'I'll empty them on your corpse,' he spat at me. I wondered whether to take him with the spear or with Hywelbane and decided the spear would be faster so long as he did not parry the blade. It was plain that he would attack soon for he had begun to swing the axe in fast intricate curves that were dazzling to watch and I suspected his intention was to charge me with that blurring blade, knock my spear aside with his shield, then bury the axe in my neck. 'My name is Wulfger,' he said formally, 'Chief of the Sarnaed tribe of Cerdic's people, and this land shall be my land.'

I slipped my left arm out of the shield loops, transferred the shield to my right arm and hefted the spear in my left hand. I did not loop the shield on my right arm, but just gripped the wooden handle tight. Wulfger of the Sarnaed was left-handed and that meant his axe would have attacked from my unguarded side if I had kept the shield on its original arm. I was not nearly so good with a spear in my left hand, but I had a notion that might finish this fight fast. 'My name,' I answered him formally, 'is Derfel, son of Aelle, King of the Aenglish. And I am the man who put the scar on Liofa's cheek.'

My boast had been intended to unsettle him, and perhaps it did, but he showed little sign of it. Instead, with a sudden roar, he attacked and his men cheered deafeningly. Wulfger's axe was whistling in the air, his shield was poised to knock my spear aside, and he was charging like a bull, but then I hurled my own shield at his face. I hurled it sideways on, so that it spun towards him like a heavy disc of metal-rimmed wood.

The sudden sight of the heavy shield flying hard at his face forced him to raise his own shield and check the violent whirling of his blurring axe. I heard my shield clatter on his, but I was already on one knee with my spear held low and lancing upwards. Wulfger of the Sarnaed had parried my shield quickly enough, but he could not stop his heavy forward rush, not could he drop his shield in time, and so he ran straight onto that long, heavy, wicked-edged blade. I had aimed at his belly, at a spot just beneath his iron breastplate where his only protection was a thick leather jerkin, and my spear went though that leather like a needle slipping through linen. I stood up as the blade sank through leather, skin, muscle and flesh to bury itself in Wulfger's lower belly. I stood and twisted the haft, roaring my own challenge now as I saw the axe blade falter. I lunged again, the spear still deep in his belly and twisted the leaf-shaped blade a second time, and Wulfger of the Sarnaed opened his mouth as he stared at me and I saw the horror come to his eyes. He tried to lift the axe, but there was only a terrible pain in his belly and a liquefying weakness in his legs, and then he stumbled, gasped and fell onto his knees.

I let go of the spear and stepped back as I drew Hywelbane. 'This is our land, Wulfger of the Sarnaed,' I said loudly enough for his men to hear me, 'and it stays our land.' I swung the blade once, but swung it hard so that it razored through the matted mass of hair at the nape of his neck and chopped into his backbone.

He fell dead, killed in an eyeblink.

I gripped my spear shaft, put a boot on Wulfger's belly and tugged the reluctant blade free. Then I stooped and wrenched the wolf skull from his helmet. I held the yellowing bone towards our enemies, then cast it on the ground and stamped it into fragments with my foot. I undid the dead man's golden collar, then took his shield, his axe and his knife and waved those trophies towards his men, who stood watching silently. My men were dancing and howling their glee. Last of all I stooped and unbuckled his heavy bronze greaves which were decorated with images of my God, Mithras.

I stood with my plunder. 'Send the children!' I shouted at the Saxons.

'Come and fetch them!' a man called back, then with a swift slash he cut a child's throat. The other two children screamed, then they too were killed and the Saxons spat on their small bodies. For a moment I thought my men would lose control and charge across the saddle, but Issa and Niall held them to the rampart. I spat on Wulfger's body, sneered at the treacherous enemy, then took my trophies back up the hill.

I gave Wulfger's shield to one of the levy, the knife to Niall and the axe to Issa. 'Don't use it in battle,' I said, 'but you can chop wood with it.'

I carried the golden collar to Ceinwyn, but she shook her head. 'I don't like dead men's gold,' she said. She was cradling our daughters and I could see she had been weeping. Ceinwyn was not a woman to betray her emotions. She had learned as a child that she could keep her fearsome father's affections by being bright-natured, and somehow that habit of cheerfulness had worked itself deep into her soul, but she could not hide her distress now. 'You could have died!' she said. I had nothing to say, so I just crouched beside her, plucked a handful of grass and scrubbed the blood from Hywelbane's edge. Ceinwyn frowned at me. 'They killed those children?'

'Yes,' I said.

'Who were they?'

I shrugged. 'Who knows? Just children captured in a raid.'

Ceinwyn sighed and stroked Morwenna's fair hair. 'Did you have to fight?'

'Would you rather I had sent Issa?'

'No,' she admitted.

'So yes, I had to fight,' I said, and in truth I had enjoyed the fight. Only a fool wants war, but once a war starts then it cannot be fought half-heartedly. It cannot even be fought with regret, but must be waged with a savage joy in defeating the enemy, and it is that savage joy that inspires our bards to write their greatest songs about love and war. We warriors dressed for battle as we decked ourselves for love; we made ourselves gaudy, we wore our gold, we mounted crests on our silver-chased helmets, we strutted, we boasted, and when the slaughtering blades came close we felt as though the blood of the Gods coursed in our veins. A man should love peace, but if he cannot fight with all his heart then he will not have peace.

'What would we have done if you had died?' Ceinwyn asked, watching as I buckled Wulfger's fine greaves over my boots.

'You would have burned me, my love,' I said, 'and sent my soul to join Dian.' I kissed her, then carried the golden collar to Guinevere, who was delighted by the gift. She had lost her jewels with her freedom, and though she had no taste for heavy Saxon work, she placed the collar about her neck.

'I enjoyed that fight,' she said, patting the golden plates into place. 'I want you to teach me some Saxon, Derfel.'

'Of course.'

'Insults. I want to hurt them.' She laughed. 'Coarse insults, Derfel, the coarsest that you know.'

And there would be plenty of Saxons for Guinevere to insult, for still more enemy spearmen were coming to the valley. My men on the southern angle called to warn me, and I went to stand on the rampart beneath our twin banners and saw two long lines of spearmen winding down the eastern hills into the river meadows. 'They started arriving a few moments ago,' Eachern told me, 'and now there's no end to them.'

Nor was there. This was no warband coming to fight, but an army, a horde, a whole people on the march. Men, women, beasts and children, all spilling from the eastern hills into Aquae Sulis's valley. The spearmen marched in their long columns, and between the columns were herds of cattle, flocks of sheep and straggling trails of women and children. Horsemen rode on the flanks, and more horsemen clustered about the two banners that marked the coming of the Saxon Kings. This was not one army, but two, the combined forces of Cerdic and Aelle, and instead of facing Arthur in the valley of the Thames they had come here, to me, and their blades were as numerous as the stars of the sky's great belt.

I watched them come for an hour and Eachern was right. There was no end to them, and I touched the bones in Hywelbane' s hilt and knew, more surely than ever, that we were doomed.

That night the lights of the Saxon fires were like a constellation fallen into Aquae Sulis's valley; a blaze of campfires reaching far to the south and deep to the west to show where the enemy encampments followed the line of the river. There were still more fires on the eastern hills, where the rearguard of the Saxon horde camped on the high ground, but in the dawn we saw those men coming down into the valley beneath us.

It was a raw morning, though it promised to be a warm day. At sunrise, when the valley was still dark, the smoke from the Saxon fires mingled with the river mist so that it seemed as if Mynydd Baddon was a green sunlit vessel adrift in a sinister grey sea. I had slept badly, for one of the women had given birth in the night and her cries had haunted me. The child was stillborn and Ceinwyn told me it should not have been delivered for another three or four months. 'They think it's a bad omen,' Ceinwyn added bleakly.

And so it probably was, I reflected, but I dared not admit as much. Instead I tried to sound confident. 'The Gods won't abandon us,' I said.

'It was Terfa,' Ceinwyn said, naming the woman who had tortured the night with her crying. 'It would have been her first child. A boy, it was. Very tiny.' She hesitated, then smiled sadly at me. 'There's a fear, Derfel, that the Gods abandoned us at Samain.'

She was only saying what I myself feared, but again I dared not admit it. 'Do you believe that?' I asked her.

'I don't want to believe it,' she said. She thought for a few seconds and was about to say something more when a shout from the southern rampart interrupted us. I did not move and the shout came again. Ceinwyn touched my arm. 'Go,' she said.

I ran to the southern rampart to find Issa, who had stood the night's last sentry watch, staring down into the valley's smoky shadows. 'About a dozen of the bastards,' he said.

'Where?'

'See the hedge?' He pointed down the bare slope to where a white-blossomed hawthorn hedge marked the end of the hillside and the beginning of the valley's cultivated land. 'They're there. We saw them cross the wheatfield.'

'They're just watching us,' I said sourly, angry that he had called me away from Ceinwyn for such a small thing.

'I don't know, Lord. There was something odd about them. There!' He pointed again and I saw a group of spearmen clamber through the hedge. They crouched on our side of the hedge and it seemed as if they looked behind them, rather than towards us. They waited for a few minutes, then suddenly ran towards us. 'Deserters?' Issa guessed. 'Surely not!'

And it did seem strange that anyone should desert that vast Saxon army to join our beleaguered band, but Issa was right, for when the eleven men were halfway up the slope they ostentatiously turned their shields upside down. The Saxon sentries had at last seen the traitors and a score of enemy spearmen were now pursuing the fugitives, but the eleven men were far enough ahead to reach us safely. 'Bring them to me when they get here,' I told Issa, then went back to the summit's centre where I pulled on my mail armour and buckled Hywelbane to my waist. 'Deserters,' I told Ceinwyn.

Issa brought the eleven men across the grass. I recognized the shields first, for they showed Lancelot's sea-eagle with the fish in its talons, and then I recognized Bors, Lancelot's cousin and champion. He smiled nervously when he saw me, then I grinned broadly and he relaxed. 'Lord Derfel,' he greeted me. His broad face was red from the climb, and his burly body heaving to draw in breath.

'Lord Bors,' I said formally, then embraced him.

'If I am to die,' he said, 'I'd rather die on my own side.' He named his spearmen, all of them Britons who had been in Lancelot's service and all men who resented being forced to carry their spears for the Saxons. They bowed to Ceinwyn, then sat while bread, mead and salted beef were brought to them. Lancelot, they said, had marched north to join Aelle and Cerdic, and now all the Saxon forces were united in the valley beneath us. 'Over two thousand men, they reckon,' Bors said.

'I have less than three hundred.'

Bors grimaced. 'But Arthur's here, yes?'

I shook my head. 'No.'

Bors stared up at me, his open mouth full of food. 'Not here?' he said at last.

'He's somewhere up north as far as I know.'

He swallowed his mouthful, then swore quietly. 'So who is here?' he asked.

'Just me.' I gestured about the hill. 'And what you can see.'

He lifted a horn of mead and drank deeply. 'Then I reckon we will die,' he said grimly.

He had thought Arthur was on Mynydd Baddon. Indeed, Bors said, both Cerdic and Aelle believed that Arthur was on the hill and that was why they had marched south from the Thames to Aquae Sulis. The Saxons, who had first driven us to this refuge, had seen Arthur's banner on Mynydd Baddon's crest and had sent news of its presence to the Saxon Kings who had been seeking Arthur in the upper reaches of the Thames. 'The bastards know what your plans are,' Bors warned me, 'and they know Arthur wanted to fight near Corinium, but they couldn't find him there. And that's what they want to do, Derfel, they want to find Arthur before Cuneglas reaches him. Kill Arthur, they reckon, and the rest of Britain will lose heart.' But Arthur, clever Arthur, had given Cerdic and Aelle the slip, and then the Saxon kings had heard that the banner of the bear was being flaunted on a hill near Aquae

Sulis and so they had turned their ponderous force southwards and sent orders for Lancelot's forces to joint them.

'Do you have any news of Culhwch?' I asked Bors.

'He's out there somewhere,' Bors said vaguely, waving to the south. 'We never found him.' He suddenly stiffened, and I looked round to see that Guinevere was watching us. She had abandoned her prison robe and was dressed in a leather jerkin, woollen trews and long boots: a man's clothes like those she had used to wear when hunting. I later discovered she had found the clothes in Aquae Sulis and, though they were of poor quality, she somehow managed to imbue them with elegance. She had the Saxon gold at her neck, a quiver of arrows on her back, the hunter's bow in her hand and a short knife at her waist.

'Lord Bors,' she greeted her old lover's champion icily.

'Lady.' Bors stood up and gave her a clumsy obeisance.

She looked at his shield that still bore Lancelot's insignia, then raised an eyebrow. 'Are you bored with him too?' she asked.

'I'm a Briton, lady,' Bors said stiffly.

'And a brave Briton,' Guinevere said warmly. 'I think we're fortunate to have you here.' Her words were precisely right and Bors, who had been embarrassed by the encounter, suddenly looked coyly pleased. He muttered something about being happy to see Guinevere, but he was not a man who made compliments elegantly and he blushed as he spoke. 'Can I assume,' Guinevere asked him, 'that your old lord is with the Saxons?'

'He is, Lady.'

'Then I pray he comes within range of my bow,' Guinevere said.

'He might not, Lady,' Bors said, for he knew Lancelot's reluctance to place himself in danger, 'but you'll have plenty of Saxons to kill before the day's out. More than enough.'

And he was right, for beneath us, where the last of the river mist was being burned away by the sun, the Saxon horde was gathering. Cerdic and Aelle, still believing that their greatest enemy was trapped on Mynydd Baddon, were planning an overwhelming assault. It would not be a subtle attack, for no spearmen were being mustered to take us in the flank, but rather it would be a simple, crude hammerblow that would come in overwhelming force straight up Mynydd Baddon's southern face. Hundreds of warriors were

196

being gathered for the attack and their close-ranked spears glinted in the early light.

'How many are there?' Guinevere asked me.

'Too many, Lady,' I said bleakly.

'Half their army,' Bors said, and explained to her that the Saxon Kings believed that Arthur and his best men were trapped on the hilltop.

'So he's fooled them?' Guinevere asked, not without a note of pride.

'Or we have,' I said glumly, indicating Arthur's banner that stirred fitfully in the small breeze.

'So now we have to beat them,' Guinevere responded briskly, though how, I could not tell. Not since I had been trapped on Ynys Mon by Diwrnach's men had I felt so helpless, but on that grim night I had possessed Merlin for an ally and his magic had seen us out of the trap. I had no magic on my side now and I could foresee nothing but doom.

All morning long I watched the Saxon warriors assemble among the growing wheat, and I watched as their wizards danced along the lines and as their chiefs harangued the spearmen. The men in the front of the Saxon battle line were steady enough, for they were the trained warriors who had sworn oaths to their lords, but the rest of that vast assembly must have been the equivalent of our levy, the *fyrd* the Saxons called it, and those men kept wandering away. Some went to the river, others back to the camps, and from our commanding height it was like watching shepherds trying to gather a vast flock; as soon as one part of the army was assembled, another would break apart and the whole business would start over again, and all the time the Saxon drums sounded. They were using great hollow logs that they thumped with wooden clubs so that their heartbeat of death echoed from the wooded slope on the valley's far side. The Saxons would be drinking ale, bolstering the courage needed to come up into our spears. Some of my own men were guzzling mead. I discouraged it, but stopping a soldier from drinking was like keeping a dog from barking, and many of my men needed the fire that mead puts into a belly for they could count as well as I. A thousand men were coming to fight fewer than three hundred.

Bors had asked that he and his men fight in the centre of our line and I had agreed. I hoped he would die swiftly, cut down by an axe or a spear, for if he was taken alive then his death would be long and horrible. He and his men had stripped their shields back to the bare wood, and now were drinking mead, and I did not blame them.

Issa was sober. 'They'll overlap us, Lord,' he said worriedly.

'They will,' I agreed, and wished I could say something more useful, but in truth I was transfixed by the enemy preparations and helpless to know what to do about the attack. I did not doubt that my men could fight against the best Saxon spearmen, but I only had enough spearmen to make a shield wall a hundred paces wide and the Saxon attack, when it came, would be three times that width. We would fight in the centre, we would kill, and the enemy would surge around our flanks to capture the hill's summit and slaughter us from behind.

Issa grimaced. His wolf-tailed helmet was an old one of mine on which he had hammered a pattern of silver stars. His pregnant wife, Scarach, had found some vervain growing near one of the springs and Issa wore a sprig on his helmet, hoping it would keep him from harm. He offered me some of the plant, but I refused. 'You keep it,' I said.

'What do we do, Lord?' he asked.

'We can't run away,' I said. I had thought of making a desperate lunge northwards, but there were Saxons beyond the northern saddle and we would have to fight our way up that slope into their spears. We had small chance of doing that, and a much greater chance of being trapped in the saddle between two enemies on higher ground. 'We have to beat them here,' I said, disguising my conviction that we could not beat them at all. I could have fought four hundred men, maybe even six hundred, but not the thousand Saxons who were now readying themselves at the foot of the slope.

'If we had a Druid,' Issa said, then let the thought die, but I knew exactly what irked him. He was thinking that it was not good to go into battle without prayers. The Christians in our ranks were praying with their arms outstretched in imitation of their God's death and they had told me they needed no priest to intercede for them, but we pagans liked to have a Druid's curses raining on our enemies before a fight. But we had no Druid, and the absence not only denied us the power of his curses, but suggested that from this day on we would have to fight without our Gods because those Gods had fled in disgust from the interrupted rites on Mai Dun.

I summoned Pyrlig and ordered him to curse the enemy. He blanched. 'But I'm a bard, Lord, not a Druid,' he protested.

'You began the Druid's training?'

'All bards do, Lord, but I was never taught the mysteries.'

'The Saxons don't know that,' I said. 'Go down the hill, hop on one leg and curse their filthy souls to the dungheap of Annwn.'

Pyrlig did his best, but he could not keep his balance and I sensed there was more fear than vituperation in his curses. The Saxons, seeing him, sent six of their own wizards to counter his magic. The naked wizards, their hair hung with small charms and stiffened into grotesque spikes with matted cow dung, clambered up the slope to spit and curse at Pyrlig who, seeing their approach, backed nervously away. One of the Saxon magicians carried a human thigh bone that he used to chase poor Pyrlig even further up the slope and, when he saw our bard's obvious terror, the Saxon jerked his body in obscene gestures. The enemy wizards came still closer so that we could hear their shrill voices over the booming thud of the drums in the valley.

'What are they saying?' Guinevere had come to stand beside me.

'They're using charms, Lady,' I said. 'They're beseeching their Gods to fill us with fear and turn our legs to water.' I listened to the chanting again. 'They beg that our eyes be blinded, that our spears be broken and our swords blunted.' The man with the thigh bone caught sight of Guinevere and he turned on her and spat a vituperative stream of obscenities.

'What's he saying now?' she asked.

'You don't wish to know, Lady.'

'But I do, Derfel, I do.'

'Then I don't wish to tell you.'

She laughed. The wizard, only thirty paces away from us now, jerked his tattooed crotch at her and shook his head, rolled his eyes, and screamed that she was a cursed witch and promised that her womb would dry to a crust and her breasts turn sour as gall, and then there was an abrupt twang beside my ear and the wizard was suddenly silent. An arrow had transfixed his gullet, going clean through his neck so that one half of the arrow jutted behind his nape and the feathered shaft stuck out beneath his chin. He stared up at Guinevere, he gurgled, and then the bone dropped from his hand. He fingered the arrow, still staring at her, then shuddered and suddenly collapsed.

'It's considered bad luck to kill an enemy's magicians,' I said in gentle reproof.

'Not now,' Guinevere said vengefully, 'not now.' She took another arrow from her quiver and fitted it to the string, but the other five wizards had seen the fate of their fellow magician and were bounding down the hill out of range. They were shrieking angrily as they went, protesting our bad faith. They had a right to protest, and I feared that the death of the one wizard would only fill the attackers with a cold anger. Guinevere took the arrow off the bow. 'So what will they do, Derfel?' she asked me.

'In a few minutes' time,' I said, 'that great mass of men will come up the hill. You can see how they'll come,' I pointed down to the Saxon formation that was still being pushed and herded into shape, 'a hundred men in their front rank, and nine or ten men in every file to push those front men onto our spears. We can face those hundred men, Lady, but our files will only have two or three men apiece, and we won't be able to push them back down the hill. We'll stop them for a while, and the shield walls will lock, but we won't drive them backwards and when they see that all our men are locked in the fighting line, they'll send their rearward files to wrap around and take us from behind.'

Her green eyes stared at me, a slightly mocking look on her face. She was the only woman I ever knew who could look me straight in the eyes, and I always found her direct gaze unsettling. Guinevere had a knack of making a man feel like a fool, though on that day, as the Saxon drums beat and the great horde steeled themselves to climb up to our blades, she wished me nothing but success. 'Are you saying we've lost?' she asked lightly.

'I'm saying, Lady, that I don't know if I can win,' I answered grimly. I was wondering whether to do the unexpected and form my men into a wedge that would charge down the hill and pierce deep into the Saxon mass. It was possible that such an attack would surprise them and even panic them, but the danger was that my men would be surrounded by enemies on the hillside and, when the last of us was dead, the Saxons would climb to the summit and take our undefended families.

Guinevere slung the bow on her shoulder. 'We can win,' she said confidently, 'we can win easily.' For a moment I did not take her seriously. 'I can tear the heart out of them,' she said more forcefully.

I glanced at her and saw the fierce joy in her face. If she was to make a fool of any man that day it would be Cerdic and Aelle, not me. 'How can we win?' I asked her.

A mischievous look came to her face. 'Do you trust me, Derfel?'

'I trust you, Lady.'

'Then give me twenty fit men.'

I hesitated. I had been forced to leave some spearmen on the northern rampart of the hill to guard against an attack across the saddle, and I could scarce lose twenty of the remaining men who faced south; but even if I had two hundred spearmen more I knew I was going to lose this battle on the hilltop, and so I nodded. 'I'll give you twenty men from the levy,' I agreed, 'and you give me a victory.' She smiled and strode away, and I shouted at Issa to find twenty young men and send them with her. 'She's going to give us a victory!' I told him loud enough for my men to hear and they, sensing hope on a day when there was none, smiled and laughed.

Yet victory, I decided, needed a miracle, or else the arrival of allies. Where was Culhwch? All day I had expected to see his troops in the south, but there had been no sign of him and I decided he must have made a wide detour around Aquae Sulis in an attempt to join Arthur. I could think of no other troops who might come to our aid, but in truth, even if Culhwch had joined me, his numbers could not have swelled ours enough to withstand the Saxon assault.

That assault was near now. The wizards had done their work and a group of Saxon horsemen now left the ranks and spurred uphill. I shouted for my own horse, had Issa cup his hands to heave me into the saddle, then I rode down the slope to meet the enemy envoys. Bors might have accompanied me, for he was a lord, but he did not want to face the men he had just deserted and so I went alone.

Nine Saxons and three Britons approached. One of the Britons was Lancelot, as beautiful as ever in his white scale armour that dazzled in the sunlight. His helmet was silvered and crested with a pair of swan's wings that were ruffled by the small wind. His two companions were Amhar and Loholt, who rode against their father beneath Cerdic's skin-hung skull and beneath my own father's great bull skull that was spattered with fresh blood in honour of this new war. Cerdic and Aelle both climbed the hill and with them were a half-dozen Saxon chieftains; all big men in fur robes and with moustaches hanging to their sword belts. The last Saxon was an interpreter and he, like the other Saxons, rode clumsily, just as I did. Only Lancelot and the twins were good horsemen.

We met halfway down the hill. None of the horses liked the slope and all shifted nervously. Cerdic scowled up at our rampart. He could see the two banners there, and a prickle of spear points above our makeshift barricade, but nothing more. Aelle gave me a grim nod while Lancelot avoided my gaze.

'Where is Arthur?' Cerdic finally demanded of me. His pale eyes looked at me from a helmet rimmed with gold and gruesomely crested with a dead man's hand. Doubtless, I thought, a British hand. The trophy had been smoked in a fire so that its skin was blackened and its fingers hooked like claws.

'Arthur is taking his ease, Lord King,' I said. 'He left it to me to swat you away while he plans how to remove the smell of your filth from Britain.' The interpreter murmured in Lancelot's ear.

'Is Arthur here?' Cerdic demanded. Convention dictated that the leaders of armies conferred before battle, and Cerdic had construed my presence as an insult. He had expected Arthur to come and meet him, not some underling.

'He's here, Lord,' I said airily, 'and everywhere. Merlin transports him through the clouds.'

Cerdic spat. He was in dull armour, with no show other than the ghastly hand on his gold-edged helmet's crest. Aelle was dressed in his usual black fur, had gold at his wrists and neck and a single bull's horn projecting from the front of his helmet. He was the older man, but Cerdic, as ever, took the lead. His clever, pinched face gave me a dismissive glance. 'It would be best,' he said, 'if you filed down the hill and laid your weapons on the road. We shall kill some of you as a tribute to our Gods and take the rest of you as slaves, but you must give us the woman who killed our wizard. She we will kill.'

'She killed the wizard on my orders,' I said, 'in return for Merlin's beard.' It had been Cerdic who had slashed off a hank of Merlin's beard, an insult I had no mind to forgive.

'Then we shall kill you,' Cerdic said.

'Liofa tried to do that once,' I said, needling him, 'and yesterday Wulfger of the Sarnaed tried to snatch my soul, but he is the one who is back in his ancestors' sty.'

Aelle intervened. 'We won't kill you, Derfel,' he growled, 'not if you surrender.' Cerdic began to protest, but Aelle hushed him with an abrupt gesture of his maimed right hand. 'We will not kill him,' he insisted. 'Did you give your woman the ring?' he asked me.

'She wears it now, Lord King,' I said, gesturing up the hill.

'She's here?' He sounded surprised.

'With your grandchildren.'

'Let me see them,' Aelle demanded. Cerdic again protested. He was here to prepare us for slaughter, not to witness a happy family meeting, but Aelle ignored his ally's protest. 'I would like to see them once,' he told me, and so I turned and shouted uphill.

Ceinwyn appeared a moment later with Morwenna in one hand and Seren in the other. They hesitated at the rampart, then stepped delicately down the grass slope. Ceinwyn was dressed simply in a linen robe, but her hair shone gold in the spring sun and I thought, as ever, that her beauty was magical. I felt a lump in my throat and tears at my eyes as she came so lightly down the hill. Seren looked nervous, but Morwenna had a defiant look on her face. They stopped beside my horse and stared up at the Saxon Kings. Ceinwyn and Lancelot looked at each other and Ceinwyn spat deliberately on the grass to void the evil of his presence.

Cerdic pretended disinterest, but Aelle clumsily slid down from his worn leather saddle. 'Tell them I am glad to see them,' he told me, 'and tell me the children's names.'

'The older is called Morwenna,' I said, 'and the younger is Seren. It means star.' I looked at my daughters. 'This King,' I told them in British, 'is your grandfather.'

Aelle fumbled in his black robe and brought out two gold coins. He gave one each to the girls, then looked mutely at Ceinwyn. She understood what he wanted and, letting go of her daughters' hands, she stepped into his embrace. He must have stunk, for his fur robe was greasy and full of filth, but she did not flinch. When he had kissed her he stepped back, lifted her hand to his lips, and smiled to see the small chip of blue-green agate in its golden ring. 'Tell her I will spare her life, Derfel,' he said.

I told her and she smiled. 'Tell him it would be better if he went back to his own land,' she said, 'and that we would take much joy in visiting him there.'

Aelle smiled when that was translated, but Cerdic just scowled. 'This is our land!' he insisted, and his horse pawed at the ground as he spoke and my daughters backed away from his venom.

'Tell them to go,' Aelle growled at me, 'for we must talk of war.' He watched them walk uphill. 'You have your father's taste for beautiful women,' he said.

'And a British taste for suicide,' Cerdic snapped. 'Your life is promised you,' he went on, 'but only if you come down from the hill now and lay your spears on the road.'

'I shall lay them on the road, Lord King,' I said, 'with your body threaded on them.'

'You mew like a cat,' Cerdic said derisively. Then he looked past me and his expression became grimmer, and I turned to see that Guinevere was now standing on the rampart. She stood tall and long-legged in her hunter's clothes, crowned with a mass of red hair and with her bow across her shoulders so that she looked like some Goddess of war. Cerdic must have recognized her as the woman who had killed his wizard. 'Who is she?' he demanded fiercely.

'Ask your lapdog,' I said, gesturing at Lancelot, and then, when I suspected that the interpreter had not translated my words accurately, I said them again in the British tongue. Lancelot ignored me.

'Guinevere,' Amhar told Cerdic's interpreter, 'and she is my father's whore,' he added with a sneer.

I had called Guinevere worse in my time, but I had no patience to listen to Amhar's scorn. I had never held any affection for

Guinevere, she was too arrogant, too wilful, too clever and too mocking to be an easy companion, but in the last few days I had begun to admire her and suddenly I heard myself spitting insults at Amhar. I do not remember now what I said, only that anger gave my words a vicious spite. I must have called him a worm, a treacherous piece of filth, a creature of no honour, a boy who would be spitted on a man's sword before the sun died. I spat at him, cursed him and drove him and his brother down the hill with my insults, and then I turned on Lancelot. 'Your cousin Bors sends you greetings,' I told him, 'and promises to pull your belly out of your throat, and you had better pray that he does, for if I take you then I shall make your soul whine.'

Lancelot spat, but did not bother to reply. Cerdic had watched the confrontation with amusement. 'You have an hour to come and grovel before me,' he finished the conference, 'and if you don't, we shall come and kill you.' He turned his horse and kicked it on down the hill. Lancelot and the others followed, leaving only Aelle standing beside his horse.

He offered me a half smile, almost a grimace. 'It seems we must fight, my son.'

'It seems we must.'

'Is Arthur really not here?'

'Is that why you came, Lord King?' I answered, though not answering his question.

'If we kill Arthur,' he said simply, 'the war is won.'

'You must kill me first, father,' I said.

'You think I wouldn't?' he asked harshly, then held his maimed hand up to me. I clasped it briefly, then watched as he led his horse down the slope.

Issa greeted my return with a quizzical look. 'We won the battle of words,' I said grimly.

'That's a start, Lord,' he said lightly.

'But they'll finish it,' I said softly and turned to watch the enemy kings going back to their men. The drums beat on. The last of the Saxons had finally been mustered into the dense mass of men that would climb to our slaughter, but unless Guinevere really was a Goddess of war, I did not know how we could beat them.

*

The Saxon advance was clumsy at first, because the hedges about the small fields at the foot of the hill broke their careful alignment. The sun was sinking in the west for it had taken all day for this attack to be prepared, but now it was coming and we could hear the rams' horns blaring their raucous challenge as the enemy spearmen broke through the hedges and crossed the small fields.

My men began singing. We always sang before battle, and on this day, as before all the greatest of our battles, we sang the War Song of Beli Mawr. How that terrible hymn can move a man! It speaks of killing, of blood in the wheat, of bodies broken to the bone and of enemies driven like cattle to the slaughter-pen. It tells of Beli Mawr's boots crushing mountains and boasts of the widows made by his sword. Each verse of the song ends in a triumphant howl, and I could not help but weep for the defiance of the singers.

I had dismounted and taken my place in the front rank, close to Bors who stood beneath our twin banners. My cheekpieces were closed, my shield was tight on my left arm and my war spear was heavy in my right. All around me the strong voices swelled, but I did not sing because my heart was too full of foreboding. I knew what was about to happen. For a time we would fight in the shield wall, but then the Saxons would break through the flimsy thorn barricades on both our flanks and their spears would come from behind and we would be cut down man by man and the enemy would taunt our dying. The last of us to die would see the first of our women being raped, yet there was nothing we could do to stop it and so those spearmen sang and some men danced the sword dance on the rampart's top where there was no thorn barricade. We had left the centre of the rampart clear of thorns in the thin hope that it might tempt the enemy to come to our spears rather than try to outflank us.

The Saxons crossed the last hedge and began their long climb up the empty slope. Their best men were in the front rank and I saw how tight their shields were locked, how thick their spears were ranked and how brightly their axes shone. There was no sign of Lancelot's men; it seemed this slaughter would be left to the Saxons alone. Wizards preceded them, rams' horns urged them on, and above them hung the bloody skulls of their kings. Some in the front rank held leashed war-dogs that would be loosed a few yards short of our line. My father was in that front rank while Cerdic was on a horse behind the Saxon mass.

They came very slowly. The hill was steep, their armour heavy, and they felt no need to rush into this slaughter. They knew it would be a grim business, however short-lived. They would come in a shield-locked wall, and once at the rampart our shields would clash and then they would try to push us backwards. Their axes would flash over our shield rims, their spears would thrust and jab and gore. There would be grunts and howls and shrieks, and men wailing and men dying, but the enemy had the greater number of men and eventually they would outflank us and so my wolftails would die.

But now my wolftails sang as they tried to drown the harsh sound of the horns and the incessant beat of the tree drums. The Saxons laboured closer. We could see the devices on their round shields now; wolf masks for Cerdic's men, bulls for Aelle's, and in between were the shields of their warlords: hawks and eagles and a prancing horse. The dogs strained at their leashes, eager to tear holes in our wall. The wizards shrieked at us. One of them rattled a cluster of rib bones, while another scrabbled on all fours like a dog and howled his curses.

I waited at the southern angle of the summit's rampart which jutted like the prow of a boat above the valley. It was here in the centre that the first Saxons would strike. I had toyed with the idea of letting them come and then, at the very last moment, pulling back fast to make a shield-ring about our women. Yet by retreating I ceded the flat hilltop as my battlefield and gave up the advantage of the higher ground. Better to let my men kill as many of the enemy as they could before we were overwhelmed.

I tried not to think of Ceinwyn. I had not kissed her farewell, or my daughters, and maybe they would live. Maybe, amidst the horror, some spearman of Aelle's would recognize the little ring and take them safe to his King.

My men began to clash their spear shafts against their shields. They had no need to lock their shields yet. That could wait till the last moment. The Saxons looked uphill as the noise battered their ears. None of them raced ahead to throw a spear – the hill was too steep for that – but one of their war-dogs broke its leash and came loping fast up the grass. Eirrlyn, who was one of my two huntsmen, pierced it with an arrow and the dog began to yelp and run in circles with the shaft sticking from its belly. Both huntsmen began shooting at other dogs and the Saxons hauled the beasts back behind the protection of their shields. The wizards scampered away to the flanks, knowing that the battle was about to begin. A huntsman's arrow smacked into a Saxon shield, then another glanced off a helmet. Not long now. A hundred paces. I licked my dry lips, blinked sweat from my eyes and stared down at the fierce bearded faces. The enemy was shouting, yet I do not remember hearing the sound of their voices. I just remember the sound of their horns, the beat of their drums, the thump of their boots on the grass, the clink of scabbards on armour and the clash of shields touching.

'Make way!' Guinevere's voice sounded behind us, and it was full of enjoyment. 'Make way!' she called again.

I turned and saw her twenty men were pushing two of the food wagons towards the ramparts. The ox-wagons were great clumsy vehicles with solid wooden discs for wheels, and Guinevere had augmented their sheer weight with two further weapons. She had stripped the pole shafts from the front of the wagons and wedged spears in their place, while the wagon beds, instead of holding food, now carried blazing fires of thorn brush. She had turned the wagons into a massive pair of flaming missiles that she planned to roll down the hill into the enemy's packed ranks, and behind her wagons, eager to see the chaos, came an excited crowd of women and children.

'Move!' I called to my men, 'move!' They ceased singing and hurried apart, leaving the whole centre of the ramparts undefended. The Saxons were now only seventy or eighty paces away and, seeing our shield wall break apart, they scented victory and quickened their pace.

Guinevere shouted at her men to hurry and more spearmen ran to put their weight behind the smoking wagons. 'Go!' she called, 'go!' and they grunted as they shoved and tugged and as the wagons began to roll faster. 'Go! Go! Go!' Guinevere screamed at them, and still more men packed in behind the wagons to force the cumbersome vehicles up across the banked earth of the ancient rampart. For a heartbeat I thought that low earth bank would defeat us, for both the wagons slowed to a halt there and their thick smoke wreathed about our choking men, but Guinevere shouted at the spearmen again and they gritted their teeth to make one last great effort to heave the wagons over the turf wall.

'Push!' Guinevere screamed, 'push!' The wagons hesitated on the rampart, then began to tip forward as men shoved from beneath. 'Now!' Guinevere shouted and suddenly there was nothing to hold the wagons, just a steep grass slope in front and an enemy beneath. The men who had been pushing reeled away exhausted as the two flaming vehicles began to roll downhill.

The wagons went slowly at first, but then quickened and began to bounce on the uneven turf so that flaming branches were flung over the burning wagon sides. The slope steepened, and the two great missiles were hurtling now; massive weights of timber and fire that thundered down onto the appalled Saxon formation.

The Saxons had no chance. Their ranks were too tight packed for men to escape the wagons, and the wagons were well aimed for they were rumbling in smoke and flame towards the very heart of the enemy attack.

'Close up!' I shouted at my men, 'make the wall! Make the wall!'

We hurried back into position just as the wagons struck. The enemy's line had stalled and some men were trying to break away, but there was no escape for those in the direct path of the wagons. I heard a scream as the long spears fixed to the wagons' fronts drove into the mass of men, then one of the wagons reared up as its front wheels bounced on fallen bodies, yet still it drove on, smashing and burning and breaking men in its path. A shield broke in two as a wheel crushed it. The second wagon veered as it struck the Saxon line. For a heartbeat it was poised on two wheels, then it tumbled onto its side to spill a wash of fire down into the Saxon ranks. Where there had been a solid, disciplined mass, there was now only chaos, fear and panic. Even where the ranks had not been struck by the wagons there was chaos, for the impact of the two vehicles had caused the careful ranks to shudder and break.

'Charge them!' I shouted. 'Come on!'

I screamed a war shout as I jumped from the rampart. I had not meant to follow the wagons down the hill, but the destruction they had caused was so great, and the enemy's horror so evident, that now was the time to add to that horror.

We screamed as we ran down the hill. It was a scream of victory, calculated to put terror into an enemy already half beaten. The Saxons still outnumbered us, but their shield wall was broken, they were winded, and we came like avenging furies from the heights. I left my spear in a man's belly, whipped Hywelbane free of her scabbard, and laid about me like a man slashing at hay. There is no calculation in such a fight, no tactics, just a soaring delight in dominating an enemy, in killing, in seeing the fear in their eyes and watching their rearward ranks running away. I was making a mad keening noise, loving the slaughter, and beside me my wolftails hacked and stabbed and jeered at an enemy that should have been dancing on our corpses.

They still could have beaten us, for their numbers were so great, but it is hard to fight in a broken shield wall going uphill and our sudden attack had broken their spirits. Too many of the Saxons were also drunk. A drunken man fights well in victory, but in defeat he panics quickly, and though Cerdic tried to hold them to the battle, his spearmen panicked and ran. Some of my youngsters were tempted to follow further down the hill, and a handful yielded to the temptation and went too far and so paid for their temerity, but I shouted at the others to stay where they were. Most of the enemy escaped, but we had won, and to prove it we stood in the blood of Saxons and our hillside was thick with their dead, their wounded and their weapons. The overturned wagon burned on the slope, a trapped Saxon screaming beneath its weight, while the other still rumbled on until it thumped into the hedge at the foot of the hill.

Some of our women came down to plunder the dead and kill the wounded. Neither Aelle nor Cerdic were among those Saxons left on the hill, but there was one great chief who was hung with gold and wore a sword with a gold-decorated hilt in a scabbard of soft black leather criss-crossed with silver; I took the belt and sword from the dead man and carried them up to Guinevere. I knelt to her, something I had never done. 'It was your victory, Lady,' I said, 'all yours.' I offered her the sword.

She strapped it on, then lifted me up. 'Thank you, Derfel,' she said.

'It's a good sword,' I said.

'I'm not thanking you for the sword,' Guinevere said, 'but for trusting me. I always knew I could fight.'

'Better than me, Lady,' I said ruefully. Why had I not thought to use the wagons?

'Better than them!' Guinevere said, indicating the beaten Saxons. She smiled. 'And tomorrow we shall do it all over again.'

The Saxons did not return that evening. It was a lovely twilight, soft and glowing. My sentries paced the wall as the Saxon fires brightened in the spreading shadows below. We ate, and after the meal I talked with Issa's wife, Scarach, and she recruited other women and between them they found some needles, knives and thread. I had given them some cloaks that I had taken from the Saxon dead and the women worked through the dusk, then on into the night by the light of our fires.

So that next morning, when Guinevere awoke, there were three banners on Mynydd Baddon's southern rampart. There was Arthur's bear and Ceinwyn's star, but in the middle, in the place of honour as befitted a victorious warlord, there was a flag showing Guinevere's badge of a moon-crowned stag. The dawn wind lifted it, she saw the badge and I saw her smile.

While beneath us the Saxons gathered their spears again.

T HE DRUMS BEGAN AT dawn and within an hour five wizards had appeared on Mynydd Baddon's lower slopes. Today, it seemed, Cerdic and Aelle were determined to exact revenge for their humiliation.

Ravens tore at more than fifty Saxon corpses that still lay on the slope close to the charred remnants of the wagon, and some of my men wanted to drag those dead to the parapet and there make a horrid array of bodies to greet the new Saxon assault, but I forbade it. Soon, I reckoned, our own corpses would be at the Saxons' disposal and if we defiled their dead then we would be defiled in turn.

It soon became clear that this time the Saxons would not risk one assault that could be turned to chaos by a tumbling wagon. Instead they were preparing a score of columns that would climb the hill from the south, the east and the west. Each group of attackers would only number seventy or eighty men, but together the small attacks must overwhelm us. We could perhaps fight off three or four of the columns, but the others would easily get past the ramparts and so there was little to do except pray, sing, eat and, for those who needed to, drink. We promised each other a good death, meaning that we would fight to the finish and sing as long as we could, but I think we all knew the end would not be a song of defiance, but a welter of humiliation, pain and terror. It would be even worse for the women. 'Should I surrender?' I asked Ceinwyn.

She looked startled. 'It isn't for me to say.'

'I have done nothing without your advice,' I told her.

'In war,' she said, 'I have no advice to give you, except maybe to ask what will happen to the women if you don't surrender.'

'They'll be raped, enslaved, or else given as wives to men who need wives.'

'And if you do surrender?'

'Much the same,' I admitted. Only the rape would be less urgent.

She smiled. 'Then you don't need my advice after all. Go and fight, Derfel, and if I don't see you till the Otherworld, then know that you cross the bridge of swords with my love.'

I embraced her, then kissed my daughters, and went back to the jutting prow of the southern rampart to watch the Saxons start up the hill. This attack was not taking nearly so long as the first, for that had needed a mass of men to be organized and encouraged, while today the enemy needed no motivation. They came for revenge and they came in such small parties that even if we had rolled a wagon down the hill they could easily have evaded it. They did not hurry, but they had no need for haste.

I had divided my men into ten bands, each responsible for two of the Saxon columns, but I doubted that even the best of my spearmen would stand for more than three or four minutes. Most likely, I thought, my men would run back to protect their women as soon as the enemy threatened to outflank them and the fight would then collapse into a miserable one-sided slaughter around our makeshift hut and its surrounding campfires. So be it, I thought, and I walked among my men and thanked them for their services and encouraged them to kill as many Saxons as they could. I reminded them that the enemies they slew in battle would be their servants in the Otherworld, 'so kill them,' I said, 'and let their survivors recall this fight with horror.' Some of them began to sing the Death Song of Werlinna, a slow and melancholy tune that was chanted about the funeral fires of warriors. I sang with them, watching the Saxons climb nearer, and because I was singing, and because my helmet clasped me tight about the ears, I did not hear Niall of the Blackshields hail me from the hill's farther rim.

It was not till I heard the women cheering that I turned. I still saw nothing unusual, but then, above the sound of the Saxon drums, I heard the shrill, high note of a horn.

I had heard that horn-call before. I had first heard it when I was a new young spearman and Arthur had ridden to save my life, and now he came again.

He had come on horseback with his men, and Niall had shouted at me when those heavily armoured horsemen had swept through the Saxons on the hill beyond the saddle and galloped on down the slope. The women on Mynydd Baddon were running to the ramparts to watch him, for Arthur did not ride up to the summit, but led his men around the upper slope of the hill. He was in his polished scale armour and wore his gold-encrusted helmet and carried his shield of hammered silver. His great war banner was unfurled, its black bear streaming stark on a linen field that was as white as the goose feathers in Arthur's helm. His white cloak billowed from his shoulders and a pennant of white ribbon was tied about the base of his spear's long blade. Every Saxon on Mynydd Baddon's lower slopes knew who he was and knew what those heavy horses could do to their small columns. Arthur had only brought forty men, for most of his big warhorses had been stolen by Lancelot in the previous year, but forty heavily armoured men on forty horses could tear infantry into horror.

Arthur reined in beneath the southern angle of the ramparts. The wind was small, so that Guinevere's banner was not visible except as an unrecognizable flag hanging from its makeshift staff. He looked for me, and finally recognized my helmet and armour. 'I have two hundred spearmen a mile or so behind!' he shouted up at me.

'Good, Lord!' I called back, 'and welcome!'

'We can hold till the spearmen come!' he shouted, then he waved his men on. He did not go down the hill, but kept riding around Mynydd Baddon's upper slopes as though daring the Saxons to climb and challenge him.

But the sight of those horses was enough to check them because no Saxon wanted to be the first to climb into the path of those galloping spears. If the enemy had come all together they could easily have overwhelmed Arthur's men, but the curve of the hill meant that most of the Saxons were invisible to each other, and each group must have hoped that another would dare to attack the horsemen first, and thus they all hung back. Once in a while a band of braver men would clamber upwards, but whenever Arthur's horsemen came back into view they would edge nervously down the hill. Cerdic himself came to rally the men immediately below the southern angle, but when Arthur's men turned to face those Saxons they faltered. They had expected an easy battle against a small number of spearmen, and were not ready to face cavalry. Not uphill, and not Arthur's cavalry. Other horse-warriors might not have scared them, but they knew the meaning of that white cloak and of the goose-feathered plume and of the shield that shone like the very sun. It meant that death had come to them, and none was willing to climb to it.

A half-hour later Arthur's infantry came to the saddle. The Saxons who had held the hill north of the saddle fled from the arrival of our reinforcements, and those tired spearmen climbed to our ramparts with our cheers deafening them. The Saxons heard the cheers and saw the new spears showing above the ancient wall, and that finished their ambitions for the day. The columns went, and Mynydd Baddon was safe for one more turn of the sun.

Arthur pulled off his helmet as he spurred a tired Llamrei up to our banners. A breath of wind gusted and he looked up and saw Guinevere's moon-crowned stag flying beside his own bear, but the broad smile on his face did not change. Nor did he say anything about the banner as he slid from Llamrei's back. He must have known that Guinevere was with me, for Balin had seen her at Aquae Sulis and the two men whom I had sent with messages could have told him, but he pretended to know nothing. Instead, just as in the old days, and as if no coolness had ever come between us, he embraced me.

All his melancholy had fled. There was life in his face again, a verve that spread amongst my men who clustered about him to hear his news, though first he demanded news from us. He had ridden among the dead Saxons on the slope and he wanted to know how and when they had died. My men forgivably exaggerated the number who had attacked the previous day, and Arthur laughed when he heard how we had pushed two flaming wagons down the slope. 'Well done, Derfel,' he said, 'well done.'

'It wasn't me, Lord,' I said, 'but her.' I jerked my head towards Guinevere's flag. 'It was all her doing, Lord. I was ready to die, but she had other ideas.'

'She always did,' he said softly, but asked nothing more. Guinevere herself was not in sight, and he did not ask where she was. He did see Bors and insisted on embracing him and hearing his news, and only then did he climb onto the turf wall and stare down at the Saxon encampments. He stood there a long time, showing himself to a dispirited enemy, but after a while he beckoned for Bors and me to join him. 'I never planned to fight them here,' he said to us, 'but it's as good a place as any. In fact it's better than most. Are they all here?' he asked Bors.

Bors had again been drinking in anticipation of the Saxon attack, but he did his best to sound sober. 'All, Lord. Except maybe the Caer Ambra garrison. They were supposed to be chasing Culhwch.' Bors jerked his beard towards the eastern hill where still more Saxons were coming down to join the encampment. 'Maybe that's them, Lord? Or perhaps they're just foraging parties?'

'The Caer Ambra garrison never found Culhwch,' Arthur said, 'for I had a message from him yesterday. He's not far away, and Cuneglas isn't far off either. In two days we'll have five hundred more men here and then they'll only outnumber us by two to one.' He laughed. 'Well done, Derfel!'

'Well done?' I asked in some surprise. I had expected Arthur's disapproval for having been trapped so far from Corinium.

'We had to fight them somewhere,' he said, 'and you chose the place. I like it. We've got the high ground.' He spoke loudly, wanting his confidence to spread amongst my men. 'I would have been here sooner,' he added to me, 'only I wasn't certain Cerdic had swallowed the bait.'

'Bait, Lord?' I was confused.

'You, Derfel, you.' He laughed and jumped down from the rampart. 'War is all accident, isn't it? And by accident you found a place we can beat them.'

'You mean they'll wear themselves out climbing the hill?' I asked.

'They won't be so foolish,' he said cheerfully. 'No, I fear we shall have to go down and fight them in the valley.'

'With what?' I asked bitterly, for even with Cuneglas's troops we would be terribly outnumbered.

'With every man we have,' Arthur said confidently. 'But no women, I think. It's time we moved your families somewhere safer.'

Our women and children did not go far; there was a village an hour to the north and most found shelter there. Even as they left Mynydd Baddon, more of Arthur's spearmen arrived from the north. These were the men Arthur had been gathering near Corinium and they were among the best in Britain. Sagramor came with his hardened warriors and, like Arthur, he went to the high southern angle of Mynydd Baddon from where he could stare down at the enemy and so that they could look up and see his lean, black-armoured figure on their skyline. A rare smile came to his face. 'Over-confidence makes them into fools,' he said scornfully. 'They've trapped themselves in the low ground and they won't move now.'

'They won't?'

'Once a Saxon builds a shelter he doesn't like being marched again. It'll take Cerdic a week or more to dig them out of that valley.' The Saxons and their families had indeed made themselves comfortable, and by now the river valley resembled two straggling villages of small thatched huts. One of those two villages was close by Aquae Sulis, while the other was two miles east where the river valley turned sharp south. Cerdic's men were in those eastern huts, while Aelle's spearmen were either quartered in the town or in the newly built shelters outside. I had been surprised that the Saxons had used the town for shelter rather than just burning it, but in every dawn a straggling procession of men came from the gates, leaving behind the homely sight of cooking smoke rising from Aquae Sulis's thatched and tiled roofs. The initial Saxon invasion had been swift, but now their impetus was gone. 'And why have they split their army into two?' Sagramor asked me, staring incredulously at the great gap between Aelle's encampment and Cerdic's huts.

'To leave us only one place to go,' I said, 'straight down there,' I pointed into the valley, 'where we'll be trapped between them.'

'And where we can keep them divided,' Sagramor pointed out happily, 'and in a few days they'll have disease down there.' Disease always seemed to spread whenever an army settled in one place. It had been just such a plague that had stopped Cerdic's last invasion of Dumnonia, and a fiercely contagious sickness that had weakened our own army when we had marched on London.

I feared that such a disease might weaken us now, but for some reason we were spared, perhaps because our numbers were still small or perhaps because Arthur scattered his army along the three miles of high crestline that ran behind Mynydd Baddon. I and my

217

men stayed on the mount, but the newly arrived spearmen held the line of northern hills. For the first two days after Arthur's arrival the enemy could still have captured those hills because their summits were thinly garrisoned, but Arthur's horsemen were continually on show and Arthur kept his spearmen moving among the crest's trees to suggest that his numbers were greater than they really were. The Saxons watched, but made no attack, and then, on the third day after Arthur's arrival, Cuneglas and his men arrived from Powys and we were able to garrison the whole long crest with strong picquets who could summon help if any Saxon attack did threaten. We were still heavily outnumbered, but we held the high ground and now had the spears to defend it.

The Saxons should have left the valley. They could have marched to the Severn and laid siege to Glevum, and we would have been forced to abandon our high ground and follow them, but Sagramor was right; men who have made themselves comfortable are reluctant to move and so Cerdic and Aelle stubbornly stayed in the river valley where they believed they were laying siege to us when in truth we were besieging them. They finally did make some attacks up the hills, but none of those assaults were pressed home. The Saxons would swarm up the hills, but when a shield line appeared at the ridge top ready to oppose them and a troop of Arthur's heavy horsemen showed on their flank with levelled spears, their ardour would fade and they would sidle back to their villages, and each Saxon failure only increased our confidence.

That confidence was so high that, after Cuneglas's army arrived, Arthur felt able to leave us. I was astonished at first, for he offered no explanation other than he had an important errand that lay a day's long ride northwards. I suppose my astonishment must have showed, for he laid an arm on my shoulders. 'We haven't won yet,' he told me.

'I know, Lord.'

'But when we do, Derfel, I want this victory to be overwhelming. No other ambition would take me away from here.' He smiled. 'Trust me?'

'Of course, Lord.'

He left Cuneglas in command of our army, but with strict orders that we were to make no attacks into the valley. The Saxons were to be left imagining that they had us cornered, and to help that deception a handful of volunteers pretended to be deserters and ran to the Saxon camps with news that our men were in such low spirits that some were running away rather than face a fight, and that our leaders were in furious dispute over whether to stay and face a Saxon attack or run north to beg for shelter in Gwent.

'I'm still not sure I see a way to end this,' Cuneglas admitted to me on the day after Arthur had left. 'We're strong enough to keep them from the high ground,' he went on, 'but not strong enough to go down into the valley and beat them.'

'So maybe Arthur's gone to fetch help, Lord King?' I suggested.

'What help?' Cuneglas asked.

'Culhwch perhaps?' I said, though that was unlikely because Culhwch was said to be east of the Saxons, and Arthur was riding north. 'Oengus mac Airem?' I offered. The King of Demetia had promised his Blackshield army, but those Irishmen had still not come.

'Oengus, maybe,' Cuneglas agreed, 'but even with the Black-shields we won't have enough men to beat those bastards.' He nodded down into the valley. 'We need Gwent's spearmen to do that.'

'And Meurig won't march,' I said.

'Meurig won't march,' Cuneglas agreed, 'but there are some men in Gwent who will. They still remember Lugg Vale.' He offered me a wry smile, for on that occasion Cuneglas had been our enemy and the men of Gwent, who were our allies, had feared to march against the army led by Cuneglas's father. Some in Gwent were still ashamed of that failure, a shame made worse because Arthur had won without their help, and I supposed it possible that, if Meurig permitted it, Arthur might lead some of those volunteers south to Aquae Sulis; but I still did not see how he could collect enough men to let us go down into that nest of Saxons and slaughter them.

'Perhaps,' Guinevere suggested, 'he's gone to find Merlin?'

Guinevere had refused to leave with the other women and children, insisting that she would see the battle through to defeat or victory. I thought Arthur might insist that she left, but whenever Arthur had come to the hilltop Guinevere had hidden herself, usually in the crude hut we had made on the plateau, and it was only after Arthur left that she reappeared. Arthur surely knew that she had remained on Mynydd Baddon, for he had watched our women leave with a careful eye and he must have seen she was not among them, but he had said nothing. Nor, when Guinevere emerged, did she mention Arthur, though she did smile whenever she saw that he had allowed her banner to remain on the ramparts. I had originally encouraged her to leave the mount, but she had scorned my suggestion and none of my men had wanted her to go. They ascribed their survival to Guinevere, and rightly too, and their reward was to equip her for battle. They had taken a fine mail shirt from a rich Saxon corpse and, once the blood was scrubbed from the mail's links, they had presented it to Guinevere, they had painted her symbol on a captured shield, and one of my men had even yielded his own prized wolftail helmet, so that she was now dressed like the rest of my spearmen, though being Guinevere she managed to make the wargear look disturbingly seductive. She had become our talisman, a heroine to all my men.

'No one knows where Merlin is,' I said, responding to her suggestion.

'There was a rumour he was in Demetia,' Cuneglas said, 'so maybe he'll come with Oengus?'

'But your Druid has come?' Guinevere asked Cuneglas.

'Malaine is here,' Cuneglas confirmed, 'and he can curse well enough. Not like Merlin, perhaps, but well enough.'

'What about Taliesin?' Guinevere asked.

Cuneglas showed no surprise that she had heard of the young bard, for clearly Taliesin's fame was spreading swiftly. 'He went to seek Merlin,' he said.

'And is he truly good?' Guinevere asked.

'Truly,' Cuneglas said. 'He can sing eagles from the sky and salmon from their pools.'

'I pray we shall hear him soon,' Guinevere said, and indeed those strange days on that sunny hilltop did seem more suited to singing than to fighting. The spring had become fine, summer was not far off, and we lazed on the warm grass and watched our enemies who seemed struck by a sudden helplessness. They attempted their few futile attacks on the hills, but made no real effort to leave the valley. We later heard they were arguing. Aelle had wanted to combine all the Saxon spearmen and strike north into the hills, so splitting our army into two parts that could be destroyed separately, but Cerdic preferred to wait until our food ran short and our confidence ebbed, though that was a vain hope for we had plenty of food and our confidence was increasing every day. It was the Saxons who went hungry, for Arthur's light horsemen harried their foraging parties, and it was Saxon confidence that waned, for after a week we saw mounds of fresh earth appear on the meadows by their huts and we knew that the enemy were digging graves for their dead. The disease that turns the bowels to liquid and robs a man of his strength had come to the enemy, and the Saxons weakened every day. Saxon women staked fish traps in the river to find food for their children, Saxon men dug graves, and we lay in the high sun and talked of bards.

Arthur returned the day after the first Saxon graves were dug. He spurred his horse across the saddle and up Mynydd Baddon's steep northern slope, prompting Guinevere to pull on her new helmet and squat among a group of my men. Her red hair flaunted itself under the helmet's rim like a banner, but Arthur pretended not to notice. I had walked to meet him and, halfway across the hill's summit, I stopped and stared at him in astonishment.

His shield was a circle of willow boards covered in leather, and over the leather was hammered a thin sheet of polished silver that shone with the reflected sunlight, but now there was a new symbol on his shield. It was the cross; a red cross, made from cloth strips that had been gummed onto the silver. The Christian cross. He saw my astonishment and grinned. 'Do you like it, Derfel?'

'You've become a Christian, Lord?' I sounded appalled.

'We've all become Christians,' he said, 'you as well. Heat a spear blade and burn the cross into your shields.'

I spat to avert evil. 'You want us to do what, Lord?'

'You heard me, Derfel,' he said, then slid off Llamrei's back and walked to the southern ramparts from where he could stare down at the enemy. 'They're still here,' he said, 'good.'

Cuneglas had joined me and overheard Arthur's previous words. 'You want us to put a cross on our shields?' he asked.

'I can demand nothing of you, Lord King,' Arthur said, 'but if you would place a cross on your shield, and on your men's shields, I would be grateful.'

'Why?' Cuneglas demanded fiercely. He was famous for his opposition to the new religion.

'Because,' Arthur said, still gazing down at the enemy, 'the cross is the price we pay for Gwent's army.'

Cuneglas stared at Arthur as though he hardly dared believe his ears.

'Meurig is coming?' I asked.

'No,' Arthur said, turning to us, 'not Meurig. King Tewdric is coming. Good Tewdric.'

Tewdric was Meurig's father, the king who had given up his throne to become a monk, and Arthur had ridden to Gwent to plead with the old man. 'I knew it was possible,' Arthur told me, 'because Galahad and I have been talking to Tewdric all winter.' At first, Arthur said, the old King had been reluctant to give up his pious, scrimped life, but other men in Gwent had added their voices to Arthur and Galahad's pleadings and, after nights spent praying in his small chapel, Tewdric had reluctantly declared he would temporarily take back his throne and lead Gwent's army south. Meurig had fought the decision, which he rightly saw as a reproof and a humiliation, but Gwent's army had supported their old King and so now they were marching south. 'There was a price,' Arthur admitted. 'I had to bow my knee to their God and promise to ascribe victory to Him, but I'll ascribe victory to any God Tewdric wants so long as he brings his spearmen.'

'And the rest of the price?' Cuneglas asked shrewdly.

Arthur made a wry face. 'They want you to let Meurig's missionaries into Powys.'

'Just that?' Cuneglas asked.

'I might have given the impression,' Arthur admitted, 'that you would welcome them. I'm sorry, Lord King. The demand was only sprung on me two days ago, and it was Meurig's idea, and Meurig's face has to be saved.' Cuneglas grimaced. He had done his best to keep Christianity from his kingdom, reckoning that Powys did not need the acrimony that always followed the new faith, but he made no protest to Arthur. Better Christians in Powys, he must have decided, than Saxons.

'Is that all you promised Tewdric, Lord?' I asked Arthur suspiciously. I was remembering Meurig's demand to be given Dumnonia's throne and Arthur's longing to be rid of that responsibility.

'These treaties always have a few details that aren't worth bothering about,' Arthur responded airily, 'but I did promise to release Sansum. He is now the Bishop of Dumnonia! And a royal counsellor again. Tewdric insisted on it. Every time I knock our good Bishop down he bobs up again.' He laughed.

'Is that all you promised, Lord?' I asked again, still suspicious.

'I promised enough, Derfel, to make sure Gwent marches to our aid,' Arthur said firmly, 'and they have undertaken to be here in two days with six hundred prime spearmen. Even Agricola decided he wasn't too old to fight. You remember Agricola, Derfel?'

'Of course I remember him, Lord,' I said. Agricola, Tewdric's old warlord, might be long in years now, but he was still one of Britain's most famous warriors.

'They're all coming from Glevum,' Arthur pointed west to where the Glevum road showed in the river valley, 'and when they come I'll join him with my men and together we'll attack straight down the valley.' He was standing on the rampart from where he stared down into the deep valley, but in his mind he was not seeing the fields and roads and wind-ruffled crops, nor the stone graves of the Roman cemetery, but instead he was watching the whole battle unfold before his eyes. 'The Saxons will be confused at first,' he went on, 'but eventually there'll be a mass of enemy hurrying along that road,' he pointed down to the Fosse Way immediately beneath Mynydd Baddon, 'and you, my Lord King,' he bowed to Cuneglas, 'and you, Derfel,' he jumped down from the low rampart and poked a finger into my belly, 'will attack them on the flank. Straight down the hill and into their shields! We'll link up with you,' he curved his hand to show how his troops would curl about the northern flank of the Saxons, 'and then we'll crush them against the river.'

Arthur would come from the west and we would attack from the north. 'And they'll escape eastwards,' I said sourly.

Arthur shook his head. 'Culhwch will march north tomorrow to join Oengus mac Airem's Blackshields, and they're coming down from Corinium right now.' He was delighted with himself, and no wonder, for if it all worked then we would surround the enemy and afterwards slaughter him. But the plan was not without risk. I guessed that once Tewdric's men arrived and Oengus's Blackshields joined us then our numbers would not be much smaller than the Saxons, but Arthur was proposing to divide our army into three parts and if the Saxons kept their heads they could destroy each part separately. But if they panicked, and if our attacks came hard and furious, and if they were confused by the noise and dust and horror, we might just drive them like cattle to the slaughter. 'Two days,' Arthur said, 'just two days. Pray that the Saxons don't hear of it, and pray that they stay where they are.' He called for Llamrei, glanced across at the red-haired spearman, then went to join Sagramor on the ridge beyond the saddle.

On the night before battle we all burned crosses onto our shields. It was a small price to pay for victory, though not, I knew, the full price. That would be paid in blood. 'I think, Lady,' I told Guinevere that night, 'that you had best stay up here tomorrow.'

She and I were sharing a horn of mead. I had found that she liked to talk late in the night and I had fallen into the habit of sitting by her fire before I slept. Now she laughed at my suggestion that she should stay on Mynydd Baddon while we went down to fight. 'I always used to think you were a dull man, Derfel,' she said, 'dull, unwashed and stolid. Now I've begun to like you, so please don't make me think I was right about you all along.'

'Lady,' I pleaded, 'the shield wall is no place for a woman.'

'Nor is prison, Derfel. Besides, do you think you can win without me?' She was sitting in the open mouth of the hut we had made from the wagons and trees. She had been given one whole end of the hut for her quarters and that night she had invited me to share a supper of scorched beef cut from the flank of one of the oxen that had hauled the wagons to Mynydd Baddon's summit. Our cooking fire was dying now, sifting smoke towards the bright stars that arched across the world. The sickle moon was low over the southern hills, outlining the sentries who paced our ramparts. 'I want to see it through to the end,' she said, her eyes bright in the shadows. 'I haven't enjoyed anything so much in years, Derfel, not in years.'

'What will happen in the valley tomorrow, Lady,' I said, 'will not be enjoyable. It will be bitter work.'

'I know,' she paused, 'but your men believe I bring them victory. Will you deny them my presence when the work is hard?'

'No, Lady,' I yielded. 'But stay safe, I beg you.'

She smiled at the vehemence of my words. 'Is that a prayer for my survival, Derfel, or a fear that Arthur will be angry with you if I come to harm?'

I hesitated. 'I think he might be angry, Lady,' I admitted.

Guinevere savoured that answer for a while. 'Did he ask about me?' she finally enquired.

'No,' I said truthfully, 'not once.'

She stared into the remnants of the fire. 'Maybe he is in love with Argante,' she said wistfully.

'I doubt he can even stand the sight of her,' I answered. A week before I would never have been so frank, but Guinevere and I were much closer now. 'She's too young for him,' I went on, 'and not nearly clever enough.'

She looked up at me, a challenge in her fire-glossed eyes. 'Clever,' she said. 'I used to think I was clever. But you all think I'm a fool, don't you?'

'No, Lady.'

'You were always a bad liar, Derfel. That's why you were never a courtier. To be a good courtier you must lie with a smile.' She stared into the fire. She was silent a long time, and when she spoke again the gentle mockery was gone from her voice. Maybe it was the nearness of battle that drove her to a layer of truth I had never heard from her before. 'I was a fool,' she said quietly, so quietly I had to lean forward to hear her over the crackling of the fire and the melody of my men's songs. 'I tell myself now that it was a kind of madness,' she went on, 'but I don't think it was. It was nothing but ambition.' She went quiet again, watching the small flickering flames. 'I wanted to be a Caesar's wife.'

'You were,' I said.

She shook her head. 'Arthur's no Caesar. He's not a tyrant, but I think I wanted him to be a tyrant, someone like Gorfyddyd.' Gorfyddyd had been Ceinwyn and Cuneglas's father, a brutal King of Powys, Arthur's enemy, and, if rumour was true, Guinevere's lover. She must have been thinking about that rumour, for she suddenly challenged me with a direct gaze. 'Did I ever tell you he tried to rape me?'

'Yes, Lady,' I said.

'It wasn't true.' She spoke bleakly. 'He didn't just try, he did rape me. Or I told myself it was rape.' Her words were coming in short spasms, as if the truth was a very hard thing to admit. 'But maybe it wasn't rape. I wanted gold, honour, position.' She was fiddling with the hem of her jerkin, stripping small lengths of linen from the frayed weave. I was embarrassed, but I did not interrupt, because I knew she wanted to talk. 'But I didn't get them from him. He knew exactly what I wanted, but knew better what he wanted for himself, and he never intended to pay my price. Instead he betrothed me to Valerin. Do you know what I was going to do with Valerin?' Her eyes challenged me again, and this time the gloss on them was not just fire, but a sheen of tears.

'No, Lady.'

'I was going to make him King of Powys,' she said vengefully. 'I was going to use Valerin to revenge myself on Gorfyddyd. I could have done it, too, but then I met Arthur.'

'At Lugg Vale,' I said carefully, 'I killed Valerin.'

'I know you did.'

'And there was a ring on his finger, Lady,' I went on, 'with your badge on it.'

She stared at me. She knew what ring I meant. 'And it had a lover's cross?' she asked quietly.

'Yes, Lady,' I said, and touched my own lover's ring, the twin of Ceinwyn's ring. Many folk wore lovers' rings incised with a cross, but not many had rings with crosses made from gold taken from the Cauldron of Clyddno Eiddyn as Ceinwyn and I did.

'What did you do with the ring?' Guinevere asked.

'I threw it in the river.'

'Did you tell anyone?'

'Only Ceinwyn,' I said. 'And Issa knows,' I added, 'because he found the ring and brought it to me.'

'And you didn't tell Arthur?'

'No.'

She smiled. 'I think you have been a better friend than I ever knew, Derfel.'

'To Arthur, Lady. I was protecting him, not you.'

'I suppose you were, yes.' She looked back into the fire. 'When this is all over,' she said, 'I shall try to give Arthur what he wants.'

'Yourself?'

My suggestion seemed to surprise her. 'Does he want that?' she asked.

'He loves you,' I said. 'He might not ask about you, but he looks for you every time he comes here. He looked for you even when you were in Ynys Wydryn. He never talked to me about you, but he wearied Ceinwyn's ears.'

Guinevere grimaced. 'Do you know how cloying love can be, Derfel? I don't want to be worshipped. I don't want every whim granted. I want to feel there's something biting back.' She spoke vehemently, and I opened my mouth to defend Arthur, but she gestured me to silence. 'I know, Derfel,' she said, 'I have no right to want anything now. I shall be good, I promise you.' She smiled. 'Do you know why Arthur is ignoring me now?'

'No, Lady.'

'Because he does not want to face me till he has victory.'

I thought she was probably right, but Arthur had shown no overt sign of his affection and so I thought it best to sound a note of warning. 'Maybe victory will be satisfaction enough for him,' I said.

Guinevere shook her head. 'I know him better than you, Derfel. I know him so well I can describe him in one word.'

I tried to think what that word would be. Brave? Certainly, but that left out all his care and dedication. I wondered if dedicated was a better word, but that did not describe his restlessness. Good? he was certainly good, but that plain word obscured the anger that could make him unpredictable. 'What is the word, Lady?' I asked.

'Lonely,' Guinevere said, and I remembered that Sagramor in Mithras's cave had used the very same word. 'He's lonely,' Guinevere said, 'like me. So let's give him victory and maybe he won't be lonely again.'

'The Gods keep you safe, Lady,' I said.

'The Goddess, I think,' she said, and saw the look of horror on my face. She laughed. 'Not Isis, Derfel, not Isis.' It had been Guinevere's worship of Isis that had led her to Lancelot's bed and to Arthur's misery. 'I think,' she went on, 'that tonight I will pray to Sulis. She seems more appropriate.'

'I'll add my prayers to yours, Lady.'

She held out a hand to check me as I rose to leave. 'We're going to win, Derfel,' she said earnestly, 'we're going to win, and everything will be changed.'

We had said that so often, and nothing ever was. But now, at Mynydd Baddon, we would try again.

We sprang our trap on a day so beautiful that the heart ached. It promised to be a long day too, for the nights were growing ever shorter and the long evening light lingered deep into the shadowed hours.

On the evening before the battle Arthur had withdrawn his own troops from all along the hills behind Mynydd Baddon. He ordered those men to leave their campfires burning so that the Saxons would believe they were still in place, then he took them west to join the men of Gwent who were approaching on the Glevum road. Cuneglas's warriors also left the hills, but they came to the summit of Mynydd Baddon where, with my men, they waited.

Malaine, Powys's chief Druid, went among the spearmen during the night. He distributed vervain, elf stones and scraps of dried mistletoe. The Christians gathered and prayed together, though I noted how many accepted the Druid's gifts. I prayed beside the ramparts, pleading with Mithras for a great victory, and after that I tried to sleep, but Mynydd Baddon was restless with the murmur of voices and the monotonous sound of stones on steel.

I had already sharpened my spear and put a new edge on Hywelbane. I never let a servant sharpen my weapons before battle, but did it myself and did it as obsessively as all my men. Once I was sure the weapons were as sharp as I could hone them I lay close to Guinevere's shelter. I wanted to sleep but I could not shake the fear of standing in a shield wall. I watched for omens, fearing to see an owl, and I prayed again. I must have slept in the end, but it was a fitful dream-racked sleep. It had been so long since I had fought in a shield wall, let alone broken an enemy's wall.

I woke cold, early and shivering. Dew lay thick. Men were grunting and coughing, pissing and groaning. The hill stank, for although we had dug latrines there was no stream to carry the dirt away. 'The smell and sound of men,' Guinevere's wry voice spoke from the shadow of her shelter.

'Did you sleep, Lady?' I asked.

'A little.' She crawled out under the low branch that served as roof and door. 'It's cold.'

'It will be warm soon.'

She crouched beside me, swathed in her cloak. Her hair was tousled and her eyes were puffy from sleep. 'What do you think about in battle?' she asked me.

'Staying alive,' I said, 'killing, winning.'

'Is that mead?' she asked, gesturing at the horn in my hand.

'Water, Lady. Mead slows a man in battle.'

She took the water from me, splashed some on her eyes and drank the rest. She was nervous, but I knew I could never persuade her to stay on the hill. 'And Arthur,' she asked, 'what does he think about in battle?'

I smiled. 'The peace that follows the fighting, Lady. He believes that every battle will be the last.'

'Yet of battles,' she said dreamily, 'there will be no end.'

'Probably never,' I agreed, 'but in this battle, Lady, stay close to me. Very close.'

'Yes, Lord Derfel,' she said mockingly, then dazzled me with a smile. 'And thank you, Derfel.'

We were in armour by the time the sun flared behind the eastern hills to touch the scrappy clouds crimson and throw a deep shadow across the valley of Saxons. The shadow thinned and shrank as the sun climbed. Wisps of mist curled from the river, thickening the smoke from the campfires amongst which the enemy moved with an unusual energy. 'Something's brewing down there,' Cuneglas said to me.

'Maybe they know we're coming?' I guessed.

'Which will make life harder,' Cuneglas said grimly, though if the Saxons did have wind of our plans, they showed no evident preparation. No shield wall was formed to face Mynydd Baddon, and no troops marched west towards the Glevum road. Instead, as the sun rose high enough to burn the mist from the river banks, it appeared as if they had at last decided to abandon the place altogether and were preparing to march, though whether they planned to go west, north or south it was hard to tell for their first task was to collect their wagons, pack-horses, herds and flocks. From our height it looked like an ant's nest kicked into chaos, but gradually some order emerged. Aelle's men gathered their baggage just outside Aquae Sulis's northern gate, while Cerdic's men organized their march beside their encampment on the river's bend. A handful of huts were burning, and doubtless they planned to fire both of their encampments before they left. The first men to go were a troop of lightly armed horsemen who rode westwards past Aquae Sulis, taking the Glevum road. 'A pity,' Cuneglas said quietly. The horsemen were scouting the route the Saxons hoped to take, and they were riding straight towards Arthur's surprise attack.

We waited. We would not go down the hill until Arthur's force was well within sight, and then we had to go fast to fill the gap between Aelle's men and Cerdic's troops. Aelle would have to face Arthur's fury while Cerdic would be prevented from helping his ally by my spearmen and by Cuneglas's troops. We would almost certainly be outnumbered, but Arthur hoped he could break through Aelle's men to bring his troops to our aid. I glanced to my left, hoping for a sight of Oengus's men on the Fosse Way, but that distant road was still empty. If the Blackshields did not come, then Cuneglas and I would be stranded between the two halves of the Saxon army. I looked at my men, noting their nervousness. They could not see down into the valley, for I had insisted they stay hidden until we launched our flank attack. Some had their eyes closed, a few Christians knelt with arms outstretched while other men stroked sharpening stones along spear blades already quickened to a razor's edge. Malaine the Druid was chanting a spell of protection, Pyrlig was praying and Guinevere was staring at me wide-eyed as though she could tell from my expression what was about to happen.

The Saxon scouts had disappeared in the west, but now they suddenly came galloping back. Dust spurted from their horses' hoofs. Their speed was enough to tell us that they had seen Arthur and soon, I thought, that tangled flurry of Saxon preparations would turn into a wall of shields and spears. I gripped my own spear's long ash shaft, closed my eyes and sent a prayer winging up through the blue to wherever Bel and Mithras were listening.

'Look at them!' Cuneglas exclaimed while I was praying, and I opened my eyes to see Arthur's attack filling the western end of the valley. The sun shone in their faces and glinted off hundreds of naked blades and polished helmets. To the south, beside the river, Arthur's horsemen were spurring ahead to capture the bridge south of Aquae Sulis while the troops of Gwent marched in a great line across the centre of the valley. Tewdric's men wore Roman gear; bronze breastplates, red cloaks and thick plumed helmets, so that from Mynydd Baddon's summit they appeared as phalanxes of crimson and gold beneath a host of banners that showed, instead of Gwent's black bull, red Christian crosses. To the north of them were Arthur's spearmen, led by Sagramor under his vast black standard that was held on a pole surmounted by a Saxon skull. To this day I can close my eyes and see that army advancing, see the wind stirring the ripple of flags above their steady lines, see the dust rising from the road behind them and see the growing crops trampled flat where they had passed.

While in front of them was panic and chaos. Saxons ran to find armour, to save their wives, to seek their chiefs or to rally in groups that slowly joined to make the first shield wall close to their encampment by Aquae Sulis, but it was a scant wall, thin and ill-manned, and I saw a horseman wave it back. To our left I could see that Cerdic's men were quicker in forming their ranks, but they were still more than two miles from Arthur's advancing troops which meant that Aelle's men would have to take the brunt of the attack. Behind that attack, ragged and dark in the distance, our levy was advancing with scythes, axes, mattocks and clubs.

I saw Aelle's banner raised among the graves of the Roman cemetery, and saw his spearmen hurry back to rally under its bloody skull. The Saxons had already abandoned Aquae Sulis, their western encampment and the baggage that had been collected outside the city, and maybe they hoped Arthur's men would pause to plunder the wagons and pack-horses, but Arthur had seen that danger and so led his men well to the north of the city's wall. Gwentian spearmen had garrisoned the bridge, leaving the heavy horsemen free to ride up behind that gold and crimson line. Everything seemed to happen so slowly. From Mynydd Baddon we had an eagle's view and we could see the last Saxons fleeing over Aquae Sulis's crumbled wall, we could see Aelle's shield wall at last hardening and we could see Cerdic's men hurrying along the road to reinforce them and we silently urged Arthur and Tewdric on, wanting them to crush Aelle's men before Cerdic could join the battle, but it seemed as though the attack had slowed to a snail's pace. Mounted messengers darted between the troops of spearmen, but no one else seemed to hurry.

Aelle's forces had pulled back a half-mile from Aquae Sulis before forming their line and now they waited for Arthur's attack. Their wizards were capering in the fields between the armies, but I could see no Druids in front of Tewdric's men. They marched under their Christian God, and at last, after straightening their shield wall, they closed on the enemy. I expected to see a conference between the lines as the leaders of the armies exchanged their ritual insults and while the two shield walls judged each other. I have known shield walls stare at each other for hours while men summoned the courage to charge, but those Christians of Gwent did not check their pace. There was no meeting of opposing leaders and no time for the Saxon wizards to cast their spells, for the Christians simply lowered their spears, hefted their oblong shields that were painted with the cross, and marched straight through the Roman graves and into the enemy's shields.

We heard the shield clash on the hill. It was a dull grinding sound, like thunder from under the earth, and it was the sound of hundreds of shields and spears striking as two great armies smashed head to head. The men of Gwent were stopped, held by the weight of the Saxons who heaved against them, and I knew men were dying down there. They were being speared, being chopped by axes, being trampled underfoot. Men were spitting and snarling over their shield rims, and the press of men would be so great that a sword could hardly be lifted in the crush.

Then Sagramor's warriors struck from the northern flank. The Numidian had plainly hoped to outflank Aelle, but the Saxon king had seen the danger and sent some of his reserve troops to form a line that took Sagramor's charge on their shields and spears. Again the splintering crash of shield striking shield sounded, and then, to us who had the eagle's view, the battle became strangely still. Two throngs of men were locked together, and those in the rear were shoving the ones in front and the ones in front were struggling to loosen their spears and thrust them forward again, and all the while Cerdic's men were hurrying along the Fosse Way beneath us. Once those men reached the battle they would easily outflank Sagramor. They could wrap around his flank and take his shield wall in the rear, and that was why Arthur had kept us on the hill.

Cerdic must have guessed we were still there. He could see nothing from the valley, for our men were hidden behind Mynydd Baddon's low ramparts, but I saw him gallop his horse to a group of men and point them up the slope. It was time, I reckoned, for us to go, and I looked at Cuneglas. He looked at me at the same time and offered me a smile. 'The Gods be with you, Derfel.'

'And you, Lord King.' I touched his offered hand, then pressed my palm against my coat of mail to feel the reassuring lump of Ceinwyn's brooch beneath.

Cuneglas stepped onto the rampart and turned to face us. 'I'm not a man for speeches,' he shouted, 'but there are Saxons down there, and you're reckoned the best killers of Saxons in Britain. So come and prove it! And remember! Once you reach the valley keep the shield wall tight! Keep it tight! Now, come!'

We cheered as we spilled over the hill's rim. Cerdic's men, those who had been sent to investigate the summit, checked, then retreated as more and more of our spearmen appeared above them. We went down that hill five hundred strong, and we went fast, angling westwards to strike against the leading troops of Cerdic's reinforcements.

The ground was tussocky, steep and rough. We did not go down in any order, but raced each other to reach the bottom, and there, after running through the field of trampled wheat and clambering through two hedges that were tangling with thorns, we formed our wall. I took the left side of the line, Cuneglas the right, and once we were properly formed and our shields were touching, I shouted at my men to go forward. A Saxon shield wall was forming in the field in front of us as men hurried from the road to oppose us. I looked to my right as we advanced and saw what a huge gap there was between us and Sagramor's men, a gap so big I could not even see his banner. I hated the thought of that gap, hated to think what horror could pour through it and so come behind us, but Arthur had been adamant. Do not hesitate, he said, do not wait for Sagramor to reach you, but just attack. It must have been Arthur, I thought, who had persuaded the Christians of Gwent to attack without pause. He was trying to panic the Saxons by denying them time, and now it was our turn to go fast into battle.

The Saxon wall was makeshift and small, maybe two hundred of Cerdic's men who had not expected to fight here, but who had thought to add their weight to Aelle's rearmost ranks. They were also nervous. We were just as nervous, but this was no time to let fear abrade valour. We had to do what Tewdric's men had done, we had to charge without stopping to take the enemy off balance, and so I roared a war shout and quickened my pace. I had drawn Hywelbane and was holding her by the upper blade in my left hand, letting the shield hang on its loops from my forearm. My heavy spear was in my right hand. The enemy shuffled together, shield against shield, spears levelled, and somewhere from my left a great war-dog was released to run at us. I heard the beast howl, then the madness of battle let me forget everything except the bearded faces in front of me.

A terrible hate wells up in battle, a hatred that comes from the dark soul to fill a man with fierce and bloody anger. Enjoyment, too. I knew that Saxon shield wall would break. I knew it long before I attacked it. The wall was too thin, had been too hurried in the making, and was too nervous, and so I broke out of our front rank and shouted my hate as I ran at the enemy. At that moment all I wanted to do was kill. No, I wanted more, I wanted the bards to sing of Derfel Cadarn at Mynydd Baddon. I wanted men to look at me and say, there is the warrior who broke the wall at Mynydd Baddon, I wanted the power that comes from reputation. A dozen men in Britain had that power; Arthur, Sagramor, Culhwch were among them, and it was a power that superseded all other except for kingship. Ours was a world where swords gave rank, and to shirk the sword was to lose honour, and so I ran ahead, madness filling my soul and exultation giving me a terrible power as I picked my victims. They were two young men, both smaller than me, both nervous, both with skimpy beards, and both were shrinking away even before I hit them. They saw a British warlord in splendour, and I saw two dead Saxons.

My spear took one in the throat. I abandoned the spear as an axe chopped into my shield, but I had seen it coming and warded off the blow, then I rammed the shield against the second man and thrust my shoulder into the shield's belly as I snatched Hywelbane with my right hand. I chopped her down and saw a splinter fly from a Saxon spear shaft, then felt my men pouring in behind me. I whirled Hywelbane over my head, chopped her down again, screamed again, swung her to the side, and suddenly in front of me there was nothing but open grass, buttercups, the road and the river meadows beyond. I was through the wall, and I was screaming my victory. I turned, rammed Hywelbane into the small of a man's back, twisted her free, saw the blood spill off her tip, and suddenly there were no more enemies. The Saxon wall had vanished, or rather it had been turned into dead and dying meat that bled onto the grass. I remember raising shield and spear towards the sun and howling a cry of thanks to Mithras.

'Shield wall!' I heard Issa bellow the order as I celebrated. I stooped to retrieve my spear, then twisted to see more Saxons hurrying from the east.

'Shield wall!' I echoed Issa's shout. Cuneglas was making his own wall, facing west to guard us from Aelle's rearward men, while I was making our line face towards the east from where Cerdic's men were coming. My men screamed and jeered. They had turned a shield wall into offal and now they wanted more. Behind me, in the space between Cuneglas's men and my own, a few wounded Saxons still lived, but three of my men were making short work of them. They cut their throats, for this was no time to take prisoners. Guinevere, I saw, was helping them.

'Lord, Lord!' That was Eachern shouting from the right-hand end of our short wall, and I looked to see him pointing at a mass of Saxons who were hurrying through the gap between us and the river. That gap was wide, but the Saxons were not threatening us, but rather hurrying to support Aelle.

'Let them be!' I shouted. I was more worried by the Saxons in

235

front of us, for they had checked to form in ranks. They had seen what we had just done and would not let us do it to them and so they packed themselves four or five ranks deep, then cheered as one of their wizards came prancing out to curse us. He was one of the mad wizards, for his face twitched uncontrollably as he spat filth at us. The Saxons prized such men, thinking they had the ear of the Gods, and their Gods must have blanched as they heard this man curse.

'Shall I kill him?' Guinevere asked me. She was fingering her bow.

'I wish you weren't here, Lady,' I said.

'A little late for that wish, Derfel,' she said.

'Let him be,' I said. The wizard's curses were not bothering my men who were shouting at the Saxons to come and test their blades, but the Saxons were in no mood to advance. They were waiting for reinforcements, and those were not far behind them. 'Lord King!' I shouted at Cuneglas. He turned. 'Can you see Sagramor?' I asked him.

'Not yet.'

Nor could I see Oengus mac Airem whose Blackshields were supposed to pour out of the hills to take the Saxons still deeper in the flank. I began to fear that we had charged too early, and that we were now trapped between Aelle's troops who were recovering from their panic and Cerdic's spearmen who were carefully thickening their shield wall before they came to overpower us.

Then Eachern shouted again and I looked south to see that the Saxons were now running east instead of west. The fields between our wall and the river were scattered with panicked men and for a heartbeat I was too puzzled to make sense of what I saw, and then I heard the noise. A noise like thunder. Hoofbeats.

Arthur's horses were big. Sagramor once told me Arthur had captured the horses from Clovis, King of the Franks, and before Clovis had owned the herd the horses had been bred for the Romans and no other horses in Britain matched their size, and Arthur chose his biggest men to ride them. He had lost many of the great warhorses to Lancelot, and I had half expected to see those huge beasts among the enemy ranks, but Arthur had scoffed at that fear. He had told me that Lancelot had captured mostly brood mares and untrained yearlings only, and it took as many years to train a horse as it did to teach a man how to fight with an unwieldy lance from the horse's back. Lancelot had no such men, but Arthur did, and now he led them from the northern slope against those of Aelle's men who were fighting Sagramor.

There were only sixty of the big horses, and they were tired for they had first ridden to secure the bridge to the south and then come to the battle's opposite flank, but Arthur spurred them into a gallop and drove them hard into the rear of Aelle's battle line. Those rearward men had been heaving forward, trying to push their forward ranks over Sagramor's shield wall, and Arthur's appearance was so sudden that they did not have time to turn and make a shield wall of their own. The horses broke their ranks wide open, and as the Saxons scattered, so Sagramor's warriors pushed back the front ranks and suddenly the right wing of Aelle's army was broken. Some Saxons ran south, seeking safety among the rest of Aelle's army, but others fled east towards Cerdic and those were the men we could see in the river meadows. Arthur and his horsemen rode those fugitives down mercilessly. The cavalrymen used their long swords to cut down fleeing men until the river meadow was littered with bodies and strewn with abandoned shields and swords. I saw Arthur gallop past my line, his white cloak spattered with blood, Excalibur reddened in his hand and a look of utter joy on his gaunt face. Hygwydd, his servant, carried the bear banner that now had a red cross marked on its lower corner. Hygwydd, normally the most taciturn of men, gave me a grin, and then he was past, following Arthur back up the hill to where the horses could recover their breath and threaten Cerdic's flank. Morfans the Ugly had died in the initial attack on Aelle's men, but that was Arthur's only loss.

Arthur's charge had broken Aelle's right wing and Sagramor was now leading his men along the Fosse Way to join his shields to mine. We had not yet surrounded Aelle's army, but we had penned him between the road and river, and Tewdric's disciplined Christians were now advancing up that corridor and killing as they came. Cerdic was still outside the trap, and it must have occurred to him to leave Aelle there and so let his Saxon rival be destroyed, but instead he decided victory was still possible. Win this day and all Britain would become Lloegyr.

Cerdic ignored the threat of Arthur's horses. He must have known that they had struck Aelle's men where they were most disordered, and that disciplined spearmen, tight in their wall, would have nothing to fear from cavalry and so he ordered his men to lock their shields, lower their spears and advance.

'Tight! Tight!' I shouted, and pushed my way into the front rank where I made sure my shield overlapped those of my neighbours. The Saxons were shuffling forward, intent on keeping shield against shield, their eyes searching our line for a weak spot as the whole mass edged towards us. There were no wizards that I could see, but Cerdic's banner was in the centre of the big formation. I had an impression of beards and horned helmets, heard a harsh ram's horn blowing continually, and watched the spear and axe blades. Cerdic himself was somewhere in the mass of men, for I could hear his voice calling to his men. 'Shields tight! Shields tight!' the King called. Two great war-dogs were loosed at us and I heard shouts and sensed disorder somewhere to my right as the dogs struck the line. The Saxons must have seen my shield wall buckle where the dogs had attacked for they suddenly cheered and surged forward.

'Tight!' I shouted, then hefted my spear over my head. At least three Saxons were looking at me as they rushed forward. I was a lord, hung with gold, and if they could send my soul to the Otherworld then they would win renown and wealth. One of them ran ahead of his fellows, intent on glory, his spear aimed at my shield and I guessed he would drop the point at the last moment to take me in the ankle. Then there was no time for such thought, only for fighting. I rammed my spear at the man's face, and pushed my shield forward and down to deflect his thrust. His blade still scored my ankle, razoring through the leather of my right boot beneath the greave I had taken from Wulfger, but my spear was bloody in his face and he was falling backwards by the time I pulled it back and the next men came to kill me.

They came just as the shields of the two lines crashed together with a noise like the sound of colliding worlds. I could smell Saxons now, the smell of leather and sweat and ordure, but I could not smell ale. This battle was too early in the morning, the Saxons had been surprised, and they had not had time to drink themselves into courage. Men heaved at my back, crushing me against my shield which pushed against a Saxon's shield. I spat at the bearded face, lunged the spear over his shoulder and felt it gripped by an enemy hand. I let it go and, by giving a huge push, freed myself just enough to draw Hywelbane. I hammered the sword down on the man in my front. His helmet was nothing but a leather cap stuffed with rags and Hywelbane's newly sharpened edge went through it to his brain. She stuck there a moment and I struggled against the dead man's weight and while I struggled a Saxon swung an axe at my head.

My helmet took the blow. There was a clanging noise that filled the universe and in my head a sudden darkness shot with streaks of light. My men said later that I was insensible for minutes, but I never fell because the press of bodies kept me upright. I remember nothing, but few men remember much of the crush of shields. You heave, you curse, you spit and you strike when you can. One of my shield neighbours said I stumbled after the axe blow and almost tripped on the bodies of the men I had killed, but the man behind me grabbed hold of my sword belt and he hauled me upright and my wolftails pressed around to give me protection. The enemy sensed I was hurt and fought harder, axes slashing at battered shields and nicked sword blades, but I slowly came out of the daze to find myself in the second rank and still safe behind the shield's blessed protection and with Hywelbane still in my hand. My head hurt, but I was unaware of it, only aware of the need to stab and slash and shout and kill. Issa was holding the gap the dogs had made, grimly killing the Saxons who had broken into our front rank and so sealing our line with their bodies.

Cerdic outnumbered us, but he could not outflank us to the north for the heavy horsemen were there and he did not want to throw his men uphill against their charge, and so he sent men to outflank us to the south, but Sagramor anticipated him and led his spearmen into that gap. I remember hearing that clash of shields. Blood had filled my right boot so that it squelched whenever I put weight on it, my skull was a throbbing thing of pain and my mouth fixed in a snarl. The man who had taken my place in the front rank would not yield it back to me. 'They're giving, Lord,' he shouted at me, 'they're giving!' And sure enough the enemy's pressure was weakening. They were not defeated, just retreating, and suddenly an enemy shout called them back and they gave a last spear lunge or axe stroke and backed hard away. We did not follow. We were too bloody, too battered and too tired to pursue, and we were obstructed by the pile of bodies that mark the tide's edge of a spear and shield battle. Some in that pile were dead, others stirred in agony and pleaded for death.

Cerdic had pulled his men back to make a new shield wall, one big enough to break through to Aelle's men, now cut off from safety by Sagramor's troops who had filled most of the gap between my men and the river. I learned later that Aelle's men were being pushed back against the river by Tewdric's spearmen, and Arthur left just enough men to keep those Saxons trapped and sent the rest to reinforce Sagramor.

My helmet had a dent across its left side and a split at the base of the dent that went clean through the iron and the leather liner. When I eased the helmet off it tugged at the blood clotting in my hair. I gingerly felt my scalp, but sensed no splintered bone, only a bruise and a pulsing pain. There was a ragged wound on my left forearm, my chest was bruised and my right ankle was still bleeding. Issa was limping, but claimed it was nothing but a graze. Niall, the leader of the Blackshields, was dead. A spear had spitted his breastplate and he lay on his back, the spear jutting skyward, with his open mouth brimming with blood. Eachern had lost an eye. He padded the open socket with a scrap of rag that he tied round his scalp, then jammed the helmet over the crude bandage and swore to revenge the eye a hundredfold.

Arthur rode down from the hill to praise my men. 'Hold them again!' he shouted to us, 'hold them till Oengus comes and then we'll finish them for ever!' Mordred rode behind Arthur, his great banner alongside the flag of the bear. Our King carried a drawn sword and his eyes were wide with the excitement of the day. For two miles along the river bank there was dust and blood, dead and dying, iron against flesh.

Tewdric's gold and scarlet ranks closed around Aelle's survivors. Those men still fought, and Cerdic now made another attempt to break through to them. Arthur led Mordred back up to the hill, while we locked shields again. 'They're eager,' Cuneglas commented as he saw the Saxon ranks advance again.

'They're not drunk,' I said, 'that's why.'

Cuneglas was unhurt and filled with the elation of a man who believes his life is charmed. He had fought in the front of the battle, he had killed, and he had not taken a scratch. He had never been famous as a warrior, not like his father, and now he believed he was earning his crown. 'Take care, Lord King,' I said as he went back to his men.

'We're winning, Derfel!' he called, and hurried away to face the attack.

This would be a far bigger attack than the first Saxon assault, for Cerdic had placed his own bodyguard at the centre of his new line and those men released huge war-dogs that raced at Sagramor whose men formed the centre of our line. A heartbeat later the Saxon spearmen struck, hacking into the gaps that the dogs had torn in our line. I heard the shields crash, then had no thought for Sagramor for the Saxon right wing charged into my men.

Again the shields banged onto one another. Again we lunged with spears or hacked down with swords, and again we were crushed against each other. The Saxon opposing me had abandoned his spear and was trying to work his short knife under my ribs. The knife could not pierce my mail armour and he was grunting, shoving, and gritting his teeth as he twisted the blade against the iron rings. I had no room to bring my right arm down to catch his wrist and so I hammered his helmet with Hywelbane's pommel, and went on hammering until he sank down at my feet and I could step on him. He still tried to cut me with the knife, but the man behind me speared him, then rammed his shield into my back to force me on into the enemy. To my left a Saxon hero was smashing left and right with his axe, savaging a path into our wall, but someone tripped him with a spear shaft and a half-dozen men pounced on the fallen man with swords or spears. He died among the bodies of his victims.

Cerdic was riding up and down behind his line, shouting at his men to push and kill. I called to him, daring him to dismount and come and fight like a man, but he either did not hear me or else ignored the taunts. Instead he spurred southwards to where Arthur was fighting alongside Sagramor. Arthur had seen the pressure on Sagramor's men and led his horsemen behind the line to reinforce the Numidian, and now our cavalry were shoving their horses into the crush of men and stabbing over the heads of the front rank with their long spears. Mordred was there, and men said later that he fought like a demon. Our King never lacked brute valour in battle, just sense and decency in life. He was no horse soldier, and so he had dismounted and taken a place in the front rank. I saw him later and he was covered in blood, none of it his own. Guinevere was behind our line. She had seen Mordred's discarded horse, mounted it, and was loosing arrows from its back. I saw one strike and shiver in Cerdic's own shield, but he brushed the thing away as if it were a fly.

Sheer exhaustion ended that second clash of the walls. There came a point where we were too tired to lift a sword again, when we could only lean on our enemy's shield and spit insults over the rim. Occasionally a man would summon the strength to raise an axe or thrust a spear, and for a moment the rage of battle would flare up, only to subside as the shields soaked up the force. We were all bleeding, all bruised, all dry-mouthed, and when the enemy backed away we were grateful for the respite.

We pulled back too, freeing ourselves from the dead who lay in a heap where the shield walls had met. We carried our wounded with us. Among our dead were a few whose foreheads had been branded by the touch of a red-hot spear blade, marking them as men who had joined Lancelot's rebellion the previous year, but they were men who now had died for Arthur. I also found Bors lying wounded. He was shuddering and complaining of the cold. His belly had been cut open so that when I lifted him his guts spilled on the ground. He made a mewing noise as I laid him down and told him that the Otherworld waited for him with roaring fires, good companions and endless mead, and he gripped my left hand hard as I cut his throat with one quick slash of Hywelbane. A Saxon crawled pitifully and blindly among the dead, blood dripping from his mouth, until Issa picked up a fallen axe and chopped down into the man's backbone. I watched one of my youngsters vomit, then stagger a few paces before a friend caught him and held him up. The youngster was crying because he had emptied his bowels and he was ashamed of himself, but he was not the only one. The field stank of dung and blood.

Aelle's men, far behind us, were in a tight shield wall with their backs to the river. Tewdric's men faced them, but were content to keep those Saxons quiet rather than fight them now, for cornered men make terrible enemies. And still Cerdic did not abandon his ally. He still hoped he could drive through Arthur's spearmen to join Aelle and then strike north to split our forces in two. He had tried twice, and now he gathered the remnants of his army for the last great effort. He still had fresh men, some of them warriors hired from Clovis's army of the Franks, and those men were now brought to the front of the battle line and we watched as the wizards harangued them, then turned to spit their maledictions at us. There was to be nothing hurried about this attack. There was no need because the day was still young, it was not even midday, and Cerdic had time to let his men eat, drink and ready themselves. One of their war drums began its sullen beat as still more Saxons formed on their army's flanks, some with leashed dogs. We were all exhausted. I sent men to the river for water and we shared it out, gulping from the helmets of the dead. Arthur came to me and grimaced at my state. 'Can you hold them a third time?' he asked.

'We have to, Lord,' I said, though it would be hard. We had lost scores of men and our wall would be thin. Our spears and swords were blunted now and there were not enough sharpening stones to make them keen again, while the enemy was being reinforced with fresh men whose weapons were untouched. Arthur slid from Llamrei, threw her reins to Hygwydd, then walked with me to the scattered tide line of the dead. He knew some of the men by name, and he frowned when he saw the dead youngsters who had scarcely had time to live before they met their enemy. He stooped and touched a finger to Bors's forehead, then walked on to pause beside a Saxon who lay with an arrow embedded in his open mouth. For a moment I thought he was about to speak, then he just smiled. He knew Guinevere was with my men, indeed he must have seen her on her horse and seen her banner that now flew alongside my starry flag. He looked at the arrow again and I saw a flicker of happiness on his face. He touched my arm and led me back towards our men who were sitting or else leaning on their spears.

A man in the gathering Saxon ranks had recognized Arthur and now strode into the wide space between the armies and shouted a challenge at him. It was Liofa, the swordsman I had faced at Thunreslea, and he called Arthur a coward and a woman. I did not translate and Arthur did not ask me to. Liofa stalked closer. He carried no shield and wore no armour, not even a helmet, and carried only his sword and that he now sheathed as if to show that he had no fear of us. I could see the scar on his cheek and I was tempted to turn and give him a bigger scar, a scar that would put him in a grave, but Arthur checked me. 'Let him be,' he said.

Liofa went on taunting us. He minced like a woman, suggesting that was what we were, and he stood with his back to us to invite a man to come and attack him. Still no one moved. He turned to face us again, shook his head with pity for our cowardice, then strode on down the tide line of the dead. The Saxons cheered him while my men watched in silence. I passed word down our line that he was Cerdic's champion, and dangerous, and that he should be left alone. It galled our men to see a Saxon so rampant, but it was better that Liofa should live now than be given a chance to humiliate one of our tired spearmen. Arthur tried to give our men heart by remounting Llamrei and, ignoring Liofa's taunts, galloping along the line of corpses. He scattered the naked Saxon wizards, then drew Excalibur and spurred yet closer to the Saxon line, flaunting his white crest and bloodied cloak. His red-crossed shield glittered and my men cheered to see him. The Saxons shrank away from him, while Liofa, left impotent in Arthur's wake, called him woman-hearted. Arthur wheeled the horse and kicked her back to me. His gesture had implied that Liofa was not a worthy opponent, and it must have stung the Saxon champion's pride because he came still nearer to our line in search of an opponent.

Liofa stopped by a pile of corpses. He stepped into the gore, then seized a fallen shield that he dragged free. He held it up so that we could all see the eagle of Powys and, when he was sure we had seen the symbol, he threw the shield down then opened his trews and pissed on the insignia of Powys. He moved his aim so that his urine fell on the shield's dead owner, and that insult proved too great.

Cuneglas roared his anger and ran out of the line.

'No!' I shouted and started towards Cuneglas. It was better, I thought, that I should fight Liofa, for at least I knew his tricks and his speed, but I was too late. Cuneglas had his sword drawn and he ignored me. He believed himself invulnerable that day. He was the king of battle, a man who had needed to show himself a hero, and he had achieved that and now he believed that everything was possible. He would strike down this impudent Saxon in front of his men, and for years the bards would sing of King Cuneglas the Mighty, King Cuneglas the Saxon-killer, King Cuneglas the Warrior.

I could not save him for he would lose face if he turned away or if another man took his place and so I watched, horrified, as he strode confidently towards the slim Saxon who wore no armour. Cuneglas was in his father's old wargear, iron trimmed with gold and with a helmet crested with an eagle's wing. He was smiling. He was soaring at that moment, filled with the day's heroics, and he believed himself touched by the Gods. He did not hesitate, but cut at Liofa and we could all have sworn that the cut must strike home, but Liofa glided from under the slash, stepped aside, laughed, then stepped aside again as Cuneglas's sword cut air a second time.

Both our men and the Saxons were roaring encouragement. Arthur and I alone were silent. I was watching Ceinwyn's brother die, and there was not a thing I could do to stop it. Or nothing I could do with honour, for if I were to rescue Cuneglas then I would disgrace him. Arthur looked down at me from his saddle with a worried face.

I could not relieve Arthur's worry. 'I fought him,' I said bitterly, 'and he's a killer.'

'You live.'

'I'm a warrior, Lord,' I said. Cuneglas had never been a warrior, which was why he wanted to prove himself now, but Liofa was making a fool of him. Cuneglas would attack, trying to smash Liofa down with his sword, and every time the Saxon just ducked or slid aside, and never once did he counter-attack; and slowly our men fell silent, for they saw that the King was tiring and that Liofa was playing with him.

Then a group of men from Powys rushed forward to save their King and Liofa took three fast backward steps and mutely gestured at them with his sword. Cuneglas turned to see his men. 'Go back!'

he shouted at them. 'Go back!' he repeated, more angrily. He must have known he was doomed, but he would not lose face. Honour is everything.

The men from Powys stopped. Cuneglas turned back to Liofa, and this time he did not rush forward, but went more cautiously. For the first time his sword actually touched Liofa's blade, and I saw Liofa slip on the grass and Cuneglas shouted his victory and raised his sword to kill his tormentor, but Liofa was spinning away, the slip deliberate, and the whirl of his swing carried his sword low above the grass so that it sliced into Cuneglas's right leg. For a moment Cuneglas stood upright, his sword faltering, and then, as Liofa straightened, he sank. The Saxon waited as the King collapsed, then he kicked Cuneglas's shield aside and stabbed down once with his sword point.

The Saxons cheered themselves hoarse, for Liofa's triumph was an omen for their victory. Liofa himself had time only to seize Cuneglas's sword, then he ran lithely away from the men who chased him for vengeance. He easily outstripped them, then turned and taunted them. He had no need to fight them, for he had won his challenge. He had killed an enemy King and I did not doubt that the Saxon bards would sing of Liofa the Terrible, the slayer of kings. He had given the Saxons their first victory of the day.

Arthur dismounted and he and I insisted on carrying Cuneglas's body back to his men. We both wept. In all the long years we had possessed no stauncher ally than Cuneglas ap Gorfyddyd, King of Powys. He had never argued with Arthur and never once failed him, while to me he had been like a brother. He was a good man, a giver of gold, a lover of justice, and now he was dead. The warriors of Powys took their dead King from us and carried him behind the shield wall. 'The name of his killer,' I said to them, 'is Liofa, and I will give a hundred gold coins to the man who brings me his head.'

Then a shout turned me. The Saxons, assured of victory, had started their advance.

My men stood. They wiped sweat from their eyes. I pulled on my battered and bloody helmet, closed its cheekpieces, and snatched up a fallen spear.

It was time to fight again.

*

246

This was the biggest Saxon attack of the day and it was made by a surge of confident spearmen who had recovered from their early surprise and who now came to splinter our lines and to rescue Aelle. They roared their war chants as they came, they beat spears on shields and they promised each other a score of British dead apiece. The Saxons knew they had won. They had taken the worst that Arthur could hurl at them, they had fought us to a standstill, they had seen their champion slay a King, and now, with their fresh troops in the lead, they advanced to finish us. The Franks drew back their light throwing-spears, readying themselves to rain a shower of sharpened iron on our shield wall.

When suddenly a horn sounded from Mynydd Baddon.

At first few of us heard the horn, so loud were the shouts and the tramp of feet and the moans of the dying, but then the horn called again, then a third time, and at the third call men turned and stared up at Mynydd Baddon's abandoned rampart. Even the Franks and Saxons stopped. They were only fifty paces from us when the horn checked them and when they, like us, turned to gaze up the long green hillside.

To see a single horseman and a banner.

There was only one banner, but it was a huge one; a wind-spread expanse of white linen on which was embroidered the red dragon of Dumnonia. The beast, all claws, tail and fire, reared on the flag that caught the wind and almost toppled the horseman who carried it. Even at this distance we could see that the horseman rode stiffly and awkwardly as though he could neither handle his black horse nor hold the great banner steady, but then two spearmen appeared behind him and they pricked his horse with their weapons and the beast sprang away down the hill and its rider was jerked hard backwards by the sudden motion. He swayed forward again as the horse raced down the slope, his black cloak flew up behind and I saw that his armour beneath the cloak was shining white, as white as the linen of his fluttering flag. Behind him, spilling off Mynydd Baddon as we had spilled just after dawn, came a shrieking mass of men with black shields and other men with tusked boars on their shields. Oengus mac Airem and Culhwch had come, though instead of striking down the Corinium road they had first worked their way onto Mynydd Baddon so that their men would link up with ours.

247

But it was the horseman I watched. He rode so awkwardly and I could see now that he was tied onto the horse. His ankles were linked under the stallion's black belly with rope, and his body was fixed to the saddle by what had to be strips of timber clamped to the saddle's tree. He had no helmet so that his long hair flew free in the wind, and beneath the hair the rider's face was nothing but a grinning skull covered by desiccated yellow skin. It was Gawain, dead Gawain, his lips and gums shrunken back from his teeth, his nostrils two black slits and his eyeballs empty holes. His head lolled from side to side while his body, to which the dragon banner of Britain was strapped, swayed from side to side.

It was death on a black horse called Anbarr, and at the sight of that ghoul coming at their flank, the Saxon confidence shuddered. The Blackshields were shrieking behind Gawain, driving the horse and its dead rider over the hedges and straight at the Saxon flank. The Blackshields did not attack in a line, but came in a howling mass. This was the Irish way of war, a terrifying assault of maddened men who came to the slaughter like lovers.

For a moment the battle trembled. The Saxons had been on the point of victory, but Arthur saw their hesitation and unexpectedly shouted us forward. 'On!' he shouted, and 'Forward!' Mordred added his command to Arthur's, 'Forward!'

Thus began the slaughter of Mynydd Baddon. The bards tell it all, and for once they do not exaggerate. We crossed our tide line of dead and carried our spears to the Saxon army just as the Blackshields and Culhwch's men hit their flank. For a few heartbeats there was the clangour of sword on sword, the thump of axe on shield, the grunting, heaving, sweating battle of locked shield walls, but then the Saxon army broke and we fought among their shredding ranks in fields made slick with Frankish and Saxon blood. The Saxons fled, broken by a wild charge led by a dead man on a black horse, and we killed them until we thought nothing of killing. We crammed the bridge of swords with Sais dead. We speared them, we disembowelled them, and some we just drowned in the river. We took no prisoners at first, but vented years of hatred on our hated enemies. Cerdic's army had shattered under the twin assault, and we roared into their breaking ranks and vied each other in killing. It was an orgy of death, a welter of slaughter. There were some Saxons so terrified that they could not move, who literally stood with wide eyes waiting to be killed, while there were others who fought like demons and others who died running and others who tried to escape to the river. We had lost all semblance of a shield wall, we were nothing but a pack of maddened war-dogs tearing an enemy to pieces. I saw Mordred limping on his clubbed foot as he cut down Saxons, I saw Arthur riding down fugitives, saw the men of Powys avenging their King a thousandfold. I saw Galahad cut left and right from horseback, his face as calm as ever. I saw Tewdric in a priest's robes, skeletally thin and with his hair tonsured, savagely slashing with a great sword. Old Bishop Emrys was there, a huge cross hanging about his neck and an old breastplate tied over his gown with horsehair rope. 'Get to hell!' he roared as he jabbed at helpless Saxons with a spear. 'Burn in the cleansing fire for ever!' I saw Oengus mac Airem, his beard soaked with Saxon blood, spearing yet more Sais. I saw Guinevere riding Mordred's horse and chopping with the sword we had given her. I saw Gawain, his head fallen clean off, slumping dead on his bleeding horse that peacefully cropped the grass among the Saxon corpses. I saw Merlin at last, for he had come with Gawain's corpse, and though he was an old man, he was striking at Saxons with his staff and cursing them for miserable worms. He had an escort of Blackshields. He saw me, smiled, and waved me on to the slaughter.

We overran Cerdic's village where women and children cowered in the huts. Culhwch and a score of men were working a stolid butcher's path through the few Saxon spearmen who tried to protect their families and Cerdic's abandoned baggage. The Saxon guards died and the plundered gold spilled like chaff. I remember dust rising like a mist, screams of women and men, children and dogs running in terror, burning huts spewing smoke and always Arthur's big horses thundering through the panic with spears dipping to take enemy spearmen in the back. There is no joy like the destruction of a broken army. The shield wall breaks and death rules, and so we killed till our arms were too tired to lift a sword and when the killing was done we found ourselves in a swamp of blood, and that was when our men discovered the ale and mead in the Saxon baggage and the drinking began. Some Saxon women found protection amongst our few sober men who carried water from the river to our wounded. We looked for friends alive and embraced them, saw friends dead and wept for them. We knew the delirium of utter victory, we shared our tears and laughter, and some men, tired as they were, danced for pure joy.

Cerdic escaped. He and his bodyguard cut through the chaos and climbed the eastern hills. Some Saxons swam south across the river, while others followed Cerdic and a few pretended death and then slipped away in the night, but most stayed in the valley beneath Mynydd Baddon and remain there to this day.

For we had won. We had turned the fields beside the river into a slaughterhouse. We had saved Britain and fulfilled Arthur's dream. We were the kings of slaughter and the lords of the dead, and we howled our bloody triumph at the sky.

For the power of the Sais was broken.

PART THREE

Nimue's Curse

QUEEN IGRAINE SAT IN my window and read the last sheets of parchment, sometimes asking me the meaning of a Saxon word, but otherwise saying nothing. She hurried through the story of the battle, then threw the parchments onto the floor in disgust. 'What happened to Aelle?' she demanded indignantly, 'or to Lancelot?'

'I shall come to their fates, Lady,' I said. I had a quill trapped on the desk with the stump of my left arm and was trimming its point with a knife. I blew the scraps onto the floor. 'All in good time.'

'All in good time!' she scoffed. 'You can't leave a story without an ending, Derfel!'

'It will have an ending,' I promised.

'It needs one here and now,' my Queen insisted. 'That's the whole point of stories. Life doesn't have neat endings, so stories must.' She is very swollen now, for her child is close to its time. I shall pray for her, and she will need my prayers for too many women die giving birth. Cows do not suffer thus, nor cats, nor bitches, nor sows, nor ewes, nor vixens, nor any creature except humankind. Sansum says that is because Eve took the apple in Eden and so soured our paradise. Women, the saint preaches, are God's punishment on men, and children his punishment on women. 'So what happened to Aelle?' Igraine demanded sternly when I did not respond to her words.

'He was killed,' I said, 'by the thrust of a spear. It struck him right here,' I tapped my ribs just above my heart. The story was longer than that, of course, but I had no mind to tell her just then for I take little pleasure in remembering my father's death, though I suppose I must set it down if the tale is to be complete. Arthur had left his men pillaging Cerdic's camp and ridden back to discover whether Tewdric's Christians had finished off Aelle's trapped army. He found the remnants of those Saxons beaten, bleeding and dying, but still defiant. Aelle himself had been wounded and could no longer hold a shield, but he would not yield. Instead, surrounded by his bodyguard and the last of his spearmen, he waited for Tewdric's soldiers to come and kill him.

The spearmen of Gwent were reluctant to attack. A cornered enemy is dangerous, and if he still possesses a shield wall, as Aelle's men did, then he is doubly dangerous. Too many spearmen of Gwent had already died, good old Agricola among them, and the survivors did not want to push forward into the Saxon shields another time. Arthur had not insisted that they try, instead he had talked with Aelle, and when Aelle refused to surrender, Arthur summoned me. I thought, when I reached Arthur's side, that he had exchanged his white cloak for a dark red one, but it was the same garment, just so spattered with blood that it looked red. He greeted me with an embrace, then, with his arm about my shoulders, led me into the space between the opposing shield walls. I remember a dying horse was there, and dead men and discarded shields and broken weapons. 'Your father won't surrender,' Arthur said, 'but I think he will listen to you. Tell him that he must be our prisoner, but that he will live with honour and can spend his days in comfort. I promise the lives of his men, too. All he needs do is give me his sword.' He looked at the beaten, outnumbered and trapped Saxons. They were silent. In their place we would have sung, but those spearmen waited for death in utter silence. 'Tell them there's been enough killing, Derfel,' Arthur said.

I unbuckled Hywelbane, laid her down with my shield and spear, then walked to face my father. Aelle looked weary, broken and hurt, but he hobbled out to meet me with his head held high. He had no shield, but held a sword in his maimed right hand. 'I thought they would send for you,' he growled. The edge of his sword was dented deep and its blade was crusted with blood. He made an abrupt gesture with the weapon when I began to describe Arthur's offer. 'I know what he wants of me,' he interrupted, 'he wants my sword, but I am Aelle, the Bretwalda of Britain, and I do not yield my sword.'

'Father,' I began again.

'You call me King!' he snarled.

I smiled at his defiance and bowed my head. 'Lord King, we offer your men their lives, and we . . .'

Once again he cut me off. 'When a man dies in battle,' he said, 'he goes to a blessed home in the sky. But to reach that great feasting hall he must die on his feet, with his sword in his hand and with his wounds to the front.' He paused, and when he spoke again his voice was much softer. 'You owe me nothing, my son, but I should take it as a kindness if you would give me my place in that feasting hall.'

'Lord King,' I said, but he interrupted me for a fourth time.

'I would be buried here,' he went on as though I had never spoken, 'with my feet to the north and my sword in my hand. I ask nothing more of you.' He turned back to his men, and I saw that he could hardly stay upright. He must have been grievously wounded, but his great bear cloak was hiding the wound. 'Hrothgar!' he called to one of his spearmen. 'Give my son your spear.' A tall young Saxon came out of the shield wall and obediently held his spear out to me. 'Take it!' Aelle snapped at me, and I obeyed. Hrothgar gave me a nervous glance then hurried back to his comrades.

Aelle closed his eyes for an instant and I saw a grimace cross his hard face. He was pale under the dirt and sweat, and he suddenly gritted his teeth as another ravaging pain seared through him, but he resisted the pain and even tried to smile as he stepped forward to embrace me. He leaned his weight on my shoulders and I could hear the breath scraping in his throat. 'I think,' he said in my ear, 'that you are the best of my sons. Now give me a gift. Give me a good death, Derfel, for I would like to go to the feasting hall of true warriors.' He stepped heavily back and propped his sword against his body, then laboriously untied the leather strings of his fur cloak. It dropped away and I saw that the whole left side of his body was soaked in blood. He had suffered a spear thrust under the breastplate, while another blow had taken him high in the shoulder, leaving his left arm hanging useless, and so he was forced to use his maimed right hand to unbuckle the leather straps that held his breastplate at his waist and shoulders. He fumbled with the buckles, but when I stepped forward to help he waved me away. 'I'm making it easy for you,' he said, 'but when I'm dead, put the breastplate back on my corpse. I shall need armour in the feasting hall, for there is much fighting there. Fighting, feasting and . . .' he stopped, racked once again by pain. He gritted his teeth, groaned, then straightened to face me. 'Now kill me,' he ordered.

'I cannot kill you,' I said, but I was thinking of my mad mother's prophecy that it would be Aelle's son who killed Aelle.

'Then I shall kill you,' he said, and he clumsily swung his sword at me. I stepped away from the swing, and he stumbled and almost fell as he tried to follow me. He stopped, panting, and stared at me. 'For the sake of your mother, Derfel,' he pleaded, 'would you have me die on the ground like a dog? Can you give me nothing?' He swung at me again, and this time the effort was too much and he began to sway and I saw there were tears in his eyes and I understood that the manner of his death was no small thing. He willed himself to stay upright and made an immense effort to lift the sword. Fresh blood gleamed at his left side, his eyes were glazing, but he kept his gaze on mine as he took one last step forward and made a feeble lunge at my midriff.

God forgive me, but I thrust the spear forward then. I put all my weight and strength into the blow, and the heavy blade took his falling weight and held him upright even as it shattered his ribs and drove deep into his heart. He gave an enormous shudder and a look of grim determination came to his dying face and I thought for a heartbeat that he wanted to lift the sword for one last blow, but then I saw he was merely making certain that his wounded right hand was fastened tight about his sword's handle. Then he fell, and he was dead before he struck the ground, but the sword, his battered and bloody sword, was still in his grip. A groan sounded from his men. Some of them were in tears.

'Derfel?' Igraine said. 'Derfel!'

'Lady?'

'You were sleeping,' she accused me.

'Age, dear Lady,' I said, 'mere age.'

'So Aelle died in the battle,' she said briskly, 'and Lancelot?'

'That comes later,' I said firmly.

'Tell me now!' she insisted.

256

'I told you,' I said, 'it comes later, and I hate stories that tell their endings before their beginnings.'

For a moment I thought she would protest, but instead she just sighed at my obstinacy and went on with her list of unfinished business. 'What happened to the Saxon champion, Liofa?'

'He died,' I said, 'very horribly.'

'Good!' she said, looking interested. 'Tell me!'

'It was a disease, Lady. Something swelled in his groin and he could neither sit nor lie, and even standing was agony. He became thinner and thinner, and finally he died, sweating and shaking. Or so we heard.'

Igraine was indignant. 'So he wasn't killed at Mynydd Baddon?'

'He escaped with Cerdic.'

Igraine gave a dissatisfied shrug, as though we had somehow failed by letting the Saxon champion escape. 'But the bards,' she said, and I groaned, for whenever my Queen mentions the bards I know I am about to be confronted with their version of history which, inevitably, Igraine prefers even though I was present when the history was made and the bards were not even born. 'The bards,' she said firmly, ignoring my groan of protest, 'all say that Cuneglas's battle with Liofa lasted the best part of a morning, and that Cuneglas killed six champions before he was struck down from behind.'

'I have heard those songs,' I said guardedly.

'And?' She glared at me. Cuneglas was her husband's grandfather and family pride was at stake. 'Well?'

'I was there, Lady,' I said simply.

'You have an old man's memory, Derfel,' she said disapprovingly, and I have no doubt that when Dafydd, the clerk of the justice who writes down the British translation of my parchments, comes to the passage on Cuneglas's death he will change it to suit my Lady's taste. And why not? Cuneglas was a hero and it will not hurt if history remembers him as a great warrior, though in reality he was no soldier. He was a decent man, and a sensible one, and wise beyond his years, but he was not a man whose heart swelled when he gripped a spear shaft. His death was the tragedy of Mynydd Baddon, but a tragedy none of us saw in the delirium of victory. We burned him on the battlefield and his balefire flamed for three days and three nights, and on the last dawn, when there were only embers amidst which were the melted remnants of Cuneglas's armour, we gathered around the pyre and sang the Death Song of Werlinna. We killed a score of Saxon prisoners too, sending their souls to escort Cuneglas in honour to the Otherworld, and I remember thinking that it was good for my darling Dian that her uncle had crossed the bridge of swords to keep her company in Annwn's towered world.

'And Arthur,' Igraine said eagerly, 'did he run to Guinevere?'

'I never saw their reunion,' I said.

'It doesn't matter what you saw,' Igraine said severely, 'we need it here.' She stirred the heap of finished parchments with her foot. 'You should have described their meeting, Derfel.'

'I told you, I didn't see it.'

'What does that matter? It would have made a very good ending to the battle. Not everyone likes to hear about spears and killing, Derfel. Tales of men fighting can get very boring after a while and a love story makes it all a lot more interesting.' And no doubt the battle will be filled with romance once she and Dafydd maul my story. I sometimes wish I could write this tale in the British tongue, but two of the monks can read and either could betray me to Sansum; so I must write in Saxon and trust that Igraine does not change the story when Dafydd provides her with the translation. I know what Igraine wants: she wants Arthur to run through the corpses, and for Guinevere to wait for him with open arms, and for the two of them to meet in ecstasy, and maybe that is how it did happen, but I suspect not, for she was too proud and he was too diffident. I imagine they wept when they met, but neither ever told me, so I shall invent nothing. I do know that Arthur became a happy man after Mynydd Baddon, and it was not just victory over the Saxons that gave him that happiness.

'And what about Argante?' Igraine wanted to know. 'You leave so much out, Derfel!'

'I shall come to Argante.'

'But her father was there. Wasn't Oengus angry that Arthur went back to Guinevere?'

'I will tell you all about Argante,' I promised, 'in due time.'

'And Amhar and Loholt? You haven't forgotten them?'

'They escaped,' I said. 'They found a coracle and paddled it across the river. I fear we shall meet them again in this tale.'

Igraine tried to prise some more details from me, but I insisted I would tell the story at my own pace and in my own order. She finally abandoned her questions and stooped to put the written parchments into the leather bag she used to carry them back to the Caer; she found stooping difficult, but refused my help. 'I shall be so glad when the baby's born,' she said. 'My breasts are sore, my legs and back ache, and I don't walk any more, I just waddle like a goose. Brochvael's bored with it too.'

'Husbands never like it when their wives are pregnant,' I said.

'Then they shouldn't try so hard to fill their bellies,' Igraine said tartly. She paused to listen as Sansum screamed at Brother Llewellyn for having left his milk pail in the passageway. Poor Llewellyn. He is a novice in our monastery and no one works harder for less thanks and now, because of a limewood bucket, he is to be condemned to a week of daily beatings from Saint Tudwal, the young man – indeed scarce more than a child – who is being groomed to be Sansum's successor. Our whole monastery lives in fear of Tudwal, and I alone escape the worst of his pique thanks to Igraine's friendship. Sansum needs her husband's protection too much to risk Igraine's displeasure.

'This morning,' Igraine said, 'I saw a stag with only one antler. It's a bad omen, Derfel.'

'We Christians,' I said, 'do not believe in omens.'

'But I see you touching that nail in your desk,' she said.

'We are not always good Christians.'

She paused. 'I'm worried about the birth.'

'We are all praying for you,' I said, and knew it was an inadequate response. But I had done more than just pray in our monastery's small chapel. I had found an eagle stone, scratched her name on its surface and buried it beside an ash tree. If Sansum knew I had made that ancient charm he would forget about his need for Brochvael's protection and have Saint Tudwal beat me bloody for a month. But then, if the saint knew I was writing this tale of Arthur he would do the same.

But write it I shall and for a time it will be easy, for now comes the happy time, the years of peace. But they were also the years of encroaching darkness, but we did not see that, for we only saw the sunlight and never heeded the shadows. We thought we had beaten the shadows, and that the sun would light Britain for ever. Mynydd Baddon was Arthur's victory, his greatest achievement, and perhaps the story should end there; but Igraine is right, life does not have tidy endings and so I must go on with this tale of Arthur, my Lord, my friend and the deliverer of Britain.

Arthur let Aelle's men live. They laid down their spears and were distributed among the winners to be slaves. I used some of them to help dig my father's grave. We dug it deep into that soft damp earth beside the river, and there we laid Aelle with his feet facing north and with his sword in his hand, and with the breastplate over his broken heart, his shield across his belly and the spear that had killed him alongside his corpse, and then we filled the grave and I said a prayer to Mithras while the Saxons prayed to their God of Thunder.

By evening the first funeral pyres were burning. I helped lay the corpses of my own men on their pyres, then left their comrades singing their souls to the Otherworld while I retrieved my horse and rode northwards through the long soft shadows. I rode towards the village where our women had found shelter and as I climbed into the northern hills the noise of the battlefield receded. It was the sound of fires crackling, of women weeping, of chanted elegies and of drunken men whooping savagely.

I took the news of Cuneglas's death to Ceinwyn. She stared at me when I told her and for a moment she showed no reaction, but then tears welled in her eyes. She pulled her cloak over her head. 'Poor Perddel,' she said, meaning Cuneglas's son who was now the King of Powys. I told her how her brother had died, and then she retreated into the cottage where she and our daughters were living. She wanted to bind up my head wound that looked much worse than it was, but she could not do it for she and her daughters must mourn Cuneglas and that meant they must shut themselves away for three days and nights in which they must hide from the sun and could neither see nor touch any man.

It was dark by then. I could have stayed in the village, but I was restless and so, under the light of a thinning moon, I rode back south. I went first to Aquae Sulis, thinking that I might find Arthur in the city, but found only the torch-lit remnants of carnage. Our levy had flooded over the inadequate wall and slaughtered whoever they found inside, but the horror ended once Tewdric's troops occupied the city. Those Christians cleaned the temple of Minerva, scooping out the entrails of three sacrificed bulls that the Saxons had left spilling bloodily across the tiles, and once the shrine was restored the Christians held a rite of thanksgiving. I heard their singing and went to find songs of my own, but my men had stayed in Cerdic's ruined camp and Aquae Sulis was filled with strangers. I could not find Arthur, or any other friend except Culhwch and he was roaring drunk, and so, in the soft dark, I rode east along the river. The air stank of blood and was filled with ghosts, but I risked the wraiths in my desperation to find a companion. I did find a group of Sagramor's men singing about a fire, but they did not know where their commander was, and so I rode on, drawn still farther eastwards by the sight of men dancing around a fire.

The dancers were Blackshields and their steps were high for they were dancing across the severed heads of their enemies. I would have ridden around the capering Blackshields, but then glimpsed two white-robed figures sitting calmly beside the fire amidst the ring of dancers. One of them was Merlin.

I tied my horse's reins to a thorn stump, then stepped through the dancing ring. Merlin and his companion were making a meal of bread, cheese and ale, and when Merlin first saw me he did not recognize me. 'Go away,' he snapped, 'or I shall turn you into a toad. Oh, it's you, Derfel!' He sounded disappointed. 'I knew if I found food that some empty belly would expect me to share it. I suppose you're hungry?'

'I am, Lord.'

He gestured for me to sit beside him. 'I suspect the cheese is Saxon,' he said dubiously, 'and it was rather covered in blood when I discovered it, but I washed it clean. Well, I wiped it anyway, and it's proving surprisingly edible. I suppose there's just enough for you.' In truth there was enough for a dozen men. 'This is Taliesin,' he curtly introduced his companion. 'He's some kind of bard out of Powys.'

I looked at the famous bard and saw a young man with a keenly

261

intelligent face. He had shaved the front part of his head like a Druid, wore a short black beard, had a long jaw, sunken cheeks and a narrow nose. His shaven forehead was circled by a thin fillet of silver. He smiled and bowed his head. 'Your fame precedes you, Lord Derfel.'

'As does yours,' I said.

'Oh, no!' Merlin groaned. 'If you two are going to grovel all over each other then go somewhere else and do it. Derfel fights,' he told Taliesin, 'because he has never really grown up, and you're famous because you happen to have a passable voice.'

'I make songs as well as sing them,' Taliesin said modestly.

'And any man can make a song if he's drunk enough,' Merlin said dismissively, then squinted at me. 'Is that blood on your hair?'

'Yes, Lord.'

'You should be grateful you weren't wounded anywhere crucial.' He laughed at that, then gestured at the Blackshields. 'What do you think of my bodyguard?'

'They dance well.'

'They have much to dance about. What a satisfying day,' Merlin said. 'And didn't Gawain play his part well? It's so gratifying when a halfwit proves to be of some use, and what a halfwit Gawain was! A tedious boy! Forever trying to improve the world. Why do the young always believe they know more than their elders? You, Taliesin, do not suffer from that tedious misapprehension. Taliesin,' Merlin now explained to me, 'has come to learn from my wisdom.'

'I have much to learn,' Taliesin murmured.

'Very true, very true,' Merlin said. He pushed a jug of ale towards me. 'Did you enjoy your little battle, Derfel?'

'No.' In truth I was feeling oddly downcast. 'Cuneglas died,' I explained.

'I heard about Cuneglas,' Merlin said. 'What a fool! He should have left the heroics to halfwits like you. Still, it's a pity he died. He wasn't exactly a clever man, not what I should call clever, but he was no halfwit and that's rare enough in these sad days. And he was always kind to me.'

'He was kindness itself to me,' Taliesin put in.

'So now you will have to find a new patron,' Merlin told the bard, 'and don't look at Derfel. He couldn't tell a decent song from a bullock's fart. The trick of a successful life,' he was now lecturing Taliesin, 'is to be born with wealthy parents. I have lived very comfortably off my rents, though come to think of it I haven't collected them for years. Do you pay me rent, Derfel?'

'I should, Lord, but never know where to send it.'

'Not that it matters now,' Merlin said. 'I'm old and feeble. Doubtless I shall be dead soon.'

'Nonsense,' I said, 'you look wonderfully fit.' He looked old, of course, but there was a spark of mischief in his eyes and a liveliness to his ancient, creased face. His hair and beard were beautifully plaited and bound in black ribbons, while his gown, except for the dried blood, was clean. He was also happy; not, I think, just because we had achieved victory, but because he enjoyed Taliesin's company.

'Victory gives life,' he said dismissively, 'but we'll soon enough forget victory. Where's Arthur?'

'No one knows,' I said. 'I heard he spent a long time talking with Tewdric, but he's not with him now. I suspect he found Guinevere.'

Merlin sneered. 'A hound returns to its vomit.'

'I'm beginning to like her,' I said defensively.

'You would,' he said scornfully, 'and I dare say she won't do any harm now. She would make you a good patron,' he told Taliesin, 'she has an absurd respect for poets. Just don't climb into bed with her.'

'No danger of that, Lord,' Taliesin said.

Merlin laughed. 'Our young bard here,' he told me, 'is celibate. He is a gelded lark. He has forsworn the greatest pleasure a man can have in order to preserve his gift.'

Taliesin saw my curiosity and smiled. 'Not my voice, Lord Derfel, but the gift of prophecy.'

'And it's a genuine gift!' Merlin said with unfeigned admiration, 'though I doubt it's worth celibacy. If I had ever been asked to pay that price I'd have abandoned the Druid's staff! I'd have taken humble employment instead, like being a bard or a spearman.'

'You see the future?' I asked Taliesin.

'He foresaw victory today,' Merlin said, 'and he knew of Cuneglas's death a month ago, though he didn't scry that a useless Saxon lump would come and steal all my cheese.' He snatched the cheese back from me. 'I suppose now,' he said, 'that you want him to forecast your future, Derfel?'

'No, Lord.'

'Quite right,' Merlin said, 'always better not to know the future. Everything ends in tears, that's all there is to it.'

'But joy is renewed,' Taliesin said softly.

'Oh, dear me, no!' Merlin cried. 'Joy is renewed! The dawn comes! The tree buds! The clouds part! The ice melts! You can do better than that sort of sentimental rubbish.' He fell silent. His bodyguard had ended their dance and gone to amuse themselves with some captured Saxon women. The women had children, and their cries were loud enough to annoy Merlin, who scowled. 'Fate is inexorable,' he said sourly, 'and everything ends in tears.'

'Is Nimue with you?' I asked him, and saw immediately from Taliesin's warning expression that I had asked the wrong question.

Merlin gazed into the fire. The flames spat an ember towards him, and he spat back to return the fire's malice. 'Do not speak to me of Nimue,' he said after he had spat. His good mood had vanished and I felt embarrassed for having asked the question. He touched his black staff, then sighed. 'She is angry with me,' he explained.

'Why, Lord?'

'Because she can't have her own way, of course. That's what usually makes people angry.' Another log cracked in the fire, spewing sparks that he brushed irritably from his robe after he had spat at the flames. 'Larchwood,' he said. 'Newly cut larch hates to be burned.' He gazed at me broodingly. 'Nimue did not approve of me bringing Gawain to this battle. She believes it was a waste, and I think, probably, that she was right.'

'He brought victory, Lord,' I said.

He closed his eyes and seemed to sigh, intimating that I was a fool too great for endurance. 'I have devoted my whole life,' he said after a while, 'to one thing. One simple thing. I wanted to restore the Gods. Is that so very hard to understand? But to do anything well, Derfel, takes a lifetime. Oh, it's all right for fools like you, you can fritter about being a magistrate one day and a spearman the next, and when it's all over, what have you achieved?

Nothing! To change the world, Derfel, you have to be single-minded. Arthur comes close, I'll say that for him. He wants to make Britain safe from Saxons, and he's probably achieved that for a while, but they still exist and they'll come back. Maybe not in my lifetime, maybe not even in yours, but your children and your children's children will have to fight this battle all over again. There is only one way to real victory.'

'The way of the Gods,' I said.

'The way of the Gods,' he agreed, 'and that was my life's work.' He gazed down at his black Druid's staff for a moment and Taliesin sat very still, watching him. 'I had a dream as a child,' Merlin said very softly. 'I went to the cave of Carn Ingli and dreamed that I had wings and could fly high enough to see all the isle of Britain, and it was so very beautiful. Beautiful and green and surrounded by a great mist that kept all our enemies away. The blessed isle, Derfel, the isle of the Gods, the one place on earth that was worthy of them, and ever since that dream, Derfel, that is all I ever wanted. To bring that blessed isle back. To bring the Gods back.'

'But,' I tried to interrupt.

'Don't be absurd!' he shouted, making Taliesin smile. 'Think!' Merlin appealed to me. 'My life's work, Derfel!'

'Mai Dun,' I said softly.

He nodded and then, for a while, he said nothing. Men were singing in the distance and everywhere there were fires. The wounded cried in the dark where dogs and scavengers preyed on the dead and the dying. In the dawn this army would wake drunk to the horror of a field after battle, but for now they sang and gorged themselves on captured ale. 'At Mai Dun,' Merlin broke his silence, 'I came so close. Very close. But I was too weak, Derfel, too weak. I love Arthur too much. Why? He isn't witty, his conversation can be as tedious as Gawain's, and he has an absurd devotion to virtue, but I do love him. You, too, as it happens. A weakness, I know. I can enjoy supple men, but I like honest men. I admire simple strength, you see, and at Mai Dun I let that liking weaken me.'

'Gwydre,' I said.

He nodded. 'We should have killed him, but I knew I couldn't do it. Not Arthur's son. That was a terrible weakness.'

'No.'

265

'Don't be absurd!' he said wearily. 'What is Gwydre's life to the Gods? Or to the prospect of restoring Britain? Nothing! But I could not do it. Oh, I had excuses. Caleddin's scroll is quite plain, it says that "the son of the land's King" must be sacrificed, and Arthur is no king, but that's a mere quibble. The rite needed Gwydre's death and I could not bring myself to do it. It was no trouble killing Gawain, it was even a pleasure stilling that virgin fool's babble, but not Gwydre, and so the rite went unfinished.' He was miserable now, hunched and miserable. 'I failed,' he added bitterly.

'And Nimue won't forgive you?' I asked hesitantly.

'Forgive? She doesn't know the word's meaning! Forgiveness is a weakness to Nimue! And now she will perform the rites, and she won't fail, Derfel. If it means killing every mother's son in Britain, she'll do it. Put them all in the pot and give it a good stir!' He half smiled, then shrugged. 'But now, of course, I've made things far more difficult for her. Like the sentimental old fool that I am, I had to help Arthur win this scuffle. I used Gawain to do it and now, I think, she hates me.'

'Why?'

He raised his eyes to the smoky sky as though appealing to the Gods to grant me some small measure of understanding. 'Do you think, you fool,' he asked me, 'that the corpse of a virgin prince is so readily available? It took me years to pump that halfwit's head full of nonsense so that he'd be ready for his sacrifice! And what did I do today? I threw Gawain away! Just to help Arthur.'

'But we won!'

'Don't be absurd.' He glared at me. 'You won? What is that revolting thing on your shield?'

I turned to look at the shield. 'The cross.'

Merlin rubbed his eyes. 'There is a war between the Gods, Derfel, and today I gave victory to Yahweh.'

'Who?'

'It's the name of the Christian God. Sometimes they call him Jehovah. So far as I can determine he's nothing but a humble fire God from some wretched far-off country who is now intent on usurping all the other Gods. He must be an ambitious little toad, because he's winning, and it was I who gave him this victory today. What do you think men will remember of this battle?'

266

'Arthur's victory,' I said firmly.

'In a hundred years, Derfel,' Merlin said, 'they will not remember whether it was a victory or a defeat.'

I paused. 'Cuneglas's death?' I offered.

'Who cares about Cuneglas? Just another forgotten king.'

'Aelle's death?' I suggested.

'A dying dog would deserve more attention.'

'Then what?'

He grimaced at my obtuseness. 'They will remember, Derfel, that the cross was carried on your shields. Today, you fool, we gave Britain to the Christians, and I was the one who gave it to them. I gave Arthur his ambition, but the price, Derfel, was mine. Do you understand now?'

'Yes, Lord.'

'And so I made Nimue's task a great deal harder. But she will try, Derfel, and she is not like me. She is not weak. There is a hardness inside Nimue, such a hardness.'

I smiled. 'She will not kill Gwydre,' I said confidently, 'for neither Arthur nor I will let her, and she won't be given Excalibur, so how can she win?'

He gazed at me. 'Do you think, idiot, that either you or Arthur are strong enough to resist Nimue? She is a woman, and what women want, they get, and if the world and all it holds must be broken in the getting, then so be it. She'll break me first, then turn her eye on you. Isn't that the truth, my young prophet?' he asked Taliesin, but the bard had closed his eyes. Merlin shrugged. 'I shall take her Gawain's ashes, and give her what help I can,' he said, 'because I promised her that. But it will all end in tears, Derfel, it will all end in tears. What a mess I have made. What a terrible mess.' He pulled his cloak about his shoulders. 'I shall sleep now,' he announced.

Beyond the fire the Blackshields raped their captives and I sat staring into the flames. I had helped win a great victory, and was inexpressibly sad.

I did not see Arthur that night and met him only briefly in the misty half-light just before the dawn. He greeted me with all his old vivacity, throwing an arm about my shoulders. 'I want to thank you,' he said, 'for looking after Guinevere these last weeks.' He was in his full armour and was making a hasty breakfast from a mildewed loaf of bread.

'If anything,' I said, 'Guinevere looked after me.'

'The wagons, you mean! I do wish I'd seen it!' He threw down the bread as Hygwydd, his servant, led Llamrei out of the gloom. 'I might see you tonight, Derfel,' Arthur said as he let Hygwydd heave him up into the saddle, 'or maybe tomorrow.'

'Where are you going, Lord?'

'After Cerdic, of course.' He settled himself on Llamrei's back, gathered her reins and took his shield and spear from Hygwydd. He kicked back his heels, going to join his horsemen who were shadowy shapes in the mist. Mordred was also riding with Arthur, no longer under guard, but accepted as a useful soldier in his own right. I watched him curb his horse and remembered the Saxon gold I had found in Lindinis. Had Mordred betrayed us? If he had I could not prove it, and the battle's result negated his treachery, but I still felt a pang of hatred for my King. He caught my malevolent gaze and turned his horse away. Arthur shouted his men on and I listened to the thunder of their departing hoofs.

I stirred my sleeping men awake with the butt of a spear and ordered them to find Saxon captives to dig more graves and build more funeral pyres. I believed I would spend my own day doing that weary business, but in mid-morning Sagramor sent a messenger begging me to bring a detachment of spearmen to Aquae Sulis where trouble had broken out. The disturbances had begun with a rumour among Tewdric's spearmen that Cerdic's treasury had been discovered and that Arthur was keeping it all for himself. Their proof was Arthur's disappearance and their revenge was a proposal to pull down the city's central shrine because it had once been a pagan temple. I managed to calm that frenzy by announcing that two chests of gold had indeed been discovered, but that they were under guard and their contents would be fairly shared once Arthur returned. At Tewdric's suggestion we sent a half-dozen of his soldiers to help guard the chests, which were still in the remnants of Cerdic's encampment.

The Christians of Gwent calmed down, but then the spearmen of Powys made new trouble by blaming Oengus mac Airem for

Cuneglas's death. The enmity between Powys and Demetia went back a long way, for Oengus mac Airem was famously fond of raiding his richer neighbour's harvest; indeed, Powys was known in Demetia as 'our larder', but this day it was the men of Powys who picked the quarrel by insisting that Cuneglas would never have died if the Blackshields had not come late to the battle. The Irish have never been reluctant to join a fight, and no sooner were Tewdric's men placated than there was a clash of swords and spears outside the law courts as Powysians and Blackshields met in a bloody skirmish. Sagramor brought an uneasy peace by the simple expedient of killing the leaders of both factions, but throughout the rest of that day there was trouble between the two nations. The discord grew worse when it was learned that Tewdric had sent a detachment of soldiers to occupy Lactodurum, a northern fortress that had not been in British hands for a lifetime, but which the leaderless men of Powys claimed had always been in their territory, not Gwent's, and a hastily raised band of Powysian spearmen set off after Tewdric's men to challenge their claim. The Blackshields, who had no dog in the Lactodurum fight, nevertheless insisted that the men of Gwent were right, only because they knew that opinion would infuriate the Powysians, and so there were more battles. They were deadly brawls about a town of which most of the combatants had never heard and which might, anyway, still be garrisoned by the Saxons.

We Dumnonians managed to avoid those battles, and so it was our spearmen who guarded the streets and thus confined the fighting to the taverns, but in the afternoon we were dragged into the disputes when Argante and a score of attendants arrived from Glevum to discover that Guinevere had occupied the bishop's house that was built behind the temple of Minerva. The bishop's palace was not the largest or most comfortable in Aquae Sulis, that distinction belonged to the palace of Cildydd, the magistrate, but Lancelot had used Cildydd's house while he was in Aquae Sulis and for that reason Guinevere avoided it. Argante nevertheless insisted that she should have the bishop's house, for it was within the sacred enclosure, and an enthusiastic party of Blackshields went to evict Guinevere, only to be met by a score of my men intent on defending her. Two men died before Guinevere announced that she did not care what house sheltered her and moved to the priests' chambers that were built alongside the great baths. Argante, victorious in that encounter, declared that Guinevere's new quarters were fitting, for she claimed that the priests' chambers had once been a brothel, and Argante's Druid, Fergal, led a crowd of Blackshields to the bath-house where they amused themselves by demanding to know the brothel's prices and shouting for Guinevere to show them her body. Another contingent of Blackshields had occupied the temple and thrown out the hastily erected cross that Tewdric had placed above the altar, and scores of red-robed spearmen of Gwent were gathering to fight their way inside and replace the cross.

Sagramor and I brought spearmen to the sacred enclosure which, in the late afternoon, promised to become a bloodbath. My men guarded the temple doors, Sagramor's protected Guinevere, but we were both outnumbered by the drunken warriors from Demetia and Gwent, while the Powysians, glad to have a cause with which they could annoy the Blackshields, shouted their support for Guinevere. I pushed through the mead-sodden crowd, clubbing down the most raucous troublemakers, but I feared the violence that grew ever more menacing as the sun sank. It was Sagramor who finally brought an uneasy peace to the evening. He climbed to the bath-house roof and there, standing tall between two statues, he roared for silence. He had stripped himself to the waist so that, contrasted with the white marble of the warriors on either side, his black skin was all the more striking. 'If any of you have an argument,' he announced in his curiously accented British, 'you will have it with me first. Man to man! Sword or spear, take your pick.' He drew his long curved sword and glared at the angry men below.

'Get rid of the whore!' an anonymous voice shouted from the Blackshields.

'You object to whores?' Sagramor shouted back. 'What kind of a warrior are you? A virgin? If you're so intent on being virtuous then come up here and I'll geld you.' That brought laughter and so ended the immediate danger.

Argante sulked in her palace. She was calling herself the Empress of Dumnonia and demanding that Sagramor and I provide her with Dumnonian guards, but she was already so thickly attended by her father's Blackshields that neither of us obeyed. Instead we both stripped naked and lowered ourselves into the great Roman bath where we lay exhausted. The hot water was wonderfully restful. Steam wisped up to the broken tiles of the roof. 'I have been told,' Sagramor said, 'that this is the largest building in Britain.'

I eyed the vast roof. 'It probably is.'

'But when I was a child,' Sagramor said, 'I was a slave in a house even bigger than this.'

'In Numidia?'

He nodded. 'Though I come from farther south. I was sold into slavery when I was very young. I don't even remember my parents.'

'When did you leave Numidia?' I asked.

'After I had killed my first man. A steward, he was. And I was ten years old? Eleven? I ran away and joined a Roman army as a slinger. I can still put a stone between a man's eyes at fifty paces. Then I learned to ride. I fought in Italy, Thrace and Egypt, then took money to join the Frankish army. That was where Arthur took me captive.' He was rarely so forthcoming. Silence, indeed, was one of Sagramor's most effective weapons, that and his hawklike face and his terrifying reputation, but in private he was a gentle and reflective soul. 'Whose side are we on?' he now asked me with a puzzled look.

'What do you mean?'

'Guinevere? Argante?'

I shrugged. 'You tell me.'

He ducked his head under the water, then came up and wiped his eyes clear. 'I suppose Guinevere,' he said, 'if the rumour is true.'

'What rumour?'

'That she and Arthur were together last night,' he said, 'though being Arthur, of course, they spent the night talking. He'll wear his tongue out long before his sword.'

'No danger of you doing that.'

'No,' he said with a smile, then the smile broadened as he looked at me. 'I hear, Derfel, that you broke a shield wall?'

'Only a thin one,' I said, 'and a young one.'

'I broke a thick one,' he said with a grin, 'a very thick one, and full of experienced warriors,' and I ducked him under the water in revenge, then splashed away before he could drown me. The baths were gloomy because no torches were lit and the very last of the day's long sunlight could not reach down through the holes in the roof. Steam misted the big room, and though I was aware that other folk were using the huge bath, I had not recognized any of them, but now, swimming across the pool, I saw a figure in white robes stooping to a man sitting on one of the underwater steps. I recognized the tufts of hair on either side of the stooping man's shaven forehead and a heartbeat later caught his words. 'Trust me on this,' he was saying with a quiet fervency, 'just leave it to me, Lord King.' He looked up at that moment and saw me. It was Bishop Sansum, newly released from his captivity and restored to all his former honours because of Arthur's promises to Tewdric. He seemed surprised to see me, but managed a sickly smile. 'The Lord Derfel,' he said, stepping cautiously back from the bath's brink, 'one of our heroes!'

'Derfel!' the man on the pool steps roared, and I saw it was Oengus mac Airem who now launched himself to offer me a bear-like embrace. 'First time I've ever hugged a naked man,' the King of the Blackshields said, 'and I can't say I see the attraction of it. First time I've taken a bath too. Do you think it will kill me?'

'No.' I said, then glanced towards Sansum. 'You keep strange company, Lord King.'

'Wolves have fleas, Derfel, wolves have fleas,' Oengus grunted.

'So in what matter,' I asked Sansum, 'should my Lord King trust you?'

Sansum did not answer, and Oengus himself looked unnaturally sheepish. 'The shrine,' he finally offered as answer. 'The good bishop was saying that he could arrange for my men to use it as a temple for a while. Isn't that right, Bishop?'

'Exactly so, Lord King,' Sansum said.

'You're both bad liars,' I said, and Oengus laughed. Sansum gave me a hostile look, then scuttled away down the flagstones. He had been a free man for just hours now, yet already he was plotting. 'What was he telling you, Lord King?' I pressed Oengus, who was a man I liked. A simple man, a strong man, a rogue, but a very good friend.

'What do you think?'

'He was talking about your daughter,' I guessed.

'Pretty little thing, isn't she?' Oengus said. 'Too thin, of course, and with a mind like a wolf bitch on heat. It's a strange world, Derfel. I breed sons dull as oxen and daughters sharp as wolves.' He paused to greet Sagramor who had followed me across the water. 'So what is to happen to Argante?' Oengus asked me.

'I don't know, Lord.'

'Arthur married her, didn't he?'

'I'm not even sure of that,' I said.

He gave me a sharp look, then smiled as he understood my meaning. 'She says they are properly married, but then she would. I wasn't sure Arthur really wanted to marry her, but I pressed him. It was one less mouth to feed, you understand.' He paused for a second. 'The thing is, Derfel,' he went on, 'that Arthur can't just send her back! That's an insult, and besides, I don't want her back. I've got plenty enough daughters without her. Half the time I don't even know which are mine and which aren't. You ever need a wife? Come to Demetia and take your pick, but I warn you they're all like her. Pretty, but with very sharp teeth. So what will Arthur do?'

'What is Sansum suggesting?' I asked.

Oengus pretended to ignore the question, but I knew he would tell us in the end because he was not a man to keep secrets. 'He just reminded me,' he eventually confessed, 'that Argante was once promised to Mordred.'

'She was?' Sagramor asked, surprised.

'It was mentioned,' I said, 'some time ago.' It had been mentioned by Oengus himself who was desperate for anything that might strengthen his alliance with Dumnonia which was his best protection against Powys.

'And if Arthur didn't marry her properly,' Oengus went on, 'then Mordred would be a consolation, wouldn't he?'

'Some consolation,' Sagramor said sourly.

'She'll be Queen,' Oengus said.

'She will,' I agreed.

'So it isn't a bad idea,' Oengus said lightly, though I suspected it was an idea he would support passionately. A marriage with Mordred would compensate Demetia's hurt pride, but it would also give Dumnonia an obligation to protect its Queen's country.

For myself I thought Sansum's proposal was the worst idea I had heard all day, for I could imagine only too well what mischief the combination of Mordred and Argante might breed, but I kept silent. 'You know what this bath lacks?' Oengus asked.

'Tell me, Lord King.'

'Women.' He chuckled. 'So where's your woman, Derfel?'

'In mourning,' I said.

'Oh, for Cuneglas, of course!' The Blackshield King shrugged. 'He never liked me, but I rather liked him. He was a rare one for believing promises!' Oengus laughed, for the promises had been ones that he had made without any intention of ever keeping them. 'Can't say I'm sorry he's dead, though. His son's just a boy and much too fond of his mother. She and those dreadful aunts of hers will rule for a while. Three witches!' He laughed again. 'I can see we might pick off a few pieces of land from those three ladies.' He slowly lowered his face into the pool. 'I'm chasing the lice upwards,' he explained, then pinched one of the little grey insects that was scrambling up his tangled beard to escape the encroaching water.

I had not seen Merlin all that day, and that night Galahad told me the Druid had already left the valley, going north. I had found Galahad standing beside Cuneglas's balefire. 'I know Cuneglas disliked Christians,' Galahad explained to me, 'but I don't think he would object to a Christian's prayer.' I invited him to sleep among my men and he walked with me to where they were camped. 'Merlin did give me a message for you,' Galahad told me. 'He says you will find what you seek among the trees that are dead.'

'I'm not sure I'm seeking anything,' I said.

'Then look among the dead trees,' Galahad said, 'and you'll find whatever it is you're not looking for.'

I looked for nothing that night, but instead slept wrapped in my cloak among my men on the battlefield. I woke early with an aching head and sore joints. The fine weather had passed and a drizzle was spitting out of the west. The rain threatened to dampen the balefires and so we began collecting wood to feed the flames, and that reminded me of Merlin's strange message, but I could see no dead trees. We were using Saxon battle axes to chop down oaks, elms and beech, sparing only the sacred ash trees, and all the trees we cut were healthy enough. I asked Issa if he had noticed any dead trees and he shook his head, but Eachern said he had seen some down by the river bend.

'Show me.'

Eachern led a whole group of us down to the bank and, where the river turned sharply west, there was a great mass of dead trees caught on the half exposed roots of a willow. The dead branches were matted with a tangle of other debris that had been washed down river, but I could see nothing of any value among the scraps. 'If Merlin says there's something there,' Galahad said, 'then we ought to look.'

'He might not have meant those trees,' I said.

'They're as good as any,' Issa said, and he stripped off his sword so that it would not get wet and jumped down onto the tangle. He broke through the brittle upper branches to splash into the river. 'Give me a spear!' he called.

Galahad handed down a spear and Issa used it to poke among the branches. In one place a stretch of frayed and tarred netting from a fish trap had been snagged to form a tent-like shape that was thick with dead leaves, and Issa needed all his strength to heave that tangled mass aside.

It was then that the fugitive broke cover. He had been hiding under the net, poised uncomfortably on a half-submerged trunk, but now, like an otter flushed by hounds, he scrambled away from Issa's spear and tried to escape up river. The dead trees tripped him, and the weight of armour slowed him, and my men, whooping on the bank, easily overtook him. If the fugitive had not been wearing armour he might have thrown himself into the river and swum to its far bank, but now he could do nothing but surrender. The man must have spent two nights and a day working his way up the river, but then discovered the hiding place and thought he could stay there until we had all left the battlefield. Now he was caught.

It was Lancelot. I first recognized him because of his long black hair of which he was so vain, then, through the mud and twigs, I saw the famous white enamel of his armour. His face showed nothing but terror. He looked from us to the river, as if contemplating throwing himself into the current, then he looked back and saw his half-brother. 'Galahad!' he called. 'Galahad!'

275

Galahad looked at me for a few heartbeats, then he made the sign of the cross, turned and walked away.

'Galahad!' Lancelot shouted again as his brother vanished from the bank above.

Galahad just kept walking.

'Bring him up,' I ordered. Issa jabbed at Lancelot with the spear and the terrified man scrambled desperately up through the nettles that grew on the bank. He still had his sword, though its blade must have been rusty after its immersion in the river. I faced him as he stumbled free of the nettles. 'Will you fight me here and now, Lord King?' I asked him, drawing Hywelbane.

'Let me go, Derfel! I'll send you money, I promise!' He babbled on, promising me gold beyond my dreams' desires, but he would not draw the sword until I prodded his chest hard with Hywelbane's point and at that moment he knew he must die. He spat at me, took one pace backwards, and drew his blade. It had once been called Tanlladwr, which means Bright Killer, but he had renamed it the Christblade when Sansum had baptized him. The Christblade was rusted now, but still a formidable weapon, and to my surprise Lancelot was no mean swordsman. I had always taken him for a coward, but that day he fought bravely enough. He was desperate, and the desperation showed itself in a series of slashing quick attacks that forced me back. But he was also tired, wet and cold, and he wearied quickly so that when his first flurry of blows had all been parried I was able to take my time as I decided on his death. He became more desperate and his blows wilder, but I ended the fight when I ducked under one of those massive cuts and held Hywelbane so that her point caught him on the arm and the momentum of his swing opened the veins from the wrist to the elbow. He yelped as the blood flowed, then his sword fell from his nerveless hand and he waited in abject terror for the killing blow.

I cleaned Hywelbane's blade with a handful of grass, dried her on my cloak, then sheathed her. 'I don't want your soul on my sword,' I told Lancelot, and for a heartbeat he looked grateful, but then I broke his hopes. 'Your men killed my child,' I told him, 'the same men you sent to try and fetch Ceinwyn to your bed. You think I can forgive you for either?'

'They were not my orders,' he said desperately. 'Believe me!'

I spat in his face. 'Shall I give you to Arthur, Lord King?'

'No, Derfel, please!' He clasped his hands. He shivered. 'Please!'

'Give him the woman's death,' Issa urged me, meaning that we should strip him, geld him and let him bleed to death between his legs.

I was tempted, but I feared to enjoy Lancelot's death. There is a pleasure in revenge, and I had given Dian's killers a terrible death and felt no pang of conscience as I enjoyed their suffering, but I had no belly for the torture of this quivering, broken man. He shook so much that I felt pity for him, and I found myself debating whether to let him live. I knew he was a traitor and a coward and that he deserved to be killed, but his terror was so abject that I actually felt sorry for him. He had always been my enemy, he had always despised me, yet as he dropped to his knees in front of me and the tears rolled down his cheeks I felt the impulse to grant him mercy and knew there would be as much pleasure in that exercise of power as there would be in ordering his death. For a heartbeat I wanted his gratitude, but then I remembered my daughter's dying face and a shudder of rage made me tremble. Arthur was famous for forgiving his enemies, but this was one enemy I could never forgive.

'The woman's death,' Issa suggested again.

'No,' I said, and Lancelot looked up at me with renewed hope. 'Hang him like a common felon,' I said.

Lancelot howled, but I hardened my heart. 'Hang him,' I ordered again, and so we did. We found a length of horsehair rope, looped it over the branch of an oak and hoisted him up. He danced as he hung, and went on dancing until Galahad returned and tugged on his half-brother's ankles to put him out of his choking misery.

We stripped Lancelot's body naked. I threw his sword and his fine scale armour into the river, burned his clothes, then used a big Saxon war axe to dismember his corpse. We did not burn him, but tossed him to the fishes so that his dark soul would not sour the Otherworld with its presence. We obliterated him from the earth, and I kept only his enamelled sword belt that had been a gift from Arthur.

I met Arthur at midday. He was returning from his pursuit of Cerdic and he and his men rode tired horses down into the valley.

'We didn't catch Cerdic,' he told me, 'but we caught some others.' He patted Llamrei's sweat-whitened neck. 'Cerdic lives, Derfel,' he said, 'but he's so weakened that he won't be a problem for a long time.' He smiled, then saw I was not matching his cheerful mood. 'What is it?' he asked.

'Just this, Lord,' I said, and held up the expensive enamelled belt.

For a moment he thought I was showing him a piece of plunder, then he recognized the sword belt which had been his own gift to Lancelot. For a heartbeat his face had the look it had borne for so many months before Mynydd Baddon: the closed, hard look of bitterness, and then he glanced up into my eyes. 'Its owner?'

'Dead, Lord. Hanged in shame.'

'Good,' he said quietly. 'And that thing, Derfel, you can throw away.' I threw the belt into the river.

And thus Lancelot died, though the songs he had paid for lived on, and to this day he is celebrated as a hero equal to Arthur. Arthur is remembered as a ruler, but Lancelot is called the warrior. In truth he was the King without land, a coward, and the greatest traitor of Britain, and his soul wanders Lloegyr to this day, screaming for its shadowbody that can never exist because we cut his corpse into scraps and fed it to the river. If the Christians are right, and there is a hell, may he suffer there for ever.

Galahad and I followed Arthur to the city, passing the balefire on which Cuneglas burned and threading the Roman graves amongst which so many of Aelle's men had died. I had warned Arthur what waited for him, but he showed no dismay when he heard that Argante had come to the city.

His arrival in Aquae Sulis prompted scores of anxious petitioners to clamour for his attention. The petitioners were men demanding recognition for acts of bravery in the battle, men demanding shares of slaves or gold, and men demanding justice in disputes that long preceded the Saxon invasion, and Arthur told them all to attend him in the temple, though once there he ignored the supplicants. Instead he summoned Galahad to an ante-chamber of the temple and, after a while, he sent for Sansum. The Bishop was jeered by the Dumnonian spearmen as he hurried across the compound. He spoke with Arthur a long time, and then Oengus mac Airem and Mordred were called to Arthur's presence. The spearmen in the enclosure were making wagers on whether Arthur would go to Argante in the Bishop's house or to Guinevere in the priests' quarters.

Arthur had not wanted my counsel. Instead, when he summoned Oengus and Mordred, he asked me to tell Guinevere that he had returned and so I crossed the yard to the priests' quarters where I discovered Guinevere in an upper room, attended by Taliesin. The bard, dressed in a clean white robe and with the silver fillet about his black hair, stood and bowed as I entered. He carried a small harp, but I sensed the two had been talking rather than making music. He smiled and backed from the room, letting the thick curtain fall across the doorway. 'A most clever man,' Guinevere said, standing to greet me. She was in a cream-coloured robe trimmed with blue ribboned hems, she wore the Saxon necklace I had given her on Mynydd Baddon, and had her red hair gathered at the crown of her head with a length of silver chain. She was not quite as elegant as the Guinevere I remembered from before the time of troubles, but she was a far cry from the armoured woman who had ridden so enthusiastically across the battlefield. She smiled as I drew near. 'You're clean, Derfel!'

'I took a bath, Lady.'

'And you live!' She mocked me gently, then kissed my cheek, and once the kiss was given she held on to my shoulders for a moment. 'I owe you a great deal,' she said softly.

'No, Lady, no,' I said, reddening and pulling away.

She laughed at my embarrassment, then went to sit in the window that overlooked the compound. Rain puddled between the stones and dripped down the temple's stained façade where Arthur's horse was tied to a ring fixed to one of the pillars. She hardly needed me to tell her that Arthur had come back, for she must have seen his arrival herself. 'Who's with him?' she asked me.

'Galahad, Sansum, Mordred and Oengus.'

'And you weren't summoned to Arthur's council?' she asked with a touch of her old mockery.

'No, Lady,' I said, trying to hide my disappointment.

'I'm sure he hasn't forgotten you.'

'I hope not, Lady,' I said and then, much more hesitantly, I told her that Lancelot was dead. I did not tell her how, simply that he was dead.

'Taliesin already told me,' she said, staring down at her hands.

'How did he know?' I asked, for Lancelot's death had only happened a brief while before and Taliesin had not been present.

'He dreamed it last night,' Guinevere said, and then she made an abrupt gesture as if ending that subject. 'So what are they discussing over there?' she asked, glancing at the temple. 'The child-bride?'

'I imagine so, Lady,' I said, then I told her what Bishop Sansum had suggested to Oengus mac Airem: that Argante should marry Mordred. 'I think it's the worst idea I've ever heard,' I protested indignantly.

'You really think that?'

'It's an absurd notion,' I said.

'It wasn't Sansum's notion,' Guinevere said with a smile, 'it was mine.'

I stared at her, too surprised to speak for a moment. 'Yours, Lady?' I finally asked.

'Don't tell anyone it was my idea,' she warned me. 'Argante wouldn't consider it for a moment if she thought the idea came from me. She'd marry a swineherd rather than someone I suggested. So I sent for little Sansum and begged him to tell me whether the rumour about Argante and Mordred was correct, and then I said how much I loathed the very thought of it and that, of course, made him all the more enthusiastic about it, though he pretended not to be. I even cried a little and begged him never to tell Argante how much I detested the very idea. By that point, Derfel, they were as good as married.' She smiled triumphantly.

'But why?' I asked. 'Mordred and Argante? They'll make nothing but trouble!'

'Whether they're married or not, they'll make trouble. And Mordred must marry, Derfel, if he's to provide an heir, and that means he must marry royally.' She paused, fingering the necklace. 'I confess I would much rather he didn't have an heir, for that would leave the throne free when he dies.' She left that thought unfinished and I gave her a curious look, to which she responded with a mask of innocence. Was she thinking that Arthur might take the throne from a childless Mordred? But Arthur had never wanted to rule. Then I realized that if Mordred did die then Gwydre, Guinevere's son, would have as good a claim as any man. That realization must have shown on my face for Guinevere smiled. 'Not that we must speculate about the succession,' she went on before I could say anything, 'for Arthur insists Mordred must be allowed to marry if he wishes, and it seems the wretched boy is attracted to Argante. They might even suit each other quite well. Like two vipers in a filthy nest.'

'And Arthur will have two enemies united in bitterness,' I said.

'No,' Guinevere said, then she sighed and looked through the window. 'Not if we give them what they want, and not if I give Arthur what he wants. And you do know what that is, don't you?'

I thought for a heartbeat, then understood everything. I understood what she and Arthur must have talked about in the long night after battle. I understood, too, what Arthur was arranging now in the temple of Minerva. 'No!' I protested.

Guinevere smiled. 'I don't want it either, Derfel, but I do want Arthur. And what he wants, I must give him. I do owe him some happiness, do I not?' she asked.

'He wants to give up his power?' I asked, and she nodded. Arthur had ever spoken of his dream of living simply with a wife, his family and some land. He wanted a hall, a palisade, a smithy and fields. He imagined himself a landowner, with no troubles other than the birds stealing his seed, the deer eating his crops and the rain spoiling his harvest. He had nurtured that dream for years and now, having beaten the Saxons, it seemed he would make the dream reality.

'Meurig also wants Arthur to give up his power,' Guinevere said.

'Meurig!' I spat. 'Why should we care what Meurig wants?'

'It is the price Meurig demanded before he agreed to let his father lead Gwent's army to war,' Guinevere said. 'Arthur didn't tell you before the battle because he knew you would argue with him.'

'But why would Meurig want Arthur to give up his power?'

'Because he believes Mordred is a Christian,' Guinevere said with a shrug, 'and because he wants Dumnonia to be ill-governed. That way, Derfel, Meurig stands a chance of taking Dumnonia's throne one day. He's an ambitious little toad.' I called him something worse, and Guinevere smiled. 'That too,' she said, 'but what he demanded, he must get, so Arthur and I will go to live in Silurian Isca where Meurig can keep an eye on us. I don't mind living in Isca. It will be better than life in some decaying hall. There are some fine Roman palaces in Isca and some very good hunting. We'll take some spearmen with us. Arthur doesn't think he needs any, but he has enemies and he needs a warband.'

I paced up and down the room. 'But Mordred!' I complained bitterly. 'He's to be given back the power?'

'It's the price we had to pay for Gwent's army,' Guinevere said, 'and if Argante is to marry Mordred then he must have his power or else Oengus will never agree to the marriage. Or at least Mordred must be given some of his power, and she must share it.'

'And all Arthur achieved will be broken!' I said.

'Arthur has freed Dumnonia of Saxons,' Guinevere said, 'and he does not want to be King. You know that, and I know that. It isn't what I want, Derfel. I always wanted Arthur to be the High King and for Gwydre to succeed him, but he doesn't want it and he won't fight for it. He wants quiet, he tells me. And if he won't rule Dumnonia, then Mordred must. Gwent's insistence and Arthur's oath to Uther ensures that.'

'So he'll just abandon Dumnonia to injustice and tyranny!' I protested.

'No,' Guinevere said, 'for Mordred will not have all the power.'

I gazed at her, and guessed from her voice that I had not understood everything. 'Go on,' I said guardedly.

'Sagramor will stay. The Saxons are defeated, but there will still be a frontier and there is no one better than Sagramor to guard it. And the rest of Dumnonia's army will swear their loyalty to another man. Mordred can rule, for he is King, but he will not command the spears, and a man without spears is a man without real power. You and Sagramor will hold that.'

'No!'

Guinevere smiled. 'Arthur knew you would say that, which is why I said I would persuade you.'

'Lady,' I began to protest, but she held up a hand to silence me.

'You are to rule Dumnonia, Derfel. Mordred will be King, but you will have the spears, and the man who commands the spears rules. You must do it for Arthur, because only if you agree can he leave Dumnonia with a clear conscience. So, to give him peace, do it for him and, maybe,' she hesitated, 'for me too? Please?'

Merlin was right. When a woman wants something, she gets it. And I was to rule Dumnonia.

TALIESIN MADE A SONG of Mynydd Baddon. He deliberately made it in the old style with a simple rhythm that throbbed with drama, heroism and bombast. It was a very long song, for it was important that every warrior who fought well received at least a half-line of praise, while our leaders had whole verses to themselves. After the battle Taliesin joined Guinevere's household and he sensibly gave his patroness her due, wonderfully describing the hurtling wagons with their heaps of fire, but avoiding any mention of the Saxon wizard she had killed with her bow. He used her red hair as an image of the blood-soaked crop of barley amongst which some Saxons died, and though I never saw any barley growing on the battlefield, it was a clever touch. He made the death of his old patron, Cuneglas, into a slow lament in which the dead King's name was repeated like a drumbeat, and he turned Gawain's charge into a chilling account of how the wraith-souls of our dead spearmen came from the bridge of swords to assail the enemy's flank. He praised Tewdric, was kind to me and gave honour to Sagramor, but above all his song was a celebration of Arthur. In Taliesin's song it was Arthur who flooded the valley with enemy blood, and Arthur who struck down the enemy King, and Arthur who made all Lloegyr cower with terror.

The Christians hated Taliesin's song. They made their own songs in which it was Tewdric who beat down the Saxons. The Lord God Almighty, the Christian songs claimed, had heard Tewdric's pleas and fetched the host of heaven to the battlefield and there His angels fought the Sais with swords of fire. Arthur received no mention in their songs, indeed the pagans were given none of the credit for the victory and to this day there are folk who declare that Arthur was not even present at Mynydd Baddon. One Christian song actually credits Meurig with Aelle's death, and

Meurig was not present at Mynydd Baddon, but at home in Gwent. After the battle Meurig was restored to his kingship, while Tewdric returned to his monastery where he was declared a saint by Gwent's bishops.

Arthur was much too busy that summer to care about making songs or saints. In the weeks following the battle we took back huge parts of Lloegyr, though we could not take it all for plenty of Saxons remained in Britain. The further east we went, the stiffer their resistance became, but by autumn the enemy was penned back into a territory only half the size they had previously ruled. Cerdic even paid us tribute that year, and he promised to pay it for ten years to come, though he never did. Instead he welcomed every boat that came across the sea and slowly rebuilt his broken forces.

Aelle's kingdom was divided. The southern portion went back into Cerdic's hands, while the northern part broke into three or four small kingdoms that were ruthlessly raided by warbands from Elmet, Powys and Gwent. Thousands of Saxons came under British rule, indeed all of Dumnonia's new eastern lands were inhabited by them. Arthur wanted us to resettle that land, but few Britons were willing to go there and so the Saxons stayed, farmed and dreamed of the day when their own Kings would return. Sagramor became the virtual ruler of Dumnonia's reclaimed lands. The Saxon chiefs knew their King was Mordred, but in those first years after Mynydd Baddon it was to Sagramor they paid their homage and taxes, and it was his stark black banner that flew above the old river fort at Pontes from where his warriors marched to keep the peace.

Arthur led the campaign to take back the stolen land, but once it was secured and once the Saxons had agreed our new frontiers, he left Dumnonia. To the very last some of us hoped he would break the promise he had given to Meurig and Tewdric, but he had no wish to stay. He had never wanted power. He had taken it as a duty at a time when Dumnonia possessed a child King and a score of ambitious warlords whose rivalry would have torn the land into turmoil, but through all the years that followed he had ever clung to his dream of living a simpler life, and once the Saxons were defeated he felt free to make his dream reality. I pleaded with him to think again, but he shook his head. 'I'm old, Derfel.'

'Not much older than I am, Lord.'

'Then you're old,' he said with a smile. 'Over forty! How many men live forty years?'

Few indeed. Yet even so I think Arthur would have wanted to stay in Dumnonia if he had received what he wanted, and that was gratitude. He was a proud man, and he knew what he had done for the country, but the country had rewarded him with a sullen discontent. The Christians had broken his peace first, but afterwards, following the fires of Mai Dun, the pagans had turned against him. He had given Dumnonia justice, he had regained much of its lost land and secured its new frontiers, he had ruled honestly, and his reward was to be derided as the enemy of the Gods. Besides, he had promised Meurig he would leave Dumnonia, and that promise reinforced the oath he had given to Uther to make Mordred King, and now he declared he would keep both promises in full. 'I'll have no happiness until the oaths are kept,' he told me, and he could not be persuaded otherwise and so, when the new frontier with the Saxons was decided and Cerdic's first tribute had been paid, he left.

He took sixty horsemen and a hundred spearmen and went to the town of Isca in Siluria, which lay north across the Severn Sea from Dumnonia. He had originally proposed to take no spearmen with him, but Guinevere's advice had prevailed. Arthur, she said, had enemies and needed protection, and besides, his horsemen were among the most potent of Britain's warriors and she did not want them falling under another man's command. Arthur let himself be persuaded, though in truth I do not think he needed much persuasion. He might dream of being a mere landowner living in a peaceful countryside with no worries other than the health of his livestock and the state of his crops, but he knew that the only peace he would ever have was of his own making and that a lord who lives without warriors will not stay at peace for long.

Siluria was a small, poor and unregarded kingdom. The last King of its old dynasty had been Gundleus, who had died at Lugg Vale, and afterwards Lancelot was acclaimed the King, but he had disliked Siluria and had happily abandoned it for the wealthier throne of the Belgic country. Lacking another King, Siluria had been divided into two client kingdoms subservient to Gwent and

Powys. Cuneglas had called himself King of Western Siluria, while Meurig was proclaimed King of Eastern Siluria, but in truth neither monarch had seen much value in its steep, cramped valleys that ran to the sea from its raw northern mountains. Cuneglas had recruited spearmen from the valleys while Meurig of Gwent had done little more than send missionaries into the territory, and the only King who had ever taken any interest in Siluria was Oengus mac Airem who had raided the valleys for food and slaves, but otherwise Siluria had been ignored. Its chieftains squabbled amongst themselves and grudgingly paid their taxes to Gwent or Powys, but the coming of Arthur changed all that. Whether he liked it or not he became Siluria's most important inhabitant and thus its effective ruler and, despite his declared ambition to be a private man, he could not resist using his spearmen to end the chieftains' ruinous squabbles. A year after Mynydd Baddon, when we first visited Arthur and Guinevere in Isca, he was wryly calling himself the Governor, a Roman title, and one that pleased him for it had no connotation of kingship.

Isca was a beautiful town. The Romans had first made a fort there to guard the river crossing, but as they pushed their legions further west and north their need for the fort diminished and they turned Isca into a place not unlike Aquae Sulis: a town where Romans went to enjoy themselves. It had an amphitheatre and though it lacked hot springs, Isca still boasted six bath-houses, three palaces and as many temples as the Romans had Gods. The town was much decayed now, but Arthur was repairing the law-courts and the palaces, and such work always made him happy. The largest of the palaces, the one where Lancelot had lived, was given to Culhwch, who had been named the commander of Arthur's bodyguard and most of those guards shared the big palace with Culhwch. The second largest palace was now home to Emrys, once Bishop of Dumnonia but now the Bishop of Isca. 'He couldn't stay in Dumnonia,' Arthur told me as he showed me the town. It was a year after Mynydd Baddon, and Ceinwyn and I were making our first visit to Arthur's new home. 'There isn't room for both Emrys and Sansum in Dumnonia,' Arthur explained, 'so Emrys helps me here. He has an insatiable appetite for administration and, better still, he keeps Meurig's Christians away.'

'All of them?' I asked.

'Most of them,' he said with a smile, 'and it's a fine place, Derfel,' he went on, gazing at Isca's paved streets, 'a fine place!' He was absurdly proud of his new home, claiming that the rain fell less hard on Isca than on the surrounding countryside. 'I've seen the hills thick with snow,' he told me, 'and the sun has shone on green grass here.'

'Yes, Lord,' I said with a smile.

'It's true, Derfel! True! When I ride out of the town I take a cloak and there comes a point where the heat suddenly fades and you must pull on the cloak. You'll see when we go hunting tomorrow.'

'It sounds like magic,' I said, gently teasing him, for normally he despised any talk of magic.

'I think it well may be!' he said in all seriousness and he led me down an alley that ran beside the big Christian shrine to a curious mound that stood in the town's centre. A spiralling path climbed to the summit of the mound where the old people had made a shallow pit. The pit held countless small offerings left for the Gods; scraps of ribbon, tufts of fleece, buttons, all of them proof that Meurig's missionaries, busy as they had been, had not entirely defeated the old religion. 'If there is magic here,' Arthur told me when we had climbed to the mound's top and were staring down into the grassy pit, 'then this is where it springs from. The local folk say it's an entrance to the Otherworld.'

'And you believe them?'

'I just know this is a blessed place,' he said happily, and so Isca was on that late summer's day. The incoming tide had swollen the river so that it flowed deep within green banks, the sun shone on the white-walled buildings and on the leafy trees that grew in their courtyards, while to the north the small hills with their busy farmlands stretched peacefully to the mountains. It was hard to believe that not so many years before a Saxon raiding party had reached those hills and slaughtered farmers, captured slaves and left the crofts burning. That raid had been during Uther's reign, and Arthur's achievement had been to thrust the enemy so far back that it seemed, that summer and for many summers to come, that no free Saxon would ever come near Isca again.

The town's smallest palace lay just to the west of the mound and it was there that Arthur and Guinevere lived. From our high point on the mysterious mound we could look down into the courtyard where Guinevere and Ceinwyn were pacing, and it was plain that it was Guinevere who was doing all the talking. 'She's planning Gwydre's marriage,' Arthur told me, 'to Morwenna, of course,' he added with a quick smile.

'She's ready for it,' I said fervently. Morwenna was a good girl, but of late she had been moody and irritable. Ceinwyn assured me that Morwenna's behaviour was merely the symptoms of a girl ready for marriage, and I for one would be grateful for the cure.

Arthur sat on the mound's grassy lip and stared westwards. His hands, I noticed, were flecked with small dark scars, all from the furnace of the smithy he had built for himself in his palace's stable yard. He had always been intrigued by blacksmithing and could enthuse for hours about its skills. Now, though, he had different matters on his mind. 'Would you mind,' he asked diffidently, 'if Bishop Emrys blesses the marriage?'

'Why would I mind?' I asked. I liked Emrys.

'Only Bishop Emrys,' Arthur said. 'No Druids. You must understand, Derfel, that I live here at Meurig's pleasure. He is, after all, the King of this land.'

'Lord,' I began to protest, but he stilled me with a raised hand and I did not pursue my indignation. I knew that the young King Meurig was an uneasy neighbour. He resented the fact that his father had temporarily relieved him of his power, resented that he had not shared in any of Mynydd Baddon's glory and was sullenly jealous of Arthur. Meurig's Gwentian territory began only yards from this mound, at the far end of the Roman bridge that crossed the River Usk, and this eastern portion of Siluria was legally another of Meurig's possessions.

'It was Meurig who wanted me to live here as his tenant,' Arthur explained, 'but it was Tewdric who gave me the rights to all the old royal rents. He, at least, is grateful for what we achieved at Mynydd Baddon, but I very much doubt that young Meurig approves of the arrangement, so I placate him by making a show of allegiance to Christianity.' He mimicked the sign of the cross and offered me a self-deprecating grimace.

'You don't need to placate Meurig,' I said angrily. 'Give me one month and I'll drag the miserable dog back here on his knees.'

Arthur laughed. 'Another war?' He shook his head. 'Meurig might be a fool, but he's never been a man to seek war, so I cannot dislike him. He will leave me in peace so long as I don't offend him. Besides, I have enough fighting on my hands without worrying about Gwent.'

His fights were small things. Oengus's Blackshields still raided across Siluria's western frontier and Arthur set small garrisons of spearmen to guard against those incursions. He felt no anger against Oengus who, indeed, he regarded as a friend, but Oengus could no more resist harvest raids than a dog could stop itself from scratching at fleas. Siluria's northern border was more troubling because that joined Powys, and Powys, since Cuneglas's death, had fallen into chaos. Perddel, Cuneglas's son, had been acclaimed King, but at least a half-dozen powerful chieftains believed they had more right to the crown than Perddel – or at least the power to take the crown – and so the once mighty kingdom of Powys had degenerated into a squalid killing ground. Gwynedd, the impover-ished country to the north of Powys, was raiding at will, warbands fought each other, made temporary alliances, broke them, massacred each other's families and, whenever they themselves were in danger of massacre, retreated into the mountains. Enough spearmen had stayed loyal to Perddel to ensure that he kept the throne, but they were too few to defeat the rebellious chieftains. 'I think we shall have to intervene,' Arthur told me.

'We, Lord?'

'Meurig and I. Oh, I know he hates war, but sooner or later some of his missionaries will be killed in Powys and I suspect those deaths will persuade him to send spearmen to Perddel's support. So long, of course, as Perddel agrees to establish Christianity in Powys, which he doubtless will if it gives him back his kingdom. And if Meurig goes to war he'll probably ask me to go. He'd much rather that my men should die than his.'

'Under the Christian banner?' I asked sourly.

'I doubt he'll want another,' Arthur said calmly. 'I've become his tax-collector in Siluria, so why shouldn't I be his warlord in Powys?' He smiled wryly at the prospect, then gave me a sheepish look. 'There is another reason to give Gwydre and Morwenna a Christian marriage,' he said after a while.

'Which is?' I had to prompt him for it was clear that this further reason embarrassed him.

'Suppose Mordred and Argante have no children?' he asked me.

I said nothing for a while. Guinevere had raised the same possibility when I had spoken to her in Aquae Sulis, but it seemed an unlikely supposition. I said as much.

'But if they are childless,' Arthur insisted, 'who would have the best claim to Dumnonia's kingship?'

'You would, of course,' I insisted. Arthur was Uther's son, even if he had been bastard born, and there were no other sons who might claim the kingdom.

'No, no,' he said quickly. 'I don't want it. I never have wanted it!'

I stared down at Guinevere, suspecting that it was she who had raised this problem of who should succeed Mordred. 'Then it would be Gwydre?' I asked.

'Then it would be Gwydre,' he agreed.

'Does he want it?' I asked.

'I think so. He listens to his mother rather than to me.'

'You don't want Gwydre to be King?'

'I want Gwydre to be whatever he wishes to be,' Arthur said, 'and if Mordred provides no heir and Gwydre wishes to make his claim then I will support him.' He was staring down at Guinevere as he spoke and I guessed that she was the real force behind this ambition. She had always wanted to be married to a King, but would accept being the mother of one if Arthur refused the throne. 'But as you say,' Arthur went on, 'it's an unlikely supposition. I hope Mordred will have many sons, but if he doesn't, and if Gwydre is called to rule, then he'll need Christian support. The Christians rule in Dumnonia now, don't they?'

'They do, Lord,' I said grimly.

'So it would be politic of us to observe the Christian rites at Gwydre's marriage,' Arthur said, then gave me a sly smile. 'You see how close your daughter is to becoming a Queen?' I had honestly never thought of that before, and it must have shown on my face, for Arthur laughed. 'A Christian marriage isn't what I would want for Gwydre and Morwenna,' he admitted. 'If it was up to me, Derfel, I would have them married by Merlin.'

'You have news of him, Lord?' I asked eagerly.

'None. I hoped you would.'

'Only rumour,' I said. Merlin had not been seen for a year. He had left Mynydd Baddon with Gawain's ashes, or at least a bundle containing Gawain's scorched and brittle bones and some ash that might have belonged to the dead Prince or might equally well have been wood ash, and since that day Merlin had not been seen. Rumour said he was in the Otherworld, other folk claimed he was in Ireland or else in the western mountains, but no one knew for certain. He had told me he was going to help Nimue, but where she was no one knew either.

Arthur stood and brushed grass off his trews. 'Time for dinner,' he said, 'and I warn you that Taliesin is liable to chant an extremely tedious song about Mynydd Baddon. Worse, it's still unfinished! He keeps adding verses. Guinevere tells me it's a masterpiece, and I suppose it must be if she says so, but why do I have to endure it at every dinner?'

That was the first time I heard Taliesin sing and I was entranced. It was, as Guinevere said to me later, as though he could pull the music of the stars down to earth. He had a wondrously pure voice, and could hold a note longer than any other bard I ever heard. He told me later that he practised breathing, a thing I would never have thought needed practice, but it meant he could linger on a dying note while he pulsed it to its exquisite end with strokes on his harp, or else he could make a room echo and shudder with his triumphant voice, and I swear that on that summer night in Isca he made the battle of Mynydd Baddon live again. I heard Taliesin sing many times, and every time I heard him with the same astonishment.

Yet he was a modest man. He understood his power and was comfortable with it. It pleased him to have Guinevere as a patroness, for she was generous and appreciated his art, and she allowed him to spend weeks at a time away from the palace. I asked him where he went during those absences and he told me he liked to visit the hills and valleys and sing to the people. 'And not just sing,' he told me, 'but listen as well. I like the old songs. Sometimes they only remember snatches of them and I try to make them whole again.' It was important, he said, to listen to the songs of the common folk, for that taught him what they liked, but he also wanted to sing his own songs to them. 'It's easy to entertain lords,' he said, 'for they need entertainment, but a farmer needs sleep before he wants song, and if I can keep him awake then I know my song has merit.' And sometimes, he told me, he just sang to himself. 'I sit under the stars and sing,' he told me with a wry smile.

'Do you truly see the future?' I asked him during that conversation.

'I dream it,' he said, as though it were no great gift. 'But seeing the future is like peering through a mist and the reward is scarcely worth the effort. Besides, I never can tell, Lord, whether my visions of the future come from the Gods or from my own fears. I am, after all, only a bard.' He was, I think, being evasive. Merlin had told me that Taliesin stayed celibate to preserve his gift of prophecy, so he must have valued it more highly than he implied, but he disparaged the gift to discourage men from asking about it. Taliesin, I think, saw our future long before any of us had a glimpse of it, and he did not want to reveal it. He was a very private man.

'Only a bard?' I asked, repeating his last words. 'Men say you are the greatest of all the bards.'

He shook his head, rejecting my flattery. 'Only a bard,' he insisted, 'though I did submit to the Druid's training. I learned the mysteries from Celafydd in Cornovia. Seven years and three I learned, and at the very last day, when I could have taken the Druid's staff, I walked from Celafydd's cave and called myself a bard instead.'

'Why?'

'Because,' he said after a long pause, 'a Druid has responsibilities, and I did not want them. I like to watch, Lord Derfel, and to tell. Time is a story, and I would be its teller, not its maker. Merlin wanted to change the story and he failed. I dare not aim so high.'

'Did Merlin fail?' I asked him.

'Not in small things,' Taliesin said calmly, 'but in the great? Yes. The Gods drift ever farther away and I suspect that neither my songs nor all Merlin's fires can summon them now. The world turns, Lord, to new Gods, and maybe that's no bad thing. A God is a God, and why should it matter to us which one rules? Only pride and habit hold us to the old Gods.'

'Are you suggesting we should all become Christians?' I asked harshly.

'What God you worship is of no importance to me, Lord,' he said. 'I am merely here to watch, listen and sing.'

So Taliesin sang while Arthur governed with Guinevere in Siluria. My task was to be a bridle on Mordred's mischief in Dumnonia. Merlin had vanished, probably into the haunting mists of the deep west. The Saxons cowered, but still yearned for our land, and in the heavens, where there is no bridle on their mischief, the Gods rolled the dice anew.

Mordred was happy in those years after Mynydd Baddon. The battle had given him a taste for warfare, and he pursued it greedily. For a time he was content to fight under Sagramor's guidance; raiding into shrunken Lloegyr or hunting down Saxon warbands that came to plunder our crops and livestock, but after a while he became frustrated by Sagramor's caution. The Numidian had no desire to start a full-scale war by conquering the territory Cerdic still possessed and where the Saxons remained strong, but Mordred desperately wanted another clash of shield walls. He once ordered Sagramor's spearmen to follow him into Cerdic's territory, but those men refused to march without Sagramor's orders and Sagramor forbade the invasion. Mordred sulked for a time, but then a plea for help arrived from Broceliande, the British kingdom in Armorica, and Mordred led a warband of volunteers to fight against the Franks who were pressing on King Budic's borders. He stayed in Armorica for over five years and in that time he made a name for himself. In battle, men told me, he was fearless, and his victories attracted yet more men to his dragon banner. They were masterless men; rogues and outlaws who could grow rich on plunder, and Mordred gave them their hearts' desires. He took back a good part of the old kingdom of Benoic and bards began to sing of him as an Uther reborn, even as a second Arthur, though other tales, never turned into song, also came home across the grey waters, and those tales spoke of rape and murder, and of cruel men given licence.

Arthur himself fought during those years for, just as he had foreseen, some of Meurig's missionaries were massacred in Powys and Meurig demanded Arthur's aid in punishing the rebels who had killed the priests, and so Arthur rode north on one of his greatest campaigns. I was not there to help him, for I had responsibilities in Dumnonia, but we all heard the stories. Arthur persuaded Oengus mac Airem to attack the rebels out of Demetia, and while Oengus's Blackshields attacked from the west, Arthur's men came from the south and Meurig's army, marching two days behind Arthur, arrived to find the rebellion quashed and most of the murderers captured, but some of the priests' killers had taken refuge in Gwynedd, where Byrthig, the King of that mountainous country, refused to hand them over. Byrthig still hoped to use the rebels to gain more land in Powys and so Arthur, ignoring Meurig's counsel for caution, surged on northwards. He defeated Byrthig at Caer Gei and then, without pause, and still using the excuse that some of the priest-killers had fled further north, he led his warband over the Dark Road into the dread kingdom of Lleyn. Oengus followed him, and at the sands of Foryd where the River Gwyrfair slides to the sea, Oengus and Arthur trapped King Diwrnach between their forces and so broke the Bloodshields of Lleyn. Diwrnach drowned, over a hundred of his spearmen were massacred, and the remainder fled in panic. In two summer months Arthur had ended the rebellion in Powys, cowed Byrthig and destroyed Diwrnach, and by doing the latter he had kept his oath to Guinevere that he would avenge the loss of her father's kingdom. Leodegan, her father, had been King of Henis-Wyren, but Diwrnach had come from Ireland, taken Henis-Wyren by storm, renamed it Lleyn, and so made Guinevere a penniless exile. Now Diwrnach was dead and I thought Guinevere might insist that his captured kingdom be given to her son, but she made no protest when Arthur handed Lleyn into Oengus's keeping in the hope that it would keep his Blackshields too busy to raid into Powys. It was better, Arthur later told me, that Lleyn should have an Irish ruler, for the great majority of its people were Irish and Gwydre would ever have been a stranger to them, and so Oengus's elder son ruled in Lleyn and Arthur carried Diwrnach's sword back to Isca as a trophy for Guinevere.

I saw none of it, for I was governing Dumnonia where my spearmen collected Mordred's taxes and enforced Mordred's justice. Issa did most of the work, for he was now a Lord in his own right and I had given him half my spearmen. He was also a father now, and Scarach his wife was expecting another child. She lived with us in Dun Caric from where Issa rode out to patrol the country, and from where, each month and ever more reluctantly, I went south to attend the Royal Council in Durnovaria. Argante presided over those meetings, for Mordred had sent orders that his Queen was to take his high place at the council. Not even Guinevere had attended council meetings, but Mordred insisted and so Argante summoned the council and had Bishop Sansum as her chief ally. Sansum had rooms in the palace and was forever whispering in Argante's ear while Fergal, her Druid, whispered in the other. Sansum proclaimed a hatred of all pagans, but when he saw that he would have no power unless he shared it with Fergal, his hatred dissolved into a sinister alliance. Morgan, Sansum's wife, had returned to Ynys Wydryn after Mynydd Baddon, but Sansum stayed in Durnovaria, preferring the Queen's confidences to his wife's company.

Argante enjoyed exercising the royal power. I do not think she had any great love for Mordred, but she did possess a passion for money, and by staying in Dumnonia she made certain that the greater part of the country's taxes passed through her hands. She did little with the wealth. She did not build as Arthur and Guinevere had built, she did not care about restoring bridges or forts, she just sold the taxes, whether they were salt, grain or hides, in return for gold. She sent some of the gold to her husband, who was forever demanding more money for his warband, but most she piled up in the palace vaults until the folk of Durnovaria reckoned their town was built on a foundation of gold. Argante had long ago retrieved the treasure I had hidden beside the Fosse Way, and to that she now added more and more, and she was encouraged in her hoarding by Bishop Sansum who, as well as being Bishop of all Dumnonia, was now named Chief Counsellor and Royal Treasurer. I did not doubt that he was using the last office to skim the treasury for his own hoard. I accused him of that one day and he immediately adopted a hurt expression. 'I do not care for gold, Lord,' he said piously. 'Did not our Lord command us not to lay up treasures on earth, but in heaven?'

I grimaced. 'He could command what he liked,' I said, 'but you would still sell your soul for gold, Bishop, and so you should, for it would prove a good bargain.'

He gave me a suspicious look. 'A good bargain? Why?'

'Because you would be exchanging filth for money, of course,' I said. I could make no pretence of liking Sansum, nor he for liking me. The mouse lord was always accusing me of trimming men's taxes in return for favours, and as proof of the accusation he cited the fact that each successive year less money came into the treasury, but that shortfall was none of my doing. Sansum had persuaded Mordred to sign a decree which exempted all Christians from taxation and I dare say the church never found a better way of making converts, though Mordred rescinded the law as soon as he realized how many souls and how little gold he was saving; but then Sansum persuaded the King that the church, and only the church, should be responsible for collecting the taxes of Christians. That increased the yield for a year, but it fell thereafter as the Christians discovered that it was cheaper to bribe Sansum than to pay their King. Sansum then proposed doubling the taxes of all pagans, but Argante and Fergal stopped that measure. Instead Argante suggested that all the taxes on the Saxons should be doubled, but Sagramor refused to collect the increase, claiming it would only provoke rebellion in those parts of Lloegyr that we had settled. It was no wonder that I hated attending council meetings, and after a year or two of such fruitless wrangling I abandoned the meetings altogether. Issa went on collecting taxes, but only the honest men paid and there seemed fewer honest men each year, and so Mordred was forever complaining of being penniless while Sansum and Argante grew rich.

Argante became rich, but she stayed childless. She sometimes visited Broceliande and, once in a long while, Mordred returned to Dumnonia, but Argante's belly never swelled after such visits. She prayed, she sacrificed and she visited sacred springs in her attempts to have a child, but she stayed barren. I remember the stink at council meetings when she wore a girdle smeared with the faeces of a newborn child, supposedly a certain remedy for barrenness, but that worked no better than the infusions of bryony and mandrake that she drank daily. Eventually Sansum persuaded her that only Christianity could bring her the miracle and so, two years after Mordred had first gone to Broceliande, Argante threw Fergal, her Druid, out of the palace and was publicly baptized in the River Ffraw that flows around Durnovaria's northern margin. For six months she attended daily services in the huge church Sansum had built in the town centre, but at the end of the six months her belly was as flat as it had been before she had waded into the river. So Fergal was summoned back to the palace and brought with him new concoctions of bat dung and weasel blood that were supposed to make Argante fertile.

By then Gwydre and Morwenna were married and had produced their first child, and that child was a boy whom they named Arthur and who was ever afterwards known as Arthur-bach, Arthur the Little. The child was baptized by Bishop Emrys, and Argante saw the ceremony as a provocation. She knew that neither Arthur nor Guinevere had any great love for Christianity, and that by baptizing their grandson they were merely currying favour with the Christians in Dumnonia whose support would be needed if Gwydre were to take the throne. Besides, Arthur-bach's very existence was a reproach to Mordred. A King should be fecund, it was his duty, and Mordred was failing in that duty. It did not matter that he had whelped bastards the length and breadth of Dumnonia and Armorica, he was not whelping an heir on Argante and the Queen spoke darkly of his crippled foot, she remembered the evil omens of his birth and she looked sourly towards Siluria where her rival, my daughter, was proving capable of breeding new Princes. The Queen became more desperate, even dipping into her treasury to pay in gold any fraudster who promised her a swollen womb, but not all the sorceresses of Britain could help her conceive and, if rumour spoke true, not half the spearmen in her palace guard either. And all the while Gwydre waited in Siluria and Argante knew that if Mordred died then Gwydre would rule in Dumnonia unless she produced an heir of her own.

I did my best to preserve Dumnonia's peace in those early years of Mordred's rule and, for a time, my efforts were helped by the King's absence. I appointed the magistrates and so made sure that Arthur's justice continued. Arthur had always loved good laws, claiming they bound a country together like the willow-boards of a shield are gripped by their leather cover, and he had taken immense trouble to appoint magistrates whom he could trust to be impartial. They were, for the most part, landowners, merchants and priests, and almost all were wealthy enough to resist the corrosive effects of gold. If men can buy the law, Arthur had always said, then the law becomes worthless, and his magistrates were famous for their honesty, but it did not take long for folk in Dumnonia to discover that the magistrates could be outflanked. By paying money to Sansum or Argante they guaranteed that Mordred would write from Armorica ordering a decision changed and so, year after year, I found myself fighting a rising sea of small injustices. The honest magistrates resigned rather than have their rulings constantly reversed, while men who might have submitted their grievances to a court preferred to settle them with spears. That erosion of the law was a slow process, but I could not halt it. I was supposed to be a bridle on Mordred's capriciousness, but Argante and Sansum were twin spurs, and the spurs were overcoming the bridle.

Yet, on the whole, that was a happy time. Few folk lived as long as forty years, yet both Ceinwyn and I did and both of us were given good health by the Gods. Morwenna's marriage gave us joy, and the birth of Arthur-bach even more, and a year later our daughter Seren was married to Ederyn, the Edling of Elmet. It was a dynastic marriage, for Seren was first cousin to Perddel, King of Powys, and the marriage was not contracted for love, but to strengthen the alliance between Elmet and Powys and though Ceinwyn opposed the marriage for she saw no evidence of affection between Seren and Ederyn, Seren had set her heart on being a Queen and so she married her Edling and moved far away from us. Poor Seren, she never did become a Queen, for she died giving birth to her first child, a daughter who lived only half a day longer than her mother. Thus did the second of my three daughters cross to the Otherworld.

We wept for Seren, though the tears were not so bitter as those we had shed at Dian's death, for Dian had died so cruelly young, but just a month after Seren died Morwenna gave birth to a second child, a daughter whom she and Gwydre named Seren, and those grandchildren were a growing brightness in our lives. They did not come to Dumnonia because there they would have been in danger from Argante's jealousy, but Ceinwyn and I went often enough to Siluria. Indeed, our visits became so frequent that Guinevere kept rooms in her palace just for our use and, after a while, we spent more time in Isca than we did in Dun Caric. My head and beard were going grey and I was content to let Issa struggle with Argante while I played with my grandchildren. I built my mother a house on Siluria's coast, but by then she was so mad that she did not know what was happening and kept trying to return to her tidewood hovel on its bluff above the sea. She died in one of the winter plagues and, as I had promised Aelle, I buried her like a Saxon with her feet to the north.

Dumnonia decayed, and there seemed little I could do to prevent the decay for Mordred had just enough power to outflank me, but Issa preserved what order and justice he could while Ceinwyn and I spent more and more of our time in Siluria. What sweet memories I keep of Isca; memories of sunny days with Taliesin singing lullabies and Guinevere gently mocking my happiness as I towed Arthur-bach and Seren in an upturned shield across the grass. Arthur would join the games, for he had ever adored children, and sometimes Galahad would be there for he had joined Arthur and Guinevere in their comfortable exile.

Galahad had still not married, though now he had a child. It was his nephew, Prince Peredur, Lancelot's son, who had been found wandering in tears among the dead of Mynydd Baddon. As Peredur grew he came more and more to resemble his father; he had the same dark skin, the same lean and handsome face, and the same black hair, but in his character he was Galahad, not Lancelot. He was a clever, grave and earnest boy, and anxious to be a good Christian. I do not know how much of his father's history he knew, but Peredur was always nervous of Arthur and Guinevere, and they, I think, found him unsettling. That was not his fault, but rather because his face reminded them of what we would all have preferred to forget, and both were grateful when, at twelve years old, Peredur was sent to Meurig's court in Gwent to learn a warrior's skills. He was a good boy, yet with his departure it was as though a shadow had gone from Isca. In later years, long after Arthur's story was done, I came to know Peredur well and to value him as highly as I have valued any man.

Peredur might have unsettled Arthur, but there were few other shadows to trouble him. In these dark days, when folk look back and remember what they lost when Arthur went, they usually speak of Dumnonia, but others also mourn Siluria, for in those years he gave that unregarded kingdom a time of peace and justice. There was still disease, and still poverty, and men did not cease from getting drunk and killing each other just because Arthur governed, but widows knew that his courts would give redress, and the hungry knew that his granaries held food to last a winter. No enemy raided across Siluria's border, and though the Christian religion spread fast through the valleys, Arthur would not let its priests defile the pagan shrines, nor allow the pagans to attack the Christian churches. In those years he made Siluria into what he had dreamed he could make all Britain: a haven. Children were not enslaved, crops were not burned and warlords did not ravage homesteads.

Yet beyond the haven's borders, dark things loomed. Merlin's absence was one. Year after year passed, and still there was no news, and after a while folk assumed the Druid must have died for surely no man, not even Merlin, could live so long. Meurig was a nagging and irritable neighbour, forever demanding higher taxes or a purge of the Druids who lived in Siluria's valleys, though Tewdric, his father, was a moderating influence when he could be stirred from his self-imposed life of near starvation. Powys stayed weak, and Dumnonia became increasingly lawless, though it was spared the worst of Mordred's rule by his absence. In Siluria alone, it seemed, there was happiness, and Ceinwyn and I began to think that we would live the rest of our days in Isca. We had wealth, we had friends, we had family and we were happy.

We were, in short, complacent, and fate has ever been the enemy of complacency, and fate, as Merlin always told me, is inexorable.

I was hunting with Guinevere in the hills north of Isca when I first heard of Mordred's calamity. It was winter, the trees were bare, and Guinevere's prized deerhounds had just run down a great red stag when a messenger from Dumnonia found me. The man handed me a letter, then watched wide-eyed as Guinevere waded among the snarling dogs to put the beast out of its misery with one merciful stab of her short spear. Her huntsmen whipped the hounds off the corpse, then drew their knives to gralloch the stag. I pulled open the parchment, read the brief message, then looked at the messenger. 'Did you show this to Arthur?'

'No, Lord,' the man said. 'The letter was addressed to you.'

'Take it to him now,' I said, handing him the sheet of parchment.

Guinevere, happily blood-streaked, stepped out of the carnage. 'You look as if it was bad news, Derfel.'

'On the contrary,' I said, 'it's good news. Mordred has been wounded.'

'Good!' Guinevere exulted. 'Badly, I hope?'

'It seems so. An axe blow to the leg.'

'Pity it wasn't to the heart. Where is he?'

'Still in Armorica,' I said. The message had been dictated by Sansum and it said that Mordred had been surprised and defeated by an army led by Clovis, High King of the Franks, and that in the battle our King had been badly wounded in the leg. He had escaped, and was now besieged by Clovis in one of the ancient hilltop forts of old Benoic. I surmised that Mordred must have been wintering in the territory that he had conquered from the Franks and which he doubtless thought would make him a second kingdom across the sea, but Clovis had led his Frankish army westwards in a surprise winter campaign. Mordred had been defeated and, though he was still alive, he was trapped.

'How reliable is the news?' Guinevere asked.

'Reliable enough,' I said. 'King Budic sent Argante a messenger.'

'Good!' Guinevere said. 'Good! Let's hope the Franks kill him.' She stepped back into the growing pile of steaming offal to find a scrap for one of her beloved hounds. 'They will kill him, won't they?' she asked me.

'Franks aren't noted for their mercy,' I said.

'I hope they dance on his bones,' she said. 'Calling himself a second Uther!'

'He fought well for a time, Lady.'

'It isn't how well you fight that matters, Derfel, it's whether or not you win the last battle.' She threw scraps of the stag's guts to her dogs, wiped her knife blade on her tunic, then thrust it back into its sheath. 'So what does Argante want of you?' she asked me. 'A rescue?' Argante was demanding exactly that, and so was Sansum which is why he had written to me. His message ordered me to march all my men to the south coast, find ships and go to Mordred's relief. I told Guinevere as much and she gave me a mocking glance. 'And you're going to tell me that your oath to the little bastard will force you to obey?'

'I have no oath to Argante,' I said, 'and certainly none to Sansum.' The mouse lord could order me as much as he liked, but I had no need to obey him nor any wish to rescue Mordred. Besides, I doubted that an army could be shipped to Armorica in winter, and even if my spearmen did survive the rough crossing they would be too few to fight the Franks. The only help Mordred might expect would be from old King Budic of Broceliande, who was married to Arthur's elder sister, Anna, but while Budic might have been happy to have Mordred killing Franks in the land that used to be Benoic, he would have no wish to attract Clovis's attention by sending spearmen to Mordred's rescue. Mordred, I thought, was doomed. If his wound did not kill him, Clovis would.

For the rest of that winter Argante harried me with messages demanding that I take my men across the sea, but I stayed in Siluria and ignored her. Issa received the same demands, but he flatly refused to obey, while Sagramor simply threw Argante's messages into the flames. Argante, seeing her power slip with her husband's waning life, became more desperate and offered gold to spearmen who would sail to Armorica. Though many spearmen took the gold, they preferred to sail westwards to Kernow or hurry north into Gwent rather than sail south to where Clovis's grim army waited. And as Argante despaired, our hopes grew. Mordred was trapped and sick, and sooner or later news must come of his death and when that news came we planned to ride into Dumnonia under Arthur's banner with Gwydre as our candidate for the kingship. Sagramor would come from the Saxon frontier to support us and no man in Dumnonia would have the power to oppose us.

But other men were also thinking of Dummonia's kingship. I learned that early in the spring when Saint Tewdric died. Arthur was sneezing and shivering with the last of the winter's colds and he asked Galahad to go to the old King's funeral rites in Burrium, the capital of Gwent which lay just a short journey up river from Isca, and Galahad pleaded with me to accompany him. I mourned for Tewdric, who had proved himself a good friend to us, yet I had no wish to attend his funeral and thus be forced to endure the interminable droning of the Christian rites, but Arthur added his pleas to Galahad's. 'We live here at Meurig's pleasure,' he reminded me, 'and we'd do well to show him respect. I would go if I could,' he paused to sneeze, 'but Guinevere says it will be the death of me.'

So Galahad and I went in Arthur's place and the funeral service did indeed seem never ending. It took place in a great barn-like church that Meurig had built in the year marking the supposed five hundredth anniversary of the appearance of the Lord Jesus Christ on this sinful earth, and once the prayers inside the church were all said or chanted, we had to endure still more prayers at Tewdric's graveside. There was no balefire, no singing spearmen, just a cold pit in the ground, a score of bobbing priests and an undignified rush to get back to the town and its taverns when Tewdric was at last buried.

Meurig commanded Galahad and me to take supper with him. Peredur, Galahad's nephew, joined us, as did Burrium's bishop, a gloomy soul named Lladarn who had been responsible for the most tedious of the day's prayers, and he began supper with yet another long-winded prayer after which he made an earnest enquiry about the state of my soul and was grieved when I assured him that it was safe in Mithras's keeping. Such an answer would normally have irritated Meurig, but he was too distracted to notice the provocation. I know he was not unduly upset by his father's death, for Meurig was still resentful that Tewdric had taken back his power at the time of Mynydd Baddon, but at least he affected to be distressed and bored us with insincere praise of his father's saintliness and sagacity. I expressed the hope that Tewdric's death had been merciful and Meurig told me that his father had starved to death in his attempt to imitate the angels.

'There was nothing of him at the end,' Bishop Lladarn elaborated, 'just skin and bone, he was, skin and bone! But the monks say that his skin was suffused with a heavenly light, praise God!'

'And now the saint is on God's right hand,' Meurig said, crossing himself, 'where one day I shall be with him. Try an oyster, Lord.' He pushed a silver dish towards me, then poured himself wine.

He was a pale young man with protuberant eyes, a thin beard and an irritably pedantic manner. Like his father he aped Roman manners. He wore a bronze wreath on his thinning hair, dressed in a toga and ate while lying on a couch. The couches were deeply uncomfortable. He had married a sad and ox-like Princess from Rheged who had arrived in Gwent a pagan, produced male twins and then had Christianity whipped into her stubborn soul. She appeared in the dimly lit supper room for a few moments, ogled us, said and ate nothing, then disappeared as mysteriously as she had arrived.

'You have any news of Mordred?' Meurig asked us after his wife's brief visit.

'We hear nothing new, Lord King,' Galahad said. 'He is penned in by Clovis, but whether he lives or not, we don't know.'

'I have news,' Meurig said, pleased to have heard it before us. 'A merchant came yesterday with news from Broceliande and he tells us that Mordred is very near death. His wound is festering.' The King picked his teeth with a sliver of ivory. 'It must be God's judgement, Prince Galahad, God's judgement.'

'Praise His name,' Bishop Lladarn intervened. The Bishop's grey beard was so long it vanished under his couch. He used the beard as a towel, wiping grease from his hands into its long, dirt-clotted strands.

'We have heard such rumours before, Lord King,' I said.

Meurig shrugged. 'The merchant seemed very sure of himself,' he said, then tipped an oyster down his throat. 'So if Mordred isn't dead already,' he went on, 'he probably will be soon, and without leaving a child!'

'True,' Galahad said.

'And Perddel of Powys is also childless,' Meurig went on.

'Perddel is unmarried, Lord King,' I pointed out.

'But does he look to marry?' Meurig demanded of us.

'There's been talk of him marrying a Princess from Kernow,' I said, 'and some of the Irish Kings have offered daughters, but his mother wishes him to wait a year or two.'

'He's ruled by his mother, is he? No wonder he's weak,' Meurig said in his petulant, high-toned voice, 'weak. I hear that Powys's western hills are filled with outlaws?'

'I hear the same, Lord King,' I said. The mountains beside the Irish Sea had been haunted by masterless men ever since Cuneglas had died, and Arthur's campaign in Powys, Gwynedd and Lleyn had only increased their numbers. Some of those refugees were spearmen from Diwrnach's Bloodshields and, united with the disaffected men from Powys, they could have proved a new threat to Perddel's throne, but so far they had been little more than a nuisance. They raided for cattle and grain, snatched children as slaves, then scampered back to their hill fastnesses to avoid retribution.

'And Arthur?' Meurig enquired. 'How did you leave him?'

'Not well, Lord King,' Galahad said. 'He would have wished to be here, but alas, he has a winter fever.'

'Not serious?' Meurig enquired with an expression that suggested he rather hoped Arthur's cold would prove fatal. 'One does hope not, of course,' he added hastily, 'but he is old, and the old do succumb to trifling things that a younger man would throw off.'

'I don't think Arthur's old,' I said.

'He must be nearly fifty!' Meurig pointed out indignantly.

'Not for a year or two yet,' I said.

'But old,' Meurig insisted, 'old.' He fell silent and I glanced round the palace chamber, which was lit by burning wicks floating in bronze dishes filled with oil. Other than the five couches and the low table there was no other furniture and the only decoration was a carving of Christ on the cross that hung high on a wall. The Bishop gnawed at a pork rib, Peredur sat silent, while Galahad watched the King with a look of faint amusement. Meurig picked his teeth again, then pointed the ivory sliver at me. 'What happens if Mordred dies?' He blinked rapidly, something he always did when he was nervous.

'A new King must be found, Lord King,' I said casually, as though the question held no real importance for me.

'I had grasped that point,' he said acidly, 'but who?'

'The Lords of Dumnonia will decide,' I said evasively.

'And will choose Gwydre?' He blinked again as he challenged me. 'That's what I hear, they'll choose Gwydre! Am I right?'

I said nothing and Galahad finally answered the King. 'Gwydre certainly has a claim, Lord King,' he said carefully.

'He has no claim, none! None!' Meurig squeaked angrily. 'His father, need I remind you, is a bastard!'

'As am I, Lord King,' I intervened.

Meurig ignored that. '"A bastard shall not enter into the congregation of the Lord"!' he insisted. 'It is written thus in the scriptures. Is that not so, Bishop?'

'"Even to the tenth generation the bastard shall not enter into the congregation of the Lord", Lord King,' Lladarn intoned, then crossed himself. 'Praise be for His wisdom and guidance, Lord King.'

'There!' Meurig said as though his whole argument was thus proved.

I smiled. 'Lord King,' I pointed out gently, 'if we were to deny kingship to the descendants of bastards, we would have no Kings.'

He stared at me with pale, bulging eyes, trying to determine whether I had insulted his own lineage, but he must have decided against picking a quarrel. 'Gwydre is a young man,' he said instead, 'and no son of a King. The Saxons grow stronger and Powys is ill-ruled. Britain lacks leaders, Lord Derfel, it lacks strong Kings!'

'We daily chant hosannas because your own dear self proves the opposite, Lord King,' Lladarn said oilily.

I thought the Bishop's flattery was nothing more than a polite rejoinder, the sort of meaningless phrase courtiers ever utter to Kings, but Meurig took it as gospel truth. 'Precisely!' the King said enthusiastically, then gazed at me with open eyes as if expecting me to echo the Bishop's sentiments.

'Who,' I asked instead, 'would you like to see on Dumnonia's throne, Lord King?'

His sudden and rapid blinking showed that he was discomfited by the question. The answer was obvious: Meurig wanted the throne for himself. He had half-heartedly tried to gain it before Mynydd Baddon, and his insistence that Gwent's army would not help Arthur fight the Saxons unless Arthur renounced his own power had been a shrewd effort to weaken Dumnonia's throne in the hope that it might one day fall vacant, but now, at last, he saw his opportunity, though he dared not announce his own candidacy openly until definite news of Mordred's death reached Britain. 'I will support,' he said instead, 'whichever candidate shows themselves to be a disciple of our Lord Jesus Christ.' He made the sign of the cross. 'I can do no other, for I serve Almighty God.'

'Praise Him!' the Bishop said hurriedly.

'And I am reliably informed, Lord Derfel,' Meurig went on earnestly, 'that the Christians in Dumnonia cry out for a good Christian ruler. Cry out!'

'And who informs you of their cry, Lord King?' I asked in a voice so acid that poor Peredur looked alarmed. Meurig gave no answer, but nor did I expect one from him, so I supplied it myself. 'Bishop Sansum?' I suggested, and saw from Meurig's indignant expression that I was right.

'Why should you think that Sansum has anything to say in this matter?' Meurig demanded, red-faced.

'Sansum comes from Gwent, does he not, Lord King?' I asked and Meurig blushed still more deeply, making it obvious that Sansum was indeed plotting to put Meurig on Dumnonia's throne, and Meurig, Sansum could be sure, would be certain to reward Sansum with yet more power. 'But I don't think the Christians of Dumnonia need your protection, Lord King,' I went on, 'nor Sansum's. Gwydre, like his father, is a friend to your faith.'

'A friend! Arthur, a friend to Christ!' Bishop Lladarn snapped at me. 'There are pagan shrines in Siluria, beasts are sacrificed to the old Gods, women dance naked under the moon, infants are passed through the fire, Druids babble!' Spittle sprayed from the Bishop's mouth as he tallied this list of iniquities.

'Without the blessings of Christ's rule,' Meurig leaned towards me, 'there can be no peace.'

'There can be no peace, Lord King,' I said directly, 'while two men want the same kingdom. What would you have me tell my son-in-law?'

Again Meurig was unsettled by my directness. He fiddled with an oyster shell while he considered his answer, then shrugged. 'You may assure Gwydre that he will have land, honour, rank and my protection,' he said, blinking rapidly, 'but I will not see him made King of Dumnonia.' He actually blushed as he spoke the last words. He was a clever man, Meurig, but a coward at heart and it must have taken a great effort for him to have expressed himself so bluntly.

Maybe he feared my anger, but I gave him a courteous reply. 'I shall tell him, Lord King,' I said, though in truth the message was not for Gwydre, but for Arthur. Meurig was not only declaring his own bid to rule Dumnonia, but warning Arthur that Gwent's formidable army would oppose Gwydre's candidacy.

Bishop Lladarn leaned towards Meurig and spoke in an urgent whisper. He used Latin, confident that neither Galahad nor I would understand him, but Galahad spoke the language and half heard what was being said. 'You're planning to keep Arthur penned inside Siluria?' he accused Lladarn in British.

Lladarn blushed. As well as being the Bishop of Burrium, Lladarn was the King's chief counsellor and thus a man of power. 'My King,' he said, bowing his head in Meurig's direction, 'cannot allow Arthur to move spearmen through Gwent's territory.'

'Is that true, Lord King?' Galahad asked politely.

'I am a man of peace,' Meurig blustered, 'and one way to secure peace is to keep spearmen at home.'

I said nothing, fearing that my anger would only make me blurt out some insult that would make things worse. If Meurig insisted that we could not move spearmen across his roads then he would have succeeded in dividing the forces that would support Gwydre. It meant that Arthur could not march to join Sagramor, nor Sagramor to join Arthur, and if Meurig could keep their forces divided then he would most likely be the next King of Dumnonia.

'But Meurig won't fight,' Galahad said scornfully as we rode down the river towards Isca the next day. The willows were hazed with their first hint of spring leaves, but the day itself was a reminder of winter with a cold wind and drifting mists.

'He might,' I said, 'if the prize is large enough.' And the prize was huge, for if Meurig ruled both Gwent and Dumnonia then he would control the richest part of Britain. 'It will depend,' I said, 'on how many spears oppose him.'

'Yours, Issa's, Arthur's, Sagramor's,' Galahad said.

'Maybe five hundred men?' I said, 'and Sagramor's are a long way away, and Arthur's would have to cross Gwent's territory to reach Dumnonia. And how many men does Meurig command? A thousand?'

'He won't risk war,' Galahad insisted. 'He wants the prize, but he's terrified of the risk.' He had stopped his horse to watch a man fishing from a coracle in the centre of the river. The fisherman cast his hand net with a careless skill and, while Galahad was admiring the fisherman's dexterity, I was weighting each cast with an omen. If this throw yields a salmon, I told myself, then Mordred will die. The throw did bring up a big struggling fish, and then I thought that the augury was a nonsense, for all of us would die, and so I told myself that the next cast must net a fish if Mordred was to die before Beltain. The net came up empty and I touched the iron of Hywelbane's hilt. The fisherman sold us a part of his catch and we pushed the salmon into our saddlebags and rode on. I prayed to Mithras that my foolish omen was misleading, then prayed that Galahad was right, and that Meurig would never dare commit his troops. But for Dumnonia? Rich Dumnonia? That was worth a risk, even for a cautious man like Meurig.

Weak kings are a curse on the earth, yet our oaths are made to kings, and if we had no oaths we would have no law, and if we had no law we would have mere anarchy, and so we must bind ourselves with the law, and keep the law by oaths, and if a man could change kings at whim then he could abandon his oaths with his inconvenient king, and so we need kings because we must have an immutable law. All that is true, yet as Galahad and I rode home through the wintry mists I could have wept that the one man who should have been a king would not be one, and that those who should never have been kings all were.

We found Arthur in his blacksmith's shed. He had built the shed himself, made a hooded furnace from Roman bricks, then purchased an anvil and a set of blacksmith's tools. He had always declared he wanted to be a blacksmith, though as Guinevere frequently remarked, wanting and being were not at all the same thing. But Arthur tried, how he tried! He employed a proper blacksmith, a gaunt and taciturn man named Morridig, whose task was to teach Arthur the skills of the trade, but Morridig had long despaired of teaching Arthur anything except enthusiasm. All of us, nevertheless, possessed items Arthur had made; iron candle-stands that had kinked shafts, misshapen cooking pots with ill-fitting handles or fire-spits that bowed over the flame. Yet the smithy made him happy, and he spent hours beside its hissing furnace, ever certain that a little more practice would make him as carelessly proficient as Morridig.

He was alone in the smithy when Galahad and I returned from Burrium. He grunted a distracted welcome, then went on hammering a shapeless piece of iron that he claimed was a shoe-plate for one of his horses. He reluctantly dropped the hammer when we presented him with one of the salmon we had bought, then interrupted our news by saying that he had already heard that Mordred was close to death. 'A bard arrived from Armorica yesterday,' he told us, 'and says the King's leg is rotting at the hip. The bard says he stinks like a dead toad.'

'How does the bard know?' I asked, for I had thought Mordred was surrounded and cut off from all the other Britons in Armorica.

'He says it's common knowledge in Broceliande,' Arthur said, then happily added that he expected Dumnonia's throne to be vacant in a matter of days, but we spoiled his cheerfulness by telling him of Meurig's refusal to allow any of our spearmen to cross Gwent's land and I furthered his gloom by adding my suspicions of Sansum. I thought for a second that Arthur was going to curse, something he did rarely, but he controlled the impulse, and instead moved the salmon away from the furnace. 'Don't want it to cook,' he said. 'So Meurig's closed all the roads to us?'

'He says he wants peace, Lord,' I explained.

Arthur laughed sourly. 'He wants to prove himself, that's what he wants. His father's dead and he's eager to show that he's a better man than Tewdric. The best way is to become a hero in battle and the second best is to steal a kingdom without a battle.' He sneezed violently, then shook his head angrily. 'I hate having a cold.'

'You should be resting, Lord,' I said, 'not working.'

'This isn't work, this is pleasure.'

'You should take coltsfoot in mead,' Galahad said.

'I've drunk nothing else for a week. Only two things cure colds: death or time.' He picked up the hammer and gave the cooling lump of iron a ringing blow, then pumped the leather-jacketed bellows that fed air into the furnace. The winter had ended, but despite Arthur's insistence that the weather was ever kind in Isca, it was a freezing day. 'What's your mouse lord up to?' he asked me as he pumped the furnace into a shimmering heat.

'He isn't my mouse lord,' I said of Sansum.

'But he's scheming, isn't he? Wants his own candidate on the throne.'

'But Meurig has no right to the throne!' Galahad protested.

'None at all,' Arthur agreed, 'but he has a lot of spears. And he'd have half a claim if he married a widowed Argante.'

'He can't marry her,' Galahad said, 'he's married already.'

'A toadstool will get rid of an inconvenient queen,' Arthur said. 'That's how Uther got rid of his first wife. A toadstool in a mushroom stew.' He thought for a few seconds, then tossed the shoe-plate into the fire. 'Fetch Gwydre for me,' he asked Galahad.

Arthur tortured the red-hot iron while we waited. A horse's shoe-plate was a simple enough object, merely a sheet of iron that protected the vulnerable hoof from stones, and all it needed was an arch of iron that slipped over the front of the hoof and a pair of lugs at the back where the leather laces were attached, but Arthur could not seem to get the thing right. His arch was too narrow and high, the plate was kinked and the lugs too big. 'Almost right,' he said after hammering the thing for another frantic minute.

'Right for what?' I asked.

He chucked the shoe-plate back into the furnace then pulled off his fire-scarred apron as Galahad returned with Gwydre. Arthur told Gwydre the news of Mordred's expected death, then of Meurig's treachery, and finished with a simple question. 'Do you want to be King of Dumnonia, Gwydre?'

Gwydre looked startled. He was a fine man, but young, very young. Nor, I think, was he particularly ambitious, though his mother was ambitious for him. He had Arthur's face, long and bony, though it was marked with an expression of watchfulness as if he always expected fate to deal him a foul blow. He was thin, but I had practised swords with him often enough to know that there was a sinewy strength in his deceptively frail body. 'I have a claim to the throne,' he answered guardedly.

'Because your grandfather bedded my mother,' Arthur said irritably, 'that's your claim, Gwydre, nothing else. What I want to know is whether you truly wish to be King.'

Gwydre glanced at me for help, found none, and looked back to his father. 'I think so, yes.'

'Why?'

Again Gwydre hesitated, and I suppose a host of reasons whirled in his head, but he finally looked defiant. 'Because I was born to it. I'm as much Uther's heir as Mordred is.'

'You reckon you were born to it, eh?' Arthur asked sarcastically. He stooped and pumped the bellows, making the furnace roar and spit sparks into its brick hood. 'Every man in this room is the son of King except you, Gwydre,' Arthur said fiercely, 'and you say you're born to it?'

'Then you be King, father,' Gwydre said, 'and then I shall be the son of a King too.'

'Well said,' I put in.

Arthur gave me an angry glance, then plucked a rag from a pile beside his anvil and blew his nose into it. He tossed the rag onto the furnace. The rest of us simply blew our noses by pinching the nostrils between finger and thumb, but he had ever been fastidious. 'Let us accept, Gwydre,' he said, 'that you are of the lineage of kings. That you are Uther's grandson and therefore have a claim on Dumnonia's throne. I have a claim too, as it happens, but I choose not to exercise it. I'm too old. But why should men like Derfel and Galahad fight to put you on Dumnonia's throne? Tell me that.'

'Because I shall be a good King,' Gwydre said, blushing, then he looked at me. 'And Morwenna will make a good Queen,' he added.

'Every man who was ever a king said he wanted to be good,' Arthur grumbled, 'and most turned out to be bad. Why should you be any different?'

'You tell me, father,' Gwydre said.

'I'm asking you!'

'But if a father doesn't know a son's character,' Gwydre riposted, 'who does?'

Arthur went to the smithy door, pushed it open and stared into the stable yard. Nothing stirred there except the usual tribe of dogs, and so he turned back. 'You're a decent man, son,' he said grudgingly, 'a decent man. I'm proud of you, but you think too well of the world. There's evil out there, true evil, and you don't credit it.'

'Did you,' Gwydre asked, 'when you were my age?'

Arthur acknowledged the acuity of the question with a half-smile. 'When I was your age,' he said, 'I believed I could make the world anew. I believed that all this world needed was honesty and kindness. I believed that if you treated folk well, that if you gave them peace and offered them justice they would respond with gratitude. I thought I could dissolve evil with good.' He paused. 'I suppose I thought of people as dogs,' he went on ruefully, 'and that if you gave them enough affection then they would be docile, but they aren't dogs, Gwydre, they're wolves. A king must rule a thousand ambitions, and all of them belong to deceivers. You will be flattered, and behind your back, mocked. Men will swear undying loyalty with one breath and plot your death with the next. And if you survive their plots, then one day you will be grey-bearded like me and you'll look back on your life and realize that you achieved nothing. Nothing. The babies you admired in their mothers' arms will have grown to be killers, the justice you enforced will be for sale, the people you protected will still be hungry and the enemy you defeated will still threaten your frontiers.' He had grown increasingly angry as he spoke, but now softened the anger with a smile. 'Is that what you want?'

Gwydre returned his father's stare. I thought for a moment that he would falter, or perhaps argue with his father, but instead he gave Arthur a good answer. 'What I want, father,' he said, 'is to treat folk well, to give them peace and offer them justice.'

Arthur smiled to hear his own words served back to him. 'Then perhaps we should try to make you King, Gwydre. But how?' He walked back to the furnace. 'We can't lead spearmen through Gwent, Meurig will stop us, but if we don't have spearmen, we don't have the throne.'

'Boats,' Gwydre said.

'Boats?' Arthur asked.

'There must be two score of fishing-boats on our coast,' Gwydre said, 'and each can take ten or a dozen men.'

'But not horses,' Galahad said, 'I doubt they can take horses.'

'Then we must fight without horses,' Gwydre said.

'We may not even need to fight,' Arthur said. 'If we reach Dumnonia first, and if Sagramor joins us, I think young Meurig might hesitate. And if Oengus mac Airem sends a warband east towards Gwent then that will frighten Meurig even more. We can probably freeze Meurig's soul by looking threatening enough.'

'Why would Oengus help us fight his own daughter?' I asked.

'Because he doesn't care about her, that's why,' Arthur said. 'And we're not fighting his daughter, Derfel, we're fighting Sansum. Argante can stay in Dumnonia, but she can't be Queen, not if Mordred's dead.' He sneezed again. 'And I think you should go to Dumnonia soon, Derfel,' he added.

'To do what, Lord?'

'To smell out the mouse lord, that's what. He's scheming, and he needs a cat to teach him a lesson, and you've got sharp claws. And you can show Gwydre's banner. I can't go because that would provoke Meurig too much, but you can sail across the Severn without rousing suspicions, and when news comes of Mordred's death you proclaim Gwydre's name at Caer Cadarn and make certain Sansum and Argante can't reach Gwent. Put them both under guard and tell them it's for their own protection.'

'I'll need men,' I warned him.

'Take a boatload, and then use Issa's men,' Arthur said, invigorated by the need to take decisions. 'Sagramor will give you troops,' he added, 'and the moment I hear that Mordred's dead I'll bring Gwydre with all my spearmen. If I'm still alive, that is,' he said, sneezing again.

'You'll live,' Galahad said unsympathetically.

'Next week,' Arthur looked up at me with red-rimmed eyes, 'go next week, Derfel.'

'Yes, Lord.'

He bent to throw another handful of coals onto the blazing furnace. 'The Gods know I never wanted that throne,' he said, 'but one way or another I consume my life fighting for it.' He sniffed. 'We'll start gathering boats, Derfel, and you assemble spearmen at Caer Cadarn. If we look strong enough then Meurig will think twice.'

'And if he doesn't?' I asked.

'Then we've lost,' Arthur said, 'we've lost. Unless we fight a war, and I'm not sure I want to do that.'

'You never do, Lord,' I said, 'but you always win them.'

'So far,' Arthur said gloomily, 'so far.'

He picked up his tongs to rescue the shoe-plate from the fire, and I went to find a boat with which to snatch a kingdom.

NEXT MORNING, ON A falling tide and in a west wind that whipped the River Usk into short steep waves, I embarked on my brother-in-law's boat. Balig was a fisherman married to Linna, my half-sister, and he was amused to have discovered that he was related to a Lord of Dumnonia. He had also profited from the unexpected relationship, but he deserved the good fortune for he was a capable and decent man. Now he ordered six of my spearmen to take the boat's long oars, and ordered the other four to crouch in the bilge. I only had a dozen of my spearmen in Isca, the rest were with Issa, but I reckoned these ten men should see me safe to Dun Caric. Balig invited me to sit on a wooden chest beside the steering oar. 'And throw up over the gunwale, Lord,' he added cheerfully.

'Don't I always?'

'No. Last time you filled the scuppers with your breakfast. Waste of fish-food, that. Cast off forrard, you worm-eaten toad!' he shouted at his crew, a Saxon slave who had been captured at Mynydd Baddon, but who now had a British wife, two children and a noisy friendship with Balig. 'Knows his boats, that I'll say for him,' Balig said of the Saxon, then he stooped to the stern line that still secured the boat to the bank. He was about to cast the rope off when a shout sounded and we both looked up to see Taliesin hurrying towards us from the grassy mound of Isca's amphitheatre. Balig held tight to the mooring line. 'You want me to wait, Lord?'

'Yes,' I said, standing as Taliesin came closer.

'I'm coming with you,' Taliesin shouted, 'wait!' He carried nothing except a small leather bag and a gilded harp. 'Wait!' he called again, then hitched up the skirts of his white robe, took off his shoes, and waded into the glutinous mud of the Usk's bank.

'Can't wait for ever,' Balig grumbled as the bard struggled through the steep mud. 'Tide's going fast.'

'One moment, one moment,' Taliesin called. He threw his harp, bag and shoes on board, hitched his skirts still higher and waded into the water. Balig reached out, clasped the bard's hand and hauled him unceremoniously over the gunwale. Taliesin sprawled on the deck, found his shoes, bag and harp, then wrung water from the skirts of his robe. 'You don't mind if I come, Lord?' he asked me, the silver fillet askew on his black hair.

'Why should I?'

'Not that I intend to accompany you. I just wish passage to Dumnonia.' He straightened the silver fillet, then frowned at my grinning spearmen. 'Do those men know how to row?'

'Course they don't,' Balig answered for me. 'They're spearmen, no use for anything useful. Do it together, you bastards! Ready? Push forward! Oars down! Pull!' He shook his head in mock despair. 'Might as well teach pigs to dance.'

It was about nine miles to the open sea from Isca, nine miles that we covered swiftly because our boat was carried by the ebbing tide and the river's swirling current. The Usk slid between glistening mudbanks that climbed to fallow fields, bare woods and wide marshes. Wicker fish traps stood on the banks where herons and gulls pecked at the flapping salmon stranded by the falling tide. Redshanks called plaintively while snipe climbed and swooped above their nests. We hardly needed the oars, for together the tide and current were carrying us fast, and once we reached the widening water where the river spilled into the Severn, Balig and his crewman hoisted a ragged brown sail that caught the west wind and made the boat surge forward. 'Ship those oars now,' he ordered my men, then he grasped the big steering oar and stood happily as the small ship dipped her blunt prow into the first big waves. 'The sea will be lively today, Lord,' he called cheerfully. 'Scoop that water out!' he shouted to my spearmen. 'The wet stuff belongs outside a boat, not in it.' Balig grinned at my incipient misery. 'Three hours, Lord, that's all, and we'll have you ashore.'

'You dislike boats?' Taliesin asked me.

'I hate them.'

'A prayer to Manawydan should avert sickness,' he said calmly.

317

He had hauled a pile of nets beside my chest and now sat on them. He was plainly untroubled by the boat's violent motion, indeed he seemed to enjoy it. 'I slept last night in the amphitheatre,' he told me. 'I like to do that,' he went on when he saw I was too miserable to respond. 'The banked seats serve like a dream tower.'

I glanced at him, my sickness somehow lessened by those last two words for they reminded me of Merlin who had once possessed a dream tower on the summit of Ynys Wydryn's Tor. Merlin's dream tower had been a hollow wooden structure that he claimed magnified the messages of the Gods, and I could understand how Isca's Roman amphitheatre with its high banked seats set about its raked sand arena might serve the same purpose. 'Were you seeing the future?' I managed to ask him.

'Some of it,' he admitted, 'but I also met Merlin in my dream last night.'

The mention of that name drove away the last qualms in my belly. 'You spoke with Merlin?' I asked.

'He spoke to me,' Taliesin corrected me, 'but he could not hear me.'

'What did he say?'

'More than I can tell you, Lord, and nothing you wish to hear.'

'What?' I demanded.

He grabbed at the stern post as the boat pitched off a steep wave. Water sprayed back from the bows and spattered on the bundles that held our armour. Taliesin made sure his harp was well protected under his robe, then touched the silver fillet that circled his tonsured head to make certain it was still in place. 'I think, Lord, that you travel into danger.' he said calmly.

'Is that Merlin's message,' I asked, touching the iron of Hywelbane's hilt, 'or one of your visions?'

'Only a vision,' he confessed, 'and as I once told you, Lord, it is better to see the present clearly than to try and discern a shape in the visions of the future.' He paused, evidently considering his next words carefully. 'You have not, I think, heard definite news of Mordred's death?'

'No.'

'If my vision was right,' he said, 'then your King is not sick at

318

all, but has recovered. I could be wrong, indeed I pray I am wrong, but have you had any omens?'

'About Mordred's death?' I asked.

'About your own future, Lord,' he said.

I thought for a second. There had been the small augury of the salmon-fisher's net, but that I ascribed to my own superstitious fears rather than to the Gods. More worryingly, the small blue-green agate in the ring that Aelle had given to Ceinwyn had fallen out, and one of my old cloaks had been stolen, and though both events could have been construed as bad omens, they could equally well be mere mishaps. It was hard to tell, and neither loss seemed portentous enough to mention to Taliesin. 'Nothing has worried me lately,' I told him instead.

'Good,' he said, rocking to the boat's motion. His long black hair flapped in the wind that was stretching the belly of our sail taut and streaming its frayed edges. The wind was also skimming the tops from the white-crested waves and driving the spray inboard, though I think more water came into the boat through its gaping seams than across its gunwales. My spearmen bailed lustily. 'But I think Mordred lives still,' Taliesin went on, ignoring the frantic activity in the boat's centre, 'and that the news of his imminent death is a ruse. But I could not swear to that. Sometimes we mistake our fears for prophecy. But I did not imagine Merlin, Lord, nor any of his words in my dream.'

Again I touched Hywelbane's hilt. I had always thought that any mention of Merlin would be reassuring, but Taliesin's calm words were chilling.

'I dreamed that Merlin was in a thick wood,' Taliesin went on in his precise voice, 'and could not find his way out; indeed, whenever a path opened before him, a tree would groan and move as though it were a great beast shifting to block his way. Merlin, the dream tells me, is in trouble. I talked to him in the dream, but he could not hear me. What that tells me, I think, is that he cannot be reached. If we sent men to find him, they would fail and they might even die. But he wants help, that I do know, for he sent me the dream.'

'Where is this wood?' I asked.

The bard turned his dark, deep-set eyes onto me. 'There may

be no wood, Lord. Dreams are like songs. Their task is not to offer an exact image of the world, but a suggestion of it. The wood, I think, tells me that Merlin is imprisoned.'

'By Nimue,' I said, for I could think of no one else who would dare challenge the Druid.

Taliesin nodded. 'She, I think, is his jailer. She wants his power, and when she has it she will use it to impose her dream on Britain.'

I was finding it difficult even to think about Merlin and Nimue. For years we had lived without them and, as a result, our world's boundaries had taken on a precise hardness. We were bounded by Mordred's existence, by Meurig's ambitions and by Arthur's hopes, not by the misty, swirling uncertainties of Merlin's dreams. 'But Nimue's dream,' I objected, 'is the same as Merlin's.'

'No, Lord,' Taliesin said gently, 'it is not.'

'She wants what he wants,' I insisted, 'to restore the Gods!'

'But Merlin,' Taliesin said, 'gave Excalibur to Arthur. And do you not see that he gave part of his power to Arthur with that gift? I have wondered about that gift for a long time, for Merlin would never explain it to me, but I think I understand it now. Merlin knew that if the Gods failed, then Arthur might succeed. And Arthur did succeed, but his victory at Mynydd Baddon was not complete. It keeps the Isle of Britain in British hands, but it did not defeat the Christians, and that is a defeat for the old Gods. Nimue, Lord, will never accept that half-victory. For Nimue it is the Gods or it is nothing. She does not care what horrors come to Britain so long as the Gods return and strike down her enemies, and to achieve that, Lord, she wants Excalibur. She wants every scrap of power so that when she relights the fires the Gods will have no choice but to respond.'

I understood then. 'And with Excalibur,' I said, 'she will want Gwydre.'

'She will indeed, Lord,' Taliesin agreed. 'The son of a ruler is a source of power, and Arthur, whether he wills it or not, is still the most famous leader in Britain. If he had ever chosen to be a king, Lord, he would have been named High King. So, yes, she wants Gwydre.'

I stared at Taliesin's profile. He actually seemed to be enjoying the boat's terrifying motion. 'Why do you tell me this?' I asked him.

My question puzzled him. 'Why should I not tell you?'

'Because by telling me,' I said, 'you warn me to protect Gwydre, and if I protect Gwydre then I prevent the return of the Gods. And you, if I'm not mistaken, would like to see those Gods return.'

'I would,' he acknowledged, 'but Merlin asked me to tell you.'

'But why would Merlin want me to protect Gwydre?' I demanded. 'He wants the Gods to return!'

'You forget, Lord, that Merlin foresaw two paths. One was the path of the Gods, the other the path of man, and Arthur is that second path. If Arthur is destroyed, then we have only the Gods, and I think Merlin knows that the Gods do not hear us any more. Remember what happened to Gawain.'

'He died,' I said bleakly, 'but he carried his banner into battle.'

'He died,' Taliesin corrected me, 'and was then placed in the Cauldron of Clyddno Eiddyn. He should have come back to life, Lord, for that is the Cauldron's power, but he did not. He did not breathe again and that surely means the old magic is waning. It is not dead, and I suspect it will cause great mischief before it dies, but Merlin, I think, is telling us to look to man, not to the Gods, for our happiness.'

I shut my eyes as a big wave shattered white on the boat's high prow. 'You're saying,' I said, when the spray had vanished, 'that Merlin has failed?'

'I think Merlin knew he had failed when the Cauldron did not revive Gawain. Why else did he bring the body to Mynydd Baddon? If Merlin had thought, for even one heartbeat, that he could use Gawain's body to summon the Gods then he would never have dissipated its magic in the battle.'

'He still took the ashes back to Nimue,' I said.

'True,' Taliesin admitted, 'but that was because he had promised to help her, and even Gawain's ashes would have retained some of the corpse's power. Merlin might know he has failed, but like any man he is reluctant to abandon his dream and perhaps he believed Nimue's energy might prove effective? But what he did not foresee, Lord, was the extent to which she would misuse him.'

'Punish him,' I said bitterly.

Taliesin nodded. 'She despises him because he failed, and she believes that he conceals knowledge from her, and so even now, Lord, in this very wind, she is forcing Merlin's secrets from him. She knows much, but she does not know all, yet if my dream is right then she is drawing out his knowledge. It might take months or years for her to learn all she needs, but she will learn, Lord, and when she knows she will use the power. And you, I think, will know it first.' He gripped the nets as the boat pitched alarmingly. 'Merlin commanded me to warn you, Lord, and so I do, but against what? I don't know.' He smiled apologetically.

'Against this voyage to Dumnonia?' I asked.

Taliesin shook his head. 'I think your danger is much greater than anything planned by your enemies in Dumnonia. Indeed, your danger is so great, Lord, that Merlin wept. He also told me he wanted to die.' Taliesin gazed up at the sail. 'And if I knew where he was, Lord, and had the power, I would send you to kill him. But instead we must wait for Nimue to reveal herself.'

I gripped Hywelbane's cold hilt. 'So what are you advising me to do?' I asked him.

'It is not my place to give advice to lords,' Taliesin said. He turned and smiled at me, and I suddenly saw that his deep-set eyes were cold. 'It does not matter to me, Lord, whether you live or die for I am the singer and you are my song, but for now, I admit, I follow you to discover the melody and, if I must, to change it. Merlin asked that of me, and I will do it for him, but I think he is saving you from one danger only to expose you to a still greater one.'

'You're not making sense,' I said harshly.

'I am, Lord, but neither of us yet understands the sense. I'm sure it will come clear.' He sounded so calm, but my fears were as grey as the clouds above and as tumultuous as the seas below. I touched Hywelbane's reassuring hilt, prayed to Manawydan, and told myself that Taliesin's warning was only a dream and nothing but a dream, and that dreams could not kill.

But they can, and they do. And somewhere in Britain, in a dark place, Nimue had the Cauldron of Clyddno Eiddyn and was using it to stir our dreams into nightmare.

*

Balig landed us on a beach somewhere on the Dumnonian coastline. Taliesin offered me a cheerful farewell, then strode long-legged off into the dunes. 'Do you know where you're going?' I called after him.

'I will when I reach there, Lord,' he called back, then disappeared.

We pulled on our armour. I had not brought my finest gear, simply an old and serviceable breastplate and a battered helmet. I slung my shield on my back, picked up my spear, and followed Taliesin inland. 'You know where we are, Lord?' Eachern asked me.

'Near enough,' I said. In the rain ahead I could make out a range of hills. 'We go south of those and we'll reach Dun Caric.'

'You want me to fly the banner, Lord?' Eachern asked. Rather than my banner of the star we had brought Gwydre's banner which showed Arthur's bear entwined with Dumnonia's dragon, but I decided against carrying it unfurled. A banner in the wind is a nuisance and, besides, eleven spearmen marching beneath a gaudy great flag would look ridiculous rather than impressive, and so I decided to wait until Issa's men could reinforce my own small band before unrolling the flag on its long staff.

We found a track in the dunes and followed it through a wood of small thorns and hazels to a tiny settlement of six hovels. The folk ran at the sight of us, leaving only an old woman who was too bent and crippled to move fast. She sank onto the ground and spat defiantly as we approached. 'You'll get nothing here,' she said hoarsely, 'we own nothing except dung-heaps. Dung-heaps and hunger, Lords, that's all you'll fetch from us.'

I crouched beside her. 'We want nothing,' I told her, 'except news.'

'News?' The very word seemed strange to her.

'Do you know who your King is?' I asked her gently.

'Uther, Lord,' she said. 'A big man, he is, Lord. Like a God!'

It was plain we would fetch no news from the hovel, or none that would make sense, and so we walked on, stopping only to eat some of the bread and dried meat that we carried in our pouches. I was in my own country, yet it felt curiously as though I walked an enemy land and I chided myself for giving too much credit to Taliesin's vague warnings, yet still I kept to the hidden wooded paths and, as evening fell, I led my small company up through a beech wood to higher ground where we might have a sight of any other spearmen. We saw none, but, far to the south, an errant ray of the dying sun lanced through a cloud bank to touch Ynys Wydryn's Tor green and bright.

We lit no fire. Instead we slept beneath the beech trees and in the morning woke cold and stiff. We walked east, staying under the leafless trees, while beneath us, in damp heavy fields, men ploughed stiff furrows, women sowed a crop and small children ran screaming to frighten the birds away from the precious seed. 'I used to do that in Ireland,' Eachern said. 'Spent half my childhood frightening birds away.'

'Nail a crow to the plough, that'll do it,' one of the other spearmen offered.

'Nail crows to every tree near the field,' another suggested.

'Doesn't stop them,' a third man put in, 'but it makes you feel better.'

We were following a narrow track between deep hedgerows. The leaves had not unfurled to hide the nests so magpies and jays were busy stealing eggs and they screeched in protest when we came close. 'The folks will know we're here, Lord,' Eachern said, 'they may not see us, but they'll know. They'll hear the jays.'

'It won't matter,' I said. I was not even sure why I was taking such care to stay hidden, except that we were so few and, like most warriors, I yearned for the security of numbers and knew I would feel a great deal more comfortable once the rest of my men were around me. Till then we would hide ourselves as best we could, though at mid-morning our route took us out of the trees and down into the open fields that led to the Fosse Way. Buck hares danced in the meadows and skylarks sang above us. We saw no one, though doubtless the peasants saw us, and doubtless the news of our passing rippled swiftly through the countryside. Armed men were ever cause for alarm, and so I had some of my men carry their shields in front so that their insignia would reassure the local people we were friends. It was not until we had crossed the Roman road and were close to Dun Caric that I saw another human, and that was a woman who, when we were still too far away for her to see the stars on our shields, ran to the woods behind the village to hide herself among the trees. 'Folks are nervous,' I said to Eachern.

'They've heard about Mordred dying,' he said, spitting, 'and they're fearing what'll happen next, but they should be happy the bastard's dying.' When Mordred was a child, Eachern had been one of his guards and the experience had given the Irish spearman a deep hatred for the King. I was fond of Eachern. He was not a clever man, but he was dogged, loyal and hard in battle. 'They reckon there'll be war, Lord,' he said.

We waded the stream beneath Dun Caric, skirted the houses, and came to the steep path that led to the palisade about the small hill. Everything was very quiet. Not even the dogs were in the village street and, more worryingly, no spearmen guarded the palisade. 'Issa's not here,' I said, touching Hywelbane's hilt. Issa's absence, by itself, was not unusual, for he spent much of his time in other parts of Dumnonia, but I doubted he would have left Dun Caric unguarded. I glanced at the village, but those doors were all shut tight. No smoke showed above the rooftops, not even from the smithy.

'No dogs on the hill,' Eachern said ominously. There was usually a pack of dogs about Dun Caric's hall and by now some should have raced down the hill to greet us. Instead there were noisy ravens on the hall roof and more of the big birds calling from the palisade. One bird flew up out of the compound with a long, red, lumpy morsel trailing from its beak.

None of us spoke as we climbed the hill. The silence had been the first indication of horror, then the ravens, and halfway up the hill we caught the sour-sweet stench of death that catches at the back of the throat, and that smell, stronger than the silence and more eloquent than the ravens, warned us of what waited inside the open gate. Death waited, nothing but death. Dun Caric had become a place of death. The bodies of men and women were strewn throughout the compound and piled inside the hall. Forty-six bodies in all, and not one still possessed a head. The ground was blood-soaked. The hall had been plundered, every basket and chest upturned, and the stables were empty. Even the dogs had been killed, though they, at least, had been left with their heads. The only living things were the cats and the ravens, and they all fled from us.

I walked through the horror in a daze. It was only after a few moments that I realized there were only ten young men among the dead. They must have been the guards left by Issa, while the rest of the corpses were the families of his men. Pyrlig was there, poor Pyrlig who had stayed at Dun Caric because he knew he could not rival Taliesin, and now he lay dead, his white robe soaked in blood and his harpist's hands deep scarred where he had tried to fend off the sword blows. Issa was not there, nor was Scarach, his wife, for there were no young women in that charnel house, neither were there any children. Those young women and children must have been taken away, either to be playthings or slaves, while the older folk, the babies and the guards had all been massacred, and then their heads had been taken as trophies. The slaughter was recent, for none of the bodies had started to bloat or rot. Flies crawled over the blood, but as yet there were no maggots wriggling in the gaping wounds left by the spears and swords.

I saw that the gate had been thrown off its hinges, but there was no sign of a fight and I suspected that the men who had done this thing had been invited into the compound as guests.

'Who did it, Lord?' one of my spearmen asked.

'Mordred,' I said bleakly.

'But he's dead! Or dying!'

'He just wants us to think that,' I said, and I could conjure up no other explanation. Taliesin had warned me, and I feared the bard was right. Mordred was not dying at all, but had returned and loosed his warband on his own country. The rumour of his death must have been designed to make people feel safe, and all the while he had been planning to return and kill every spearman who might oppose him. Mordred was throwing off his bridle, and that meant, surely, that after this slaughter at Dun Caric he must have gone east to find Sagramor, or maybe south and west to discover Issa. If Issa still lived.

It was our fault, I suppose. After Mynydd Baddon, when Arthur had given up his power, we had thought that Dumnonia would be protected by the spears of men loyal to Arthur and his beliefs, and that Mordred's power would be curtailed because he had no spearmen. None of us had foreseen that Mynydd Baddon would give our King a taste for war, nor that he would be so successful at battle that he would attract spearmen to his banner. Mordred now had spears, and spears give power, and I was seeing the first exercise of that new power. Mordred was scouring the country of the folk who had been set to limit his power and who might support Gwydre's claim to the throne.

'What do we do, Lord?' Eachern asked me.

'We go home, Eachern,' I said, 'we go home.' And by 'home' I meant Siluria. There was nothing we could do here. We were only eleven men, and I doubted we had any chance of reaching Sagramor whose forces lay so far to the east. Besides, Sagramor needed no help from us in looking after himself. Dun Caric's small garrison might have given Mordred easy pickings, but he would find plucking the Numidian's head a much harder task. Nor could I hope to find Issa, if Issa even lived, and so there was nothing to do but go home and feel a frustrated fury. It is hard to describe that fury. At its heart was a cold hate for Mordred, but it was an impotent and aching hate because I knew I could do nothing to give swift vengeance to these folk who had been my people. I felt, too, as though I had let them down. I felt guilt, hate, pity and an aching sadness.

I put one man to stand guard at the open gate while the rest of us dragged the bodies into the hall. I would have liked to burn them, but there was not enough fuel in the compound and we had no time to collapse the hall's thatched roof onto the corpses, and so we contented ourselves with putting them into a decent line, and then I prayed to Mithras for a chance to bring these folk a fitting revenge. 'We'd better search the village,' I told Eachern when the prayer was done, but we were not given the time. The Gods, that day, had abandoned us.

The man at the gate had not been keeping proper watch. I cannot blame him. None of us were in our right minds on that hilltop, and the sentry must have been looking into the blood-soaked compound instead of watching out of the gate, and so he saw the horsemen too late. I heard him shout, but by the time I ran out of the hall the sentry was already dead and a dark-armoured horseman was pulling a spear from his body. 'Get him!' I shouted, and started running towards the horseman, and I expected him to turn his horse and ride away, but instead he abandoned his spear and spurred further into the compound and more horsemen immediately followed him.

'Rally!' I shouted, and my nine remaining men crowded about me to make a small shield circle, though most of us had no shields for we had dropped them while we hauled the dead into the hall. Some of us did not even have spears. I drew Hywelbane, but I knew there was no hope for there were more than twenty horsemen in the compound now and still more were spurring up the hill. They must have been waiting in the woods beyond the village, maybe expecting Issa's return. I had done the same myself in Benoic. We would kill the Franks in some remote outpost, then wait in ambush for more, and now I had walked into an identical trap.

I recognized none of the horsemen, and none bore an insignia on their shields. A few of the horsemen had covered their leather shield faces with black pitch, but these men were not Oengus mac Airem's Blackshields. They were a scarred group of veteran warriors, bearded, ragged-haired and grimly confident. Their leader rode a black horse and had a fine helmet with engraved cheekpieces. He laughed when one of his men unfurled Gwydre's banner, then he turned and spurred his horse towards me. 'Lord Derfel,' he greeted me.

For a few heartbeats I ignored him, looking about the blood-soaked compound in a wild hope that there might still be some means of escape, but we were ringed by the horsemen who waited with spears and swords for the order to kill us. 'Who are you?' I asked the man in the decorated helmet.

For answer he simply turned back his cheekpieces. Then smiled at me.

It was not a pleasant smile, but nor was he was a pleasant man. I was staring at Amhar, one of Arthur's twin sons. 'Amhar ap Arthur,' I greeted him, then spat.

'Prince Amhar,' he corrected me. Like his brother Loholt, Amhar had ever been bitter about his illegitimate birth and he must now have decided to adopt the title of Prince even though his father was no king. It would have been a pathetic pretension had not Amhar changed so much since my last brief glimpse of him on the slopes of Mynydd Baddon. He looked older and much more formidable. His beard was fuller, a scar had flecked his nose and his breastplate was scored with a dozen spear strikes. Amhar, it seemed to me, had grown up on the battlefields of Armorica, but maturity had not decreased his sullen resentment. 'I have not forgotten your insults at Mynydd Baddon,' he told me, 'and have longed for the day when I could repay them. But my brother, I think, will be even more pleased to see you.' It had been I who had held Loholt's arm while Arthur struck off his hand.

'Where is your brother?' I asked.

'With our King.'

'And your King is who?' I asked. I knew the answer, but wanted it confirmed.

'The same as yours, Derfel,' Amhar said. 'My dear cousin, Mordred.' And where else, I thought, would Amhar and Loholt have gone after the defeat at Mynydd Baddon? Like so many other masterless men of Britain they had sought refuge with Mordred, who had welcomed every desperate sword that came to his banner. And how Mordred must have loved having Arthur's sons on his side!

'The King lives?' I asked.

'He thrives!' Amhar said. 'His Queen sent money to Clovis, and Clovis preferred to take her gold than to fight us.' He smiled and gestured at his men. 'So here we are, Derfel. Come to finish what we began this morning.'

'I shall have your soul for what you did to these folk,' I said, gesturing with Hywelbane at the blood that still lay black in Dun Caric's yard.

'What you will have, Derfel,' Amhar said, leaning forward on his saddle, 'is what I, my brother and our cousin decide to give you.'

I stared up at him defiantly. 'I have served your cousin loyally.'

Amhar smiled. 'But I doubt he wants your services any more.'

'Then I shall leave his country,' I said.

'I think not,' Amhar said mildly. 'I think my King would like to meet you one last time, and I know my brother is eager to have words with you.'

'I would rather leave,' I said.

'No,' Amhar insisted. 'You will come with me. Put the sword down.'

'You must take it, Amhar.'

'If I must,' he said, and did not seem worried by the prospect, but why should he have been worried? He outnumbered us, and at least half my men had neither shields nor spears.

I turned to my men. 'If you wish to surrender,' I told them, 'then step out of the ring. But as for me, I will fight.' Two of my unarmed men took a hesitant step forward, but Eachern snarled at them and they froze. I waved them away. 'Go,' I said sadly. 'I don't want to cross the bridge of swords with unwilling companions.' The two men walked away, but Amhar just nodded to his horsemen and they surrounded the pair, swung their swords and more blood flowed on Dun Caric's summit. 'You bastard!' I said, and ran at Amhar, but he just twitched his reins and spurred his horse out of my reach, and while he evaded me his men spurred in towards my spearmen.

It was another slaughter, and there was nothing I could do to prevent it. Eachern killed one of Amhar's men, but while his spear was still fixed in that man's belly, another horseman cut Eachern down from behind. The rest of my men died just as swiftly. Amhar's spearmen were merciful in that, at least. They did not let my men's souls linger, but chopped and stabbed with a ferocious energy.

I knew little of it, for while I pursued Amhar one of his men spurred behind me and gave me a huge blow across the back of my head. I fell, my head reeling in a black fog shot through with streaks of light. I remember falling to my knees, then a second blow struck my helmet and I thought I must be dying. But Amhar wanted me alive, and when I recovered my wits I found myself lying on one of Dun Caric's dung-heaps with my wrists tied with rope and Hywelbane's scabbard hanging at Amhar's waist. My armour had been taken, and a thin gold torque stolen from around my neck, but Amhar and his men had not found Ceinwyn's brooch that was still safely pinned beneath my jerkin. Now they were busy sawing off the heads of my spearmen with their swords. 'Bastard,' I spat the insult at Amhar, but he just grinned and turned back to his grisly work. He chopped through Eachern's spine with Hywelbane,

330

then gripped the head by the hair and tossed it onto the pile of heads that were being gathered into a cloak. 'A fine sword,' he told me, balancing Hywelbane in his hand.

'Then use it to send me to the Otherworld.'

'My brother would never forgive me for showing such mercy,' he said, then he cleaned Hywelbane's blade on his ragged cloak and thrust it into the scabbard. He beckoned three of his men forward, then drew a small knife from his belt. 'At Mynydd Baddon,' he said, facing me, 'you called me a bastard cur and a worm-ridden puppy. Do you think I am a man to forget insults?'

'The truth is ever memorable,' I told him, though I had to force the defiance into my voice for my soul was in terror.

'Your death will certainly be memorable,' Amhar said, 'but for the moment you must be content with the attentions of a barber.' He nodded at his men.

I fought them, but with my hands bound and my head still throbbing, there was little I could do to resist them. Two men held me fast against the dung-heap while the third gripped my head by the hair as Amhar, his right knee braced against my chest, cut off my beard. He did it crudely, slicing into the skin with each stroke, and he tossed the cut hanks of hair to one of his grinning men who teased the strands apart and wove them into a short rope. Once the rope was finished it was made into a noose that was put about my neck. It was the supreme insult to a captured warrior, the humiliation of having a slave's leash made from his own beard. They laughed at me when it was done, then Amhar hauled me to my feet by tugging on the beard-leash. 'We did the same to Issa,' he said.

'Liar,' I retorted feebly.

'And made his wife watch,' Amhar said with a smile, 'then made him watch while we dealt with her. They're both dead now.'

I spat in his face, but he just laughed at me. I had called him a liar, but I believed him. Mordred, I thought, had worked his return to Britain so efficiently. He had spread the tale of his imminent death, and all the while Argante had been shipping her hoarded gold to Clovis, and Clovis, thus purchased, had let Mordred go free. And Mordred had sailed to Dumnonia and was now killing his enemies. Issa was dead, and I did not doubt that most of his spearmen, and the spearmen I had left in Dumnonia, had died with him. I was a prisoner. Only Sagramor remained.

They tied my beard-leash to the tail of Amhar's horse, then marched me southwards. Amhar's forty spearmen formed a mocking escort, laughing whenever I stumbled. They dragged Gwydre's banner through the mud from the tail of another horse.

They took me to Caer Cadarn, and once there they threw me into a hut. It was not the hut in which we had imprisoned Guinevere so many years before, but a much smaller one with a low door through which I had to crawl, helped by the boots and spear staves of my captors. I scrambled into the hut's shadows and there saw another prisoner, a man brought from Durnovaria whose face was red from weeping. For a moment he did not recognize me without my beard, but then he gasped in astonishment. 'Derfel!'

'Bishop,' I said wearily, for it was Sansum, and we were both Mordred's prisoners.

'It's a mistake!' Sansum insisted. 'I shouldn't be here!'

'Tell them,' I said, jerking my head towards the guards outside the hut, 'not me.'

'I did nothing. Except serve Argante! And look how they reward me!'

'Be quiet,' I said.

'Oh, sweet Jesus!' He fell on his knees, spread his arms and gazed up at the cobwebs in the thatch. 'Send an angel for me! Take me to Thy sweet bosom.'

'Will you be quiet?' I snarled, but he went on praying and weeping, while I stared morosely towards Caer Cadarn's wet summit where a heap of severed heads was being piled. My men's heads were there, joining scores of others that had been fetched from all across Dumnonia. A chair draped in a pale blue cloth was perched on top of the pile; Mordred's throne. Women and children, the families of Mordred's spearmen, peered at the grisly heap, and some then came to look through our hut's low door and laugh at my beardless face.

'Where's Mordred?' I asked Sansum.

'How would I know?' he answered, interrupting his prayer.

'Then what do you know?' I asked. He shuffled back onto the

bench. He had done me one small service by fumbling the rope free from my wrists, but the freedom gave me little comfort for I could see six spearmen guarding the hut, and I did not doubt that there were others I could not see. One man just sat facing the hut's open entrance with a spear, begging me to try and crawl through the low door and thus give him a chance of skewering me. I had no chance of overpowering any of them. 'What do you know?' I asked Sansum again.

'The King came back two nights ago,' he said, 'with hundreds of men.'

'How many?'

He shrugged. 'Three hundred? Four? I couldn't count them, there were so many. They killed Issa in Durnovaria.'

I closed my eyes and said a prayer for poor Issa and his family. 'When did they arrest you?' I asked Sansum.

'Yesterday.' He looked indignant. 'And for nothing! I welcomed him home! I didn't know he was alive, but I was glad to see him. I rejoiced! And for that they arrested me!'

'So why do they think they arrested you?' I asked him.

'Argante claims I was writing to Meurig, Lord, but that can't be true! I have no skill with letters. You know that.'

'Your clerks do, Bishop.'

Sansum adopted an indignant look. 'And why should I talk to Meurig?'

'Because you were plotting to give him the throne, Sansum,' I said, 'and don't deny it. I talked with him two weeks ago.'

'I was not writing to him,' he said sulkily.

I believed him, for Sansum had ever been too canny to put his schemes on paper, but I did not doubt he had sent messengers. And one of those messengers, or perhaps a functionary at Meurig's court, had betrayed him to Argante who had doubtless craved Sansum's hoarded gold. 'You deserve whatever you're going to get,' I told him. 'You've plotted against every king who ever showed you kindness.'

'All I ever wanted was the best for my country, and for Christ!'

'You worm-ridden toad,' I said, spitting on the floor. 'You just wanted power.'

333

He made the sign of the cross and stared at me with loathing. 'It's all Fergal's fault,' he said.

'Why blame him?'

'Because he wants to be treasurer!'

'You mean he wants to be wealthy like you?'

'Me?' Sansum stared with feigned surprise. 'Me? Wealthy? In the name of God all I ever did was put a pittance aside in case the kingdom was in need! I was prudent, Derfel, prudent.' He went on justifying himself, and it gradually dawned on me that he believed every word he said. Sansum could betray people, he could scheme to have them killed as he had tried to kill Arthur and me when we had gone to arrest Ligessac, and he could bleed the Treasury dry, yet all the time he somehow persuaded himself that his actions were justified. His only principle was ambition, and it occurred to me, as that miserable day slunk into night, that when the world was bereft of men like Arthur and of Kings like Cuneglas, then creatures like Sansum would rule everywhere. If Taliesin was right then our Gods were vanishing, and with them would go the Druids, and after them the great Kings, and then would come a tribe of mouse lords to rule over us.

The next day brought sunshine and a fitful wind that fetched the stench of the heaped heads to our hut. We were not allowed out of the hut and so were forced to relieve ourselves in a corner. We were not fed, though a bladder of stinking water was thrown in to us. The guards were changed, but the new men were as watchful as the old. Amhar came to the hut once, but only to gloat. He drew Hywelbane, kissed her blade, polished her on his cloak, then fingered her newly honed edge. 'Sharp enough to take your hands off, Derfel,' he said. 'I'm sure my brother would like a hand of yours. He could mount it on his helmet! And I could have the other. I need a new crest.' I said nothing and after a time he became bored with trying to provoke me and walked away, slashing at thistles with Hywelbane.

'Maybe Sagramor will kill Mordred,' Sansum whispered to me.

'I pray so.'

'That's where Mordred's gone, I'm sure. He came here, sent Amhar to Dun Caric, then rode eastwards.'

'How many men does Sagramor have?'

'Two hundred.'

'Not many,' I said.

'Or perhaps Arthur will come?' Sansum suggested.

'He'll know Mordred's back by now,' I said, 'but he can't march through Gwent because Meurig won't let him, which means he has to ship his men by boat. And I doubt he'll do that.'

'Why not?'

'Because Mordred is the rightful King, Bishop, and Arthur, however much he hates Mordred, won't deny him that right. He won't break his oath to Uther.'

'He won't try and rescue you?'

'How?' I asked. 'The moment these men saw Arthur approaching they'd cut both our throats.'

'God save us,' Sansum prayed. 'Jesus, Mary and the Saints protect us.'

'I'd rather pray to Mithras,' I said.

'Pagan!' Sansum hissed, but he did not try to interrupt my prayer.

The day drew on. It was a spring day of utter loveliness, but to me it was bitter as gall. I knew my head would be added to the heap on Caer Cadarn's summit, but that was not the keenest cause of my misery; that came from the knowledge that I had failed my people. I had led my spearmen into a trap, I had seen them die, I had failed. If they greeted me in the Otherworld with reproach, then that was what I deserved, but I knew they would welcome me with joy, and that only made me feel more guilty. Yet the prospect of the Otherworld was a comfort to me. I had friends there, and two daughters, and when the torture was over and my soul was released to its shadowbody, I would have the happiness of reunion. Sansum, I saw, could find no consolation in his religion. All that day he whined, moaned, wept and railed, but his noise achieved nothing. We could only wait through one more night and another long hungry day.

Mordred returned late in the afternoon of that second day. He rode in from the east, leading a long column of marching spearmen who shouted greetings to Amhar's warriors. A group of horsemen accompanied the King and among them was one-handed Loholt. I confess I was frightened to see him. Some of Mordred's men carried bundles that I suspected would contain severed heads, and

335

so they did, but the heads were far fewer than I had feared. Maybe twenty or thirty were tipped onto the fly-buzzing heap, and not one of them looked to be black-skinned. I guessed that Mordred had surprised and butchered one of Sagramor's patrols, but he had missed his main prize. Sagramor was free, and that was a consolation. Sagramor was a wonderful friend and a terrible enemy. Arthur would have made a good enemy, for he was ever prone to forgiveness, but Sagramor was implacable. The Numidian would pursue a foe to the world's end.

Yet Sagramor's escape was of small use to me that evening. Mordred, on hearing of my capture, shouted for joy, then demanded to be shown Gwydre's mud-soiled banner. He laughed at the sight of the bear and dragon, then ordered the banner laid flat on the grass so that he and his men could piss on it. Loholt even danced a few steps at the news of my capture, for it was here, on this very hilltop, that his hand had been struck off. The mutilation had been a punishment for daring to rebel against his father and now he could revenge himself on his father's friend.

Mordred demanded to see me and Amhar came to fetch me, bringing the leash made from my beard. He was accompanied by a huge man, wall-eyed and toothless, who ducked through the hut's door, seized my hair and forced me down onto all fours then pushed me through the low door. Amhar circled my neck with the beard-leash and then, when I tried to stand, forced me back down. 'Crawl,' he commanded. The toothless brute forced my head down, Amhar tugged on the leash, and so I was forced to crawl towards the summit through jeering lines of men, women and children. All spat on me as I passed, some kicked me, others thrashed me with spear butts, but Amhar prevented them from crippling me. He wanted me whole for his brother's pleasure.

Loholt waited by the pile of heads. The stump of his right arm was sheathed in silver, and at the sheath's end, where his hand had been, a pair of bear claws was fixed. He grinned as I crawled close to his feet, but was too incoherent with joy to speak. Instead he babbled and spat at me, and all the time he kicked me in the belly and ribs. There was force in his kicks, but he was so angry that he attacked blindly and thus did little more than bruise me. Mordred watched from his throne which was set at the top of the fly-buzzing pile of severed heads. 'Enough!' he called after a while and Loholt gave me one last kick and stood aside. 'Lord Derfel,' Mordred greeted me with a mocking courtesy.

'Lord King,' I said. I was flanked by Loholt and Amhar, while all around the pile of heads a greedy crowd had gathered to watch my humiliation.

'Stand, Lord Derfel,' Mordred ordered me.

I stood and gazed up at him, but I could see nothing of his face for the sun was westering behind him and it dazzled me. I could see Argante standing to one side of the piled heads, and with her was Fergal, her Druid. They must have ridden north from Durnovaria during the day for I had not seen them earlier. She smiled to see my beardless face.

'What happened to your beard, Lord Derfel?' Mordred asked with pretended concern.

I said nothing.

'Speak!' Loholt ordered me, and cuffed me around the face with his stump. The bear claws raked my cheek.

'It was cut, Lord King,' I said.

'Cut!' He laughed. 'And do you know why it was cut, Lord Derfel?'

'No, Lord.'

'Because you are my enemy,' he said.

'Not true, Lord King.'

'You are my enemy!' he screamed in a sudden tantrum, banging one arm of the chair and watching to see whether I showed any fear at his anger. 'As a child,' he announced to the crowd, 'this thing raised me. He beat me! He hated me!' The crowd jeered until Mordred held up a hand to still them. 'And this man,' he said, pointing at me with his finger to add bad luck to his words, 'helped Arthur cut off Prince Loholt's hand.' Again the crowd shouted angrily. 'And yesterday,' Mordred went on, 'Lord Derfel was found in my kingdom with a strange banner.' He jerked his right hand and two men ran forward with Gwydre's urine-soaked flag. 'Whose banner is that, Lord Derfel?' Mordred asked.

'It belongs to Gwydre ap Arthur, Lord.'

'And why is Gwydre's banner in Dumnonia?'

For a heartbeat or two I thought of telling a lie. Perhaps I could

337

claim that I was bringing the banner as a form of tribute to Mordred, but I knew he would not believe me and, worse, I would despise myself for the lie. So instead I raised my head. 'I was hoping to raise it on news of your death, Lord King.'

My truth took him by surprise. The crowd murmured, but Mordred just drummed the chair's arm with his fingers. 'You declare yourself a traitor,' he said after a while.

'No, Lord King,' I said, 'I might have hoped for your death, but I did nothing to bring it about.'

'You didn't come to Armorica to rescue me!' he shouted.

'True,' I said.

'Why?' he asked dangerously.

'Because I would have thrown good men after bad,' I said, gesturing at his warriors. They laughed.

'And did you hope Clovis would kill me?' Mordred asked when the laughter had died.

'Many hoped for that, Lord King,' I said, and again my honesty seemed to surprise him.

'So give me one good reason, Lord Derfel, why I should not kill you now,' Mordred commanded me.

I stayed silent for a short while, then shrugged. 'I can think of no reason, Lord King.'

Mordred drew his sword and laid it across his knees, then put his hands flat on the blade. 'Derfel,' he announced, 'I condemn you to death.'

'It is my privilege, Lord King!' Loholt demanded eagerly. 'Mine!' And the crowd bayed their support for him. Watching my slow death would give them a fine appetite for the supper that was being prepared on the hilltop.

'It is your privilege to take his hand, Prince Loholt,' Mordred decreed. He stood and limped carefully down the pile of heads with the drawn sword in his right hand. 'But it is my privilege,' he said when he was close to me, 'to take his life.' He lifted the sword blade between my legs and gave me a crooked smile. 'Before you die, Derfel,' he said, 'we shall take more than your hands.'

'But not tonight!' a sharp voice called from the back of the crowd. 'Lord King! Not tonight!' There was a murmur from the crowd. Mordred looked astonished rather than offended at the interruption

338

and said nothing. 'Not tonight!' the man called again, and I turned to see Taliesin walking calmly through the excited throng that parted to give him passage. He carried his harp and his small leather bag, but now had a black staff as well so that he looked exactly like a Druid. 'I can give you a very good reason why Derfel should not die tonight, Lord King,' Taliesin said as he reached the open space beside the heads.

'Who are you?' Mordred demanded.

Taliesin ignored the question. Instead he walked to Fergal and the two men embraced and kissed, and it was only when that formal greeting was done that Taliesin looked back to Mordred. 'I am Taliesin, Lord King.'

'A thing of Arthur's,' Mordred sneered.

'I am no man's thing, Lord King,' Taliesin said calmly, 'and as you choose to insult me, then I shall leave my words unsaid. It is all one to me.' He turned his back on Mordred and began to walk away.

'Taliesin!' Mordred called. The bard turned to look at the King, but said nothing. 'I did not mean to insult you,' Mordred said, not wanting the enmity of a sorcerer.

Taliesin hesitated, then accepted the King's apology with a nod. 'Lord King,' he said, 'I thank you.' He spoke gravely and, as befitted a Druid speaking to a King, without deference or awe. Taliesin was famous as a bard, not as a Druid, but everyone there treated him as though he were a full Druid and he did nothing to correct their misapprehension. He wore the Druidical tonsure, he carried the black staff, he spoke with a sonorous authority and he had greeted Fergal as an equal. Taliesin plainly wanted them to believe his deception, for a Druid cannot be killed or maltreated, even if he is an enemy's Druid. Even on a battlefield Druids may walk in safety and Taliesin, by playing the Druid, was guaranteeing his own safety. A bard did not have the same immunity.

'So tell me why this thing,' Mordred pointed to me with his sword, 'should not die tonight.'

'Some years ago, Lord King,' Taliesin said, 'the Lord Derfel paid me gold to cast a spell on your wife. The spell caused her to be barren. I used the womb of a doe that I had filled with the ashes of a dead child to perform the charm.'

339

Mordred looked at Fergal, who nodded. 'That is certainly one way it can be done, Lord King,' the Irish Druid confirmed.

'It isn't true!' I shouted and, for my pains, received another raking blow from the bear claws on Loholt's silver-sheathed stump.

'I can lift the charm,' Taliesin went on calmly, 'but it must be lifted while Lord Derfel lives, for he was the petitioner of the charm, and if I lift it now, while the sun sets, it cannot be done properly. I must do it, Lord King, in the dawn, for the enchantment must be removed while the sun is rising, or else your Queen will stay childless for ever.'

Mordred again glanced at Fergal and the small bones woven into the Druid's beard rattled as he nodded his assent. 'He speaks true, Lord King.'

'He lies!' I protested.

Mordred pushed his sword back into its scabbard. 'Why do you offer this, Taliesin?' he asked.

Taliesin shrugged. 'Arthur is old, Lord King. His power wanes. Druids and bards must seek patronage where the power is rising.'

'Fergal is my Druid,' Mordred said. I had thought him a Christian, but was not surprised to hear that he had reverted to paganism. Mordred was never a good Christian, though that, I suspect, was the very least of his sins.

'I shall be honoured to learn more skills from my brother,' Taliesin said, bowing to Fergal, 'and I will swear to follow his guidance. I seek nothing, Lord King, but a chance to use my small powers for your great glory.'

He was smooth. He spoke with honey on his tongue. I had paid him no gold for charms, but everyone there believed him, and none more so than Mordred and Argante. It was thus that Taliesin, the bright-browed, bought me an extra night of life. Loholt was disappointed, but Mordred promised him my soul as well as my hand in the dawn and that gave him some consolation.

I was made to crawl back to the hut. I took a beating and kicking on the way, but I lived.

Amhar took the leash of hair from my neck, then booted me into the hut. 'We shall meet in the dawn, Derfel,' he said.

With the sun in my eyes and a blade at my throat.

*

That night Taliesin sang to Mordred's men. They had gathered in the half-finished church that Sansum had started to build on Caer Cadarn, and which now served as a roofless, broken-walled hall, and there Taliesin charmed them with his music. I had never before, and have never since, heard him sing more beautifully. At first, like any bard entertaining warriors, he had to fight the babble of voices, but gradually his skill silenced them. He accompanied himself on his harp and he chose to sing laments, but laments of such loveliness that Mordred's spearmen listened in awestruck silence. Even the dogs ceased their yelping and lay silent as Taliesin the Bard sang into the night. If he ever paused too long between songs the spearmen demanded more, and so he would sing again, his voice dying on the melody's endings, then surging again with the new verses, but forever soothing, and Mordred's folk drank and listened, and the drink and the songs made them weep, and still Taliesin sang to them. Sansum and I listened too, and we also wept for the ethereal sadness of the laments, but as the night stretched on Taliesin began to sing lullabies, sweet lullabies, delicate lullabies, lullabies to put drunken men to sleep, and while he sang the air grew colder and I saw that a mist was forming over Caer Cadarn.

The mist thickened and still Taliesin sang. If the world is to last through the reigns of a thousand kings I doubt men will ever hear songs so wondrously sung. And all the while the mist wrapped about the hilltop so that the fires grew dim in the vapour and the songs filled the dark like wraith songs echoing from the land of the dead.

Then, in the dark, the songs ended and I heard nothing but sweet chords being struck on the harp and it seemed to me that the chords drew closer and closer to our hut and to the guards who had been sitting on the damp grass listening to the music.

The sound of the harp came nearer still and at last I saw Taliesin in the mist. 'I have brought you mead,' he said to my guards, 'share it.' And he took from his bag a stoppered jar that he handed to one of the guards and, while they passed the jar to and fro, he sang to them. He sang the softest song of all that song-haunted night, a lullaby to rock a troubled world to sleep, and sleep they did. One by one the guards tipped sideways, and still Taliesin sang, his voice enchanting that whole fortress, and only when one of the guards began to snore did he stop singing and lower his hand from the harp. 'I think, Lord Derfel, that you can come out now,' he said very calmly.

'Me too!' Sansum said, and pushed past me to scramble first through the door.

Taliesin smiled when I appeared. 'Merlin ordered me to save you, Lord,' he said, 'though he says you may not thank him for it.'

'Of course I will,' I said.

'Come on!' Sansum yelped, 'no time to talk. Come! Quick!'

'Wait, you misery,' I said to him, then stooped and took a spear from one of the sleeping guards. 'What charm did you use?' I asked Taliesin.

'A man hardly needs a charm to make drunken folk sleep,' he said, 'but on these guards I used an infusion of mandrake root.'

'Wait for me here,' I said.

'Derfel! We must go!' Sansum hissed in alarm.

'You must wait, Bishop,' I said, and I slipped away into the mist, going towards the blurred glow of the biggest fires. Those fires burned in the half-built church that was nothing more than stretches of unfinished log-walls with great gaps between the timbers. The space inside was filled with sleeping people, though some were now waking and staring bleary-eyed like folk stirring from an enchantment. Dogs were rooting among the sleepers for food and their excitement was waking still more people. Some of the newly woken folk watched me, but none recognized me. To them I was just another spearman walking in the night.

I discovered Amhar by one of the fires. He slept with his mouth open, and he died the same way. I thrust the spear into his open mouth, paused long enough for his eyes to open and for his soul to recognize me, and then, when I saw that he knew me, I pushed the blade through his neck and spine so that he was pinned to the ground. He jerked as I killed him, and the last thing his soul saw on this earth was my smile. Then I stooped, took the beard leash from his belt, unbuckled Hywelbane, and stepped out of the church. I wanted to look for Mordred and Loholt, but more sleepers were waking now, and one man called out to ask who I was, and so I just went back into the misted shadows and hurried uphill to where Taliesin and Sansum waited.

'We must go!' Sansum bleated.

'I have bridles by the ramparts, Lord,' Taliesin told me.

'You think of everything,' I said admiringly. I paused to throw the remnants of my beard on the small fire that had warmed our guards, and when I saw that the last of the strands had flared and burned to ash I followed Taliesin to the northern ramparts. He found the two bridles in the shadows, then we climbed to the fighting platform and there, hidden from the guards by the mist, we clambered over the wall and dropped to the hillside. The mist ended halfway down the slope and we hurried on to the meadow where most of Mordred's horses were sleeping in the night. Taliesin woke two of the beasts, gently stroking their noses and chanting in their ears, and they calmly let him put the bridles over their heads.

'You can ride without a saddle, Lord?' he asked me.

'Without a horse, tonight, if necessary.'

'What about me?' Sansum demanded as I heaved myself onto one of the horses.

I looked down at him. I was tempted to leave him in the meadow for he had been a treacherous man all his life and I had no wish to prolong his existence, but he could also be useful to us on this night and so I reached down and hauled him onto the horse's back behind me. 'I should leave you here, Bishop,' I said as he settled himself. He offered me no answer, but just wrapped his arms tight round my waist. Taliesin was leading the second horse towards the meadow's gate that he tugged open. 'Did Merlin tell you what we should do now?' I asked the bard as I kicked my horse through the opening.

'He did not, Lord, but wisdom suggests we should go to the coast and find a boat. And that we hurry, Lord. The sleep on that hilltop will not last long, and once they find you missing, they will send men to search for us.' Taliesin used the gate as a mounting-block.

'What do we do?' Sansum asked in panic, his grip fierce about me.

343

'Kill you?' I suggested. 'Then Taliesin and I can make better time.'

'No, Lord, no! Please, no!'

Taliesin glanced up at the misted stars. 'We ride west?' he suggested.

'I know just where we're going,' I said, kicking the horse towards the track that led to Lindinis.

'Where?' Sansum demanded.

'To see your wife, Bishop,' I said, 'to see your wife.' That was why I saved Sansum's life that night, because Morgan was now our best hope. I doubted she would help me, and was certain she would spit in Taliesin's face if he asked for aid, but for Sansum she would do anything.

And so we rode to Ynys Wydryn.

We woke Morgan from sleep and she came to the door of her hall in a bad temper, or rather in a worse than usual temper. She did not recognize me without a beard and did not see her husband who, sore from the ride, was lagging behind us; instead Morgan saw Taliesin as a Druid who had dared to come into the sacred confines of her shrine. 'Sinner!' she screeched at him, her newly woken state proving no barrier to the full force of her vituperation. 'Defiler! Idolater! In the name of the holy God and His blessed Mother I order you to go!'

'Morgan!' I called, but just then she saw the bedraggled, limping figure of Sansum and she gave a small mew of joy and hurried towards him. The quarter moon glinted on the golden mask with which she covered her fire-ravaged face.

'Sansum!' she called. 'My sweet!'

'Precious!' Sansum said, and the two clasped each other in the night.

'Dear one,' Morgan babbled, stroking his face, 'what have they done to you?'

Taliesin smiled, and even I, who hated Sansum and had no love for Morgan, could not resist a smile at their evident pleasure. Of all the marriages I have ever known, that was the strangest. Sansum was as dishonest a man as ever lived, and Morgan as honest as any woman in creation, yet they plainly adored each other, or Morgan, at least, adored Sansum. She had been born fair, but the terrible fire that had killed her first husband had twisted her body and scarred her face into horror. No man could have loved Morgan for her beauty, or for her character which had been as fire-twisted into bitterness as her face had been ravaged into ugliness, but a man could love Morgan for her connections for she was Arthur's sister, and that, I ever believed, was what drew Sansum towards her. But if he did not love her for herself, he nevertheless made a show of love that convinced her and gave her happiness, and for that I was willing to forgive even the mouse lord his dissimulation. He admired her, too, for Morgan was a clever woman and Sansum prized cleverness, and thus both gained from the marriage; Morgan received tenderness, Sansum received protection and advice, and as neither sought the pleasures of the other's flesh, it had proved a better marriage than most.

'Within an hour,' I brutally broke their happy reunion apart, 'Mordred's men will be here. We must be far away by then, and your women, Lady,' I said to Morgan, 'should seek safety in the marshes. Mordred's men won't care that your women are holy, they will rape them all.'

Morgan glared at me with her one eye that glinted in the mask's hole. 'You look better without a beard, Derfel,' she said.

'I shall look worse without a head, Lady, and Mordred is making a pile of heads on Caer Cadarn.'

'I don't know why Sansum and I should save your sinful lives,' she grumbled, 'but God commands us to be merciful.' She turned from Sansum's arms and shrieked in a terrible voice to wake her women. Taliesin and I were ordered into the church, given a basket, and told to fill it with the shrine's gold while Morgan sent women into the village to wake the boatmen. She was wonderfully efficient. The shrine was suffused with panic, but Morgan controlled all, and it took only minutes before the first women were being helped into the flat-bottomed marsh boats that then headed into the mist-shrouded mere.

We left last of all, and I swear I heard hoofbeats to the east as our boatman poled the punt into the dark waters. Taliesin, sitting in the bow, began to sing the lament of Idfael, but Morgan snapped at him to cease his pagan music. He lifted his fingers from the small harp. 'Music knows no allegiance, Lady,' he chided her gently.

'Yours is the devil's music,' she snarled.

'Not all of it,' Taliesin said, and he began to sing again, but this time a song I had never heard before. 'By the rivers of Babylon,' he sang, 'where we sat down, we shed bitter tears to remember our home,' and I saw that Morgan was pushing a finger beneath her mask as if she was brushing away tears. The bard sang on and the high Tor receded as the marsh mists shrouded us and as our boatman poled us through whispering reeds and across the black water. When Taliesin ended his song there was only the sound of the lake rippling down the hull and the splash of the boatman's pole thumping down to surge us forward again.

'You should sing for Christ,' Sansum said reprovingly.

'I sing for all the Gods,' Taliesin said, 'and in the days to come we will need all of them.'

'There is only one God!' Morgan said fiercely.

'If you say so, Lady,' Taliesin said mildly, 'but I fear He has served you ill tonight,' and he pointed back towards Ynys Wydryn and we all turned to see a livid glow spreading in the mist behind. I had seen that glow before, seen it through these same mists on this same lake. It was the glow of buildings being put to the torch, the glow of burning thatch. Mordred had followed us and the shrine of the Holy Thorn, where his mother was buried, was being burned to ashes, but we were safe in the marshes where no man dared to go unless he possessed a guide.

Evil had again gripped Dumnonia.

But we were safe, and in the dawn we found a fisherman who would sail to Siluria in return for gold. And so I went home to Arthur.

And to new horror.

CEINWYN WAS SICK.

The sickness had come swiftly, Guinevere told me, just hours after I had sailed from Isca. Ceinwyn had begun to shiver, then to sweat, and by that evening she no longer had the strength to stand, and so she had taken to her bed and Morwenna had nursed her, and a wise-woman had fed her a concoction of coltsfoot and rue and put a healing charm between her breasts, but by morning Ceinwyn's skin had broken into boils. Every joint ached, she could not swallow, and her breath rasped in her throat. She began to rave then, thrashing in the bed and screaming hoarsely of Dian.

Morwenna tried to prepare me for Ceinwyn's death. 'She believes she was cursed, father,' she told me, 'because on the day you left a woman came and asked us for food. We gave her barley grains, but when she left there was blood on the doorpost.'

I touched Hywelbane's hilt. 'Curses can be lifted.'

'We fetched the Druid from Cefu-crib,' Morwenna told me, 'and he scraped the blood from the door and gave us a hagstone.' She stopped, staring tearfully at the pierced stone that now hung above Ceinwyn's bed. 'But the curse won't go!' she cried. 'She's going to die!'

'Not yet,' I said, 'not yet.' I could not believe in Ceinwyn's imminent death for she had always been so healthy. Not a hair on Ceinwyn's head had turned grey, she still possessed most of her teeth, and she had been as lithe as a girl when I had left Isca, but now, suddenly, she looked old and ravaged. And she was in pain. She could not tell us of the pain, but her face betrayed it, and the tears that ran down her cheeks cried it aloud.

Taliesin spent a long time staring at her and he agreed that she had been cursed, but Morgan spat on that opinion. 'Pagan superstition!' she croaked, and busied herself finding new herbs

347

that she boiled in mead and fed on a spoon through Ceinwyn's lips. Morgan, I saw, was very gentle, even though, as she dripped the liquid, she harangued Ceinwyn as a pagan sinner.

I was helpless. All I could do was sit by Ceinwyn's side, hold her hand and weep. Her hair became lank and, two days after my return, it began to drop out in handfuls. Her boils burst, soaking the bed with pus and blood. Morwenna and Morgan made new beds with fresh straw and new linen, but each day Ceinwyn would soil the bed and the old linen had to be boiled in a vat. The pain went on, and the pain was so hard that after a while even I began to wish that death would snatch her from its torment, but Ceinwyn did not die. She just suffered, and sometimes she would scream because of the pain, and her hand would tighten on my fingers with a terrible force and I could only wipe her forehead, say her name and feel the fear of loneliness creep through me.

I loved my Ceinwyn so much. Even now, years later, I smile to think of her, and sometimes I wake in the night with tears on my face and know they are due to her. We had begun our love in a blaze of passion and wise folk say that such passion must ever end, but ours had not ended, but had instead changed into a long, deep love. I loved and admired her, the days seemed brighter because of her presence, and suddenly I could only watch as the demons racked her and the pain made her shudder and the boils grew red and taut and burst into filth. And still she would not die.

Some days Galahad or Arthur relieved me at the bedside. Everyone tried to help. Guinevere sent for the wisest women in Siluria's hills and put gold into their palms so that they would bring new herbs or vials of water from some remote sacred spring. Culhwch, bald now, but still coarse and belligerent, wept for Ceinwyn and gave me an elf-bolt that he had found in the hills to the west, though when Morgan found that pagan charm in Ceinwyn's bed she threw it out, just as she had thrown out the Druid's hagstone and the charm she had discovered between Ceinwyn's breasts. Bishop Emrys prayed for Ceinwyn, and even Sansum, before he left for Gwent, joined him in prayer, though I doubt that his pleas were as heartfelt as those that Emrys called to God. Morwenna was devoted to her mother, and no one fought harder for a cure. She nursed her, cleaned her, prayed for her, wept with her. Guinevere, of

348

course, could not stand the sight of Ceinwyn's disease, or the smell
of the sick-room, but she walked with me for hours while Galahad
or Arthur held Ceinwyn's hand. I remember one day we had walked
to the amphitheatre and were pacing around its sandy arena when,
somewhat clumsily, Guinevere tried to console me. 'You are fortunate, Derfel,' she said, 'for you experienced a rare thing. A great
love.'

'So did you, Lady,' I said.

She grimaced, and I wished I had not invited the unspoken
thought that her great love had been spoiled, though in truth both
she and Arthur had outlived that unhappiness. I suppose it must
have been there still, a shadow deep back and sometimes during
those years a fool would mention Lancelot's name and a sudden
silence would embarrass the air, and once a visiting bard had
innocently sung us the Lament of Blodeuwedd, a song that tells of
a wife's unfaithfulness, and the smoky air in the feasting-room had
been taut with silence at the song's end, but for most of that time
Arthur and Guinevere were truly happy. 'Yes,' Guinevere said,
'I'm lucky too.' She spoke curtly, not out of dislike for me, but
because she was always uncomfortable with intimate conversations.
Only at Mynydd Baddon had she overcome that reserve, and she
and I had very nearly become friends at that time, but since then
we had drifted apart, not into our old hostility, but into a wary,
though affectionate, acquaintanceship. 'You look good without a
beard,' she said now, changing the subject, 'it makes you look
younger.'

'I have sworn to grow it again only after Mordred's death,' I
said.

'May it be soon. How I would hate to die before that worm
fetches his deserts.' She spoke savagely, and with a real fear that
old age might kill her before Mordred died. We were all in our
forties now, and few folk lived longer. Merlin, of course, had lasted
twice forty years and more, and we all knew others who had made
fifty or sixty or even seventy years, but we thought of ourselves as
old. Guinevere's red hair was heavily streaked with grey, but she
was still a beauty and her strong face looked on the world with all
its old force and arrogance. She paused to watch Gwydre, who had
ridden a horse into the arena. He raised a hand to her, then put

the horse through its paces. He was training the stallion to be a warhorse; to rear and kick with its hoofs and to keep its legs moving even when it was stationary so that no enemy could slice its hamstrings. Guinevere watched him for a while. 'Do you think he'll ever be King?' she asked wistfully.

'Yes, Lady,' I said. 'Mordred will make a mistake sooner or later and then we'll pounce.'

'I hope so,' she said, slipping her arm into mine. I do not think she was trying to give me comfort, but rather to take it for herself. 'Has Arthur spoken to you of Amhar?' she asked.

'Briefly, Lady.'

'He doesn't blame you. You do know that, don't you?'

'I'd like to believe it,' I said.

'Well you can,' she said brusquely. 'His grief is for his failings as a father, not for the death of that little bastard.'

Arthur, I suspect, was far more grieved for Dumnonia than he was for Amhar, for he had been deeply embittered by the news of the massacres. Like me, he wanted revenge, but Mordred commanded an army and Arthur had fewer than two hundred men who would all need to cross the Severn by boat if they were to fight Mordred. In all honesty, he could not see how it was to be done. He even worried about the legality of such vengeance. 'The men he killed,' he told me, 'were his oath-men. He had a right to kill them.'

'And we have a right to avenge them,' I insisted, but I am not sure Arthur entirely agreed with me. He always tried to elevate the law above private passion, and according to our law of oaths, which makes the King the source of all law and thus of all oaths, Mordred could do as he wished in his own land. That was the law, and Arthur, being Arthur, worried about breaking it, but he also wept for the men and women who had died and for the children who had been enslaved, and he knew that still more would die or be slave-chained while Mordred lived. The law, it seemed, would have to be bent, but Arthur did not know how to bend it. If we could have marched our men through Gwent, and then led them so far east that we could drop down into the border lands with Lloegyr and so have joined forces with Sagramor, we would have had the strength to beat down Mordred's savage army, or at least

350

meet it on equal terms, but King Meurig obstinately refused to let us cross his lands. If we crossed the Severn by boat we must go without our horses, and then we would find ourselves a long way from Sagramor and divided from him by Mordred's army. Mordred could defeat us first, then turn back to deal with the Numidian.

At least Sagramor still lived, but that was small consolation. Mordred had slaughtered some of Sagramor's men, but he had failed to find Sagramor himself and he had pulled his men back from the frontier country before Sagramor could launch a savage reprisal. Now, we heard, Sagramor and a hundred and twenty of his men had taken refuge in a fort in the south country. Mordred feared to make an assault on the fort, and Sagramor lacked the strength to sally out and defeat Mordred's army, and so they watched each other but did not fight, while Cerdic's Saxons, encouraged by Sagramor's impotence, again spread west into our land. Mordred detached warbands to oppose those Saxons, oblivious of the messengers who dared cross his land to link Arthur and Sagramor. The messages reflected Sagramor's frustration – how could he extricate his men and bring them to Siluria? The distance was great and the enemy, far too numerous, lay in his path. We truly did seem helpless to revenge the killings, but then, three weeks after my return from Dumnonia, news came from Meurig's court.

The rumour reached us from Sansum. He had come to Isca with me, but had found Arthur's company too galling and so, leaving Morgan in her brother's care, the Bishop had fled to Gwent and now, perhaps to show us how close to the King he was, he sent us a message saying that Mordred was seeking Meurig's permission to bring his army through Gwent to attack Siluria. Meurig, Sansum said, had not yet decided on an answer.

Arthur repeated Sansum's message to me. 'Is the mouse lord plotting again?' he asked me.

'He's supporting both you and Meurig, Lord,' I said sourly, 'so that both of you will be grateful to him.'

'But is it true?' Arthur wondered. He hoped it was, for if Mordred attacked Arthur, then no law could condemn Arthur for fighting back, and if Mordred marched his army north into Gwent then we could sail south across the Severn Sea and link forces with

Sagramor's men somewhere in southern Dumnonia. Both Galahad and Bishop Emrys doubted that Sansum spoke truly, but I disagreed. Mordred hated Arthur above all men, and I thought that he would be unable to resist the attempt to defeat Arthur in battle.

So, for a few days we made plans. Our men trained with spear and sword, and Arthur sent messengers to Sagramor outlining the campaign he hoped to fight, but either Meurig denied Mordred the permission he needed, or else Mordred decided against an attack on Siluria, for nothing happened. Mordred's army stayed between us and Sagramor, we heard no more rumours from Sansum and all we could do was wait.

Wait and watch Ceinwyn's agony. Watch her face sink into gauntness. Listen to her raving, feel the terror in her grip and smell the death that would not come.

Morgan tried new herbs. She laid a cross on Ceinwyn's naked body, but the touch of the cross made Ceinwyn scream. One night, when Morgan was sleeping, Taliesin made a counter-charm to avert the curse he still believed was the cause of Ceinwyn's sickness, but though we killed a hare and painted its blood on Ceinwyn's face, and though we touched her boil-ravaged skin with the burnt tip of an ash wand, and though we surrounded her bed with eagle-stones and elf-bolts and hagstones, and though we hung a bramble sprig and a bunch of mistletoe cut from a lime tree over her bed, and though we laid Excalibur, one of the Treasures of Britain, by her side, the sickness did not lift. We prayed to Grannos, the God of healing, but our prayers were unanswered and our sacrifices ignored. 'It is a magic too strong,' Taliesin said sadly. The next night, while Morgan slept again, we brought a Druid from northern Siluria into the sick chamber. He was a country Druid, all beard and stink, and he chanted a spell, then crushed the bones of a skylark into a powder that he stirred into an infusion of mugwort in a holly cup. He trickled the mixture into Ceinwyn's mouth, but the medicine achieved nothing. The Druid tried feeding her scraps of a black cat's roasted heart, but she spat them out and so he used his strongest charm, the touch of a corpse's hand. The hand, which reminded me of the crest of Cerdic's helmet, was blackened. The Druid touched it on Ceinwyn's forehead, on her nose and her throat, then pressed it against her scalp as he muttered an incantation, but all he achieved was to transfer a score of his lice from his beard onto her scalp and when we tried to comb them from her head we pulled out the last of her hair. I paid the Druid, then followed him into the courtyard to escape the smoke of the fires on which Taliesin was burning herbs. Morwenna came with me. 'You must rest, father,' she said.

'There'll be time for rest later,' I said, watching the Druid shuffle off into the dark.

Morwenna put her arms around me and rested her head on my shoulder. She had hair as golden as Ceinwyn's had been, and it smelt like Ceinwyn's. 'Maybe it isn't a magic at all,' she said.

'If it weren't magic,' I said, 'then she would have died.'

'There's a woman in Powys who is said to have great skills.'

'Then send for her,' I said wearily, though I had no faith in any sorcerers now. A score had come and taken gold, but not one had lifted the sickness. I had sacrificed to Mithras, I had prayed to Bel and to Don, and nothing had worked.

Ceinwyn moaned, and the moan rose to a scream. I flinched at the sound, then gently pushed Morwenna away. 'I must go to her.'

'You rest, father,' Morwenna said. 'I'll go to her.'

It was then that I saw the cloaked figure standing in the centre of the courtyard. Whether it was a man or a woman I could not tell, nor could I say how long the figure had stood there. It seemed to me that only a moment before the courtyard had been empty, but now the cloaked stranger was in front of me with a face dark shadowed from the moon by a deep hood, and I felt a sudden dread that this was death appearing. I stepped towards the figure. 'Who are you?' I demanded.

'No one you know, Lord Derfel Cadarn.' It was a woman who spoke, and as she spoke she pushed back the hood and I saw that she had painted her face white, then smeared soot about her eye sockets so that she looked like a living skull. Morwenna gasped.

'Who are you?' I demanded again.

'I am the breath of the west wind, Lord Derfel,' she said in a sibilant voice, 'and the rain that falls on Cadair Idris, and the frost that edges Eryri's peaks. I am the messenger from the time before kings, I am the Dancer.' She laughed then, and her laughter was like a madness in the night. The sound of it brought Taliesin and

Galahad to the door of the sickroom where they stood and stared at the white-faced laughing woman. Galahad made the sign of the cross while Taliesin touched the iron latch of the door. 'Come here, Lord Derfel,' the woman commanded me, 'come to me, Lord Derfel.'

'Go, Lord,' Taliesin encouraged me, and I had a sudden hope that the lice-ridden Druid's spells might have worked after all, for though they had not lifted the sickness from Ceinwyn, they had brought this apparition to the courtyard and so I stepped into the moonlight and went close to the cloaked woman.

'Embrace me, Lord Derfel,' the woman said, and there was something in her voice that spoke of decay and dirt, but I shuddered and took another step and placed my arms around her thin shoulders. She smelt of honey and ashes. 'You want Ceinwyn to live?' she whispered in my ear.

'Yes.'

'Then come with me now,' she whispered back, and pulled out of my embrace. 'Now,' she repeated when she saw my hesitation.

'Let me fetch a cloak and a sword,' I said.

'You will need no sword where we go, Lord Derfel, and you may share my cloak. Come now, or let your lady suffer.' With those words she turned and walked out of the courtyard.

'Go!' Taliesin urged me, 'go!'

Galahad tried to come with me, but the woman turned in the gate and ordered him back. 'Lord Derfel comes alone,' she said, 'or he does not come at all.'

And so I went, following death in the night, going north.

All that night we walked so that by dawn we were at the edge of the high hills, and still she pressed on, choosing paths that took us far from any settlement. The woman who called herself the Dancer walked barefoot, and skipped sometimes as if she was filled with an unquenchable joy. An hour after the dawn, when the sun was flooding the hills with new gold, she stopped beside a small lake and dashed water onto her face and scrubbed at her cheeks with handfuls of grass to wash away the mix of honey and ashes with which she had whitened her skin. Till that moment I had not known whether she was young or old, but now I saw she was a woman in her twenties, and very beautiful. She had a delicate face, full of life, with happy eyes and a quick smile. She knew her own beauty and laughed when she saw that I recognized it too. 'Would you lie with me, Lord Derfel?' she asked.

'No,' I said.

'If it would cure Ceinwyn,' she asked, 'would you lie with me?'

'Yes.'

'But it won't!' she said, 'it won't!' And she laughed and ran ahead of me, dropping her heavy cloak to reveal a thin linen dress clinging to a lissom body. 'Do you remember me?' she asked, turning to face me.

'Should I?'

'I remember you, Lord Derfel. You stared at my body like a hungry man, but you were hungry. So hungry. Remember?' And with that she closed her eyes and walked down the sheep path towards me, and she made her steps high and precise, pointing her toes out with each high step, and I immediately recalled her. This was the girl whose naked skin had shone in Merlin's darkness. 'You're Olwen,' I said, her name coming back to me across the years. 'Olwen the Silver.'

'So you do remember me. I am older now. Older Olwen,' she laughed. 'Come, Lord! Bring the cloak.'

'Where are we going?' I asked.

'Far, Lord, far. To where the winds spring and the rains begin and the mists are born and no kings rule.' She danced on the path, her energy apparently endless. All that day she danced, and all that day she spoke nonsense to me. I think she was mad. Once, as we walked through a small valley where silver-leaved trees shivered in the little wind, she pulled off the dress and danced naked across the grass, and she did it to stir and tempt me, and when I doggedly walked on and showed no hunger for her, she just laughed, slung the dress across her shoulder and walked beside me as though her nakedness was no strange thing. 'I was the one who carried the curse to your home,' she told me proudly.

'Why?'

'Because it had to be done, of course,' she said in all apparent sincerity, 'just as now it has to be lifted! Which is why we're going to the mountains, Lord.'

'To Nimue?' I asked, knowing already, as I think I had known ever since Olwen had first appeared in the courtyard, that it was to Nimue we were going.

'To Nimue,' Olwen agreed happily. 'You see, Lord, the time has come.'

'What time?'

'Time for the end of all things, of course,' Olwen said, and thrust her dress into my arms so that she was unencumbered. She skipped ahead of me, turning sometimes to give me a sly look, and taking pleasure in my unchanging expression. 'When the sun shines,' she told me, 'I like to be naked.'

'What is the end of all things?' I asked her.

'We shall make Britain into a perfect place,' Olwen said. 'There will be no sickness and no hunger, no fears and no wars, no storms and no clothes. Everything will end, Lord! The mountains will fall and the rivers will turn on themselves and the seas will boil and the wolves will howl, but at its ending the country will be green and gold and there will be no more years, and no more time, and we shall all be Gods and Goddesses. I shall be a tree Goddess. I shall rule the larch and the hornbeam, and in the mornings I shall dance, and in the evenings I shall lie with golden men.'

'Were you not supposed to lie with Gawain?' I asked her. 'When he came from the Cauldron? I thought you were to be his Queen.'

'I did lie with him, Lord, but he was dead. Dead and dry. He tasted of salt.' She laughed. 'Dead and dry and salty. One whole night I warmed him, but he did not move. I did not want to lie with him,' she added in a confiding voice, 'but since that night, Lord, I have known nothing but happiness!' She turned lightly, dancing a twisting step on the spring grass.

Mad, I thought, mad and heartbreakingly beautiful, as beautiful as Ceinwyn had once been, though this girl, unlike my pale-skinned and golden-haired Ceinwyn, was black-haired and her skin was sun-darkened. 'Why do they call you Olwen the Silver?' I asked her.

'Because my soul is silver, Lord. My hair is dark, but my soul is silver!' She spun on the path, then ran lithely on. I paused a few moments later to catch my breath and stared down into a deep valley where I could see a man herding sheep. The shepherd's dog

356

raced up the slope to gather in a straggler, and beneath the milling flock I could see a house where a woman laid wet clothes to dry on furze bushes. That, I thought, was real, while this journey through the hills was a madness, a dream, and I touched the scar on my left palm, the scar that held me to Nimue, and I saw that it had reddened. It had been white for years, now it was livid.

'We must go on, Lord!' Olwen called me. 'On and on! Up into the clouds.' To my relief she took her dress back and pulled it over her head and shook it down over her slim body. 'It can be cold in the clouds, Lord,' she explained, and then she was dancing again and I gave the shepherd and his dog a last rueful glance and followed the dancing Olwen up a narrow track that led between high rocks.

We rested in the afternoon. We stopped in a steep-sided valley where ash, rowan and sycamore grew, and where a long narrow lake shivered black under the small wind. I leaned against a boulder and must have slept for a while, for when I woke I saw that Olwen was naked again, but this time she was swimming in the cold black water. She came shuddering from the lake, scrubbed herself dry with her cloak, then pulled on her dress. 'Nimue told me,' she said, 'that if you lay with me, Ceinwyn would die.'

'Then why did you ask me to lie with you?' I asked harshly.

'To see if you loved your Ceinwyn, of course.'

'I do,' I said.

'Then you can save her,' Olwen said happily.

'How did Nimue curse her?' I asked.

'With a curse of fire and a curse of water and the curse of the blackthorn,' Olwen said, then crouched at my feet and stared into my eyes, 'and with the dark curse of the Otherbody,' she added ominously.

'Why?' I asked angrily, not caring about the details of the curses, only that any curse at all should have been put on my Ceinwyn.

'Why not?' Olwen said, then laughed, draped her damp cloak about her shoulders and walked on. 'Come, Lord! Are you hungry?'

'Yes.'

'You shall eat. Eat, sleep and talk.' She was dancing again, making delicate barefoot steps on the flinty path. I noticed that her feet were bleeding, but she did not seem to mind. 'We are going backwards,' she told me.

'What does that mean?'

She turned so that she was skipping backwards and facing me. 'Backwards in time, Lord. We unspool the years. Yesterday's years are flying past us, but so fast you cannot see their nights or their days. You are not born yet, your parents are not born, and back we go, ever back, to the time before there were kings. That, Lord, is where we go. To the time before kings.'

'Your feet are bleeding,' I said.

'They heal,' and she turned and skipped on. 'Come!' she called. 'Come to the time before kings!'

'Does Merlin wait for me there?' I asked.

That name stopped Olwen. She stood, turned back again, and frowned at me. 'I lay with Merlin once,' she said after a while. 'Often!' she added in a burst of honesty.

That did not surprise me. He was a goat. 'Is he waiting for us?' I asked.

'He is at the heart of the time before kings,' Olwen said seriously. 'At its utter heart, Lord. Merlin is the cold in the frost, the water in the rain, the flame in the sun, the breath in the wind. Now come,' she plucked at my sleeve with a sudden urgency, 'we cannot talk now.'

'Is Merlin a prisoner?' I asked, but Olwen would not answer. She raced ahead of me, and waited impatiently for me to catch up with her, and as soon as I did she ran ahead again. She took those steep paths lightly while I laboured behind, and all the time we were going deeper into the mountains. By now, I reckoned, we had left Siluria behind and had come into Powys, but into a part of that unhappy country where young Perddel's rule did not reach. This was the land without law, the lair of brigands, but Olwen skipped carelessly through its dangers.

The night fell. Clouds filled from the west so that soon we were in a complete darkness. I looked about me and saw nothing. No lights, not even the glimmer of a distant flame. It was thus, I imagine, that Bel found the isle of Britain when he first came to bring it life and light.

Olwen put her hand into mine. 'Come, Lord.'

'You can't see!' I protested.

'I see everything,' she said, 'trust me, Lord,' and with that she led me onwards, sometimes warning me of an obstacle. 'We must cross a stream here, Lord. Tread gently.'

I knew that our path was climbing steadily, but little else. We crossed a patch of treacherous shale, but Olwen's hand was firm in mine, and once we seemed to walk along the spine of a high ridge where the wind whistled about my ears and Olwen sang a strange little song about elves. 'There are still elves in these hills,' she told me when the song ended. 'Everywhere else in Britain they were killed, but not here. I've seen them. They taught me to dance.'

'They taught you well,' I said, not believing a word she said, but strangely comforted by the warm grip of her small hand.

'They have cloaks of gossamer,' she said.

'They don't dance naked?' I asked, teasing her.

'A gossamer cloak hides nothing, Lord,' she reproved me, 'but why should we hide what is beautiful?'

'Do you lie with the elves?'

'One day I shall. Not yet. In the time after the kings, I shall. With them and with golden men. But first I must lie with another salty man. Belly to belly with another dry thing from the Cauldron's heart.' She laughed and tugged at my hand and we left the ridge and climbed a smooth slope of grass to reach a higher crest. There, for the first time since the clouds had hidden the moon, I saw light.

Far across a dark saddle of land there lay a hill, and in the hill there must have been a valley that was filled with fire so that the nearer brow of the hill was edged with its glow. I stood there, my hand unconsciously in Olwen's hand, and she laughed with delight as she saw me gazing at that sudden light. 'That is the land before kings, Lord,' she told me. 'You will find friends there, and food.'

I took my hand from hers. 'What friend would put a curse on Ceinwyn?'

She took my hand back. 'Come, Lord, not far now,' she said, and she tugged me down the slope, trying to make me run, but I would not. I went slowly, remembering what Taliesin had told me in the magical mist he had drawn across Caer Cadarn; that Merlin had ordered him to save me, but that I might not thank him for it, and as I walked ever nearer that hollow of fire I feared I would discover Merlin's meaning. Olwen chivvied me, she laughed at my fears and her eyes sparkled with the reflection of the fire's glow, but I climbed towards the livid skyline with a heavy heart.

Spearmen guarded the edge of the valley. They were savage-looking men swathed in furs and carrying rough-shafted spears with crudely fashioned blades. They said nothing as we passed, though Olwen greeted them cheerfully, then she led me down a path into the valley's smoky heart. There was a long slender lake in the valley's bed, and all around the black lake's shores were fires, and by the fires were small huts among groves of stunted trees. An army of people was camped there, for there were two hundred fires or more.

'Come, Lord,' Olwen said and drew me on down the slope. 'This is the past,' she told me, 'and this is the future. This is where the hoop of time meets.'

This is a valley, I told myself, in upland Powys. A hidden place where a desperate man might find shelter. The hoop of time did nothing here, I assured myself, yet even so I felt a shiver of apprehension as Olwen took me down to the huts beside the lake where the army camped. I had thought the folk here must be sleeping, for we were deep into the night, but as we walked between the lake and the huts a crowd of men and women swarmed from the huts to watch us pass. They were strange things, those people. Some laughed for no reason, some gibbered meaninglessly, some twitched. I saw goitred faces, blind eyes, hare lips, tangled masses of hair, and twisted limbs. 'Who are they?' I asked Olwen.

'The army of the mad, Lord,' she said.

I spat towards the lake to avert evil. They were not all mad or crippled, those poor folk, for some were spearmen, and a few, I noticed, had shields covered with human skin and blackened with human blood; the shields of Diwrnach's defeated Bloodshields. Others had Powys's eagle on their shields, and one man even boasted the fox of Siluria, a badge that had not been carried into battle since Gundleus's time. These men, just like Mordred's army, were the scourings of Britain: defeated men, landless men, men with nothing to lose and everything to win. The valley reeked of human waste. It reminded me of the Isle of the Dead, that place where Dumnonia sent its terrible mad, and the place where I had once gone to rescue Nimue. These folk had the same wild look and gave the same unsettling impression that at any moment they might leap and claw for no apparent reason.

'How do you feed them?' I asked.

'The soldiers fetch food,' Olwen said, 'the proper soldiers. We eat a lot of mutton. I like mutton. Here we are, Lord. Journey's end!' And with those happy words she took her hand away from mine and skipped ahead of me. We had reached the end of the lake and in front of me now was a grove of great trees that grew in the shelter of a high rocky cliff.

A dozen fires burned under the trees and I saw that the trunks of the trees formed two lines, giving the grove the appearance of a vast hall, and at the hall's far end were two rearing grey stones like the high boulders that the old people erected, though whether these were ancient stones, or newly raised, I could not tell.

Between the stones, enthroned on a massive wooden chair, and holding Merlin's black staff in one hand, was Nimue. Olwen ran to her and threw herself down at Nimue's feet and put her arms about Nimue's legs and laid her head on Nimue's knees. 'I brought him, Lady!' she said.

'Did he lie with you?' Nimue asked, talking to Olwen but staring fixedly at me. Two skulls surmounted the standing stones, each thickly covered in melted wax.

'No, Lady,' Olwen said.

'Did you invite him?' Still Nimue's one eye gazed at me.

'Yes, Lady.'

'Did you show yourself to him?'

'All day I showed myself to him, Lady.'

'Good girl,' Nimue said, and patted Olwen's hair and I could almost imagine the girl purring as she lay so contentedly at Nimue's feet. Nimue still stared at me, and I, as I paced between those tall fire-lit tree trunks, stared back at her.

Nimue looked as she had looked when I had fetched her from the Isle of the Dead. She looked as though she had not washed, or combed her hair, or taken any care of herself in years. Her empty eye socket had no patch, or any false eye, but was a shrunken, shrivelled scar in her haggard face. Her skin was deeply ingrained with dirt, her hair was a greasy, matted tangle that fell to her waist. Her hair had once been black, but now it was bone white, all but

361

for one black streak. Her white robe was filthy, but over it she wore a misshapen sleeved coat, much too big for her, which I suddenly realized must be the Coat of Padarn, one of the Treasures of Britain, while on a finger of her left hand was the plain iron Ring of Eluned. Her nails were long and her few teeth black. She looked much older, or perhaps that was just the dirt accentuating the grim lines of her face. She had never been what the world would call beautiful, but her face had been quickened by intelligence and that had made her attractive, but now she looked repulsive and her once lively face was bitter, though she did offer me a shadow of a smile as she held up her left hand. She was showing me the scar, the same scar that I bore on my left hand, and in answer I held up my own palm and she nodded in satisfaction. 'You came, Derfel.'

'Did I have any choice?' I asked bitterly, then pointed to the scar on my hand. 'Doesn't this pledge me to you? Why attack Ceinwyn to bring me to you, when you already had this?' I tapped the scar again.

'Because you wouldn't have come,' Nimue said. Her mad creatures flocked about her throne like courtiers, others fed the fires and one sniffed at my ankles like a dog. 'You have never believed,' Nimue accused me. 'You pray to the Gods, but you don't believe in them. No one believes properly now, except us.' She waved her purloined staff at the halt, the half-blind, the maimed and the mad, who stared at her in adoration. 'We believe, Derfel,' she said.

'I too believe,' I replied.

'No!' Nimue screamed the word, making some of the creatures under the trees call out in terror. She pointed the staff at me. 'You were there when Arthur took Gwydre from the fires.'

'You could not expect Arthur to see his son killed,' I said.

'What I expected, fool, was to see Bel come from the sky with the air scorched and crackling behind him and the stars tossed like leaves in a tempest! That's what I expected! That's what I deserved!' She put her head back and shrieked at the clouds, and all the crippled mad howled with her. Only Olwen the Silver was silent. She gazed at me with a half-smile, as though to suggest that she and I alone were sane in this refuge of the mad. 'That's what I wanted!' Nimue shouted at me over the cacophony of wailing and yelping. 'And that is what I shall have,' she added, and with those

362

words she stood, shook Olwen's embrace free and beckoned me with her staff. 'Come.'

I followed her past the standing stones to a cave in the cliff. It was not a deep cave, just large enough to hold a man lying on his back, and at first I thought I did see a naked man lying in the cave's shadows. Olwen had come to my side and was trying to take my hand, but I pushed her away as, all around me, the mad pressed close to see what lay on the cave's stone floor.

A small fire smouldered in the cave, and in its dim light I saw that it was not a man lying on the rock, but the clay figure of a woman. It was a life-size figure with crude breasts, spread legs and a rudimentary face. Nimue ducked into the cave to crouch beside the clay figure's head. 'Behold, Derfel Cadarn,' she said, 'your woman.'

Olwen laughed and smiled up at me. 'Your woman, Lord!' Olwen said, in case I did not understand.

I stared at the grotesque clay figure, then at Nimue. 'My woman?'

'That is Ceinwyn's Otherbody, you fool!' Nimue said, 'and I am Ceinwyn's bane.' There was a frayed basket at the back of the cave, the Basket of Garanhir, another Treasure of Britain, and Nimue took from it a bunch of dried berries. She stooped and pressed one into the unfired clay of the woman's body. 'A new boil, Derfel!' she said, and I saw that the clay's surface was pitted with other berries. 'And another, and another!' She laughed, pressing the dry berries into the red clay. 'Shall we give her pain, Derfel? Shall we make her scream?' And with those words she drew a crude knife from her belt, the Knife of Laufrodedd, and she stabbed its chipped blade into the clay woman's head. 'Oh, she is screaming now!' Nimue told me. 'They are trying to hold her down, but the pain is so bad, so bad!' And with that she wriggled the blade about and suddenly I was enraged and stooped into the cave's mouth and Nimue immediately let go of the knife and poised two fingers over the clay eyes. 'Shall I blind her, Derfel?' she hissed at me. 'Is that what you want?'

'Why are you doing this?' I asked her.

She took the Knife of Laufrodedd from the tortured clay skull. 'Let her sleep,' she crooned, 'or maybe not?' And with that she gave a mad laugh and snatched an iron ladle from the Basket of

Garanhir, scooped some burning embers from the smoky fire and scattered the burning scraps over the body and I imagined Ceinwyn shuddering and screaming, her back arching with the sudden pain, and Nimue laughed to see my impotent rage. 'Why am I doing it?' she asked. 'Because you stopped me from killing Gwydre. And because you can bring the Gods to earth. That is why.'

I stared at her. 'You're mad too,' I said softly.

'What do you know of madness?' Nimue spat at me. 'You and your little mind, your pathetic little mind. You can judge me? Oh, pain!' And she stabbed the knife into the clay breasts. 'Pain! Pain!' The mad things behind me joined in her cry. 'Pain! Pain!' they exulted, some clapping their hands and others laughing with delight.

'Stop!' I shouted.

Nimue crouched over the tortured figure, her knife poised. 'Do you want her back, Derfel?'

'Yes,' I was close to tears.

'She is most precious to you?'

'You know she is.'

'You would rather lie with that,' Nimue gestured at the grotesque clay figure, 'than with Olwen?'

'I lie with no woman but Ceinwyn,' I said.

'Then I will give her back to you,' Nimue said, and she tenderly stroked the clay figure's forehead. 'I will restore your Ceinwyn to you,' Nimue promised, 'but first you must give me what is most precious to me. That is my price.'

'And what is most precious to you?' I asked, knowing the answer before she gave it to me.

'You must bring me Excalibur, Derfel,' Nimue said, 'and you must bring me Gwydre.'

'Why Gwydre?' I demanded. 'He's not a ruler's son.'

'Because he was promised to the Gods, and the Gods demand what was promised to them. You must bring him to me before the next moon is full. You will take Gwydre and the sword to where the waters meet beneath Nant Dduu. You know the place?'

'I know it,' I said grimly.

'And if you do not bring them, Derfel, then I swear to you that Ceinwyn's sufferings will increase. I shall plant worms in her belly, I shall turn her eyes to liquid, I shall make her skin peel and her

364

flesh rot on her crumbling bones, and though she will beg for death I will not send it, but only give her pain instead. Nothing but pain.' I wanted to step forward and kill Nimue there and then. She had been a friend and even, once, a lover, but now she had gone so far from me into a world where the spirits were real and the real were playthings. 'Bring me Gwydre and bring me Excalibur,' Nimue went on, her one eye glittering in the cave's gloom, 'and I shall free Ceinwyn of her Otherbody and you of your oath to me, and I shall give you two things.' She reached behind her and pulled out a cloth. She shook it open and I saw it was the old cloak that had been stolen from me in Isca. She fumbled in the cloak, found something, and held it up between a finger and thumb and I saw she was holding the little missing agate from Ceinwyn's ring. 'A sword and a sacrifice,' she said, 'for a cloak and a stone. Will you do that, Derfel?' she asked.

'Yes,' I said, and not meaning it, but not knowing what else I could say. 'Will you leave me with her now?' I demanded.

'No,' Nimue said, smiling. 'But you want her to rest tonight? Then this one night, Derfel, I shall give her respite.' She blew the ashes off the clay, picked out the berries and plucked the charms that had been pinned to the body. 'In the morning,' Nimue said, 'I shall replace them.'

'No!'

'Not all of them,' she said, 'but more each day until I hear you are come to where the waters meet at Nant Dduu.' She pulled a burnt scrap of bone from the clay belly. 'And when I have the sword,' she went on, 'my army of the mad will make such fires that the night of Samain Eve will turn to day. And Gwydre will come back to you, Derfel. He will rest in the Cauldron and the Gods will kiss him to life and Olwen will lie with him and he will ride in glory with Excalibur in his hand.' She took a pitcher of water and spilt a little onto the figure's brow, then smoothed it gently into the glistening clay. 'Go now,' she said, 'your Ceinwyn will sleep and Olwen has another thing to show you. At dawn you will leave.'

I stumbled after Olwen, pushing through the grinning crowd of horrid things that pressed about the cave and following the dancing girl along the cliff face to another cave. Inside I saw a second clay figure, this one a man, and Olwen gestured to it, then giggled. 'Is it me?' I asked, for I saw the clay was smooth and unmarked, but then, peering closer into the darkness, I saw the clay man's eyes had been gouged out.

'No, Lord,' Olwen said, 'it is not you.' She stooped beside the figure and picked up a long bone needle that had been lying beside its legs. 'Look,' she said, and she slid the needle into the clay foot. From somewhere behind us a man wailed in pain. Olwen giggled. 'Again,' she said, and slid the bone into the other foot and once again the voice cried in pain. Olwen laughed, then reached for my hand. 'Come,' she said, and led me into a deep cleft that opened in the cliff. The cleft narrowed, then seemed to end abruptly ahead of us, for I could see only the dim sheen of reflected firelight on high rock, but then I saw a kind of cage had been made at the gorge's end. Two hawthorns grew there, and rough baulks of timber had been nailed across their trunks to make crude prison bars. Olwen let go of my hand and pushed me forward. 'I shall come for you in the morning, Lord. There's food waiting there.' She smiled, turned and ran away.

At first I thought the crude cage was some kind of shelter, and that when I got close I would find an entrance between the bars, but there was no door. The cage barred the last few yards of the gorge, and the promised food was waiting under one of the hawthorns. I found stale bread, dried mutton and a jar of water. I sat, broke the loaf, and suddenly something moved inside the cage and I twitched with alarm as a thing scrabbled towards me.

At first I thought the thing was a beast, then I saw it was a man, and then I saw that it was Merlin.

'I shall be good,' Merlin said to me, 'I shall be good.' I understood the second clay figure then, for Merlin was blind. No eyes at all. Just horror. 'Thorns in my feet,' he said, 'in my feet,' then he collapsed beside the bars and whimpered. 'I shall be good, I promise!'

I crouched. 'Merlin?' I said.

He shuddered. 'I will be good!' he said in desperation, and when I put a hand through his bars to stroke his tangled filthy hair, he jerked back and shivered.

'Merlin?' I said again.

'Blood in the clay,' he said, 'you must put blood in the clay. Mix it well. A child's blood works best, or so I'm told. I never did it, my dear. Tanaburs did, I know, and I talked to him once about it. He was a fool, of course, but he knew some few tawdry things. The blood of a red-haired child, he told me, and preferably a crippled child, a red-haired cripple. Any child will do at a pinch, of course, but the red-haired cripple is best.'

'Merlin,' I said, 'it's Derfel.'

He babbled on, giving instructions on how best to make the clay figure so that evil could be sent from afar. He spoke of blood and dew and the need to mould the clay during the sound of thunder. He would not listen to me, and when I stood and tried to prise the bars away from the trees, two spearmen came grinning from the cleft's shadows behind me. They were Bloodshields, and their spears told me to stop my efforts to free the old man. I crouched again. 'Merlin!' I said.

He crept nearer, sniffing. 'Derfel?' he asked.

'Yes, Lord.'

He groped for me, and I gave him my hand and he clutched it hard. Then, still holding my hand, he sank onto the ground. 'I'm mad, you know?' he said in a reasonable voice.

'No, Lord,' I said.

'I have been punished.'

'For nothing, Lord.'

'Derfel? Is it really you?'

'It is me, Lord. Do you want food?'

'I have much to tell you, Derfel.'

'I hope so, Lord,' I said, but he seemed incapable of ordering his wits, and for the next few moments he talked of the clay again, then of other charms, and he again forgot who I was for he called me Arthur, and then he was silent for a long while. 'Derfel?' he finally asked again.

'Yes, Lord.'

'Nothing must be written, do you understand?'

'You've told me so many times, Lord.'

'All our lore must be remembered. Caleddin had it all written down, and that's when the Gods began to retreat. But it is in my head. It was. And she took it. All of it. Or almost all.' He whispered the last three words.

'Nimue?' I asked, and he gripped my hand so terribly hard at the mention of her name and again he fell silent.

'She blinded you?' I asked.

'Oh, she had to!' he said, frowning at the disapproval in my voice. 'No other way to do it, Derfel. I should have thought that was obvious.'

'Not to me,' I said bitterly.

'Quite obvious! Absurd to think otherwise,' he said, then let go of my hand and tried to arrange his beard and hair. His tonsure had disappeared beneath a layer of matted hair and dirt, his beard was straggly and flecked with leaves, while his white robe was the colour of mud. 'She's a Druid now,' he said in a tone of wonder.

'I thought women couldn't be Druids,' I said.

'Don't be absurd, Derfel. Just because women never have been Druids doesn't mean they can't be! Anyone can be a Druid! All you need do is memorize the six hundred and eighty-four curses of Beli Mawr and the two hundred and sixty-nine charms of Lleu and carry in your head about a thousand other useful things, and Nimue, I must say, was an excellent pupil.'

'But why blind you?'

'We have one eye between us. One eye and one mind.' He fell silent.

'Tell me about the clay figure, Lord,' I said.

'No!' He shuffled away from me, terror in his voice. 'She has told me not to tell you,' he added in a hoarse whisper.

'How do I defeat it?' I asked.

He laughed at that. 'You, Derfel? You would fight my magic?'

'Tell me how,' I insisted.

He came back to the bars and turned his empty eye sockets left and right as though he were looking for some enemy who might be overhearing us. 'Seven times and three,' he said, 'I dreamed on Carn Ingli.' He had gone back into madness, and all that night I discovered that if I tried to prise out of him the secrets of Ceinwyn's sickness he would do the same. He would babble of dreams, of the wheat-girl he had loved by the waters of Claerwen or of the hounds of Trygwylth who he was persuaded were hunting him. 'That is why I have these bars, Derfel,' he said, pounding the wooden slats, 'so that the hounds cannot reach me, and why I have no eyes, so they cannot see me. The hounds can't see you, you know, not if you have no eyes. You should remember that.'

'Nimue,' I said at one point, 'will bring the Gods back?'

'That is why she has taken my mind, Derfel,' Merlin said.

'Will she succeed?'

'A good question! An excellent question. A question I ask myself constantly.' He sat and hugged his bony knees. 'I lacked the nerve, didn't I? I betrayed myself. But Nimue won't. She will go to the bitter end, Derfel.'

'But will she succeed?'

'I would like to have a cat,' he said after a while. 'I do miss cats.'

'Tell me about the summoning.'

'You know it all already!' he said indignantly. 'Nimue will find Excalibur, she will fetch poor Gwydre, and the rites will be done properly. Here, on the mountain. But will the Gods come? That is the question, isn't it? You worship Mithras, don't you?'

'I do, Lord.'

'And what do you know of Mithras?'

'The God of soldiers,' I said, 'born in a cave. He is the God of the sun.'

Merlin laughed. 'You know so little! He is the God of oaths. Did you know that? Or do you know the grades of Mithraism? How many grades do you have?' I hesitated, unwilling to reveal the secrets of the mysteries. 'Don't be absurd, Derfel!' Merlin said, his voice as sane as it had ever been in all his life. 'How many? Two? Three?'

'Two, Lord.'

'So you've forgotten the other five! What are your two?'

'Soldier and Father.'

'*Miles* and *Pater*, they should be called. And once there were also *Leo*, *Corax*, *Perses*, *Nymphus* and *Heliodromus*. How little you know of your miserable God, but then, your worship is a mere shadow worship. Do you climb the seven-runged ladder?'

'No, Lord.'

'Do you drink the wine and bread?'

'That is the Christian way, Lord,' I protested.

'The Christian way! What halfwits you all are! Mithras's mother was a virgin, shepherds and wise men came to see her newborn child, and Mithras himself grew to become a healer and a teacher. He had twelve disciples, and on the eve of his death he gave them a final supper of bread and wine. He was buried in a rock tomb and rose again, and he did all this long before the Christians nailed their God to a tree. You let the Christians steal your God's clothes, Derfel!'

I gazed at him. 'Is this true?' I asked him.

'It is true, Derfel,' Merlin said, and raised his ravaged face to the crude bars. 'You worship a shadow God. He is going, you see, just as our Gods are going. They all go, Derfel, they go into the void. Look!' He pointed up into the clouded sky. 'The Gods come and the Gods go, Derfel, and I no longer know if they hear us or see us. They pass by on the great wheel of heaven and now it is the Christian God who rules, and He will rule for a while, but the wheel will also take Him into the void and mankind will once again shiver in the dark and look for new Gods. And they will find them, for the Gods come and they go, Derfel, they go and they come.'

'But Nimue will turn the wheel back?' I asked.

'Perhaps she will,' Merlin said sadly, 'and I would like that, Derfel. I would like to have my eyes back, and my youth, and my joy.' He rested his forehead on the bars. 'I will not help you break the enchantment,' he said softly, so softly I almost did not hear him. 'I love Ceinwyn, but if Ceinwyn must suffer for the Gods, then she is doing a noble thing.'

'Lord,' I began to plead.

'No!' He shouted so loudly that in the encampment behind us some dogs howled in reply. 'No,' he said more quietly. 'I compromised once and I will not compromise again, for what was the price of compromise? Suffering! But if Nimue can perform the rites, then all our suffering will be done. Soon be done. The Gods will return, Ceinwyn will dance and I shall see.'

He slept for a while and I slept too, but after a time he woke me by putting a claw-like hand through the bars and seizing my arm. 'Are the guards asleep?' he asked me.

'I think so, Lord.'

'Then look for the silver mist,' he whispered to me.

I thought for a heartbeat he had slipped back into madness. 'Lord?' I asked him.

'I sometimes think,' he said, and his voice was quite sane, 'that there is only so much magic left on the earth. It fades like the Gods fade. But I did not give Nimue everything, Derfel. She thinks I did, but I saved one last enchantment. And I have worked it for you and for Arthur, for you two I loved above all men. If Nimue fails, Derfel, then look for Caddwg. You remember Caddwg?'

Caddwg was the boatman who had rescued us from Ynys Trebes so many years before, and the man who had hunted Merlin's piddocks. 'I remember Caddwg,' I said.

'He lives at Camlann now,' Merlin said in a whisper. 'Look for him, Derfel, and seek the silver mist. Remember that. If Nimue fails and horror comes, then take Arthur to Camlann, find Caddwg and look for the silver mist. It is the last enchantment. My last gift to those who were my friends.' His fingers tightened on my arm. 'Promise me you will seek it?'

'I shall, Lord,' I promised him.

He seemed relieved. He sat for a time, clutching my arm, then sighed. 'I wish I could come with you. But I can't.'

'You can, Lord,' I said.

'Don't be absurd, Derfel. I am to stay here and Nimue will use me one last time. I might be old, blind, half mad and nearly dead, but there is still power in me. She wants it.' He uttered a horrid little whimper. 'I cannot even weep any longer,' he said, 'and there are times when all I wish to do is weep. But in the silver mist, Derfel, in that silver mist, you will find no weeping and no time, just joy.'

He slept again, and when he woke it was dawn and Olwen had come for me. I stroked Merlin's hair, but he was gone into the madness again. He yapped like a dog, and Olwen laughed to hear it. I wished there had been something I could give him, some small thing to give him comfort, but I had nothing. So I left him, and took his last gift with me even though I did not understand what it was; the last enchantment.

Olwen did not take me back by the same path that had brought me to Nimue's encampment, but instead led me down a steep combe, and then into a dark wood where a stream tumbled between rocks. It had begun to rain and our path was treacherous, but Olwen danced ahead of me in her damp cloak. 'I like the rain!' she called out to me once.

'I thought you liked the sun,' I said sourly.

'I like both, Lord,' she said. She was her usual merry self, but I scarcely listened to most of what she said. I was thinking of Ceinwyn, and of Merlin, and of Gwydre and Excalibur. I was thinking that I was in a trap, and I saw no way out. Must I choose between Ceinwyn and Gwydre? Olwen must have guessed what I was thinking because she came and slipped her arm through mine. 'Your troubles will soon be over, Lord,' she said comfortingly.

I took my arm away. 'They are just beginning,' I said bitterly.

'But Gwydre won't stay dead!' she said encouragingly. 'He will lie in the Cauldron, and the Cauldron gives life.' She believed, but I did not. I still believed in the Gods, but I no longer believed we could bend them to our will. Arthur, I thought, had been right. It is to ourselves we must look, not to the Gods. They have their own amusements, and if we are not their toys, then we should be glad.

Olwen stopped beside a pool under the trees. 'There are beavers here,' she said, staring at the rain-pitted water, and when I said nothing she looked up and smiled. 'If you keep walking down the stream, Lord, you will come to a track. Follow it down the hill and you will find a road.'

I followed the track and the road, emerging from the hills near the old Roman fort of Cicucium that was now home to a group of nervous families. Their menfolk saw me and came from the fort's broken gate with spears and dogs, but I waded the stream and scrambled uphill and when they saw I meant no harm, had no weapons and was evidently not the scout for a raiding party, they contented themselves with jeering at me. I could not remember being so long without a sword since childhood. It made a man feel naked.

It took me two days to reach home; two days of bleak thinking without any answer. Gwydre was the first to see me coming down Isca's main street and he ran to greet me. 'She's better than she was, Lord,' he called.

'But getting worse again,' I said.

372

He hesitated. 'Yes. But two nights ago we thought she was recovering.' He looked at me anxiously, worried by my grim appearance.

'And each day since,' I said, 'she has slipped back.'

'There must be hope, though,' Gwydre tried to encourage me.

'Maybe,' I said, though I had none. I went to Ceinwyn's bedside and she recognized me and tried to smile, but the pain was building in her again and the smile showed as a skull-like grimace. She had a fine layer of new hair, but it was all white. I bent, dirty as I was, and kissed her forehead.

I changed my clothes, washed and shaved, strapped Hywelbane to my waist and then sought Arthur. I told him all that Nimue had told me, but Arthur had no answers, or none he would tell me. He would not surrender Gwydre, and that condemned Ceinwyn, but he could not say that to my face. Instead he looked angry. 'I've had enough of this nonsense, Derfel.'

'A nonsense that is giving Ceinwyn agony, Lord,' I reproved him.

'Then we must cure her,' he said, but conscience gave him pause. He frowned. 'Do you believe Gwydre will live again if he is placed in the Cauldron?'

I thought about it and could not lie to him. 'No, Lord.'

'Nor I,' he said, and called for Guinevere, but the only suggestion she could make was that we should consult Taliesin.

Taliesin listened to my tale. 'Name the curses again, Lord,' he said when I was done.

'The curse of fire,' I said, 'the curse of water, the curse of the blackthorn and the dark curse of the Otherbody.'

He flinched when I said the last. 'The first three I can lift,' he said, 'but the last? I know of no one who can lift that.'

'Why not?' Guinevere demanded sharply.

Taliesin shrugged. 'It is the higher knowledge, Lady. A Druid's learning does not cease with his training, but goes on into new mysteries. I have not trodden that path. Nor, I suspect, has any man in Britain other than Merlin. The Otherbody is a great magic and to counter it we need a magic just as great. Alas, I don't have it.'

I stared at the rainclouds above Isca's roofs. 'If I cut off Ceinwyn's head, Lord,' I spoke to Arthur, 'will you cut off mine a heartbeat later?'

'No,' he said in disgust.

'Lord!' I pleaded.

'No!' he said angrily. He was offended by the talk of magic. He wanted a world in which reason ruled, not magic, but none of his reason helped us now.

Then Guinevere spoke softly. 'Morgan,' she said.

'What of her?' Arthur asked.

'She was Merlin's priestess before Nimue,' Guinevere said. 'If anyone knows Merlin's magic, it is Morgan.'

So Morgan was summoned. She limped into the courtyard, as ever managing to bring an aura of anger with her. Her gold mask glinted as she looked at each of us in turn and, seeing no Christian present, she made the sign of the cross. Arthur fetched her a chair, but she refused it, implying that she had little time for us. Since her husband had gone to Gwent, Morgan had busied herself in a Christian shrine to the north of Isca. Sick folk went there to die and she fed them, nursed them and prayed for them. Folk call her husband a saint to this day, but I think the wife is called a saint by God.

Arthur told her the tale and Morgan grunted with each revelation, but when Arthur spoke of the curse of the Otherbody she made the sign of the cross, then spat through the mask's mouthpiece. 'So what do you want of me?' she asked belligerently.

'Can you counter the curse?' Guinevere asked.

'Prayer can counter it!' Morgan declared.

'But you have prayed,' Arthur said in exasperation, 'and Bishop Emrys has prayed. All the Christians of Isca have prayed and Ceinwyn lies sick still.'

'Because she is a pagan,' Morgan said vituperatively. 'Why should God waste his mercy on pagans when He has His own flock to look after?'

'You have not answered my question,' Guinevere said icily. She and Morgan hated each other, but for Arthur's sake pretended to a chill courtesy when they met.

Morgan was silent for a while, then abruptly nodded her head.

374

'The curse can be countered,' she said, 'if you believe in these superstitions.'

'I believe,' I said.

'But even to think of it is a sin!' Morgan cried and made the sign of the cross again.

'Your God will surely forgive you,' I said.

'What do you know of my God, Derfel?' she asked sourly.

'I know, Lady,' I said, trying to remember all the things Galahad had told me over the years, 'that your God is a loving God, a forgiving God, and a God who sent His own Son to earth so that others should not suffer.' I paused, but Morgan made no reply. 'I know too,' I went on gently, 'that Nimue works a great evil in the hills.'

The mention of Nimue might have persuaded Morgan, for she had ever been angry that the younger woman had usurped her place in Merlin's entourage. 'Is it a clay figure?' she asked me, 'made with a child's blood, dew, and moulded beneath the thunder?'

'Exactly,' I said.

She shuddered, spread her arms and prayed silently. None of us spoke. Her prayer went on a long time, and perhaps she was hoping we would abandon her, but when none of us left the courtyard, she dropped her arms and turned on us again. 'What charms is the witch using?'

'Berries,' I said, 'slivers of bone, embers.'

'No, fool! What charms? How does she reach Ceinwyn?'

'She has the stone from one of Ceinwyn's rings and one of my cloaks.'

'Ah!' Morgan said, interested despite her revulsion for the pagan superstition. 'Why one of your cloaks?'

'I don't know.'

'Simple, fool,' she snapped, 'the evil flows through you!'

'Me?'

'What do you understand?' she snapped. 'Of course it flows through you. You have been close to Nimue, have you not?'

'Yes,' I said, blushing despite myself.

'So what is the symbol of that?' she asked. 'She gave you a charm? A scrap of bone? Some piece of pagan rubbish to hang about your neck?'

'She gave me this,' I said, and showed her the scar on my left hand.

Morgan peered at the scar, then shuddered. She said nothing.

'Counter the charm, Morgan,' Arthur pleaded with her.

Morgan was silent again. 'It is forbidden,' she said after a while, 'to dabble in witchcraft. The holy scriptures tell us that we should not suffer a witch to live.'

'Then tell me how it is done,' Taliesin pleaded.

'You?' Morgan cried. 'You? You think you can counter Merlin's magic? If it is to be done, then let it be done properly.'

'By you?' Arthur asked and Morgan whimpered. Her one good hand made the sign of the cross, and then she shook her head and it seemed she could not speak at all. Arthur frowned. 'What is it,' he asked, 'that your God wants?'

'Your souls!' Morgan cried.

'You want me to become a Christian?' I asked.

The gold mask with its incised cross snapped up to face me. 'Yes,' Morgan said simply.

'I will do it,' I said just as simply.

She pointed her hand at me. 'You will be baptized, Derfel?'

'Yes, Lady.'

'And you will swear obedience to my husband.'

That checked me. I gazed at her. 'To Sansum?' I asked feebly.

'He is a bishop!' Morgan insisted. 'He has God's authority! You will agree to swear obedience to him, you will agree to be baptized, and only then will I lift the curse.'

Arthur stared at me. For a few heartbeats I could not swallow the humiliation of Morgan's demand, but then I thought of Ceinwyn and I nodded. 'I will do it,' I told her.

So Morgan risked her God's anger and lifted the curse.

She did it that afternoon. She came to the palace courtyard in a black robe and without any mask so that the horror of her fire-ravaged face, all red and scarred and ridged and twisted, was visible to us all. She was furious with herself, but committed to her promise, and she hurried about her business. A brazier was lit and fed with coals and, while the fire heated, slaves fetched baskets of potter's clay that Morgan moulded into the figure of a woman. She used blood

376

from a child that had died in the town that morning, and water that a slave swept up from the courtyard's damp grass, and mixed both with the clay. There was no thunder, but Morgan said the counter-charm did not need thunder. She spat in horror at what she had made. It was a grotesque image, that thing, a woman with huge breasts, spread legs and a gaping birth canal, and in the figure's belly she dug a hole that she said was the womb where the evil must rest. Arthur, Taliesin and Guinevere watched enthralled as she moulded the clay and then as she walked three times round the obscene figure. After the third sunwise circuit she stopped, raised her head to the clouds and wailed. For a moment I thought she was in such pain that she could not proceed and that her God was commanding her to stop the ceremony, but then she turned her twisted face towards me. 'I need the evil now,' she said.

'What is it?' I asked.

The slit that was her mouth seemed to smile. 'Your hand, Derfel.'

'My hand?'

I saw now that the lipless slit was a smile. 'The hand that binds you to Nimue,' Morgan said. 'How else do you think the evil is channelled? You must cut it off, Derfel, and give it to me.'

'Surely,' Arthur began to protest.

'You force me to sin!' Morgan turned on her brother with a shriek, 'then you challenge my wisdom?'

'No,' Arthur said hurriedly.

'It is nothing to me,' she said carelessly, 'if Derfel wants to keep his hand, so be it. Ceinwyn can suffer.'

'No,' I said, 'no.'

We sent for Galahad and Culhwch, then Arthur led the three of us to his smithy where the forge burned night and day. I took my lover's ring from the finger of my left hand and gave it to Morridig, Arthur's smith, and asked him to seal the ring about Hywelbane's pommel. The ring was of common iron, a warrior's ring, but it had a cross made of gold that I had stolen from the Cauldron of Clyddno Eiddyn and it was the twin of a ring Ceinwyn wore.

We placed a thick piece of timber on the anvil. Galahad held me tight, his arms about me, and I bared my arm and laid my left hand on the timber. Culhwch gripped my forearm, not to keep it still, but for afterwards.

Arthur raised Excalibur. 'Are you sure, Derfel?' he asked.

'Do it, Lord,' I said.

Morridig watched wide-eyed as the bright blade touched the rafters above the anvil. Arthur paused, then hacked down once. He hacked down hard, and for a second I felt no pain, none, but then Culhwch took my spurting wrist and thrust it into the burning coals of the forge and that was when the pain whipped through me like a spear thrust. I screamed, and then I remember nothing at all.

I heard later how Morgan took the severed hand with its fatal scar and sealed it in the clay womb. Then, to a pagan chant as old as time, she pulled the bloody hand out through the birth canal and tossed it onto the brazier.

And thus I became a Christian.

PART FOUR

The Last Enchantment

SPRING HAS COME to Dinnewrac. The monastery warms, and the silence of our prayers is broken by the bleating of lambs and the song of larks. White violets and stitchwort grow where snow lay for so long, but best of all is the news that Igraine has given birth to a child. It is a boy, and both he and his mother live. God be thanked for that, and for the season's warmth, but for little else. Spring should be a happy season, but there are dark rumours of enemies.

The Saxons have returned, though whether it was their spearmen who started the fires we saw on our eastern horizon last night, no one knows. Yet the fires burned bright, flaring in the night sky like a foretaste of hell. A farmer came at dawn to give us some split logs of lime that we can use to make a new butter churn, and he told us the fires were set by raiding Irish, but we doubt that for there have been too many stories of Saxon warbands in the last few weeks. Arthur's achievement was to keep the Saxons at bay for a whole generation, and to do it he taught our Kings courage, but how feeble our rulers have become since then! And now the Sais return like a plague.

Dafydd, the clerk of the justice who translates these parchments into the British tongue, arrived to collect the newest skins today and he told me that the fires were almost certainly Saxon mischief, and afterwards informed me that Igraine's new son is to be named Arthur. Arthur ap Brochvael ap Perddel ap Cuneglas; a good name, though Dafydd plainly did not approve of it, and at first I was not sure why. He is a small man, not unlike Sansum, with the same busy expression and the same bristly hair. He sat in my window to read the finished parchments and kept tutting and shaking his head at my handwriting. 'Why,' he finally asked me, 'did Arthur abandon Dumnonia?'

'Because Meurig insisted on it,' I explained, 'and because Arthur himself never wanted to rule.'

'But it was irresponsible of him!' Dafydd said sternly.

'Arthur was not a king,' I said, 'and our laws insist that only kings can rule.'

'Laws are malleable,' Dafydd said with a sniff, 'I should know, and Arthur should have been a king.'

'I agree,' I said, 'but he was not. He was not born to it and Mordred was.'

'Then nor was Gwydre born to the kingship,' Dafydd objected.

'True,' I said, 'but if Mordred had died, Gwydre had as good a claim as anyone, except Arthur, of course, but Arthur did not want to be King.' I wondered how often I had explained this same thing. 'Arthur came to Britain,' I said, 'because he took an oath to protect Mordred, and by the time he went to Siluria he had achieved all that he had set out to do. He had united the kingdoms of Britain, he had given Dumnonia justice and he had defeated the Saxons. He might have resisted Meurig's demands to yield his power, but in his heart he didn't want to, and so he gave Dumnonia back to its rightful King and watched all that he had achieved fall apart.'

'So he should have remained in power,' Dafydd argued. Dafydd, I think, is very like Saint Sansum, a man who can never be in the wrong.

'Yes,' I said, 'but he was tired. He wanted other men to carry the burden. If anyone was to blame, it was me! I should have stayed in Dumnonia instead of spending so much time in Isca. But at the time none of us saw what was happening. None of us realized Mordred would prove a good soldier, and when he did we convinced ourselves that he would die soon enough and Gwydre would become King. Then all would have been well. We lived in hope rather than in the real world.'

'I still think Arthur let us down,' Dafydd said, his tone explaining why he disapproved of the new Edling's name. How many times have I been forced to listen to that same condemnation of Arthur? If only Arthur had stayed in power, men say, then the Saxons would still be paying us tribute and Britain would stretch from sea to sea, but when Britain did have Arthur it just grumbled about him. When he gave folk what they wanted, they complained because

382

it was not enough. The Christians attacked him for favouring the pagans, the pagans attacked him for tolerating the Christians, and the Kings, all except Cuneglas and Oengus mac Airem, were jealous of him. Oengus's support counted for little, but when Cuneglas died Arthur lost his most valuable royal supporter. Besides, Arthur did not let anyone down. Britain let itself down. Britain let the Saxons creep back, Britain squabbled amongst itself and then Britain whined that it was all Arthur's fault. Arthur, who had given them victory!

Dafydd skimmed through the last few pages. 'Did Ceinwyn recover?' he asked me.

'Praise God, yes,' I said, 'and lived for many years after.' I was about to tell Dafydd something of those last years, but I could see he was not interested and so I kept my memories to myself. In the end Ceinwyn died of a fever. I was with her, and I wanted to burn her corpse, but Sansum insisted that she was buried in the Christian manner. I obeyed him, but a month later I arranged for some men, the sons and grandsons of my old spearmen, to dig up her corpse and burn it on a pyre so that her soul could go to join her daughters in the Otherworld and for that sinful action I have no regrets. I doubt that any man will do as much for me, though perhaps Igraine, if she reads these words, will have my balefire built. I pray so.

'Do you change the tale when you translate it?' I asked Dafydd.

'Change it?' He looked indignant. 'My Queen won't let me change a syllable!'

'Truly?' I asked.

'I might correct some infelicities of grammar,' he said, collecting the skins, 'but nothing else. I presume the ending of the story is close now?'

'It is.'

'Then I shall return in a week,' he promised, and pushed the parchments into a bag and hurried away. A moment later Bishop Sansum scurried into my room. He was carrying a strange bundle which at first I took to be a stick wrapped up in an old cloak. 'Did Dafydd bring news?' he asked.

'The Queen is well,' I said, 'as is her child.' I decided against telling Sansum that the child was to be named Arthur, for it would only annoy the saint and life is much easier in Dinnewrac when Sansum is in a good temper.

'I asked for news,' Sansum snapped, 'not women's gossip about a child. What about the fires? Did Dafydd mention the fires?'

'He knows no more than we do, Bishop,' I said, 'but King Brochvael believes they are Saxons.'

'God preserve us,' Sansum said, and walked to my window from where the smear of smoke was still just visible in the east. 'God and His saints preserve us,' he prayed, then came to my desk and put the strange bundle on top of this skin. He pulled away the cloak and I saw, to my astonishment, and almost to the provocation of my tears, that it was Hywelbane. I did not dare show my emotion, but instead crossed myself as if I was shocked by the appearance of a weapon in our monastery. 'There are enemies near,' Sansum said, explaining the sword's presence.

'I fear you are right, Bishop,' I said.

'And enemies provoke hungry men in these hills,' Sansum went on, 'so at night you will stand guard on the monastery.'

'So be it, Lord,' I said humbly. But me? Stand guard? I am white-haired, old and feeble. One might as well ask a toddling child to stand guard as to rely on me, but I made no protest and once Sansum had left the room I slid Hywelbane from her scabbard and thought how heavy she had become during the long years she had lain in the monastery's treasure cupboard. She was heavy and clumsy, but she was still my sword, and I peered at the yellowed pig bones set into her hilt and then at the lover's ring that was bound about its pommel and I saw, on that flattened ring, the tiny scraps of gold I had stolen from the Cauldron so long ago. She brought back so many stories, that sword. There was a patch of rust on her blade and I carefully scraped it away with the knife I use for sharpening my quills, and then I cradled her for a long time, imagining that I was young again and still strong enough to wield her.

But me? Stand guard? In truth Sansum did not want me to stand guard, but rather to stand like a fool to be sacrificed while he scuttled out of the back door with Saint Tudwal in one hand and the monastery's gold in the other. But if that is to be my fate I will not complain. I would rather die like my father with my sword in my hand, even if my arm is weak and the sword blunt. That was not the fate Merlin wanted for me, nor what Arthur wanted, but it is not a bad way for a soldier to die, and though I have been a monk these many years and a Christian even longer, in my sinful soul I am still a spearman of Mithras. And so I kissed my Hywelbane, glad to see her after all these years.

So now I shall write the tale's ending with my sword beside me and I shall hope that I am given time to finish this tale of Arthur, my Lord, who was betrayed, reviled and, after his departure, missed like no other man was ever missed in all of Britain's history.

I fell into a fever after my hand was struck off, and when I woke I discovered Ceinwyn sitting beside my bed. At first I did not recognize her, for her hair was short and had gone as white as ash. But it was my Ceinwyn, she was alive and her health was coming back, and when she saw the light in my eyes she leaned forward and laid her cheek on mine. I put my left arm around her and discovered I had no hand to stroke her back, only a stump bound in bloody cloth. I could feel the hand, I could even feel it itching, but there was no hand there. It had been burned.

A week later I was baptized in the River Usk. Bishop Emrys performed the ceremony, and once he had dipped me in the cold water, Ceinwyn followed me down the muddy bank and insisted on being baptized as well. 'I will go where my man goes,' she told Bishop Emrys, and so he folded her hands on her breasts and tipped her back into the river. A choir of women sang as we were baptized and that night, dressed in white, we received the Christian bread and wine for the first time. After the mass Morgan produced a parchment on which she had written my promise to obey her husband in the Christian faith and she demanded that I sign my name.

'I've already given you my word,' I objected.

'You will sign, Derfel,' Morgan insisted, 'and you will swear the oath on a crucifix as well.'

I sighed and signed. Christians, it seemed, did not trust the older form of oath-making, but demanded parchment and ink. And so I acknowledged Sansum as my Lord and, after I had written my name, Ceinwyn insisted on adding her own. Thus began the second half of my life, the half in which I have kept my oath to Sansum, though not as well as Morgan hoped. If Sansum knew I was writing this tale he would construe it as a breaking of the promise and punish me accordingly, but I no longer care. I have committed many sins, but breaking oaths was not one of them.

After my baptism I half expected a summons from Sansum, who was still with King Meurig in Gwent, but the mouse lord simply kept my written promise and demanded nothing, not even money. Not then.

The stump of my wrist healed slowly, and I did not help the healing by insisting on practising with a shield. In battle a man puts his left arm through the two shield loops and grips the wooden handle beyond, but I no longer had fingers to grip the shield and so I had the loops remade as buckled straps that could be tightened about my forearm. It was not as secure as the proper way, but it was better than having no shield, and once I had become used to the tight straps I practised with sword and shield against Galahad, Culhwch or Arthur. I found the shield clumsy, but I could still fight, even though every practice bout left the stump bleeding so that Ceinwyn would scold me as she put on a new dressing.

The full moon came and I took no sword or sacrifice to Nant Dduu. I waited for Nimue's vengeance, but none came. The feast of Beltain was a week after the full moon and Ceinwyn and I, obedient to Morgan's orders, did not extinguish our fires or stay awake to see the new fires lit, but Culhwch came to us next morning with a brand of the new fire that he tossed into our hearth. 'You want me to go to Gwent, Derfel?' he asked.

'Gwent?' I asked. 'Why?'

'To murder that little toad, Sansum, of course.'

'He's not troubling me.'

'Yet,' Culhwch grumbled, 'but he will. Can't imagine you as a Christian. Does it feel different?'

'No.'

Poor Culhwch. He rejoiced to see Ceinwyn well, but hated the bargain I had made with Morgan to make her well. He, like many others, wondered why I did not simply break my promise to Sansum, but I feared Ceinwyn's sickness would return if I did and so I stayed true. In time that obedience became a habit, and once

Ceinwyn was dead I found I had no will to break the promise, even though her death had loosed the promise's grip on me.

But this lay far in the unknown future on that day when the new fires warmed cold hearths. It was a beautiful day of sunshine and blossom. I remember we bought some goslings in the market-place that morning, thinking our grandchildren would like to see them grow in the small pond that lay behind our quarters, and afterwards I went with Galahad to the amphitheatre where I practised again with my clumsy shield. We were the only spearmen there, for most of the others were still recovering from a night of drinking. 'Goslings aren't a good idea,' Galahad said, rattling my shield with a solid blow of his spear butt.

'Why not?'

'They grow up to be bad-tempered.'

'Nonsense,' I said. 'They grow up to become supper.'

Gwydre interrupted us with a summons from his father, and we strolled back into the town to discover Arthur had gone to Bishop Emrys's palace. The Bishop was seated, while Arthur, in shirt and trews, was leaning on a big table that was covered with wood shavings on which the Bishop had written lists of spearmen, weapons and boats. Arthur looked up at us and for a heartbeat he said nothing, but I remember his grey-bearded face was very grim. Then he uttered one word. 'War.'

Galahad crossed himself, while I, still accustomed to my old ways, touched Hywelbane's hilt. 'War?' I asked.

'Mordred is marching on us,' Arthur said. 'He's marching right now! Meurig gave him permission to cross Gwent.'

'With three hundred and fifty spearmen, we hear,' Emrys added.

To this day I believe it was Sansum's persuasion that convinced Meurig to betray Arthur. I have no proof of that, and Sansum has ever denied it, but the scheme reeked of the mouse lord's cunning. It is true that Sansum had once warned us of the possibility of just such an attack, but the mouse lord was forever cautious in his betrayals and if Arthur had won the battle that Sansum confidently expected to be fought in Isca then he would have wanted a reward from Arthur. He certainly wanted no reward from Mordred, for Sansum's scheme, if it was indeed his, was intended to benefit Meurig. Let Mordred and Arthur fight to the death, then Meurig could take over Dumnonia and the mouse lord would rule in Meurig's name.

And Meurig did want Dumnonia. He wanted its rich farmlands and its wealthy towns, and so he encouraged the war, though he strenuously denied any such encouragement. If Mordred wanted to visit his uncle, he said, who was he to stop it? And if Mordred wanted an escort of three hundred and fifty spearmen, who was Meurig to deny a King his entourage? And so he gave Mordred the permission he wanted, and by the time we first heard of the attack the leading horsemen of Mordred's army were already past Glevum and hurrying west towards us.

Thus by treachery, and through the ambition of a weak King, Arthur's last war began.

We were ready for that war. We had expected the attack to come weeks before, and though Mordred's timing surprised us our plans were all made. We would sail south across the Severn Sea and march to Durnovaria where we expected Sagramor's men to join us. Then, with our forces united, we would follow Arthur's bear north to confront Mordred as he returned from Siluria. We expected a battle, we expected to win, and afterwards we would acclaim Gwydre as King of Dumnonia on Caer Cadarn. It was the old story; one more battle, then everything would change.

Messengers were sent to the coast demanding that every Silurian fishing-boat be brought to Isca, and while those boats rowed up river on the flood tide, we readied for our hasty departure. Swords and spears were sharpened, armour was polished and food was put into baskets or sacks. We packed the treasures from the three palaces and the coins from the treasury, and warned Isca's inhabitants to be ready to flee westwards before Mordred's men arrived.

Next morning we had twenty-seven fishing-boats moored in the river beneath Isca's Roman bridge. A hundred and sixty-three spearmen were ready to embark, and most of those spearmen had families, but there was room in the boats for them all. We were forced to leave our horses behind, for Arthur had discovered that horses make bad sailors. While I had been travelling to meet Nimue he had tried loading horses onto one of the fishing-boats, but the animals panicked in even the gentlest waves, and one had even kicked its way through the boat's hull and so on the day before we sailed we drove the animals to pastures on a distant farm and promised ourselves we would return for them once Gwydre was made King. Morgan alone refused to sail with us, but instead went to join her husband in Gwent.

We began loading the boats at dawn. First we placed the gold in the bottom of the boats, and on top of the gold we piled our armour and our food, and then, under a grey sky and in a brisk wind, we began to embark. Most of the boats took ten or eleven people, and once the boats were filled they pulled into the middle of the river and anchored there so that the whole fleet could leave together.

The enemy arrived just as the last boat was being loaded. That was the largest boat and it belonged to Balig, my sister's husband. In it were Arthur, Guinevere, Gwydre, Morwenna and her children, Galahad, Taliesin, Ceinwyn and me, together with Culhwch, his one remaining wife and two of his sons. Arthur's banner flew from the boat's high prow and Gwydre's standard flapped at the stern. We were in high spirits, for we were sailing to give Gwydre his kingdom, but just as Balig was shouting at Hygwydd, Arthur's servant, to hurry aboard, the enemy came.

Hygwydd was bringing a last bundle from Arthur's palace and he was only fifty paces from the river bank when he looked behind and saw the horsemen coming from the town gate. He had time to drop the bundle and half draw his sword, but then the horses were on him and a spear took him in the neck.

Balig threw the gangplank overboard, pulled a knife from his belt and slashed the stern mooring line. His Saxon crewman threw off the bow line and our boat drifted out into the current as the horsemen reached the bank. Arthur was standing and staring in horror at the dying Hygwydd, but I was looking towards the amphitheatre where a horde had appeared.

It was not Mordred's army. This was a swarm of the insane; a scrabbling rush of bent, broken and bitter creatures who surged round the amphitheatre's stone arches and ran down to the river bank yelping small cries. They were in rags, their hair was wild and their eyes filled with a fanatical rage. It was Nimue's army of the mad. Most were armed with nothing but sticks, though a few had spears. The horsemen were all armed with spears and shields, and they were not mad. They were fugitives from Diwrnach's Bloodshields and still wore their ragged black cloaks and carried their blood-darkened shields, and they scattered the mad people as they spurred down the bank to keep pace with us.

Some of the mad went down beneath the horses' hoofs, but dozens more just plunged into the river and swam clumsily towards our boats. Arthur shouted at the boatmen to let go their anchors, and one by one the heavily laden boats cut themselves free and began to drift. Some of the crews were reluctant to abandon the heavy stones that served as anchors and tried to haul them up, and so the drifting boats crashed into the stationary ones and all the time the desperate, sad, mad things were thrashing clumsily towards us. 'Spear butts!' Arthur shouted, and seized his own spear, turned it, and thrust it hard down onto a swimmer's head.

'Oars!' Balig called, but no one heeded him. We were too busy pushing the swimmers away from the hull. I worked one-handed, thrusting attackers under the water, but one madman seized my spear shaft and almost pulled me into the water. I let him have the weapon, drew Hywelbane and sliced her down. The first blood flowed on the river.

The river's north bank was now thick with Nimue's howling, capering followers. Some threw spears at us, but most just screamed their hate, while others followed the swimmers into the river. A long-haired man with a hare lip tried to climb aboard our bows, but the Saxon kicked him in the face, then kicked him again so that he fell. Taliesin had found a spear and was using its blade on other swimmers. Downstream of us a boat drifted onto the muddy bank where its crew desperately tried to pole themselves free of the mud, but they were too slow and Nimue's spearmen scrambled aboard. They were led by Bloodshields, and those practised killers screamed defiance as they carried their spears down the stranded boat's length. It was Bishop Emrys's boat and I saw the white-haired Bishop parry a spear with a sword, but then he was killed and a score of mad things followed the Bloodshields onto the slippery deck. The Bishop's wife screamed briefly, then was savaged by a spear. Knives slashed and ripped and stabbed, and blood trickled from the scuppers to flow towards the sea. A man in a deerskin tunic balanced himself on the stern of the captured boat, and, as we drifted past, leapt towards our gunwale. Gwydre raised his spear and the man shrieked as he impaled himself on the long shaft. I remember his hands gripping the spear pole while his body writhed on the point, then Gwydre dropped both spear and man into the river and drew his sword. His mother was thrusting a spear into the thrashing arms beside the boat. Hands clung to our gunwale and we stamped on them, or cut them with swords, and gradually our boat drew away from its attackers. All the boats were drifting now, some sideways, some stern first, and the boatmen were swearing and shouting at each other or else screaming at the spearmen to use the oars. A spear flew from the bank and thumped into our hull, and then the first arrows flew. They were hunters' arrows, and they hummed as they whipped over our heads.

'Shields!' Arthur shouted, and we made a wall of shields along the boat's gunwale. The arrows spat into them. I was crouching beside Balig, protecting both of us, and my shield quivered as the small arrows thumped home.

We were saved by the river's swift current and by the ebbing tide which carried our jumbled mass of boats downstream and so out of the bowmen's range. The cheering, raving horde followed us, but west of the amphitheatre there was a stretch of boggy ground and that slowed our pursuers and gave us time in which we could at last make order out of chaos. The cries of our attackers followed us, and their bodies drifted in the current beside our small fleet, but at last we had oars and could pull the boat's bow around and follow the other vessels towards the sea. Our two banners were stuck thick with arrows.

'Who are they?' Arthur demanded, staring back at the horde.

'Nimue's army,' I said bitterly. Thanks to Morgan's skill, Nimue's charms had failed and so she had unleashed her followers to fetch Excalibur and Gwydre.

'Why didn't we see them coming?' Arthur wanted to know.

'A charm of concealment, Lord?' Taliesin guessed, and I remembered how often Nimue had worked such charms.

Galahad scoffed at the pagan explanation. 'They marched through the night,' he suggested, 'and hid in the woods until they were ready, and we were all too busy to look for them.'

'The bitch can fight Mordred now instead of us,' Culhwch suggested.

'She won't,' I said, 'she'll join him.'

But Nimue had not finished with us yet. A group of horsemen were galloping on the road that led northwards about the swamp, and a horde of folk followed those spearmen on foot. The river did not run straight to the sea, but made vast loops through the coastal plain and I knew that at every western curve we would find the enemy waiting.

The horsemen did indeed wait for us, but the river widened as it neared the sea and the water ran swiftly, and at each bend we were swept safely past them. The horsemen called curses down on us, then galloped on to find the next bend from where they could launch their spears and arrows at us. Just before the sea there was a long straight stretch of the river and Nimue's horsemen kept pace with us all down the length of that reach, and that was when I first saw Nimue herself. She rode a white horse, was dressed in a white robe, and had her hair tonsured like a Druid. She carried Merlin's staff and wore a sword at her side. She shouted at us, but the wind snatched her words away, and then the river curved eastwards and we slid away from her between the reed-thick banks. Nimue turned away and spurred her horse towards the river's mouth.

'We're safe now,' Arthur said. We could smell the sea, gulls called above us, ahead was the endless sound of waves breaking on a shore, and Balig and the Saxon were hitching the sail's yard to the ropes that hoisted it up the mast. There was one last great loop of the river to negotiate, one last encounter with Nimue's horsemen to endure, and then we would be swept out into the Severn Sea.

'How many men did we lose?' Arthur wanted to know, and we shouted questions and answers back and forth between the small fleet. Only two men had been struck by arrows, and the one stranded boat had been overwhelmed, but most of his small army was safe. 'Poor Emrys,' Arthur said, and then was silent for a while, but he pushed the melancholy aside. 'In three days,' he said, 'we'll be with Sagramor.' He had sent messages eastwards and, now that Mordred's army had left Dumnonia, there was surely nothing to stop Sagramor coming to meet us. 'We shall have a small army,'

Arthur said, 'but a good one. Good enough to beat Mordred, and then we start all over again.'

'Start over again?' I asked.

'Beat back Cerdic once more,' he said, 'and knock some sense into Meurig.' He laughed bitterly. 'There's always one more battle. Have you noticed that? Whenever you think everything is settled, it all seethes up again.' He touched Excalibur's hilt. 'Poor Hygwydd. I shall miss him.'

'You'll miss me too, Lord,' I said gloomily. The stump of my left wrist was throbbing painfully and my missing hand was unaccountably itching with a sensation so real that I kept trying to scratch it.

'I'll miss you?' Arthur asked, raising an eyebrow.

'When Sansum summons me.'

'Ah! The mouse lord.' He gave me a quick smile. 'I think our mouse lord will want to come back to Dumnonia, don't you? I can't see him gaining preferment in Gwent, they have too many bishops already. No, he'll want to come back, and poor Morgan will want the shrine at Ynys Wydryn again, so I shall make a bargain with them. Your soul for Gwydre's permission for them to live in Dumnonia. We'll free you of the oath, Derfel, never you mind.' He slapped my shoulder, then clambered forward to where Guinevere sat beneath the mast.

Balig plucked an arrow from the sternpost, twisted away its iron head that he tucked into a pocket for safe keeping, then tossed the feathered shaft overboard. 'Don't like the look of that,' he said to me, jerking his chin towards the west. I turned and saw there were black clouds far out to sea.

'Rain coming?' I asked.

'Could be a bite of wind in it, too,' he said ominously, then spat overboard to avert the ill-luck. 'But we don't have far to go. We could miss it.' He leaned on the steering oar as the boat was swept about the last great loop of the river. We were going west now, hard into the wind, and the river's surface was choppy with small, white-flecked waves that shattered on our bow and splashed back across the deck. The sail was still lowered. 'Pull now!' Balig called to our oarsmen. The Saxon had one oar, Galahad another, Taliesin and Culhwch had the middle bench and Culhwch's two sons completed the crew. The six men pulled hard, fighting the wind, but the current and tide still helped us. The banners at prow and stern snapped hard in the wind, rattling the arrows trapped in their weave.

Ahead of us the river turned southwards and it was there, I knew, that Balig would hoist the sail so that the wind would help us down the long sea reach. Once at sea we would be forced to keep inside the withy-marked channel that ran between the wide shallows until we reached the deep water where we could turn away from the wind and race across to the Dumnonian shore. 'It won't take long to cross,' Balig said comfortingly, glancing at the clouds, 'not long. Should outrun that bit of wind.'

'Can the boats stay together?' I asked.

'Near enough.' He jerked his head at the boat immediately in front of us. 'That old tub will lag behind. Sails like a pregnant pig, she does, but near enough, near enough.'

Nimue's horsemen waited for us on a spit of land that lay where the river turned south towards the sea. As we came closer she rode out from the mass of spearmen and urged her horse into the shallow water, and as we came closer still I saw two of her spearmen drag a captive into the shallows beside her.

At first I thought it must be one of our men taken from the stranded boat, but then I saw that the prisoner was Merlin. His beard had been cut off and his unkempt white hair blew ragged in the rising wind as he stared blindly towards us, but I could have sworn that he was smiling. I could not see his face clearly, for the distance was too great, but I do swear he was smiling as he was pulled into the small waves. He knew what was about to happen.

Then, suddenly, so did I, and there was nothing I could do to prevent it.

Nimue had been carried from this sea as a child. She had been captured in Demetia by a band of slave-raiders, then brought across the Severn Sea to Dumnonia, but on the voyage a storm rose and all the raiders' ships were sunk. The crews and their captives drowned, all but for Nimue who had come safe from the sea onto Ynys Wair's rocky shore and Merlin, rescuing the child, had called her Vivien because she was so plainly beloved by Manawydan, the sea God, and Vivien is a name that belongs to Manawydan. Nimue, being cross-grained, had ever refused to use the name, but I remembered it now, and I remembered that Manawydan loved her, and I knew she was about to use the God's help to work a great curse on us.

'What is she doing?' Arthur asked.

'Don't watch, Lord,' I said.

The two spearmen had waded back to shore, leaving the blinded Merlin alone beside Nimue's horse. He made no attempt to escape. He just stood there, his hair streaming white, while Nimue drew a knife from her sword belt. It was the Knife of Laufrodedd.

'No!' Arthur shouted, but the wind carried his protest back in our boat's path, back across the marshes and the reeds, back to nowhere. 'No!' he called again.

Nimue pointed her Druid's staff towards the west, raised her head to the skies and howled. Still Merlin did not move. Our fleet swept past them, each boat coming close to the shallows where Nimue's horse stood before being snatched southwards as the crews hoisted their sails. Nimue waited until our flag-hung boat came near and then she lowered her head and gazed at us with her one eye. She was smiling, and so was Merlin. I was close enough to see clearly now, and he was still smiling as Nimue leaned down from her saddle with the knife. One hard stroke was all it needed.

And Merlin's long white hair and his long white robe turned red.

Nimue howled again. I had heard her howl many times, but never like that, for this howl mingled agony with triumph. She had worked her spell.

She slid off the horse and let go of her staff. Merlin must have died quickly, but his body still thrashed in the small waves and for a few heartbeats it looked as though Nimue was wrestling with the dead man. Her white robe was spattered with red, and the red was instantly diluted by the sea as she heaved and pushed Merlin's corpse further into the water. At last, free of the mud, he floated and she pushed him out into the current as a gift for her Lord, Manawydan.

And what a gift she gave. The body of a Druid is powerful magic, as powerful as any that this poor world possesses, and Merlin was the last and the greatest of the Druids. Others came after him, of course, but none had his knowledge, and none his wisdom, and none had half his power. And all that power was now given to one spell, one incantation to the God of the sea who had rescued Nimue so many years before.

She plucked the staff from where it floated on the waves and pointed it at our boat, then she laughed. She put her head back and laughed like the mad who had followed her from the mountains to this killing in the waters. 'You will live!' she called to our boat, 'and we shall meet again!'

Balig hoisted the sail and the wind caught it and snatched us down the sea reach. None of us spoke. We just stared back towards Nimue and to where, white in the turmoil of the grey waves, the body of Merlin followed us towards the deep.

Where Manawydan waited for us.

We turned our boat south-east to let the wind drive into the tattered sail's belly and my stomach heaved with every lurching wave.

Balig was struggling with the steering oar. We had shipped the other oars, letting the wind do the work, but the strong tide was driving against us and it kept pushing our boat's head round to the south where the wind would make the sail slap, and the steering oar would bend alarmingly, but slowly the boat would come back, the sail would crack like a great whip as it filled again, and the bows would dip into a wave trough and my belly would churn and the bile rise in my throat.

The sky darkened. Balig looked up at the clouds, spat, then heaved on the steering oar again. The first rain came, great drops that spattered on the deck and darkened the dirty sail. 'Pull in those banners!' Balig shouted, and Galahad furled the forward flag while I struggled to free the flag at the stern. Gwydre helped me bring it down, then lost his balance as the boat tipped on a wave crest. He fell against the gunwale as the water broke over the bow. 'Bail!' Balig shouted, 'bail!'

The wind was rising now. I vomited over the boat's quarter, then looked up to see the rest of the fleet tossing in a grey nightmare of broken water and flying spindrift. I heard a crack above me, and looked up to see that our sail had split in two. Balig cursed. Behind us the shore was a dark line, and beyond it, lit by sunlight, the hills of Siluria glowed green, but all around us was dark and wet and threatening.

'Bail!' Balig shouted again, and those who were in the belly of the boat used helmets to scoop the water from around the bundles of treasure, armour and food.

And then the storm hit. Till now we had suffered only from the storm's outriders, but now the wind howled across the sea and the rain came flat and stinging above the whitened waves. I lost sight of the other boats, so thick was the rain and so dark the sky. The shore disappeared, and all I could see was a nightmare of short, high, white-crested waves from which the water flew to drench our boat. The sail flogged itself to ragged shreds that streamed from the spar like broken banners. Thunder split the sky and the boat fell off a wave crest and I saw the water, green and black, surging up to spill across the gunwales, but somehow Balig steered the bow into the wave and the water hesitated at the boat's rim, then dropped away as we rose to the next wind-tortured crest.

'Lighten the boat!' Balig screamed over the storm's howl.

We threw the gold overboard. We jettisoned Arthur's treasure, and my treasure, and Gwydre's treasure and Culhwch's treasure. We gave it all to Manawydan, pouring coins and cups and candlesticks and gold bars into his greedy maw, and still he wanted more, and so we hurled the baskets of food and the furled banners overboard, but Arthur would not give him his armour, and nor would I, and so we stowed the armour and our weapons in the tiny cabin under the after deck and instead threw some of the ship's stone ballast after the gold. We reeled about the boat like drunken men, tossed by the waves and with our feet sliding in a slopping mix of vomit and water. Morwenna clutched her children, Ceinwyn and Guinevere prayed, Taliesin bailed with a helmet, while Culhwch and Galahad helped Balig and the Saxon crewman to lower the remnants of the sail. They threw the sail overboard, spar and all, but tied its wreckage to a long horse-hair rope that they looped about the boat's sternpost, and the drag of the spar and sail somehow turned our boat's head into the wind so that we faced the storm and rode its anger in great swooping lurches.

'Never known a storm move so quick!' Balig shouted to me. And no wonder. This was no usual storm, but a fury brought by a

Druid's death, and the world shrieked air and sea about our ears as our creaking ship rose and fell to the pounding waves. Water spurted between the planks of the hull, but we bailed it out as fast as it came.

Then I saw the first wreckage on the crest of a wave, and a moment later glimpsed a man swimming. He tried to call to us, but the sea drove him under. Arthur's fleet was being destroyed. Sometimes, as a squall passed and the air momentarily cleared, we could see men bailing madly, and see how low their boats rode in the turmoil, and then the storm would blind us again, and when it lifted again there were no boats visible at all, just floating timbers. Arthur's fleet, boat by boat, was sunk and his men and women drowned. The men who wore their armour died the quickest.

And all the while, just beyond the sea-fretted wreckage of our sail that dragged behind our labouring boat, Merlin's body followed us. He appeared sometime after we had hurled the sail overboard, and then he stayed with us and I would see his white robe on the face of a wave, see it vanish, only to glimpse it again as the seas moved on. Once it seemed as though he lifted his head from the water and I saw the wound in his throat had been washed white by the ocean, and he stared at us from his empty sockets, but then the waters dipped him down and I touched an iron nail in the sternpost and begged Manawydan to take the Druid down to the sea's bed. Take him down, I prayed, and send his soul to the Otherworld, but every time I looked he was still there, his white hair fanning about his head on the swirling sea.

Merlin was there, but no more boats. We peered through the rain and flying spray, but there was nothing there except a dark churning sky, a grey and dirty white sea, wreckage, and Merlin, always Merlin, and I think he was protecting us, not because he wanted us safe, but because Nimue had still not finished with us. Our boat carried what she most desired, and so our boat alone must be preserved through Manawydan's waters.

Merlin did not disappear until the storm itself had vanished. I saw his face one last time and then he just went down. For a heartbeat he was a white shape with spread arms in the green heart of a wave, and then he was gone. And with his disappearance the wind's spite died and the rain ceased.

The sea still tossed us, but the air cleared and the clouds turned from black to grey, and then to broken white, and all about us was an empty sea. Ours was the only boat left and as Arthur stared around the grey waves I saw the tears in his eyes. His men were gone to Manawydan, all of them, all his brave men save we few. A whole army was gone.

And we were alone.

We retrieved the spar and the remnants of the sail, and then we rowed for the rest of that long day. Every man except me had blistered hands, and even I tried to row, but found my one good hand was not enough to manage an oar, and so I sat and watched as we pulled southwards through the rolling seas until, by evening, our keel grated on sand and we struggled ashore with what few possessions we still had left.

We slept in the dunes, and in the morning we cleaned the salt off our weapons and counted what coins we still had. Balig and his Saxon stayed with their boat, claiming they could salvage her, and I gave him my last piece of gold, embraced him, and then followed Arthur south.

We found a hall in the coastal hills and the lord of that hall proved to be a supporter of Arthur's, and he gave us a saddle horse and two mules. We tried to give him gold, but he refused it. 'I wish,' he said, 'I had spearmen to give you, but alas.' He shrugged. His hall was poor and he had already given us more than he could afford. We ate his food, dried our clothes by his fire, and afterwards sat with Arthur under the apple blossom in the hall's orchard. 'We can't fight Mordred now,' Arthur told us bleakly. Mordred's forces numbered at least three hundred and fifty spearmen, and Nimue's followers would help him so long as he pursued us, while Sagramor had fewer than two hundred men. The war was lost before it had even properly begun.

'Oengus will come to help us,' Culhwch suggested.

'He'll try,' Arthur agreed, 'but Meurig will never let the Black-shields march through Gwent.'

'And Cerdic will come,' Galahad said quietly. 'As soon as he hears that Mordred is fighting us, he'll march. And we shall have two hundred men.'

'Fewer,' Arthur interjected.

'To fight how many?' Galahad asked. 'Four hundred? Five? And our survivors, even if we win, will have to turn and face Cerdic.'

'Then what do we do?' Guinevere asked.

Arthur smiled. 'We go to Armorica,' he said. 'Mordred won't pursue us there.'

'He might,' Culhwch growled.

'Then we face that problem when it comes,' Arthur said calmly. He was bitter that morning, but not angry. Fate had given him a terrible blow, so all he could do now was reshape his plans and try to give us hope. He reminded us that King Budic of Broceliande was married to his sister, Anna, and Arthur was certain the King would give us shelter. 'We shall be poor,' he gave Guinevere an apologetic smile, 'but we have friends and they will help us. And Broceliande will welcome Sagramor's spearmen. We shan't starve. And who knows?' he gave his son a smile, 'Mordred might die and we can come back.'

'But Nimue,' I said, 'will pursue us to the world's end.'

Arthur grimaced. 'Then Nimue must be killed,' he said, 'but that problem must also wait its time. What we need to do now is decide how we reach Broceliande.'

'We go to Camlann,' I said, 'and ask for Caddwg the boatman.'

Arthur looked at me, surprised by the certainty in my voice. 'Caddwg?'

'Merlin arranged it, Lord,' I said, 'and told me of it. It is his final gift to you.'

Arthur closed his eyes. He was thinking of Merlin and for a heartbeat or two I thought he was going to shed tears, but instead he just shuddered. 'To Camlann, then,' he said, opening his eyes.

Einion, Culhwch's son, took the saddle horse and rode eastwards in search of Sagramor. He took new orders that instructed Sagramor to find boats and go south across the sea to Armorica. Einion would tell the Numidian that we sought our own boat at Camlann and would look to meet him on Broceliande's shore. There was to be no battle against Mordred, no acclamation on Caer Cadarn, just an ignominious flight across the sea.

When Einion had left we put Arthur-bach and little Seren on one of the mules, heaped our armour on the other, and walked south. By now, Arthur knew, Mordred would have discovered that we had fled from Siluria and Dumnonia's army would already be retracing its steps. Nimue's men would doubtless be with them, and they had the advantage of the hard Roman roads while we had miles of hilly country to cross. And so we hurried.

Or we tried to hurry, but the hills were steep, the road was long, Ceinwyn was still weak, the mules were slow, and Culhwch had limped ever since the long-ago battle we had fought against Aelle outside London. We made a slow journey of it, but Arthur seemed resigned to his fate now. 'Mordred won't know where to seek us,' he said.

'Nimue might,' I suggested. 'Who knows what she forced Merlin to tell her at the end?'

Arthur said nothing for a while. We were walking through a wood bright with bluebells and soft with the new year's leaves. 'You know what I should do?' he said after a while. 'I should find a deep well and throw Excalibur into its depths, and then cover her with stones so that no one will ever find her between now and the world's ending.'

'Why don't you, Lord?'

He smiled and touched the sword's hilt. 'I'm used to her now. I shall keep her till I need her no more. But if I must, I shall hide her. Not yet, though.' He walked on, pensive. 'Are you angry with me?' he asked after a long pause.

'With you? Why?'

He gestured as if to encompass all Dumnonia, all that sad country that was so bright with blossom and new leaf on that spring morning. 'If I had stayed, Derfel,' he said, 'if I had denied Mordred his power, this would not have happened.' He sounded regretful.

'But who was ever to know,' I asked, 'that Mordred would prove a soldier? Or raise an army?'

'True,' he admitted, 'and when I agreed to Meurig's demand I thought Mordred would rot away in Durnovaria. I thought he'd drink himself into his grave or fall into a quarrel and fetch a knife in the back.' He shook his head. 'He should never have been King, but what choice did I have? I had sworn Uther's oath.'

It all went back to that oath and I remembered the High Council, the last to be held in Britain, where Uther had devised the oath that would make Mordred King. Uther had been an old man then, gross and sick and dying, and I had been a child who wanted nothing more than to become a spearman. It was all so long ago, and Nimue had been my friend in those days. 'Uther didn't even want you to be one of the oath-takers,' I said.

'I never thought he did,' Arthur said, 'but I took it. And an oath is an oath, and if we purposefully break one then we break faith with all.' More oaths had been broken, I thought, than had ever been kept, but I said nothing. Arthur had tried to keep his oaths and that was a comfort to him. He smiled suddenly, and I saw that his mind had veered off onto a happier subject. 'Long ago,' he told me, 'I saw a piece of land in Broceliande. It was a valley leading to the south coast and I remember a stream and some birches there, and I thought what a good place it would be for a man to build a hall and make a life.'

I laughed. Even now all he really wanted was a hall, some land, and friends about him; the very same things he had always desired. He had never loved palaces, nor rejoiced in power, though he had loved the practice of war. He tried to deny that love, but he was good at battle and quick in thought and that made him a deadly soldier. It was soldiering that had made him famous, and had let him unite the Britons and defeat the Saxons, but then his shyness about power, and his perverse belief in the innate goodness of man, and his fervent adherence to the sanctity of oaths, had let lesser men undo his work.

'A timber hall,' he said dreamily, 'with a pillared arcade facing the sea. Guinevere loves the sea. The land slopes southwards, towards a beach, and we can make our hall above it so that all day and night we can hear the waves falling on the sand. And behind the hall,' he went on, 'I shall build a new smithy.'

'So you can torture more metal?' I asked.

'*Ars longa*,' he said lightly, '*vita brevis*.'

'Latin?' I asked.

He nodded. 'The arts are long, life is short. I shall improve, Derfel. My fault is impatience. I see the form of the metal I want, and hurry it, but iron won't be hurried.' He put a hand on my bandaged arm. 'You and I have years yet, Derfel.'

'I hope so, Lord.'

'Years and years,' he said, 'years to grow old and listen to songs and tell stories.'

'And dream of Britain?' I asked.

'We served her well,' he said, 'and now she must serve herself.'

'And if the Sais come back,' I asked, 'and men call for you again, will you return?'

He smiled. 'I might return to give Gwydre his throne, but otherwise I shall hang Excalibur on the highest rafter of my hall's high roof, Derfel, and let the cobwebs shroud her. I shall watch the sea and plant my crops and see my grandchildren grow. You and I are done, my friend. We've discharged our oaths.'

'All but one,' I said.

He looked at me sharply. 'You mean my oath to help Ban?'

I had forgotten that oath, the one, the only one, that Arthur had failed to keep, and his failure had ridden him hard ever since. Ban's kingdom of Benoic had gone down to the Franks, and though Arthur had sent men, he had not gone to Benoic himself. But that was long in the past, and I for one had never blamed Arthur for the failure. He had wanted to help, but Aelle's Saxons had been pressing hard at the time and he could not have fought two wars at once. 'No, Lord,' I said, 'I was thinking of my oath to Sansum.'

'The mouse lord will forget you,' Arthur said dismissively.

'He forgets nothing, Lord.'

'Then we shall have to change his mind,' Arthur said, 'for I do not think I can grow old without you.'

'Nor I without you, Lord.'

'So we shall hide ourselves away, you and I, and men will ask, where is Arthur? And where is Derfel? And where is Galahad? Or Ceinwyn? And no one will know, for we shall be hidden under the birch trees beside the sea.' He laughed, but he could see that dream so close now and the hope of it drove him on through the last miles of our long journey.

It took us four days and nights, but at last we reached Dumnonia's southern shore. We had skirted the great moor and we came to the ocean while walking on the ridge of a high hill. We paused at the ridge's crest while the evening light streamed over our shoulders to light the wide river valley that opened to the sea beneath us. This was Camlann.

I had been here before, for this was the southern country below Dumnonian Isca where the local folk tattooed their faces blue. I had served Lord Owain when I first came, and it was under his leadership that I had joined the massacre on the high moors. Years later I had ridden close to this hill when I went with Arthur to try and save Tristan's life, though my attempt failed and Tristan had died, and now I had returned a third time. It was lovely country, as beautiful as any I had seen in Britain, though for me it held memories of murder and I knew I would be glad to see it fade behind Caddwg's boat.

We stared down at our journey's end. The River Exe flowed to the sea beneath us, but before it reached the ocean it formed a great wide sea-lake that was penned from the ocean by a narrow spit of sand. That spit was the place men called Camlann, and at its tip, just visible from our high perch, the Romans had built a small fortress. Inside the fort they had raised a great high becket of iron that had once held a fire at night to warn approaching galleys of the treacherous sandspit.

Now we gazed down at the sea-lake, the sandspit and the green shore. No enemy was in sight. No spear blade reflected the day's late sun, no horsemen rode the shore tracks and no spearmen darkened the narrow tongue of sand. We could have been alone in all the universe.

'You know Caddwg?' Arthur asked me, breaking the silence.

'I met him once, Lord, years ago.'

'Then find him, Derfel, and tell him we shall wait for him at the fort.'

I looked southwards towards the sea. Huge and empty and glittering, it was the path to take us from Britain. Then I went downhill to make the voyage possible.

The last glimmering light of evening lit my way to Caddwg's house. I had asked folk for directions and had been guided to a small cabin that lay on the shore north of Camlann and now, because the tide was only halfway in, the cabin faced a gleaming expanse of empty mud. Caddwg's boat was not in the water, but perched high and dry on land with its keel supported by rollers and its hull by wooden poles. '*Prydwen*, she's called,' Caddwg said, without any greeting.

He had seen me standing beside his boat and now came from his house. The old man was thickly bearded, deeply suntanned and dressed in a woollen jerkin that was stained with pitch and glittering with fish scales.

'Merlin sent me,' I said.

'Reckoned he would. Said he would. Is he coming himself?'

'He's dead,' I said.

Caddwg spat. 'Never thought to hear that.' He spat a second time. 'Thought death would give him a miss.'

'He was murdered,' I said.

Caddwg stooped and threw some logs on a fire that burned under a bubbling pot. The pot held pitch, and I could see that he had been caulking the gaps between *Prydwen's* planks. The boat looked beautiful. Her wooden hull had been scraped clean and the shining new layer of wood contrasted with the deep black of the pitch-soaked caulking that stopped the water spurting between her timbers. She had a high prow, a tall sternpost and a long, newly made mast that now rested on trestles beside the stranded hull. 'You'll be wanting her, then,' Caddwg said.

'There are thirteen of us,' I told him, 'waiting at the fort.'

'Tomorrow this time,' he said.

'Not till then?' I asked, alarmed at the delay.

'I didn't know you were coming,' he grumbled, 'and I can't launch her till high water, and that'll be tomorrow morning, and by the time I get her mast shipped and the sail bent on and the steerboard shipped, the tide'll be ebbed again. She'll float again by mid afternoon, she will, and I'll come for you quick as I can, but like as not it'll be dusk. You should have sent me word.'

That was true, but none of us had thought to send a warning to Caddwg for none of us understood boats. We had thought to come here, find the boat and sail away, and we had never dreamed that the boat might be out of the water. 'Are there other boats?' I asked.

'Not for thirteen folk,' he said, 'and none that can take you where I'm going.'

'To Broceliande,' I said.

'I'll take you where Merlin told me to take you,' Caddwg said obstinately, then stumped around to *Prydwen's* bow and pointed up to a grey stone that was about the size of an apple. There was

405

nothing remarkable about the stone except that it had been skilfully worked into the ship's stem where it was held by the oak like a gem clasped by a gold setting. 'He gave me that bit of rock,' Caddwg said, meaning Merlin. 'A wraithstone, that is.'

'Wraithstone?' I asked, never having heard of such a thing.

'It'll take Arthur where Merlin wanted him to go, and nothing else will take him there. And no other boat can take him there, only a boat that Merlin named,' Caddwg said. The name Prydwen meant Britain. 'Arthur is with you?' Caddwg asked me, suddenly anxious.

'Yes.'

'Then I'll bring the gold as well,' Caddwg said.

'Gold?'

'The old man left it for Arthur. Reckoned he'd want it. No good to me. Gold can't catch a fish. It bought me a new sail, I'll say that for it, and Merlin told me to buy the sail and so he had to give me gold, but gold don't catch fish. It catches women,' he chuckled, 'but not fish.'

I looked up at the stranded boat. 'Do you need help?' I asked.

Caddwg offered a humourless laugh. 'And what help can you give? You and your short arm? Can you caulk a boat? Can you step a mast or bend on a sail?' He spat. 'I only have to whistle and I'll have a score of men helping me. You'll hear us singing in the morning, and that'll mean we're hauling her down the rollers into the water. Tomorrow evening,' he nodded curtly to me, 'I'll look for you at the fort.' He turned and went back to his hut.

And I went to join Arthur. It was dark by then and all the stars of heaven pricked the sky. A moon shimmered a long trail across the sea and lit the broken walls of the little fort where we would wait for *Prydwen*.

We had one last day in Britain, I thought. One last night and one last day, and then we would sail with Arthur into the moon's path and Britain would be nothing but a memory.

The night wind blew soft across the fort's broken wall. The rusted remnant of the ancient beacon tilted on its bleached pole above us, the small waves broke on the long beach, the moon slowly dropped into the sea's embrace and the night darkened.

We slept in the small shelter of the ramparts. The Romans had made the walls of the fort out of sand on which they had mounded turf planted with sea grass, and then they had placed a wooden palisade along the wall's top. The wall must have been feeble even when it had been built, but the fort had never been anything more than a look-out station and a place where a small detachment of men could shelter from the sea winds as they tended the beacon. The wooden palisade was almost all decayed now, and the rain and wind had worn much of the sand wall down, but in a few places it still stood four or five feet high.

The morning dawned clear and we watched as a cluster of small fishing-boats put out to sea for their day's work. Their departure left only *Prydwen* beside the sea-lake. Arthur-bach and Seren played on the lake's sand where there were no breakers, while Galahad walked with Culhwch's remaining son up the coast to find food. They came back with bread, dried fish and a wooden pail of warm fresh milk. We were all oddly happy that morning. I remember the laughter as we watched Seren roll down the face of a dune, and how we cheered when Arthur-bach tugged a great bunch of seaweed out of the shallows and up onto the sand. The huge green mass must have weighed as much as he did, but he pulled and jerked and somehow dragged the heavy tangle right up to the fort's broken wall. Gwydre and I applauded his efforts, and afterwards we fell to talking. 'If I'm not meant to be King,' Gwydre said, 'then so be it.'

'Fate is inexorable,' I said and, when he looked quizzically at me, I smiled. 'That was one of Merlin's favourite sayings. That and "Don't be absurd, Derfel." I was always absurd to him.'

'I'm sure you weren't,' he said loyally.

'We all were. Except perhaps Nimue and Morgan. The rest of us simply weren't clever enough. Your mother, maybe, but she and he were never really friends.'

'I wish I'd known him better.'

'When you're old, Gwydre,' I said, 'you can still tell men that you met Merlin.'

'No one will believe me.'

'No, they probably won't,' I said. 'And by the time you're old they'll have invented new stories about him. And about your father

407

too.' I tossed a scrap of shell down the face of the fort. From far off across the water I could hear the strong sound of men chanting and knew I listened to the launching of *Prydwen*. Not long now, I told myself, not long now. 'Maybe no one will ever know the truth,' I said to Gwydre.

'The truth?'

'About your father,' I said, 'or about Merlin.' Already there were songs that gave the credit for Mynydd Baddon to Meurig, of all people, and many songs that extolled Lancelot above Arthur. I looked around for Taliesin and wondered if he would correct those songs. That morning the bard had told us that he had no intention of crossing the sea with us, but would walk back to Siluria or Powys, and I think Taliesin had only come with us that far so that he could talk with Arthur and thus learn from him the tale of his life. Or perhaps Taliesin had seen the future and had come to watch it unfold, but whatever his reasons, the bard was talking with Arthur now, but Arthur suddenly left Taliesin's side and hurried towards the shore of the sea-lake. He stood there for a long while, peering northwards. Then, suddenly, he turned and ran to the nearest high dune. He clambered up its face, then turned and stared northwards again.

'Derfel!' Arthur called, 'Derfel!' I slithered down the fort's face and hurried over the sand and up the dune's flank. 'What do you see?' Arthur asked me.

I stared northwards across the glittering sea-lake. I could see *Prydwen* halfway down its slip, and I could see the fires where salt was panned and the daily catches were smoked, and I could see some fishermen's nets hanging from spars planted in the sand, and then I saw the horsemen.

Sunlight glittered off a spear point, then another, and suddenly I could see a score of men, maybe more, pounding along a road that led well inland of the sea-lake's shore. 'Hide!' Arthur shouted, and we slid down the dune, snatched up Seren and Arthur-bach, and crouched like guilty things inside the fort's crumbling ramparts.

'They'll have seen us, Lord,' I said.

'Maybe not.'

'How many men?' Culhwch asked.

'Twenty?' Arthur guessed, 'thirty? Maybe more. They were

coming from some trees. There could be a hundred of them.'

There was a soft scraping noise and I turned to see that Culhwch had drawn his sword. He grinned at me. 'I don't care if it's two hundred men, Derfel, they're not cutting my beard.'

'Why would they want your beard?' Galahad asked. 'A smelly thing full of lice?'

Culhwch laughed. He liked to tease Galahad, and to be teased in return, and he was still thinking of his reply when Arthur cautiously raised his head above the rampart and stared west towards the place where the approaching spearmen would appear. He went very still, and his stillness quieted us, then suddenly he stood and waved. 'It's Sagramor!' he called to us, and the joy in his voice was unmistakable. 'It's Sagramor!' he said again, and he was so excited that Arthur-bach took up the happy cry. 'It's Sagramor!' the small boy shouted, and the rest of us clambered over the rampart to see Sagramor's grim black flag streaming from a skull-tipped spear shaft. Sagramor himself, in his conical black helmet, was in the lead and, seeing Arthur, he spurred forward across the sand. Arthur ran to greet him, Sagramor vaulted from his horse, stumbled to his knees and clasped Arthur about the waist.

'Lord!' Sagramor said in a rare display of feeling, 'Lord! I thought not to see you again.'

Arthur raised him, then embraced him. 'We would have met in Broceliande, my friend.'

'Broceliande?' Sagramor said, then spat. 'I hate the sea.' There were tears on his black face and I remembered him telling me once why he followed Arthur. Because, he had said, when I had nothing, Arthur gave me everything. Sagramor had not come here because he was reluctant to board a ship, but because Arthur needed help.

The Numidian had brought eighty-three men, and Einion, Culhwch's son, had come with them. 'I only had ninety-two horses, Lord,' Sagramor told Arthur. 'I've been collecting them for months.' He had hoped he could outride Mordred's forces and so bring all his men safe to Siluria, but instead he had brought as many as he could to this dry spit of sand between the sea-lake and the ocean. Some of the horses had collapsed on the way, but eighty-three had come through safe.

'Where are your other men?' Arthur asked.

'They sailed south yesterday with all our families,' Sagramor said, then pulled back from Arthur's embrace and looked at us. We must have appeared a sorry and battered group, for he offered one of his rare smiles before bowing low to Guinevere and Ceinwyn.

'We have only one boat coming,' Arthur said worriedly.

'Then you will take that one boat, Lord,' Sagramor said calmly, 'and we shall ride west into Kernow. We can find boats there and follow you south. But I wanted to meet you this side of the water in case your enemies found you too.'

'We've seen none so far,' Arthur said, touching Excalibur's hilt, 'at least, not this side of the Severn Sea. And I pray we shall see none all day. Our boat comes at dusk, and then we leave.'

'So I shall guard you till dusk,' Sagramor said, and his men slid from their saddles, took their shields from their backs and planted their spears in the sand. Their horses, sweat-whitened and panting, stood exhausted while Sagramor's men stretched their tired arms and legs. We were now a warband, almost an army, and our banner was Sagramor's black flag.

But then, just an hour later, on horses as tired as Sagramor's, the enemy came to Camlann.

CEINWYN HELPED ME pull on my armour for it was hard to manage the heavy mail shirt with only one hand, and impossible to buckle the bronze greaves that I had taken at Mynydd Baddon and which protected my legs from the spear thrust that comes under the shield rim. Once the greaves and the mail were in place, and once Hywelbane's belt was buckled around my waist, I let Ceinwyn fasten the shield to my left arm. 'Tighter,' I told her, instinctively pressing against my mail coat to feel the small lump where her brooch was attached to my shirt. It was safely there, a talisman that had seen me through countless battles.

'Maybe they won't attack,' she said, tugging the shield straps as tight as they would go.

'Pray that they don't,' I said.

'Pray to whom?' she asked with a grim smile.

'To whichever God you trust the most, my love,' I said, then kissed her. I pulled on my helmet, and she fastened the strap under my chin. The dent made in the helmet's crown at Mynydd Baddon had been hammered smooth and a new iron plate riveted to cover the gash. I kissed Ceinwyn again, then closed the cheekpieces. The wind blew the wolftail plume in front of the helmet's eyes slits, and I flicked my head back to throw the long grey hair aside. I was the very last wolftail. The others had been massacred by Mordred or taken down into Manawydan's keeping. I was the last, just as I was the last warrior alive to carry Ceinwyn's star on my shield. I hefted my war spear, its shaft as thick as Ceinwyn's wrist and its blade a sharpened wedge of Morridig's finest steel. 'Caddwg will be here soon,' I told her, 'we won't have long to wait.'

'Just all day,' Ceinwyn said, and she glanced up the sea-lake to where *Prydwen* floated at the edge of the mudbank. Men were hauling her mast upright, but soon the falling tide would strand the boat again and we would have to wait for the waters to rise. But at least the enemy had not bothered Caddwg, and had no reason to do so. To them he was doubtless just another fisherman and no business of theirs. We were their business.

There were sixty or seventy of the enemy, all of them horsemen, and they must have ridden hard to reach us, but now they were waiting at the spit's landward end and we all knew that other spearmen would be following them. By dusk we could face an army, maybe two, for Nimue's men would surely be hurrying with Mordred's spearmen.

Arthur was in his war finery. His scale armour, which had tongues of gold amidst the iron plates, glinted in the sun. I watched him pull on his helmet that was crested with white goose feathers. Hygwydd would usually have armoured him, but Hygwydd was dead so Guinevere strapped Excalibur's cross-hatched scabbard about his waist and hung the white cloak on his shoulders. He smiled at her, leaned to hear her speak, laughed, then closed the helmet's cheekpieces. Two men helped him up into the saddle of one of Sagramor's horses, and once he was mounted they passed him his spear and his silver-sheeted shield from which the cross had long been stripped away. He took the reins with his shield hand, then kicked the horse towards us. 'Let's stir them up,' he called down to Sagramor, who stood beside me. Arthur planned to lead thirty horsemen towards the enemy, then feint a panicked withdrawal that he hoped would tempt them into a trap.

We left a score of men to guard the women and children in the fort while the rest of us followed Sagramor to a deep hollow behind a dune that fronted the sea's beach. The whole sandspit west of the fort was a confusion of dunes and hollows that formed a maze of traps and blind alleys, and only the spit's final two hundred paces, east of the fort, offered level ground.

Arthur waited until we were hidden, then led his thirty men west along the sea-rippled sand that lay close to the breaking waves. We crouched under the high dune's cover. I had left my spear at the fort, preferring to fight this battle with Hywelbane alone. Sagramor also planned to fight with sword alone. He was scrubbing a patch of rust from his curved blade with a handful of sand. 'You lost your beard,' he grunted at me.

'I exchanged it for Amhar's life.'

I saw a flash of teeth as he grinned behind the shadow of his helmet's cheekpieces. 'A good exchange,' he said, 'and your hand?'

'To magic.'

'Not your sword hand, though.' He held the blade to catch the light, was satisfied that the rust was gone, then cocked his head, listening, but we could hear nothing except the breaking waves. 'I shouldn't have come,' he said after a while.

'Why not?' I had never known Sagramor to shirk a fight.

'They must have followed me,' he said, jerking his head westwards to indicate the enemy.

'They might have known we were coming here anyway,' I said, trying to comfort him, though unless Merlin had betrayed Camlann to Nimue, it seemed more likely that Mordred would indeed have left some lightly armoured horsemen to watch Sagramor and that those scouts must have betrayed our hiding place. Whatever, it was too late now. Mordred's men knew where we were and now it was a race between Caddwg and the enemy.

'Hear that?' Gwydre called. He was in armour and had his father's bear on his shield. He was nervous, and no wonder, for this would be his first real battle.

I listened. My leather padded helmet muffled sound, but at last I heard the thud of hoofs on sand.

'Keep down!' Sagramor snarled at those men who were tempted to peer over the crest of the dune.

The horses were galloping down the sea's beach, and we were hidden from that beach by the dune. The sound drew nearer, rising to a thunder of hoofs as we gripped our spears and swords. Sagramor's helmet was crested with the mask of a snarling fox. I stared at the fox, but heard only the growing noise of the horses. It was warm and sweat was trickling down my face. The mail coat felt heavy, but it always did until the fighting started.

The first hoofs pounded past, then Arthur was shouting from the beach. 'Now!' he called, 'Now! Now! Now!'

'Go!' Sagramor shouted and we all scrambled up the dune's inner face. Our boots slipped in the sand, and it seemed I would never reach the top, but then we were over the crest and running down onto the beach where a swirl of horsemen churned the hard wet sand beside the sea. Arthur had turned and his thirty men had clashed with their pursuers who outnumbered Arthur's men by two to one, but those pursuers now saw us running towards their flank and the more prudent immediately turned and galloped west towards safety. Most stayed to fight.

I screamed a challenge, took a horseman's spear point plumb on the centre of my shield, raked Hywelbane across the horse's rear leg to hamstring the animal, and then, as the horse tipped towards me, I swept Hywelbane hard into the rider's back. He yelped in pain, and I jumped back as horse and man collapsed in a flurry of hoofs, sand and blood. I kicked the twitching man in the face, stabbed down with Hywelbane, then backswung the sword at a panicked horseman who feebly stabbed at me with his spear. Sagramor was keening a terrible war cry and Gwydre was spearing a fallen man at the sea's edge. The enemy were breaking from the fight and spurring their horses to safety through the sea's shallows where the receding water sucked a swirl of sand and blood back into the collapsing waves. I saw Culhwch spur his horse to an enemy and haul the man bodily from his saddle. The man tried to stand, but Culhwch backswung the sword, turned his horse and chopped down again. The few enemy who had survived were trapped between us and the sea now, and we killed them grimly. Horses screamed and thrashed their hoofs as they died. The small waves were pink and the sand was black with blood.

We killed twenty of them and took sixteen prisoners, and when the prisoners had told us all they knew, we killed them too. Arthur grimaced as he gave the order, for he disliked killing unarmed men, but we could spare no spearmen to guard prisoners, nor did we have any mercy for these foes who carried unmarked shields as a boast of their savagery. We killed them quickly, forcing them to kneel on the sand where Hywelbane or Sagramor's sharp sword took their heads. They were Mordred's men, and Mordred himself had led them down the beach, but the King had wheeled his horse at the first sign of our ambush and shouted at his men to retreat. 'I came close to him,' Arthur said ruefully, 'but not close enough.' Mordred had escaped, but the first victory was ours, though three of our men had died in the fight and another seven were bleeding badly. 'How did Gwydre fight?' Arthur asked me.

'Bravely, Lord, bravely,' I said. My sword was thick with blood that I tried to scrape off with a handful of sand. 'He killed, Lord,' I assured Arthur.

'Good,' he said, then crossed to his son and put an arm around his shoulders. I used my one hand to scrub the blood from Hywelbane, then tugged the buckle of my helmet loose and pulled it off my head.

We killed the wounded horses, led the uninjured beasts back to the fort, then collected our enemy's weapons and shields. 'They won't come again,' I told Ceinwyn, 'not unless they're reinforced.' I looked up at the sun and saw that it was climbing slowly through the cloudless sky.

We had very little water, only what Sagramor's men had brought in their small baggage, and so we rationed the water-skins. It would be a long and thirsty day, especially for our wounded. One of them was shivering. His face was pale, almost yellow, and when Sagramor tried to trickle a little water into the man's mouth he bit convulsively at the skin's lip. He began to moan, and the sound of his agony grated on our souls and so Sagramor hastened the man's death with his sword. 'We must light a pyre,' Sagramor said, 'at the spit's end.' He nodded his head towards the flat sand where the sea had left a tangle of sun-bleached driftwood.

Arthur did not seem to hear the suggestion. 'If you want,' he said to Sagramor, 'you can go west now.'

'And leave you here?'

'If you stay,' Arthur said quietly, 'then I don't know how you will leave. We have only one boat coming. And more men will come to Mordred. None to us.'

'More men to kill,' Sagramor said curtly, but I think he knew that by staying he was assuring his own death. Caddwg's boat might take twenty people to safety, but certainly no more. 'We can swim to the other shore, Lord,' he said, jerking his head towards the eastern bank of the channel that ran deep and fast about the tip of the sandspit. 'Those of us who can swim,' he added.

'Can you?'

'Never too late to learn,' Sagramor said, then spat. 'Besides, we're not dead yet.'

Nor were we beaten yet, and every minute that passed took us nearer safety. I could see Caddwg's men carrying the sail to *Prydwen*, which was canted at the edge of the sea. Her mast was now upright, though men still rigged lines from the masthead, and in an hour or two the tide would turn and she would float again, ready for the voyage. We just had to endure till the late afternoon. We occupied ourselves by making a huge pyre from the driftwood, and when it was burning we heaved the bodies of our dead into the flames. Their hair flared bright, then came the smell of roasting flesh. We threw on more timber until the fire was a roaring, white-hot inferno.

'A ghost fence might deter the enemy,' Taliesin remarked when he had chanted a prayer for the four burning men whose souls were drifting with the smoke to find their shadowbodies.

I had not seen a ghost fence in years, but we made one that day. It was a grisly business. We had thirty-six dead enemy bodies and from them we took thirty-six severed heads which we rammed onto the blades of the captured spears. Then we planted the spears across the spit and Taliesin, conspicuous in his white robe and carrying a spear shaft so that he resembled a Druid, walked from one bloody head to the next so that the enemy would think that an enchantment was being made. Few men would willingly cross a ghost fence without a Druid to avert its evil, and once the fence was made we rested more easily. We shared a scanty midday meal and I remember Arthur looking ruefully at the ghost fence as he ate. 'From Isca to this,' he remarked softly.

'From Mynydd Baddon to this,' I said.

He shrugged. 'Poor Uther,' he said, and he must have been thinking of the oath that had made Mordred King, the oath that had led to this sun-warmed spit beside the sea.

Mordred's reinforcements arrived in the early afternoon. They mostly came on foot in a long column that straggled down the sea-lake's western shore. We counted over a hundred men and knew that more would be following.

'They'll be tired,' Arthur told us, 'and we have the ghost fence.'

But the enemy now possessed a Druid. Fergal had arrived with the reinforcements, and an hour after we first saw the column of spearmen, we watched as the Druid crept near the fence and sniffed the salt air like a dog. He threw handfuls of sand towards the nearest head, hopped on one leg for a moment, then ran to the spear and toppled it. The fence was broken, and Fergal tipped his head to the sun and gave a great cry of triumph. We pulled on helmets, found our shields and passed sharpening stones amongst ourselves.

The tide had turned, and the first fishing-boats were coming home. We hailed them as they passed the spit, but most ignored our calls, for common folk all too often have good reason to fear spearmen, but Galahad waved a gold coin and that lure did bring one boat which nosed gingerly into the shore and grounded on the sand near the blazing balefire. Its two crewmen, both with heavily tattooed faces, agreed to take the women and children to Caddwg's craft, which was almost afloat again. We gave the fishermen gold, handed the women and children into the boat, and sent one of the wounded spearmen to guard them. 'Tell the other fishermen,' Arthur told the tattooed men, 'that there's gold for any man who brings his boat with Caddwg.' He made a brief farewell to Guinevere, as I did to Ceinwyn. I held her close for a few heartbeats and found I had no words.

'Stay alive,' she told me.

'For you,' I said, 'I will,' and then I helped push the grounded boat into the sea and watched it slowly pull away into the channel.

A moment later one of our mounted scouts came galloping back from the broken ghost fence. 'They're coming, Lord!' he shouted.

I let Galahad buckle my helmet strap, then held out my arm so he could bind the shield tight. He gave me my spear. 'God be with you,' he said, then picked up his own shield that was blazoned with the Christian cross.

We would not fight in the dunes this time because we did not have enough men to make a shield wall that would stretch right across the hilly part of the sandspit, and that meant Mordred's horsemen could have galloped around our flanks, surrounded us, and we would have been doomed to die in a tightening ring of enemies. Nor did we fight in the fort, for there too we could have been surrounded and thus cut off from the water when Caddwg arrived, and so we retreated to the narrow tip of the spit where our shield wall could stretch from one shore to the other. The balefire still blazed just above the line of weed that marked the high-tide limit, and while we waited for the enemy Arthur ordered still more driftwood to be heaped on its flames. We went on feeding that fire until we saw Mordred's men approaching, and then we made our shield wall just a few paces in front of the flames. We set Sagramor's dark banner in the centre of our line, touched our shields edge to edge and waited.

We were eighty-four men and Mordred brought over a hundred to attack us, but when they saw our shield wall formed and ready, they stopped. Some of Mordred's horsemen spurred into the shallows of the sea-lake, hoping to ride about our flank, but the water deepened swiftly where the channel ran close beside the southern shore and they found they could not ride around us; so they slid out of their saddles and carried their shields and spears to join Mordred's long wall. I looked up to see that the sun was at last sliding down towards the high western hills. *Prydwen* was almost afloat, though men were still busy in her rigging. It would not be long, I thought, before Caddwg came, but already there were more enemy spearmen straggling down the western road. Mordred's forces grew stronger, and we could only grow weaker.

Fergal, his beard woven with fox fur and hung with small bones, came to the sand in front of our shield wall and there he hopped on one leg, held one hand in the air and kept one eye closed. He cursed our souls, promising them to the fire-worm of Crom Dubh and to the wolfpack that hunts Eryri's Pass of Arrows. Our women would be given as playthings to the demons of Annwn and our children would be nailed to the oaks of Arddu. He cursed our spears and our swords, and threw an enchantment to shatter our shields and turn our bowels to water. He screamed his spells, promising that for food in the Otherworld we would have to scavenge the droppings of the hounds of Arawn and that for water we would lick the bile of Cefydd's serpents. 'Your eyes will be blood,' he crooned, 'your bellies shall be filled with worms, and your tongues will turn black! You will watch the rape of your women and the murder of your children!' He called some of us by name, threatening torments unimaginable, and to counter his spells we sang the War Song of Beli Mawr.

From that day to this I have not heard that song sung again by warriors, and never did I hear it better sung than on that sea-wrapped stretch of sun-warmed sand. We were few, but we were the best warriors Arthur ever commanded. There were only one or two young men in that shield wall; the rest of us were seasoned, hardened men who had been through battle and smelt the slaughter and knew how to kill. We were the lords of war. There was not a weak man there, not a single man who could not be trusted to protect his neighbour, and not a man whose courage would break, and how we sang that day! We drowned Fergal's curses, and the strong sound of our voices must have carried across the water to where our women waited on *Prydwen*. We sang to Beli Mawr who had harnessed the wind to his chariot, whose spear shaft was a tree and whose sword slaughtered the enemy like a reaping hook cutting thistles. We sang of his victims scattered dead in the wheatfields and rejoiced for the widows made by his anger. We sang that his boots were like millstones, his shield an iron cliff and his helmet's plume tall enough to scrape the stars. We sang tears into our eyes and fear into our enemy's hearts.

The song ended in a feral howl, and even before that howl had ended Culhwch had limped out of our shield wall and shaken his spear at the enemy. He derided them as cowards, spat on their lineage and invited them to taste his spear. The enemy watched him, but none moved to take his challenge. They were a tattered, fearsome band, as hardened to killing as we were, though not, maybe, to the war of shield walls. They were the scourings of Britain and Armorica, the brigands, outlaws and masterless men who had flocked to Mordred's promise of plunder and rape. Minute by minute their ranks swelled as men came down the spit, but the newcomers were footsore and weary, and the narrowing of the spit restricted the number of men who could advance into our spears. They might push us back, but they could not outflank us.

Nor, it seemed, would any come to face Culhwch. He planted himself opposite Mordred, who stood in the centre of the enemy line. 'You were born of a toad-whore,' he called to the King, 'and fathered by a coward. Fight me! I limp! I'm old! I'm bald! But you daren't face me!' He spat at Mordred, and still not one of Mordred's men moved. 'Children!' Culhwch jeered at them, then turned his back on the enemy to show his scorn of them.

It was then that a youngster rushed from the enemy ranks. His helmet was too big for his beardless head, his breastplate a poor thing of leather and his shield had a gaping split between two of its boards. He was a young man who needed to kill a champion to find wealth and he ran at Culhwch, screaming hatred, and the rest of Mordred's men cheered him on.

Culhwch turned back, half crouched, and held his spear towards his enemy's crotch. The young man raised his own spear, thinking to drive it down over Culhwch's low shield, then shouted in triumph as he thrust down hard, but his shout turned into a choking scream as Culhwch's spear flicked up to snatch the youngster's soul from his open mouth. Culhwch, old in war, stepped back. His own shield had not even been touched. The dying man stumbled, the spear stuck in his throat. He half turned towards Culhwch, then fell. Culhwch kicked his enemy's spear out of his hand, jerked his own spear free and stabbed down hard into the youngster's neck. Then he smiled at Mordred's men. 'Another?' he called. No one moved. Culhwch spat at Mordred and walked back to our cheering ranks. He winked at me as he came near. 'See how it's done, Derfel?' he called, 'watch and learn,' and the men near me laughed.

Prydwen was floating now, her pale hull shimmering its reflection on the water that was being ruffled by a small western wind. That wind brought us the stench of Mordred's men; the mingled smells of leather, sweat and mead. Many of the enemy would be drunk, and many would never dare face our blades if they were not drunk. I wondered if the youngster whose mouth and gullet were now black with flies had needed mead-courage to face Culhwch.

Mordred was cajoling his men forward now, and the bravest among them were encouraging their comrades to advance. The sun seemed much lower suddenly, for it was beginning to dazzle us; I had not realized how much time had passed while Fergal cursed us and Culhwch taunted the enemy, and still that enemy could not find the courage to attack. A few would start forward, but the rest would lag behind, and Mordred would then curse them as he closed up the shield wall and urged them on again. It was ever thus. It takes great courage to close on a shield wall, and ours, though small, was close-knit and full of famous warriors. I glanced at *Prydwen* and saw her sail fall from the yard, and saw too that the new sail was dyed scarlet like blood and was decorated with Arthur's black bear. Caddwg had spent much gold for that sail, but then I had no time to watch the distant ship for Mordred's men were at last coming close and the brave ones were urging the rest into a run.

'Brace hard!' Arthur shouted, and we bent our knees to take the shock of the shield blow. The enemy was a dozen paces away, ten, and about to charge screaming when Arthur shouted again. 'Now!' he called, and his voice checked the enemy's rush for they did not know what he meant, and then Mordred screamed at them to kill, and so at last they closed with us.

My spear hit a shield and was knocked down. I let it go and snatched up Hywelbane that I had stuck into the sand in front of me. A heartbeat later Mordred's shields struck our shields and a short sword flailed at my head. My ears rang from a blow on my helmet as I stabbed Hywelbane under my shield to find my attacker's leg. I felt her blade bite, twisted her hard and saw the man stagger as I crippled him. He flinched, but stayed on his feet. He had black curly hair crammed under a battered iron helmet and he was spitting at me as I managed to pull Hywelbane up from behind my shield. I parried a wild blow of his short sword, then beat my heavy blade down on his head. He sank to the sand. 'In front of me,' I shouted to the man behind me, and he used his spear to kill the crippled man who could otherwise have stabbed up into my groin, and then I heard men shouting in pain or alarm and I glanced left, my view obscured by swords and axes, and saw that great burning baulks of driftwood were being hurled over our heads into the enemy line. Arthur was using the balefire as a weapon, and his last word of command before the shield walls clashed had ordered the men by the fire to seize the logs by their unburned ends and hurl them into Mordred's ranks. The enemy spearmen instinctively flinched away from the flames, and Arthur led our men into the gap that was made.

'Make way!' a voice shouted behind me, and I ducked aside as a spearman ran through our ranks with a great burning shaft of wood. He thrust it at the enemy's faces, they twisted aside from the glowing tip, and we jumped into the gap. The fire scorched our faces as we hacked and thrusted. More flaming brands flew over us. The enemy closest to me had twisted away from the heat, opening his unprotected side to my neighbour, and I heard his ribs snap under the spear's thrust and saw the blood bubble at his lips as he dropped. I was in the enemy's second rank now, and the fallen timber was burning my leg, but I let the pain turn into a rage that drove Hywelbane hard into a man's face, and then the men behind me kicked sand onto the flames as they pushed forward, driving me on into the third rank. I had no room now to use my sword, for I was crushed shield to shield against a swearing man who spat at me and tried to work his own sword past my shield's edge. A spear came over my shoulder to strike the swearing man's cheek and the pressure of his shield yielded just enough to let me push my own shield forward and swing Hywelbane. Later, much later, I remember screaming an incoherent sound of rage as I hammered that man into the sand. The madness of battle was on us, the desperate madness of fighting men trapped in a small place, but it was the enemy who was giving way. Rage was turned into horror and we fought like Gods. The sun blazed just above the western hill.

'Shields! Shields! Shields!' Sagramor roared, reminding us to keep the wall continuous, and my right-hand neighbour knocked his shield on mine, grinned, and stabbed forward with his spear. I saw an enemy's sword being drawn back for a mighty blow and I met it with Hywelbane on the man's wrist and she cut through that wrist as though the enemy's bones were made of reed. The sword flew into our rear ranks with a bloody hand still gripping its hilt. The man on my left fell with an enemy spear in his belly, but the second rank man took his place and shouted a great oath as he slammed his shield forward and swung his sword down.

Another burning log flew low over us and fell on two of the enemy, who reeled apart. We leapt into the gap, and suddenly there was empty sand ahead of us. 'Stay together!' I shouted, 'stay together!' The enemy was breaking. Their front rank was dead or wounded, their second rank was dying, and the men in the rear were those who least wanted to fight and so were the ones who were easiest to kill. Those rear ranks were filled by men who were skilled at rape and clever at pillage, but had never faced a shield wall of hardened killers. And how we were killing now. Their wall was breaking, corroded by fire and fear, and we were screaming a victor's chant. I stumbled on a body, fell forward and rolled over

422

with my shield held above my face. A sword slammed into the shield, the sound deafening, then Sagramor's men stepped over me and a spearman hauled me upright. 'Wounded?' he asked.

'No.'

He pushed on. I looked to see where our wall needed strengthening, but everywhere it was at least three men deep, and those three ranks were grinding forward over the carnage of a slaughtered enemy. Men grunted as they swung, as they stabbed and as they drove the blades into enemy flesh. It is the beguiling glory of war, the sheer exhilaration of breaking a shield wall and slaking a sword on a hated enemy. I watched Arthur, a man as kind as any I have known, and saw nothing but joy in his eyes. Galahad, who prayed each day that he could obey Christ's commandment to love all men, was now killing them with a terrible efficiency. Culhwch was roaring insults. He had discarded his shield so that he could use both hands on his heavy spear. Gwydre was grinning behind his cheekpieces, while Taliesin was singing as he killed the enemy wounded left behind by our advancing shield wall. You do not win the fight of the shield wall by being sensible and moderate, but by a Godlike rush of howling madness.

And the enemy could not stand our madness, and so they broke and ran. Mordred tried to hold them, but they would not stay for him, and he fled with them back towards the fort. Some of our men, the rage of battle still seething inside them, began to pursue, but Sagramor called them back. He had been wounded on his shield shoulder, but he shook off any attempt we made to help him and bellowed at his men to stop their pursuit. We dared not follow them, beaten though they were, for then we would have found ourselves in the wider part of the spit and so have invited the enemy to surround us. Instead we stayed where we had fought and we jeered at our enemies, calling them cowards.

A gull pecked at the eyes of a dead man. I looked away to see that *Prydwen* was bows on to us now and free of her mooring, though her bright sail was hardly stirring in the gentle wind. But she was just moving, and the colour of her sail shivered its long reflection on the glassy water.

Mordred saw the boat, saw the great bear on her sail, and he knew his enemy might escape to sea and so he screamed at his men to make a new wall. Reinforcements were joining him minute by minute, and some of the newcomers were Nimue's men for I saw two Bloodshields take their place in the new line that formed to charge us.

We fell back to where we had started, making our shield wall in the blood-soaked sand just in front of the fire that had helped us win the first attack. The bodies of our first four dead were only half burned and their scorched faces grinned foully at us through lips shrivelled back from discoloured teeth. We left the enemy's dead on the sand as obstacles in the path of the living, but hauled our own dead back and piled them beside the fire. We had sixteen dead and a score of badly wounded, but we still had enough men to form a shield wall, and we could still fight.

Taliesin sang to us. He sang his own song of Mynydd Baddon, and it was to that hard rhythm that we touched our shields together again. Our swords and spears were blunted and bloodied, the enemy was fresh, but we cheered as they came towards us. *Prydwen* was scarcely moving. She looked like a ship poised on a mirror, but then I saw long oars unfold like wings from her hull.

'Kill them!' Mordred screamed, and he now had the battle rage himself and it drove him onto our line. A handful of brave men supported him, and they were followed by some of Nimue's demented souls, so it was a ragged charge that first fell on our line, but among the men who came were new arrivals who wanted to prove themselves, and so again we bent our knees and crouched behind our shield rims. The sun was blinding now, but in the moment before the crazed rush struck home, I saw flashes of light from the western hill and knew that there were still more spearmen on that high ground. I gained the impression that a whole new army of spearmen had come to the summit, but from where, or who led them, I could not tell, and then I had no time to think of the newcomers, for I was thrusting my shield forward and the blow of shield on shield made the stump of my arm sing in pain and I keened a sound of agony as I sliced Hywelbane down. A Bloodshield opposed me, and I cut him down hard, finding the gap between his breastplate and helmet, and when I had jerked Hywelbane free of his flesh I slashed wildly at the next enemy, a mad creature, and spun him away with blood spurting from his cheek, nose and eye.

Those first enemies had run ahead of Mordred's shield wall, but now the bulk of the enemy struck us and we leaned into their attack and screamed defiance as we lunged our blades across our shield rims. I recall confusion and the noise of sword ringing on sword, and the crash of shield striking shield. Battle is a matter of inches, not miles. The inches that separate a man from his enemy. You smell the mead on their breath, hear the breath in their throats, hear their grunts, feel them shift their weight, feel their spittle on your eyes, and you look for danger, look back into the eyes of the next man you must kill, find an opening, take it, close the shield wall again, step forward, feel the thrust of the men behind, half stumble on the bodies of those you have killed, recover, push forward, and afterwards you recall little except the blows that so nearly killed you. You work and push and stab to make an opening in their shield wall, and then you grunt and lunge and slash to widen the gap, and only then does the madness take over as the enemy breaks and you can begin to kill like a God because the enemy is scared and running, or scared and frozen, and all they can do is die while you harvest souls.

And beat them back again we did. Again we used flames from our balefire, and again we broke their wall, but we broke our own in the doing of it. I remember the sun bright behind the high western hill, and I remember staggering into an open patch of sand and shouting at men to support me, and I remember slashing Hywelbane onto the exposed nape of an enemy's neck and watching his blood well up through severed hair and seeing his head jerk back, and then I saw that the two battle lines had broken each other and we were nothing but small struggling groups of bloody men on a bloody stretch of fire-littered sand.

But we had won. The rearmost ranks of the enemy ran rather than take more of our swords, but in the centre, where Mordred fought, and Arthur fought, they did not run and the fight became grim around those two leaders. We tried to surround Mordred's men, but they fought back, and I saw how few we were and how many of us would never fight again because we had spilt our blood into Camlann's sands. A crowd of the enemy watched us from the dunes, but they were cowards and would not come forward to help their comrades, and so the last of our men fought the last of

Mordred's, and I saw Arthur hacking with Excalibur, trying to reach the King, and Sagramor was there, and Gwydre too, and I joined in the fight, throwing a spear away with my shield, stabbing Hywelbane forward, and my throat was dry as smoke and my voice a raven's croak. I struck at another man, and Hywelbane left a scar across his shield and he staggered back and did not have the strength to step forward again, and my own strength was ebbing and so I just stared at him through sweat-stung eyes. He came forward slowly, I stabbed, he staggered back from the blow on his shield and thrust a spear at me, and it was my turn to go backwards. I was panting, and all across the spit tired men fought tired men.

Galahad was wounded, his sword arm broken and his face bloody. Culhwch was dead. I did not see it, but I found his body later with two spears in his unarmoured groin. Sagramor was limping, but his quick sword was still deadly. He was trying to shelter Gwydre, who bled from a cut on his cheek and was attempting to reach his father's side. Arthur's goose-feather plumes were red with blood and his white cloak streaked with it. I watched him cut down a tall man, kick away the enemy's despairing lunge and slice down hard with Excalibur.

It was then that Loholt attacked. I had not seen him till that moment, but he saw his father and he spurred his horse and drew his spear back with his one remaining hand. He screamed a chant of hate as he charged into the tangle of tired men. The horse was white-eyed and terrified, but the spurs drove it on as Loholt aimed his blade at Arthur, but then Sagramor plucked up a spear and hurled it so that the horse's legs were tangled by the heavy staff and the animal fell in a shower of sand. Sagramor stepped into the flailing hoofs and scythed his sword's dark blade sideways and I saw blood spurt up from Loholt's neck, but just as Sagramor snatched Loholt's soul, so a Bloodshield darted forward and lunged at Sagramor with a spear. Sagramor backhanded his sword, spraying Loholt's blood from its tip, and the Bloodshield went down screaming, but then a shout announced that Arthur had reached Mordred and the rest of us instinctively turned to watch as the two men confronted each other. A lifetime of hatred rankled between them.

Mordred reached his sword out lowly, then swept it back to show his men he wanted Arthur for himself. The enemy obediently stumbled away. Mordred, just as he had been on the day when he had been acclaimed on Caer Cadarn, was all in black. A black cloak, black breastplate, black trews, black boots and a black helmet. In places the black armour had been scarred where blades had cut through the dried pitch to fleck open the bare metal. His shield was covered in pitch, and his only touches of colour were a shrivelled sprig of vervain that showed at his neck and the eye sockets of the skull that crested his helmet. A child's skull, I thought, for it was so small, and its eye sockets had been stuffed with scraps of red cloth. He limped forward on his clubbed foot, swinging his sword, and Arthur gestured at us to step back to give him room to fight. He hefted Excalibur, and raised his silver shield that was torn and bloody. How many of us were left by then? I do not know. Forty? Maybe less, and *Prydwen* had reached the turn in the river channel and was now gliding towards us with the wraithstone grey in her prow and her sail barely stirring in the small wind. The oars dipped and rose. The tide was almost full.

Mordred lunged, Arthur parried, lunged with his own blade, and Mordred stepped back. The King was quick, and he was young, but his clubbed foot and the deep thigh wound he had taken in Armorica made him less agile than Arthur. He licked dry lips, came forward again, and the swords rang loud in the evening air. One of the watching enemy suddenly staggered and fell for no apparent reason, but he did not move again as Mordred stepped fast forward and swung his sword in a blinding arc. Arthur met the blade with Excalibur, then shoved his shield forward to strike the King and Mordred staggered away. Arthur drew his arm back for the lunge, but Mordred somehow kept his footing and scrambled back with his sword countering the lunge and flicking fast forward in reply.

I could see Guinevere standing in *Prydwen's* prow with Ceinwyn just behind her. In the lovely evening light it seemed as though the hull was made of silver and the sail of finest scarlet linen. The long oars dipped and rose, dipped and rose, and slowly she came until a breath of warm wind at last filled the bear on her sail and the water rippled faster down her silver flanks, and just then Mordred screamed and charged, the swords clashed, shields banged, and Excalibur swept the grisly skull from the crest of

Mordred's helm. Mordred swung hard back and I saw Arthur flinch as his enemy's blade struck home, but he pushed the King away with his shield and the two men stepped apart.

Arthur pressed his sword hand against his waist where he had been struck, then shook his head as though denying that he was hurt. But Sagramor was hurt. He had been watching the fight, but now he suddenly bent forward and stumbled down into the sand. I crossed to him. 'Spear in my belly,' he said, and I saw he was clutching his stomach with both hands to stop his guts from spilling onto the sand. Just as he had killed Loholt, so the Bloodshield had struck Sagramor with his spear and had died in that achievement, but Sagramor was dying now. I put my one good arm about him and turned him onto his back. He gripped my hand. His teeth chattered, and he groaned, then he forced up his helmeted head to watch as Arthur went cautiously forward.

There was blood at Arthur's waist. Mordred's last swing had cut up into the scale armour, up between the scale-like flakes of metal, and it had bitten deeply into Arthur's side. Even as Arthur went forward new blood glistened and welled where the sword had torn through his armoured coat, but Arthur suddenly leapt forward and turned his threatened lunge into a downwards chop that Mordred parried on his shield. Mordred threw the shield wide to throw Excalibur clear and stabbed forward with his own sword, but Arthur took that lunge on his shield, drew back Excalibur, and it was then that I saw his shield tilt backwards and saw Mordred's sword scrape up the torn silver cover. Mordred shouted and pushed the blade harder and Arthur did not see the sword tip coming until it broke over the shield's edge and stabbed up into the eyehole of his helmet.

I saw blood. But I also saw Excalibur come down from the sky in a blow as strong as Arthur ever struck.

Excalibur cut through Mordred's helmet. It slit the black iron as though it were parchment, then broke the King's skull and sliced into his brain. And Arthur, with blood glistening at his helmet's eyehole, staggered, recovered, then wrenched Excalibur free in a spray of bloody droplets. Mordred, dead from the moment Excalibur had split his helmet, fell forward at Arthur's feet. His blood gushed onto the sand and onto Arthur's boots, and his men, seeing their King dead and Arthur still on his feet, gave a low moan and stepped backwards.

I took my hand from Sagramor's dying grip. 'Shield wall!' I shouted, 'shield wall!' And the startled survivors of our small warband closed ranks in front of Arthur and we touched our ragged shields together and snarled forward over Mordred's lifeless body. I thought the enemy might come back for vengeance, but they stepped backwards instead. Their leaders were dead, and we were still showing defiance, and they had no belly for more death that evening.

'Stay here!' I shouted at the shield wall, then went back to Arthur.

Galahad and I eased the helmet from his head and so released a rush of blood. The sword had missed his right eye by a finger's breadth, but it had broken the bone outside the eye and the wound was pulsing blood. 'Cloth!' I shouted, and a wounded man ripped a length of linen from a dead man's jerkin and we used it to pad the wound. Taliesin bound it up, using a strip torn from the skirts of his robe. Arthur looked up at me when Taliesin was finished and tried to speak.

'Quiet, Lord,' I said.

'Mordred,' he said.

'He's dead, Lord,' I said, 'he's dead.'

I think he smiled, and then *Prydwen*'s bow scraped on the sand. Arthur's face was pale and bloody rivulets laced his cheek.

'You can grow a beard now, Derfel,' he said.

'Yes, Lord,' I said, 'I will. Don't speak.' There was blood at his waist, far too much blood, but I could not take his armour off to find that wound, even though I feared it was the worse of his two injuries.

'Excalibur,' he said to me.

'Quiet, Lord,' I said.

'Take Excalibur,' he said. 'Take it and throw it into the sea. Promise me?'

'I will, Lord, I promise.' I took the bloodied sword from his hand, then stepped back as four unwounded men lifted Arthur and carried him to the boat. They passed him over the gunwale, and Guinevere helped to take him and to lay him on *Prydwen*'s deck.

She made a pillow of his blood-soaked cloak, then crouched beside him and stroked his face. 'Are you coming, Derfel?' she asked me.

I gestured to the men who still formed a shield wall on the sand. 'Can you take them?' I asked. 'And can you take the wounded?'

'Twelve men more,' Caddwg called from the stern. 'No more than twelve. Don't have space for more.'

No fishing-boats had come. But why should they have come? Why should men involve themselves in killing and blood and madness when their job is to take food from the sea? We only had *Prydwen* and she would have to sail without me. I smiled at Guinevere. 'I can't come, Lady,' I said, then turned and gestured again towards the shield wall. 'Someone must stay to lead them over the bridge of swords.' The stump of my left arm was oozing blood, there was a bruise on my ribs, but I was alive. Sagramor was dying, Culhwch was dead, Galahad and Arthur were injured. There was no one but me. I was the last of Arthur's warlords.

'I can stay!' Galahad had overheard our conversation.

'You can't fight with a broken arm,' I said. 'Get in the boat, and take Gwydre. And hurry! The tide's falling.'

'I should stay,' Gwydre said nervously.

I seized him by the shoulders and pushed him into the shallows. 'Go with your father,' I said, 'for my sake. And tell him I was true to the end.' I stopped him suddenly, and turned him back to face me, and I saw there were tears on his young face. 'Tell your father,' I said, 'that I loved him to the end.'

He nodded, then he and Galahad climbed aboard. Arthur was with his family now, and I stepped back as Caddwg used one of the oars to pole the ship back into the channel. I looked up at Ceinwyn and I smiled, and there were tears in my eyes, but I could think of nothing to say except to tell her that I would wait for her beneath the apple trees of the Otherworld; but just as I was phrasing the clumsy words, and just as the ship slipped off the sand, she stepped lightly onto the bow and leapt into the shallows.

'No!' I shouted.

'Yes,' she said, and reached out a hand so that I would help her onto the shore.

'You know what they'll do to you?' I asked.

She showed me a knife in her left hand, meaning she would kill herself before she was taken by Mordred's men. 'We've been together too long, my love, to part now,' she said and then she stood beside me to watch as *Prydwen* edged into the deep water. Our last daughter and her children were sailing away. The tide had turned and the first of the ebb was creeping the silver ship towards the sea reach.

I stayed with Sagramor as he died. I cradled his head, held his hand and talked his soul onto the bridge of swords. Then, with my eyes brimming with tears, I walked back to our small shield wall and saw that Camlann was filled with spearmen now. A whole army had come, but they had come too late to save their King, though they still had time enough to finish us. I could see Nimue at last, her white robe and her white horse bright in the shadowed dunes. My friend and one-time lover was now my final enemy.

'Fetch me a horse,' I told a spearman. There were stray horses everywhere and he ran, grabbed a bridle and brought a mare back to me. I asked Ceinwyn to unstrap my shield, then had the spearman help me onto the mare's back and, once mounted, I tucked Excalibur under my left arm and took the reins with my right. I kicked back and the horse leapt ahead, and I kicked her again, scattering sand with her hoofs and men from her path. I was riding among Mordred's men now, but there was no fight in them for they had lost their Lord. They were masterless and Nimue's army of the mad was behind them, and behind Nimue's ragged forces there was a third army. A new army had come to Camlann's sands.

It was the same army I had seen on the high western hill, and I realized it must have marched south behind Mordred to take Dumnonia for itself. It was an army that had come to watch Arthur and Mordred destroy themselves, and now that the fighting was done the army of Gwent moved slowly forward beneath their banners of the cross. They came to rule Dumnonia and to make Meurig its King. Their red cloaks and scarlet plumes looked black in the twilight, and I looked up to see that the first faint stars were pricking the sky.

I rode towards Nimue, but stopped a hundred paces short of my old friend. I could see Olwen watching me, and Nimue's baleful stare, and then I smiled at her and took Excalibur into my right

431

hand and held up the stump of my left so that she would know what I had done. Then I showed her Excalibur.

She knew what I planned then. 'No!' she screamed, and her army of the mad wailed with her and their gibbering shook the evening sky.

I put Excalibur under my arm again, picked up the reins and kicked the mare as I turned her about. I urged her on, driving her fast onto the sand of the sea-beach, and I heard Nimue's horse galloping behind me, but she was too late, much too late.

I rode towards *Prydwen*. The small wind was filling her sail now and she was clear of the spit and the wraithstone at her bows was rising and falling in the sea's endless waves. I kicked again and the mare tossed her head and I shouted her on into that darkening sea, and kept kicking her until the waves broke cold against her chest and only then did I drop the reins. She quivered under me as I took Excalibur in my right hand.

I drew my arm back. There was blood on the sword, yet her blade seemed to glow. Merlin had once said that the Sword of Rhydderch would turn to flame at the end, and perhaps she did, or perhaps the tears in my eyes deceived me.

'No!' Nimue wailed.

And I threw Excalibur, threw her hard and high towards the deep water where the tide had scoured the channel through Camlann's sands.

Excalibur turned in the evening air. No sword was ever more beautiful. Merlin swore she had been made by Gofannon in the smithy of the Otherworld. She was the Sword of Rhydderch and a Treasure of Britain. She was Arthur's sword and a Druid's gift, and she wheeled against the darkening sky and her blade flashed blue fire against the brightening stars. For a heartbeat she was a shining bar of blue flame poised in the heavens, and then she fell.

She fell true in the channel's centre. There was hardly a splash, just a glimpse of white water, and she was gone.

Nimue screamed. I turned the mare away and drove her back to the beach and back across the litter of battle to where my last warband waited. And there I saw that the army of the mad was drifting away. They were going, and Mordred's men, those that survived, were fleeing down the beach to escape the advance of

Meurig's troops. Dumnonia would fall, a weak King would rule and the Saxons would return, but we would live.

I slid from the horse, took Ceinwyn's arm, and led her to the top of a nearby dune. The sky in the west was a fierce red glow for the sun was gone, and together we stood in the world's shadow and watched as *Prydwen* rose and fell to the waves. Her sail was full now, for the evening wind was blowing from the west and *Prydwen*'s prow broke water white and her stern left a widening wake across the sea. Full south she sailed, and then she turned into the west, but the wind was from the west and no boat can sail straight into the wind's eye, yet I swear that boat did. She sailed west, and the wind was blowing from the west, yet her sail was full and her high prow cut the water white, or maybe I did not know what it was that I saw for there were tears in my eyes and more tears running down my cheeks.

And while we watched we saw a silver mist form on the water.

Ceinwyn gripped my arm. The mist was just a patch, but it grew and it glowed. The sun was gone, there was no moon shining, just the stars and the twilight sky and the silver-flecked sea and the dark-sailed boat, yet the mist did glow. Like the silver spindrift of stars, it glowed. Or maybe it was just the tears in my eyes.

'Derfel!' Sansum snapped at me. He had come with Meurig and now he scrambled across the sand towards us. 'Derfel!' he called. 'I want you! Come here! Now!'

'My dear Lord,' I said, but not to him. I spoke to Arthur. And I watched and wept, my arm around Ceinwyn, as the pale boat was swallowed by the shimmering silver mist.

And so my Lord was gone.

And no one has seen him since.

Gildas, the historian who probably wrote his *De Excidio et Conquestu Brittaniae* (Of the Ruin and Conquest of Britain) within a generation of the Arthurian period, records that the Battle of Badonici Montis (usually translated today as Mount Badon) was a siege, but, tantalizingly, he does not mention that Arthur was present at the great victory which, he laments, 'was the last defeat of the wretches'. The *Historia Brittonum* (History of the Britons) which might or might not have been written by a man called Nennius, and which was compiled at least two centuries after the Arthurian period, is the first document to claim that Arthur was the British commander at 'Mons Badonis' where 'in one day nine hundred and sixty men were killed by an attack of Arthur's, and no one but himself laid them low'. In the tenth century some monks in western Wales compiled the *Annales Cambriae* (Annals of Wales) where they record 'the Battle of Badon in which Arthur bore the cross of our Lord Jesus Christ on his shoulders for three days and three nights, and the Britons were the victors'. The Venerable Bede, a Saxon whose *Historia Ecclesiastica Gentis Anglorum* (Ecclesiastical History of the English) appeared in the eighth century, acknowledges the defeat, but does not mention Arthur, though that is hardly surprising because Bede seems to have taken most of his information from Gildas. Those four documents are just about our only early sources (and three of them are not early enough) for information on the battle. Did it happen?

Historians, while reluctant to admit that the legendary Arthur ever existed, do seem to agree that sometime close to the year 500 AD the British fought and won a great battle against the encroaching Saxons at a place called Mons Badonicus, or Mons Badonis, or Badonici Montis, or Mynydd Baddon or Mount Badon or, simply, Badon. Further, they suggest that this was an important battle because it appears to have effectively checked the Saxon conquest of British land for a generation. It also, as Gildas laments, seems to have been the 'last defeat of the wretches', for in the two hundred years following that defeat the Saxons spread across what is now called England and so dispossessed the native Britons. In all the dark period of the darkest age of Britain's history, this one battle stands out as an important event, but sadly we have no idea where it took place. There have been many suggestions. Liddington Castle in Wiltshire and Badbury Rings in Dorset are candidates for the site, while Geoffrey of Monmouth, writing in the twelfth century, places the battle at Bath, probably because Nennius describes the hot springs at Bath as *balnea Badonis*. Later historians have proposed Little Solsbury Hill, just west of Batheaston in the valley of the Avon near Bath, as the battlefield and I have adopted that suggestion for the site described in the novel. Was it a siege? No one really knows, any more than we can know who besieged whom. There just seems to be a general agreement that it is likely a battle took place at Mount Badon, wherever that is, that it may have been a siege, but may not, that it probably occurred very near the year 500 AD, though no historian would stake a reputation on that assertion, that the Saxons lost and that possibly Arthur was the architect of that great victory.

Nennius, if he was indeed the author of the *Historia Brittonum*, ascribes twelve battles to Arthur, most of them in unidentifiable locations, and he does not mention Camlann, the battle that traditionally ends Arthur's tale. The *Annales Cambriae* are our earliest source for that battle, and those annals were written much too late to be authoritative. The Battle of Camlann, then, is even more mysterious than Mount Badon, and it is impossible to identify any location where it might have taken place, if indeed it happened at all. Geoffrey of Monmouth said it was fought beside the River Camel in Cornwall, while in the fifteenth century Sir Thomas Malory placed it on Salisbury Plain. Other writers have suggested Camlan in Merioneth in Wales, the River Cam which flows near South Cadbury ('Caer Cadarn'), Hadrian's Wall or even sites in Ireland. I placed it at Dawlish Warren, in South Devon, for no other reason than that I once kept a boat in the Exe estuary and reached the sea by sailing past the Warren. The name Camlann might mean 'crooked river', and the channel of the Exe estuary is as crooked as any, but my choice is plainly capricious.

The *Annales Cambriae* have only this to say of Camlann; 'the battle of Camlann in which Arthur and Medraut (Mordred) perished'. And so, perhaps, they did, but legend has ever insisted that Arthur survived his wounds and was carried to the magical isle of Avalon where he still sleeps with his warriors. We have clearly moved far beyond the realm where any self-respecting historian would venture, except to suggest that the belief in Arthur's survival reflects a deep and popular nostalgia for a lost hero, and in all the isle of Britain no legend is more persistent than this notion that Arthur still lives. 'A grave for Mark,' the Black Book of Carmarthen records, 'a grave for Gwythur, a grave for Gwgawn of the red sword, but, perish the thought, a grave for Arthur.' Arthur was probably no king, he may not have lived at all, but despite all the efforts of historians to deny his very existence, he is still, to millions of folk about the world, what a copyist called him in the fourteenth century, *Arturus Rex Quondam, Rexque Futurus*: Arthur, our Once and Future King.